ON THE TRAIL
OF THE TRUTH

Also published in Large Print
from G.K. Hall by Michael Phillips:

The Journals of Corrie Belle Hollister

My Father's World
Daughter of Grace

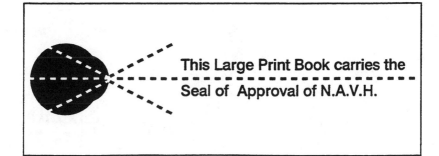

**This Large Print Book carries the
Seal of Approval of N.A.V.H.**

ON THE TRAIL
OF THE TRUTH

Michael Phillips

G.K. Hall & Co.
Thorndike, Maine

Published in 1995 by arrangement with Bethany House Publishers.

G.K. Hall Large Print Inspirational Collection.

The text of this Large Print edition is unabridged.
Other aspects of the book may vary from the original edition.

Set in 16 pt. News Plantin by Warren Doersam.

Printed in the United States on permanent paper.

Library of Congress Cataloging in Publication Data

Phillips, Michael R., 1946–
    On the trail of the truth / Michael Phillips.
        p.   cm. — (The Journals of Corrie Belle Hollister ; 3)
    ISBN 0-7838-1490-9 (lg. print : hc)
    1. Frontier and pioneer life — California — Fiction.
2. California — History — 1850–1950 — Fiction.   3. Large
type books.   I. Title.   II. Series: Phillips, Michael R.,
1946–   Journals of Corrie Belle Hollister ; 3.
[PS3566.H492O5   1995]
813'.54—dc20   95-34710

To
Gregory Erich Phillips

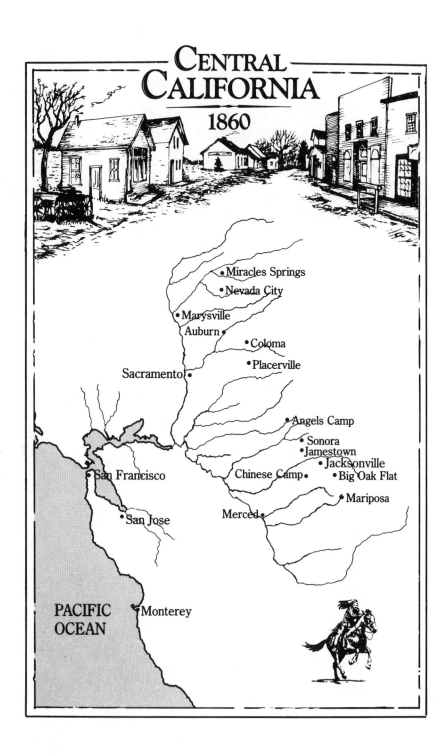

CENTRAL CALIFORNIA
1860

• Miracles Springs
• Nevada City
• Marysville
Auburn •
• Coloma
• Placerville
Sacramento •
• Angels Camp
• Sonora
• Jamestown
• Jacksonville
Chinese Camp • • Big Oak Flat
• Mariposa
Merced •
San Francisco •
• San Jose

PACIFIC
OCEAN   Monterey

Contents

Chapter 1

REFLECTIONS

I remember the last time I was here listening to Miss Stansberry play the wedding march on the church piano. Two months ago, back in June, I was sitting down in the front row waiting for what I thought was going to be my pa's wedding to Katie Morgan.

But that wedding never happened. Uncle Nick crashed in, shouting that Katie should marry *him*, not my pa, and to my amazement, Pa agreed. I was filled with a lot of feelings that seemed to be fighting inside my head. I wanted Pa to be happy, but down inside I just didn't feel right about him and Katie. Right from the beginning they somehow didn't seem like the kind of man and woman that were meant to be together. Not married, at least. Not when I thought of Ma. An hour later, I was there again — only this time sitting *next* to Pa, watching Katie becoming Mrs. Nicholas Belle. Instead of marrying Pa, Katie had ended up married to Uncle Nick.

So this day in the second week of August 1854,

I felt a heap different than I had the last time I heard the wedding march. No seventeen-year-old girl could have been happier than I was standing up there in front of the church alongside Mrs. Parrish. Uncle Nick stood on the other side next to Pa, with Rev. Rutledge in between. It was the perfect ending to the last eight or nine months, since that day toward the end of last year when Pa announced to us kids that he was planning to get married again. For weeks — ever since Nick and Katie's wedding, ever since I saw Pa and Mrs. Parrish walking quietly away from the church after Uncle Nick had busted in — I'd been so happy and distracted, I hadn't been able to think straight. And on the big day, even standing there in front of the church, I couldn't keep my mind focused on what was going on. All of a sudden I realized the music had stopped and Rev. Rutledge was talking and telling folks about what the wedding vows were supposed to mean. By the time I started listening in earnest, he was already getting on with the business of what we were all doing here! As he said the words, my brain was racing, remembering so many things. I had to stand there, straight and quiet next to Mrs. Parrish, smiling and acting calm. But inside I was anything but calm.

"Do you, Drummond . . ."

When I thought back to the first day I heard that name, and how Pa and Mrs. Parrish squared off on the street in front of the Gold Nugget, I just wanted to laugh. He was *Mr.* Drum then. None of us knew who he was or what was to come from that day. He and Mrs. Parrish sure didn't like each other much at first!

"So, Mr. Drum, what might be your intentions now?" I could still hear her stern voice, her glaring eyes bearing down on Pa's bewildered face.

And he roared back, "I reckon it ain't none of your dad-blamed business!"

Mrs. Parrish said she aimed to *make* us kids her business and told him he ought to be ashamed of himself. Pa said he had no intention of having a woman tell him what to do, and then he rode off through the middle of town.

What a beginning that had been! Who'd have ever figured it would come to this?

"Take this woman to be your wedded wife . . ."

Wife . . . his *wife!* My first thought was of Ma. But instead of showing sadness or regret or sorrow when her face came into my memory, she was smiling. I knew she understood and was watching with pleasure, glad that the Lord had sent such a good woman to this man and his kids.

At first Pa was looking mostly at Rev. Rutledge, but now he glanced over toward me and Mrs. Parrish. He wasn't looking at me but her, and he looked right into her eyes. I couldn't see her

11

face looking back at him, but from the look of love in Pa's eyes, I didn't see how he could possibly concentrate on what the minister was saying. Pa's eyes were so full it must have taken all his concentration just to fill them with that look. I don't think I'd ever seen such a look in his eyes before.

I couldn't help remembering the meeting of their eyes on that day he and Katie were supposed to be married, after Uncle Nick had run in and the uproar had started. Pa had a sheepish, embarrassed look on his face as he stood next to where Mrs. Parrish was sitting, and she looked back at him sort of half-crying.

That memory sent me back further, to a day when Pa and I were talking in the barn. He told me that when he looked into Katie's eyes, it just wasn't the same as it used to be with Ma.

Now as I saw Pa and Mrs. Parrish looking at each other, everything seemed to be coming right after a long time of wondering how it would all turn out. No one would ever replace Ma, but you could sure tell there was something pretty special for both Pa and Mrs. Parrish.

"*. . . to have and to hold from this day forward, for better, for worse, for richer, for poorer, in sickness and in health . . .*"

During the last few weeks, getting ready for the wedding, I often found myself wondering when Pa actually started thinking differently about Mrs. Parrish. I thought back to that day of the first church service in Miracle Springs, when there wasn't even a church yet, when he stuck up for the minister. I wondered if he had done that for her, maybe without even knowing it himself. Or that first Christmas dinner at Mrs. Parrish's house, when Pa got mad and we all left early. I wondered if they really liked each other back then, if some of their arguments were just to cover up feelings that might have been sneaking up on them from behind. I guess that's something I'll *never* know!

> ". . . *to love and to cherish, till death do you part, according to God's holy ordinance?*"

I asked Pa about three weeks before the wedding, "When did you first notice Mrs. Parrish?" He looked at me as if to say *What are you talking about, girl?* But he knew well enough what I was driving at. "When did you look at her different than just another woman, Pa? You know what I mean."

He kept eyeing me, serious as could be, then a little grin broke out on his lips. Once he got to talking about it, I think he enjoyed the memories. We talked about the meetings for the school committee, and he sheepishly admitted that we had gone early a couple of times so he'd be able to see Mrs. Parrish before the minister got there, just like I figured. "And you got all cleaned up and shaved and smelling good too, didn't you,

Pa?" I asked. "And that was on account of her, wasn't it?"

"I reckon," he answered. "But don't tell no one."

"Everyone knows by now, Pa," I laughed. "There ain't nothing more to hide!"

He blustered a bit after I said that, but in a little while he started talking again, and this time it was about Katie. He said almost the minute she got to California, he realized he'd made a mistake, but he didn't know what to do about fixing it.

"Why didn't you just call the whole thing off?" I asked.

He said he could see it all perfectly clear now and couldn't imagine he could have been such a fool, thinking it might work if he just went ahead and didn't say anything. "But by then, Corrie," he said, "my head was so blamed full of that Parrish woman I couldn't even think straight. I was so muddled I pretty near got myself hitched to the wrong woman, just like Nick said. I was just a downright nincompoop 'bout the whole thing!"

"It's a good thing Uncle Nick came when he did," I said.

"Tarnation, you're right there, girl! Yes, sir, Nick saved my hide but good! And that more'n made up for all the times I hauled him outta his share of the scrapes we got ourselves into. Yep, I figure we're about even now."

It was quiet for a minute, then I asked Pa,

14

"How come you wrote off for Katie in the first place, Pa?"

Pa thought a minute, scratched his head, and finally said, "I don't know, Corrie . . . I just don't know. I been wonderin' that same thing myself for quite a spell."

"Maybe for Uncle Nick," I suggested with a grin.

"Yeah, probably," said Pa. "But you know, Corrie, folks sometimes say there's times a man's just gotta do what he's gotta do — which is just another way of saying that a man is sometimes determined to go his own fool-headed way no matter how stupid it might be. And I reckon that's how it was with me back then. I was already startin' to feel something inside for the Parrish lady, and I reckon it scared me a little. At the same time, I wasn't sure if I even liked her, 'cause she could sure be ornery sometimes. So maybe I figured gettin' me a bride like Katie would put a stop to the crazy thoughts I was havin'. But it didn't work at all! The minute Katie got here I found myself thinkin' of Almeda all the more."

I smiled, and that was the end of my conversation with Pa.

Whatever his mistakes and uncertainties back then, he sure wasn't making one now. And he wasn't having any more second thoughts. For when the words *I do* came out of his mouth, the whole church heard them, and I couldn't keep from crying.

Then the minister and all the eyes of the people

15

turned toward Mrs. Parrish.

Do you, Almeda . . .

Poor Rev. Rutledge! It must have been hard for him to utter those words. Mrs. Parrish had brought him here, and they had been together so much the whole first year. It was hardly any secret that he was sweet on her. Everybody in town figured they were going to get married one day. And now he was having to marry her to somebody *else!* But ever since Rev. Rutledge came to Miracle Springs, folks have been surprised at what a fine man he turned out to be — building the church, pitching in with all the rest of the men when anything needed to be done, helping folks, going to visit anybody who was sick. I think he'd earned the respect of just about everybody in the whole community. And now he was marrying Mrs. Parrish to Drummond Hollister with his head high and being a real man about how things had turned out.

". . . take this man to be your wedded hus-band . . ."

Only about a week before the wedding, one Sunday afternoon Mrs. Parrish came out to our house for dinner. Of course she'd been spending a lot of time with us, but she wouldn't come there to live till after the wedding. She was there, along with Katie and Nick and everybody else,

16

and the talk was getting lively and everybody was laughing. Katie asked the question, but I'd wondered about it too, just like I had with Pa.

"Now tell us, Almeda," she said, "when did you first fall in love with this cantankerous gold miner?"

Mrs. Parrish laughed, and Uncle Nick chimed in, "Yeah, that's somethin' I'd like to know! How any woman in her right mind could think o' marryin' a coot like him, I can't figure it!"

"Aw, keep your no-good opinions to yourself, Nick!" Pa shot back, but neither of them were serious.

When it quieted down a bit, Mrs. Parrish told about how much she'd admired him when he stood up in church, and even when he'd stomped out after Christmas dinner that time. She said part of her was angry with him for ruining her nice dinner, but at the same time she couldn't help respecting him for wanting to stand up for what he thought was right, and for not wanting things said about him that he didn't think were true. "But I suppose the very first time my heart thought about fluttering must have been that day, not long after the children and I had gone on a picnic out in the country, when I was getting ready to leave on a business trip. Drum rode up in a great flurry of dust and noise, jumped off his horse, and came striding up to me so determined-looking I didn't know what he was about to do! But when he took me aside and told me he was the children's father, and then apologized for not coming forward sooner — well, right then I think something began telling me this was an unusual man."

"No, you were already after me sooner'n that!" said Pa seriously, but with a twinkle in his eye.

"What do you mean, I was *after* you?"

"You know perfectly well what I mean. You always were a mighty headstrong woman, and you —"

"Headstrong! Drummond Hollister, I ought to —"

"You know well and good you're headstrong. And you know you were out to get me right from the start."

"There is no truth in that whatsoever."

"Come on, Almeda, don't lie in front o' the children." Pa threw a wink at us. "Do you deny you went out on that picnic intentionally to get near to my place here?"

"I simply said that —"

"There! You can't deny it! Right from the start you were trying to weasel in closer toward me."

"It was only for the sake of the children. I've told you that before."

Pa laughed. "I don't believe that for a minute. You had your sights set long ago. Once you took a look at me, you couldn't help yourself. Go on, tell Katie the truth."

By now everybody was laughing at their good-natured argument. Mrs. Parrish didn't say anything for a minute. I was beginning to wonder if Pa'd hurt her feelings. But I guess she was just trying to think up some good way to get the best of him. Finally she burst out:

"Well, it worked, didn't it? I got you in the end!"

". . . to have and to hold from this day forward, for better, for worse, for richer, for poorer, in sickness and in health. . . ."

I suppose after the incident with Becky's kidnapping by Buck Krebbs and the thing with Royce and the ransom money, there could hardly be any doubt that Mrs. Parrish was prepared and willing to give everything she had for Pa and us kids, even if it meant she *would* be poor from then on. After what she did that day, the minister hardly needed to ask if she was pledged to Pa for better or worse and richer or poorer. She'd proved that already!

Pa didn't realize what she'd done right at first. He didn't know how she'd twisted Royce's arm to give her the money. If I hadn't seen her go into the bank with that parcel of papers, and then seen that horrible look on Mr. Royce's face later when she left, none of us might have ever known, because Pa and Uncle Nick had already gone to the sheriff's.

But later that night when I told Pa what I'd seen, he jumped up and, hurt as he was, rode into town right then to get the money back to her. And almost as quickly, she lit off out of

19

town for Royce's home, even though it was past banking hours.

Pa told us later that she'd signed over the deeds to all her property, her business, her home and office, and all her supplies and equipment as collateral against the $50,000. If she hadn't gotten the full amount of money back to Royce within twenty-four hours, everything she owned would have become his! That was how much she cared about Becky's safety, and how much she trusted Pa!

The minute Pa learned what she'd done, he must have known that their lives were made to be intertwined together somehow. After that, his future could have no one in it besides her — not after all they'd already been through together, and how close it had brought them toward each other.

That's when, he told me later, he suddenly realized he loved Mrs. Parrish *himself*, and not just because she was nice to us kids.

So when Mrs. Parrish answered the minister's question, every single person in that church knew the depth of love behind the vows.

". . . *to love, to cherish, and to obey till death do you part according to God's holy ordinance?*"

And with eyes brimming full of tears, and a radiant smile of love and thanksgiving spread all across her face, Mrs. Parrish answered: *"I do."*

20

Ten minutes later, as I walked back down the aisle in time to Miss Stansberry's playing, my hand on Uncle Nick's arm, I was following my pa and my brand-new mother!

Chapter 2

Rice, Bouquets, and Garters

As Pa and Mrs. Parrish walked through the front door of the church and outside, I heard shouts and yells, followed by Pa's loud voice and then Mrs. Parrish's laughing.

Uncle Nick and I were right behind. As the sunlight hit our faces, there were six or eight of the saloon girls gathered around, tossing handfuls of rice in the air at them. The whole rest of the church was right on our heels, and within a minute or two they were all getting into the act. Katie had made sure everyone in Miracle Springs under the age of fifteen — and a lot of those older, too! — had a good supply of rice. And before you knew it the whole town was after them, whooping and hollering.

Mrs. Parrish could hardly move fast enough to get away in her beautiful white wedding dress, the same one as she'd worn in Boston and which she had packed away all this time. Most of the folks weren't after her at all. Pa had by far the worst time of it with the rice! But I knew he loved every second, yelling and running and pretending to be trying to get away, while at the same time letting Tad and Becky and the other kids get him good a few times. When it was all done, and people were laughing and panting and handshaking and backslapping, Pa's hair and black broadcloth suit looked as if he'd walked out in the middle of a hailstorm.

There'd been a big afternoon of festivities planned. Pa had fussed about it ahead of time. "Let's just get the thing done, and then slip outta town, Almeda," he'd said. "There don't need to be a big to-do on our account."

Pa still didn't understand. Mrs. Parrish took me aside and said, "Your father, bless him, is so humble he has no idea how folks around here look up to him!"

She was right! If people around Miracle Springs were interested in Pa's getting married before, *now* with him marrying Mrs. Parrish — and almost two months after Nick and Katie's wedding for word to spread about it — why, folks had hardly been talking of anything else! The little church was packed, with people standing up all around the outside walls. Lots of folks from the hills and neighboring towns knew there'd be no room inside, so they just came and waited around outside for the festivities afterward. Rev. Rutledge had made sure the doors and all the windows were open, and so folks peered in however they could. Then afterwards the tables were set up and filled with food, with the big wedding cake in the middle. When everyone started gathering around, I reckon there were more people than would have filled the church three or four times over, and a lot of faces I'd never seen. Mrs. Parrish herself was a pretty well-known woman, so no doubt lots of people were there on account of her.

It's not often a man gets married with his kids right there with him. Pa had the five of us — me and Zack and Emily and Becky and Tad — come stand beside him and Mrs. Parrish. It was such a proud, happy moment! We were a *whole* family again! Uncle Nick stood right there in front of us with his arm around Katie. Zack's best friend, Little Wolf, was there, as well as Miss Stansberry and her brother and Rev. Rutledge and all the other folks that we'd come to know. I hardly know how to describe what I was feeling — complete, I reckon. None of the pieces were out of place or missing anymore.

Then Mrs. Parrish took Pa's hand and together they began to cut the cake. Uncle Nick and Alkali Jones kept the men stirred up with their catcalls and poking fun at Pa, and there was plenty of laughter to go around, with Pa getting in his share of jibes back at his two friends. Then they handed out slices of the cake, first to the kids and then to everybody else, and there was more handshaking and well-wishing and congratulations offered to the bride and groom. A few of the women cried again, but most of the tears, mine included, had come and gone in the church. By now everybody's spirits were pretty high.

"Time to throw the bouquet!" someone called out.

I glanced up, but couldn't see who it was. It had been a woman's voice — probably someone wanting to get it herself! Mrs. Parrish had told us earlier about the custom of the bride throwing the bouquet over her shoulder to the women of her wedding party and family and whoever else wanted to join in. "And whoever catches it," she said, and eleven-year-old Becky's eyes were big and wide listening to every word, "that woman's going to be the *next* one to get married."

"Really?" said Becky slowly, full of wonder.

"That's what they say," answered Mrs. Parrish.

"Then *I'm* going to catch it!" said Becky, more as if she was speaking fact than hope.

Emily didn't say anything. She was thirteen, and turning into a pretty young lady. It wouldn't be long before fellas would be turning their heads to look at her twice. And I couldn't help wondering what *she* was thinking about the bouquet. Flowers or not, I had no doubts she'd have half a dozen handsome young men courting and sweet-talking her before *anybody* threw a second look toward me. Maybe that's why I had the feeling that Mrs. Parrish would try to toss her bouquet in my direction.

"All right . . . all right," she answered to the call, coming out from behind the cake table. "Ladies, girls — all of you gather round right over here in front of me!"

A scurry and bustle followed. All the little girls came running, some of the saloon girls, laughing to themselves but wanting to join in the fun and maybe hoping for a chance to grab at the bouquet, the three of us Hollister girls, and the few unmarried women that were there.

"Are you all ready?" she said, and as she did her eyes caught mine. I wasn't sure I *wanted* to catch it.

A chorus of high-pitched shouts went up.

Mrs. Parrish turned around, her back to us, picked up her bouquet from the table, and gave it a mighty heave up in the air back over her head.

I was right; it did come in my direction — but not nearly close enough that I could even have jumped up and touched it. The bouquet went sailing over my head!

Becky cried out in disappointment. Sounds of *oohs* and *aahs* and various cheers went up. I spun around to see a red-faced Miss Stansberry, standing far toward the rear, holding Mrs. Parrish's flowers with a look of shock and surprise in her eyes.

We all clamored around her, while the men clapped and cheered, and a few winked and kidded each other with knowing expressions of significance on their faces.

"And now, Drummond, it's time for you to throw my garter," said Mrs. Parrish.

26

"Yeah, Drum!" several called out. "The garter
. . . throw it to me!"

Now the men *really* erupted with shouts and
yells and laughter. Above it all I could hear Mr.
Jones's *hee, hee, hee!* and Uncle Nick's whooping.
All the men were having a good time trying to
make Pa feel as uncomfortable as they could!

Mrs. Parrish pulled up the corner of her dress
to the knee, and now all the yelling changed to
whistling, while the women tried to shush up
their husbands. But nobody was going to be de-
nied making sport of anything they could on this
day. Mrs. Parrish took her time, throwing Pa a
smile as she slowly slipped the garter down over
her calf and ankle.

"Here, Drum, will you help me a moment?"
she said coyly. Pa stepped up and lent a steadying
hand to her free arm to keep her balanced.

"No, Drum," she said. "I want *you* to slip the
garter over my shoe."

A red flush crept over his face. Pa stooped
down to one knee and began the process, while
the whistling and calling out doubled in volume.

When he finally stood up, the garter in hand,
he shouted, "Cut out all your hollerin', you pack
of baboons! Can't you see there's ladies present!"

But the men just fired off more teasing and
jesting at Pa all the louder.

"All right, then, you loco varmints!" shouted
Pa back. "Any of you characters who's fool
enough to want to get yourself hitched come up
here and get yourselves ready, 'cause I'm about

to give this little thing the heave-ho."

All the boys hustled forward, nine-year-old Tad right in the front.

"Throw it to me, Pa!" he cried.

"You gotta fight for it with everyone else, boy," Pa answered. "Get in there, Zack . . . Little Wolf . . . come on, all of you get ready."

Not nearly so many men gathered around as women, even though there were twenty times more men available for marrying than women.

Pa turned his back to them and threw the garter in the air behind him. Zack made a halfhearted reach for it, Tad leaped up in the air, but neither was even close. Like the bouquet, the garter flew over the top of them, and I saw it hit Rev. Rutledge on the back of the head. He'd been talking to Patrick Shaw and wasn't even paying attention to what was going on behind him.

The minute it hit his head, the minister's hand unconsciously shot up to investigate the disturbance he'd felt. He then turned around to see every face upon him, the garter hanging from two of his fingers, a bewildered expression on his face.

When the truth of what happened dawned on him, a broad grin spread over his face, followed by an embarrassed laugh.

"Well, Reverend," called out Uncle Nick, "I reckon you're next!"

"No, no, not me," insisted the minister. "Here, this souvenir ought to be your pa's," he said, leaning down and handing the garter to Tad, who had scampered through legs and bodies and now stood next to Rev. Rutledge.

"Yes, sir!" exclaimed Tad, taking it from him, a happy smile on his face. He ran back to Pa and held it out to him.

"No, boy, you keep it," said Pa. "Who knows? Maybe you *will* be next — with the Reverend there performing the ceremony!"

Everyone laughed again, and then settled down to the serious business of consuming the cake and other food people had brought.

Chapter 3

A Glimpse Ahead

Pa's marriage to Mrs. Parrish was just about the happiest day of my life.

By the time we all got to bed that night, I was exhausted, and I think everyone else was too. Being too happy for too long at one stretch can wear a body out just as much as hard work.

But as I lay in my bed on that warm August evening, even though I was so tired I didn't think I could have kept on my feet another minute, sleep didn't come for a long time. Once my feet and hands quit being so active, my brain figured it had to get some exercise. The instant my head rested against the pillow, my mind raced off and I had no choice but to follow.

This day wasn't just the first day of Pa's and Mrs. Parrish's life together as husband and wife, I thought. It was also *my* first day, I guess you'd say, as a grown-up.

I *wasn't* grown up yet, of course. And it's ridiculous to say that all of a sudden, on a *certain* day, you just up and become an adult. I was only seventeen, and plenty of seventeen-year-olds *did* have to fend for themselves and were a lot closer to full grown and independent than I was. But I knew on the day of the wedding that a lot of things were going to be changing for me real soon.

I'd been so busy the last two years since Ma died, acting like a mother to the other kids, helping Pa with the chores and the cooking and cleaning. Suddenly I realized time was passing quickly and I was getting older in a hurry. Ma had been right about the prospects of my marrying. And even if I did have any prospects — which I didn't — I don't think I'd have relished the idea anyhow. If I ever did get married one day, it'd have to be the Lord who saw to that part of my life, because there was a heap of living I wanted to do, things I wanted to see, places I dreamed of going.

It began to dawn on me that maybe now I *could* do some of those things, go to some of those places. Now that Pa was married, Mrs. Parrish would be taking care of everything that I'd been doing — all those housekeeping and wife and mothering things I'd sorta done because there was nobody else to do them.

Pretty soon I'd *have* to figure out something to do besides just being underfoot around the house. I was pretty close to being past schooling age, and I suppose I could study to be a teacher someplace else, like Miss Stansberry. Pa and Mrs. Parrish would have kept me at home till I was fifty — that's just how wonderful they both were. But somehow I wasn't sure that'd be exactly right — or if it was what I wanted.

Something inside me started stirring that night. Ma and Uncle Nick and Pa — they all used to talk about the "Belle blood," as if when your name was Belle, you had no choice but to get ornery and stubborn and independent every so often. I didn't think I ever got too much that way, but once in a while when I'd get riled or headstrong over something, Pa'd mutter about the Belle blood.

Maybe it was my Belle blood stirring. I started thinking about going off alone to some strange new place just to see what it was like, thinking about meeting new people, about being a grown-up who had to take care of herself because she didn't have to tend to her Pa and brothers and sisters anymore. I found myself wondering what Los Angeles was like, and thinking about the Oregon territory folks were talking about. I wanted to know more about the mountains and the miners and Indians and trappers who lived in them and what kind of people they were.

Even a month earlier I would have been afraid at the prospect of going someplace by myself, of being away from Pa and the others, of having a job of my own somewhere besides Miracle Springs. But it didn't frighten me now. It was kind of exciting, adventurous.

Maybe that was what the Belle blood did to folks. Maybe that's why Uncle Nick was always in trouble and then came out here — that adventurous spirit in his blood.

So when I say it was my first day as a grown-up, I don't mean that anything really *changed* all at once. But my thoughts and my outlook toward things began to change — no longer a little girl way of viewing. I began to think, *This is my life, and I'm getting older. Pretty soon I'm going to be out doing things and going places because I decide to, not because my ma and pa decide for me.*

Maybe that's what growing up is more than anything else — being on your own, relying on *yourself* to decide what's going to become of you instead of looking to somebody else like you've always done. And as I lay there that night, that was the question that kept coming to me: *What AM I going to do with myself now?*

It wasn't as if I needed to decide anything before I got up the next morning. With Uncle Nick and Aunt Katie still there in the cabin with us, and with Pa and Mrs. Parrish off to Sacramento and San Francisco for a week, for a while it'd be just like the last six months. School would be starting up again in a few weeks, and I had already agreed to help Miss Stansberry again this year.

But Uncle Nick was already building a new cabin for him and Katie up past the mine in a little clearing in the woods, about five or six hundred yards from ours. Zack was now fifteen and had been growing like a weed. He was still quiet, but his voice had deepened and he was apt to be as tall as Pa in another six months. He'd be thinking man-thoughts before long.

Mrs. Parrish and I'd already laughed several times over what I should call her. She told me, "I would be honored, Corrie, to have you call me *Mother,* but only when you feel comfortable doing so. And you must never call me what you called your real mother."

"I called her *Ma,*" I said.

"Then you call me whatever you like." She smiled and put her arm around me. "I will always call you just Corrie. But I want you to know that I do think of you as a very special daughter — a spiritual daughter, a daughter whom the Lord gave me first as a friend . . . a daughter of grace."

"Thank you," I replied. "But I'm afraid you will keep being *Mrs. Parrish* for a while yet."

She laughed, that laugh that always seemed to have music at the back of it. "Oh, I do love you, Corrie Belle! I will be as happy as can be to keep being *Mrs. Parrish* to you forever!"

I gave her a tight squeeze. I loved her too — differently, but I think by now probably just as much as I loved Ma and Pa. I couldn't believe how good it was of God to bring together the two people I loved most in the world.

Just then some of Ma's last words came back to me. It had been two years, but I could almost hear her voice saying them like it had been yesterday.

You turned out to be a right decent-looking girl, she said. *You're gonna get along just fine, Corrie. I know you'll make me and your pa proud.*

I cried thinking about her. It was still the happiest day of my life, but sometimes happiness and sadness get all mixed up in a girl's heart, and then tears come out and you don't quite know why.

Then Ma's words about women getting on in the world came to my mind, her telling me — as she did more than once — to be strong and have courage and to try things.

"Don't be afraid to go out and do things, Corrie. And never worry what folks'll say or think. How else is a woman gonna get on in the world if she don't try?" That wasn't the kind of thing you heard most women talking about. But I guess Ma had plenty of the Belle blood in her too!

When I finally began to get drowsy, the last thought I can remember was praying that God would make me strong and would give me the courage to go out and do whatever it was he might want me to.

But I don't think my prayers were completely finished when I fell asleep.

Chapter 4

Possibilities

That next week I found myself wondering even more about what my future held. Katie and I took care of things, the kids played, Uncle Nick worked on his new cabin, but most of the time I kept thinking about Pa and Mrs. Parrish getting back home. Now that they were married, it didn't seem *right* with them not here.

But their being gone did give me and Katie a good chance to get to know each other better. I reckon with it all settled between Pa and Mrs. Parrish, I found myself able to see a lot in Aunt Katie that I hadn't seen before when my feelings were getting in the way placing her up alongside Mrs. Parrish and comparing the two. Now, Katie was . . . just Katie! And I discovered I really liked her a lot more than I ever thought I would. We talked about many things, and she told me about growing up in the East, and even some about her and Uncle Nick. She treated me like a friend, and I found myself thinking about her as mine too.

But she also had an annoying side. Now that she and Uncle Nick and Pa and Mrs. Parrish were married, she seemed to figure it was *my* turn. That whole week whenever we'd get to talking, she'd make little comments how I needed to be practical and look ahead to the time when I'd be starting my *own* family, and how I oughtn't wait as long as either of them. According to Katie, it was high time I either got a job or got married.

"There's that new young fellow up the pass, Corrie," she reminded me more than once, "not much older than you, and a nice young man. He's going to be looking to settle down with a wife before long."

She just didn't understand that I wasn't interested in marriage yet. Maybe I would be later, maybe I wouldn't. I didn't know. But right now there were other things I wanted to think about. Still, Katie kept whispering these kinds of things in my ear. She was determined to be practical, a realist, while Mrs. Parrish had always encouraged me to think about my dreams.

As much as I missed Pa and Mrs. Parrish, the time without them helped me to see this difference between Katie and Mrs. Parrish, and to think more about myself too. Mrs. Parrish was always telling me that *everything* has a good side, if you know how to look for it and find it, and I reckon this was one of those times.

Mrs. Parrish had asked me to go into town once or twice while they were gone to check in at the Freight Company, just to make sure everything was in order. I thought it a mite strange — she'd gone on lots of trips before without anyone having to check up on the business. But I wouldn't find out why she'd asked me to do that until a few days after they got back.

In the meantime, I did ride into Miracle Springs one afternoon. When I walked into the Parrish Mine and Freight Company office, Mr. Ashton immediately stood up from the desk where he was sitting and gave me a very pleasant, though awfully formal, greeting.

"Good morning, Miss Hollister," he said.

Miss Hollister! I thought. *It's only me, Mr. Ashton — Corrie Belle!*

But instead of saying what came into my mind, I just answered, "Howdy, Mr. Ashton. Mrs. Parrish said I should come in to see you while they were gone and see how you were doing."

"Everything is smooth as can be, Miss Hollister," he replied, still in a stiff but friendly voice. "Marcus loaded up the Jefferson order this morning and is off to Nevada City with it. And the invoices for the shipment of tools and that sample for the new kind of sluice box came —" He picked up some papers off his desk as he spoke and held them up to show me. "So I have no doubt the merchandise will be arriving in the next day or two. Several of the men are anxious to see the new box."

I hardly had a notion what he was talking about, but when he was done he kept looking at me like he was expecting me to say something.

I gave a halfway sort of nod. "Uh . . . so Marcus Weber's not here today?" I said. I had intended to say hi to him too.

"That's right, Miss. On his way to Nevada City. When do you expect Mrs. Parr—"

Mr. Ashton caught himself and smiled with an embarrassed grin.

"When do you expect Mrs. *Hollister* back, I should say, shouldn't I, Miss Hollister!"

"Takes a heap of getting used to the idea, doesn't it, Mr. Ashton?" I said. "I don't know what to call her either."

"Yes, indeed! Many changes, indeed."

"I don't know exactly, Mr. Ashton," I said, finally answering his question. "I figured it'd be about a week, like maybe we'd see them back on Sunday or Monday."

"Yes, yes, that's what I thought, too. I only wondered if you, now that you and Mrs. — Mrs. — *Hollister* — now that you are family, you know — I thought perhaps you might have heard something differently. But yes, Sunday or Monday . . . I'm sure that's about right."

As I left the office I couldn't ever recollect seeing Mr. Ashton act so strangely. He was talking to me like a perfect stranger! And I was at a loss to figure how Mrs. Parrish marrying Pa would make him behave so downright peculiar to me.

But it started to come a little more clear after she and Pa got back from their honeymoon trip.

On Thursday, after they got back to Miracle

39

on Tuesday, Mrs. Parrish said, "Corrie, it's time you and I had a talk."

"Woman to woman?" I said, smiling. I loved the chances we had to be alone and talk for a long time, especially about living as a Christian and thinking more about God in the things that went on every day. I wanted to be a woman like Mrs. Parrish, a godly woman who was different than other folks. I had already learned so much from her, but there was still a lot I didn't understand. She was teaching me to find out answers for myself by praying and searching in the Bible. So I was expecting another talk like that when she took me aside.

"Yes, woman to woman," she replied. "But perhaps even more . . . mother to daughter," she added.

"I like the sound of that," I said.

"So do I." But from the look on her face and the serious tone of her voice I could tell something different was coming than the kind of things we'd talked about before.

There was a long pause. A knot twisted in my stomach, as if something bad was about to come, although Mrs. Parrish had never said or done anything to make me afraid. Finally she spoke up.

"This is very difficult for me, Corrie," she said, then paused again. "You know how much I love you — both your father and I?"

"Yes, ma'am — of course," I said.

"Well then, Corrie, you must take what I'm

about to say as coming from a heart that loves you very much."

I nodded.

"Well, Corrie," she went on, "I have to be honest with you and say that I've been thinking a great deal about you — about your future. Both your father and I have. And we have discussed what some of the possibilities might be for you — alternatives, things you might do."

I didn't like the sound of her words. Was she going to start getting like Katie and try to marry me off? Had she and Pa spent their week away planning out my whole future?

But I kept my first feelings to myself and decided to hear her out. And I realized after a while that nothing had changed at all, and that she still wanted me to be able to dream, yet to be practical at the same time.

"You see, Corrie, most women don't spend a great deal of time thinking about what they might like to do. They just live a day at a time and life comes along, and they just do what they do without ever stopping to wonder if they might do something *else*. Or if they might *have to* do something else. I have thought about this because of losing Mr. Parrish. Women are more vulnerable. They need to be prepared in case they are suddenly on their own. But most women never think of that until it is too late. I certainly never did. Do you see what I mean?"

"I think so."

"Men don't do that, at least not most of the

men I've known. Men plan and dream and work to see their dreams fulfilled. Most of the men around in these parts have dreamed of getting rich in the gold fields. Now, most of them won't, and their dreams will never come true. But at least they think and plan and *try* to do what they dream of doing. Other men want to get a spread of land they can call their own, maybe have a farm or a ranch and raise horses or cows or grow wheat. I've known other men who dream of going to sea. Some of the things they want to do happen, others don't. But most men are thinking and planning about how they want their lives to go.

"But most women, Corrie, they just take life as it comes. They're so dependent on men that they figure what happens to them will depend on what the men in their lives do — brothers, fathers, husbands. They think the men have to make the plans and do the figuring and try the new things and explore the new places and make the money and stake the claims . . . and all the while the women just have to follow along."

She stopped, this time for longer. She took a couple of deep breaths, and I could tell she was still thinking.

"I'm not saying that's wrong. In one sense, God made men to be the leaders and the doers and he made women to be the followers. God made the woman to be man's helper, that's exactly how the Bible says it, Corrie. The men are supposed to be the ones that are in charge of how the world goes, and the women are supposed to help them, not run off trying to do their own kinds of things independent of men.

"But not every woman gets married. And, married or single, a woman's still got to know how to think and how to make decisions. How else can she be a good *helpmeet*, as the Bible calls it, if she doesn't use the mind God has given her?

"And some women — and this is what I wanted to get to, Corrie — some women don't have men to depend on. Women like me, when my husband died — and like your mother, after your father left. Some women find themselves in circumstances where they *have* to be able to make their own decisions, to fend for themselves. If they take life just as it happens to come to them, well, they never know what is going to become of them.

"When my first husband died, Corrie, I had to do a lot of thinking and praying. I began to realize that a woman's got to be able to think and plan and have alternatives too. Some women more than others. When I suddenly found myself all alone, I realized that *I* had to make the decisions about what was going to become of me. I had no man to depend on. My life was *mine*. That's when I started thinking that a woman needs dreams and plans and thoughts of her own. You can never tell when *you're* going to be making the decisions that will determine what becomes of you. Do you see what I mean?"

"Alternatives?" I asked.

"Yes. Possibilities — different things you can do, choices you can make. Most women don't *have* many alternatives because they never give life or their future enough thought, and never think about the different possibilities. But some women have to. If there's no man to do it for them, they have to take hold of the reins of their own lives. And they do so because they *want* to — they *want* to make the choices that will decide what they do. Most men nowadays aren't too comfortable with women doing that. But more women than ever are getting an education and even getting jobs everyone figured were just for men."

"Like Miss Stansberry?"

"Yes. Harriet said she had wanted to be a schoolteacher ever since she was young. And though she has her brother with her, I have the feeling she probably would have come out here anyway, even if she was by herself."

"She is an adventurous lady," I said.

"But women are doing things other than just what folks figure are women-things, like teaching."

"Running a business like you do sure isn't what too many women are doing."

Mrs. Parrish laughed. "I'll say! And it was hard for many of the men around here to accept at first. But like I said, after Mr. Parrish died, I *had* to think of my options — should I go back East, take over my husband's business, try to get married again? I decided to become a businesswoman, and I've never regretted it. I love what I have done, and I am so thankful that such a possibility was available to me, even though my first husband had been the one to open the door to it for me.

"Your mother too, Corrie — it was much the same for her. She was left without a man, with a family, with decisions to make."

"Ma didn't have many things she could have done," I said. "We just stayed on the land like always. Of course, she had kin there to help us."

"What if there hadn't been kin, or what if you hadn't had the farm? Then she would have had to consider other possibilities."

"But we did decide to come west in the end."

"Exactly! You see your mother *was* a strong, thinking, deciding, trying-to-figure-what-was-best kind of woman. She did more than just take life as it happened to come. She made decisions about what she thought was best for her and her family. And, Corrie, I suspect there are a lot more women like that than some of the men realize. That's why men always seem so surprised when women like your ma or Miss Stansberry —"

"Or you!"

She laughed. "*And* me — why they seem so surprised when a women stands up and does something different than 'the weaker sex' does."

She laughed again, a humorous laugh, as though she and I were in on a secret no one else knew about. "But we have to be patient with them," she said, still chuckling. "It may take them a while, but in the end men usually come around to seeing things reasonably, as long as women aren't too pushy to begin with. Why, nearly all of my customers are men, and by now they are used to doing business with a woman, used to the fact that I have men working for me who consider me their boss. And I think most of my customers have learned to respect me as a fair and honest and intelligent businesswoman, though most of them laughed at the very notion when I first announced my plans to continue the company after my husband's death. Men just sometimes need a little time to get used to things, that's all."

A silence fell between us. I was thinking about everything she had said. I guess Mrs. Parrish was considering what to say next, because she started in from a whole new angle, talking about me this time.

"Do you see what all this has to do with you, Corrie?" she asked at length, very serious sounding again.

She stopped and waited a long time for me to answer.

"I think maybe," I replied slowly. "You figure maybe I ought to be thinking about my possibilities, too, because I'm not —"

"No, Corrie," she interrupted, "not for any reason other than because I love you very much, and I think you are an extremely gifted young woman. I want only the absolute best for you, and so I think we — your father and I *and* you

— all ought to be thinking and praying about what that might be. We need to consider choices, alternatives, that are before you."

I laughed sheepishly. "I've told you what Ma said, haven't I?"

"About you not being of a marrying sort? Yes, Corrie. But if your mother could see you now — and I believe she *can!* — she would know you are the most beautiful, wonderful daughter she could ever have hoped for! That's not at all what I had in mind, Corrie."

"I'm not sure I want to get married, Mrs. Parrish," I said.

"I know. But whether you do or don't, I think a young woman still owes it to herself to think about things *she* might want to do in life — even if she does get married."

"Is it because of you and Pa getting married," I asked, "that you figure now it's maybe time for me — you know, with me getting older and getting past school age, that I move — ?"

"Oh no, Corrie!" She put her arm around me and squeezed me tight. "I love you so much! I would keep you here with us forever if I could. I never want you to go someplace away from us. Never, Corrie! And I know your pa feels the same way, too. He's real proud of you, Corrie."

You can't imagine how happy it made me to hear that! "So it isn't that you think I ought to be finding myself a man, or looking for a job someplace, since I'm not a kid anymore?"

"No, Corrie. It's just that we want the best

for you. We want you to be happy. And more than anything, I want to see you become the woman I think God had in his mind when he made you — a woman doing some exciting things."

"What kinds of things?" I asked.

"That's just it — I don't know, Corrie. I simply think there's a life full of opportunities out there waiting for you. And as much as I would like to always have you by my side, you're right about one thing — you aren't a child anymore. And that's why your pa and I have been talking about some of the ways you might begin preparing for whatever the future holds."

"I have wondered about teaching school," I said. "Seems that's about the only thing a young woman like me could do — like Miss Stansberry."

"Teaching is one possibility."

"I'd have to go to college."

"I thought of that," she replied. "Your father and I would have enough money to send you away to a normal school to get your certificate. Though I would hate to see you have to go away."

"There's always the newspaper writing," I added.

"That's what you *really* want to do, isn't it?"

"Oh yes!"

"But how to get you started . . . ?" Again her finger found her lips, pursed together now.

"That's another one of those areas where men don't figure a woman has much place, isn't it?"

Mrs. Parrish laughed. "Men figure that about

48

everything! I'll let you in on a secret. I think they are uncomfortable because they don't like the competition. They're afraid a woman might do something just as well as they! But I fear you are right — it could be very difficult for a newspaperman to take articles by a woman seriously."

"Like Singleton," I sighed.

"There is something else I've been thinking about, Corrie," said Mrs. Parrish.

I looked at her, just waiting.

"You've had some experience teaching, helping Harriet. So that's one alternative you might explore. You've helped your pa with your brothers and sisters for two years, so we already know you could make a good wife and mother. You want to write for a newspaper, but maybe the time hasn't come quite yet for that. What would you think of learning a little about my business?"

"The Freight Company?" I asked, surprised.

"Yes. How would you like to work with me?"

"I'd never thought of that before," I said. Then I couldn't help smiling. "Did you talk to Mr. Ashton about this?" I asked.

"I think I may have mentioned it to him," she answered. "Why?"

"Well, I went in to your office last week, like you asked me to — Say, is *this* why you wanted me to do that?"

Mrs. Parrish nodded.

"I wondered what you could possibly want me

to check up on. I don't know anything about the business."

"I just wanted to see what you'd think about being my family representative while I was out of town. But go on, tell me about Mr. Ashton."

"He talked to me real peculiar, all formal and stiff, calling me *Miss* Hollister! No one ever calls me that!"

Mrs. Parrish laughed loudly. "He probably thinks I'm going to make all sorts of changes now that I'm married again. He probably figures I'll turn it into a family business and he'll be out of a job."

"That's why he was being so polite."

"I'll have to talk to him and put his mind at ease," she said. "But I did speak to him about the possibility of your working in the office a little — when you're not helping Miss Stansberry, of course. What do you think, Corrie?"

"I — I don't know . . . it's such a new idea."

"I'd pay you, of course."

"You wouldn't have to do that, ma'am," I told her.

"But I *would* do it, Corrie. You're old enough now to have a money-earning job. It would be good experience. There's nothing like being in business to gain valuable knowledge. You meet people, you learn how things are run, you sometimes travel to new places. Whatever other things the Lord may in time lead you into — and we must be faithful to pray for *his* guidance — helping in the Mine and Freight Company will give you experiences you'll be able to use anywhere. And perhaps one day you'll be running the business in my place, who can tell? I've suddenly got a family to manage. I might find myself with more than I can handle."

"I'm willing to try, I reckon," I said finally, "if you think I can do it."

"I know you can, Corrie."

Chapter 5

Adjustments

For the whole next year I worked with Mrs. Parrish at the Freight Company. I kept going to school every day, both to learn and to help Miss Stansberry. But most days after school I worked a couple of hours, and I even got to make some deliveries with Mrs. Parrish and Marcus Weber to some of the outlying areas in the hills.

Mrs. Parrish had been right. I learned things and met a lot of new people. I still didn't figure I was cut out to be a businesswoman like her, but it never hurt to have a few more possibilities of things I might be able to do if I needed to.

That fall after the wedding, Pa and us kids all moved into Miracle Springs to Mrs. Parrish's house so that Uncle Nick and Katie could have the cabin to themselves while they finished building their own place. Mrs. Parrish's house had seemed so huge before, but all of a sudden it was a pretty tiny place with seven of us living there!

Pa went out to the claim every morning, the

kids and I went to school, and Mrs. Parrish went to the freight office. Pa and Uncle Nick would work mornings at the mine, and then afternoons on the two cabins — finishing Uncle Nick's and adding on to Pa's to make more room. Alkali Jones was there most days, and on weekends several of the other men would come out and help too. Usually Rev. Rutledge was there pounding nails or carrying lumber just about every Saturday.

Katie stayed at the claim nearly all the time, helping too, feeding the men. The grass and trees she'd brought us from the East were all growing, and she'd started clearing a garden spot up by their new place for next year. She had plenty to keep her busy, though she started feeling poorly later in the fall and had to keep to her bed a lot. Pa said it was probably just the weather starting to turn cold.

Mr. Alkali Jones, who always seemed to know everything about everything, was now ranting every day about what a miserable winter we were fixing to have. "Them squirrels got twice the winter fur I seen on 'em in fifteen years," he'd go on. "An' they're hidin' acorns in places I ain't seen afore. I tell ya, we're in fer a heap o' snow an' cold!"

They finished the adding on to our place about the middle of October, and then with the work concentrating all at Uncle Nick's, they got his and Katie's new home closed in and the roof and the doors and windows on by about the second week of November, just before any of the big rains Mr. Jones predicted began to fall.

Two days after they moved and got Katie comfortably settled — though she was feeling better by this time — a huge storm came through. It rained for two days and the streets around Miracle turned to mud. Up in the hills to the east a lot of snow had fallen. Alkali Jones said that with a start like this — as early as it was — it was "unmistakably gonna be the dad-blamest, coldest, most ornery winter ya ever done seen!" He finished off his words with that high-pitched cackle and gave his beard a scratch with his dirty fingers. But what he said sure turned out to be right!

Once the storm had passed and the sun came back out to start drying up the mud and grass and fields, leaving big ruts in the roads with muddy water standing in brown pools in the low spots, I figured we'd all be moving back out to the cabin, especially since now it was bigger and they'd added on a couple of rooms. That's what Pa'd been thinking too.

But Mrs. Parrish was having some second thoughts about it. It was so hard not to keep calling her Mrs. Parrish! I knew someday I'd probably have to start calling her either *Mother* or *Almeda*. But right then I wasn't ready for the first or old enough for the second, and I just couldn't keep from calling her Mrs. Parrish like I'd always thought of her.

Anyway, one morning I heard Pa and my new mother, Almeda Parrish Hollister — that ought to take care of just about anything I might think of calling her! — talking. The conversation was getting louder than usual. I'd never heard them argue before, and I didn't figure they ever *would* argue! But I suppose even married people who love each other have differences of opinion now and then, though never having been married I can't say for certain.

They began talking about the two houses, but pretty soon they were talking about lots of other things.

"It only seems, Drummond," Mrs. Parrish was saying, "that since we are all here now, and since the children and I all have to be in town every day, perhaps it would make more sense just to stay here in my house — at least through the winter, as long as the children are in school."

Pa was quiet for a minute. I had to admit what she said made sense, even though I hadn't thought of it before. I'd never stopped to consider what would happen to Mrs. Parrish's house when we all went back out to the claim.

Finally Pa spoke.

"I reckon you got a good point there," he said, "but I got the place all fixed up so there's more space. You and I can have a room off to ourselves, and the boys got a room, Emily and Becky can share a room, and the little one Corrie can have by herself. It's a dang sight more space than we got here, Almeda."

"But the trips back and forth into town every day, and in the cold and wet of winter . . ."

She didn't finish the sentence.

"Yep, I know. But it just don't seem right somehow, livin' at a woman's house when a man's got a place of his own."

"The woman's house is not as good as the man's?"

"I didn't say that. I just said it don't seem altogether right. It's kinda like it'd be if you kept on with your Freight Company and I quit working the mine. I know we talked this out a while back. But I been doing a lot o' thinkin' on it since."

"As I told you when we discussed this before, I intend to keep my Freight Company, Drummond."

"I know, for a while. But you know as well as I do that it ain't right for a woman to support a man, and that's kinda like it'd be if we kept on living in —"

"What do you mean *for a while?*" she interrupted, her voice sounding a little agitated.

"I mean I know you can't just shut down an operation that size right away. It'll take you some time."

"Shut down? Drummond, I have no intention of shutting down my operation at all. You didn't think my marrying you meant I would give up my business? There was never any talk of that when we discussed it before the wedding."

"I guess I figured that was sort of understood." Pa's voice was quiet. I couldn't tell if he was embarrassed or was slowly getting riled. He got the same kind of quiet in both moods.

"It was not understood by me," said Mrs. Parrish. "I thought it was understood that we both had been married before, we both were involved in livelihoods of our own — your claim and my company — and I had no idea you were thinking that any of that would change. Why, I would never think of asking you to give up *your* claim or *your* cabin because of marrying me."

"That's different. I'm a man."

"What's different about it?"

"A man's work — well, it's more important than a woman's. Maybe you had to run your company so as to provide for yourself. But you got me now. You got a husband to take care of you, so you don't have to anymore."

"And if I want to?"

"Women ain't supposed to be out doin' what men do, not unless they have to, and you don't have to no more."

"Maybe I *want* to. Did you ever consider that I enjoy what I do, that maybe I'm a good businesswoman, and that I don't *want* to just be at home sweeping the floor and fixing a supper for you to eat when you're through with *your* work? Did you ever consider that?"

"I reckon I never did. Women are supposed to be at home, men are supposed to be out working. What you're saying just ain't natural. I know I never said this to you before, but it just ain't done that way."

A long pause followed. When Mrs. Parrish

spoke again, her voice was calm but determined.

"Look, Drummond," she said. "I know most men, and even most women, might agree with what you say. But I'm not most women. I'm *me!* And after my first husband died, I found out some things about myself. I found out that I had a strength down inside that I could depend on. I found out that I was a good businesswoman, that I could fend for myself in this rough California world, a man's world. I found out a lot about the person I am down inside by having to stand up for myself and make it on my own when my husband was suddenly gone. I liked what I found, Drummond. The things God built into me during that time — I'm just not willing to let go of. I love you, Drummond Hollister. You are the best thing that has happened to me since my first husband died. I will love and obey and cherish you all my life. But that doesn't mean I will stop being myself — a woman, a person with my *own* dreams and goals and things I want to do in life. Please don't ask me to give up my business for you, Drummond. I would do it if you asked, because I will obey you. But I don't know what would become of me if I did. A piece of me would die. Please, don't ask me to do that."

It got quiet for a long time. The next thing I heard was the sound of Pa's boots on the wood floor, and then the back door opening and then shutting again. I guess he had to think about it all. And usually when Pa was thinking he went someplace alone, outside or in the barn or on the back of one of his favorite horses.

I never heard the two of them discussing the business or the houses again for a long time. I think they did, though, because every so often I could tell from the quiet between them that they'd been talking and had seen things differently.

But however they decided to work it out, nothing much changed. Most of the time they were as loving and pleasant as could be to each other. Mrs. Parrish went to her office every day and the Mine and Freight Company kept doing business just as before. I went on working there after school. And Pa seemed pleased with me learning different aspects of the business. Pa kept mining with Uncle Nick and Mr. Jones, and they continued to bring gold out of the stream and out of the mountain the deeper into it they dug.

I guess Pa saw that Mrs. Parrish's idea about the houses was pretty smart. Most of the time that winter we stayed at the house in town — Mrs. Parrish's house — during the week, and then on Friday night Pa'd come in to fetch us all with the big wagon and take us out to the claim. Since there was no school, Mrs. Parrish didn't go into her office on Saturday, and so we'd stay there all weekend, and ride back in on Monday morning for the week. During the week, Pa'd come into town every evening for the night.

It was a bit of a cumbersome arrangement. But we were kind of an unusual family, and it was gonna take some time for things to get figured out.

Chapter 6

Winter 1854–55

Without even thinking about it, Christmas dinner was becoming a kind of tradition. Maybe our Christmases stand out in my mind because each of the three was so different, and every time I remembered them it reminded me of how fast things had changed since we'd been in California, and how much the Lord had done for us.

This Christmas was no exception. It was the best ever!

Now we were two happy families, and Mrs. Parrish was there with us. I hadn't been happier since her and Pa's wedding day. All morning she and us three girls worked and sang away in the kitchen, baking pies and sweet potatoes and a big ham, while Pa was outside with Zack and Tad. Pa'd got Zack a new rifle for his very own, and Zack could hardly stand it, he was so excited. So as we were working, we heard the shots firing in the woods where Pa was giving him a lot of instructions about aiming, which Zack really didn't need.

We loaded the food and some extra chairs into the wagon about noon, and took it up to Nick and Katie's new place where we were going to eat. It was their first chance to show off the new cabin, and they'd invited a couple of other families, and of course the Stansberrys and the minister. Katie had been excited for days, planning and telling us she had a surprise for everyone.

We got there first, and soon the others began to gather. When Rev. Rutledge's buggy drove up, Miss Stansberry was with him, alone, with the news about her brother. Hermon Stansberry had taken sick and wasn't going to come. We all prayed for his health before sitting down to dinner, and Miss Stansberry took a nice basket of food back with her for him when the day was over.

But Katie's announcement was the highlight of the whole day!

"I have some big news to tell you all," she said, with a wider smile than I'd ever seen on her already wide mouth. "Some time along about the middle of next summer" — she looked at the five of us kids — "your Uncle Nick is going to stop being *just* an uncle and start being a pa himself!"

Mrs. Parrish was on her feet, exclaiming excitedly almost before the words had left Katie's lips. She gave Katie a great hug, which was followed by the other women doing the same, while Becky tugged at my arm asking me what all the yelling was about. I whispered to her that Katie was going to have a little baby. "And it'll be *your* cousin," I said.

The men were slapping Uncle Nick on the shoulder and shaking hands. Then Uncle Nick went to the fireplace where he picked up a small box from on top of one of the stones, and started passing out cigars that he'd bought. The minister didn't take one, but Uncle Nick shoved one into Zack's hand with a laugh.

"It's high time you tried it, Zack, my boy!" he said.

"Can I, Pa?" said Zack, expecting the usual answer.

Pa shrugged. "Maybe your Uncle Nick's right, son. I guess if he's finally old enough to be a pa, I reckon you're old enough to try one of those things."

Uncle Nick wasted no time. With a grin on his face, he struck a match and held it up to the end of the cigar that was now sticking six inches out of Zack's mouth. Zack sucked in a couple times, got a few puffs going as the tobacco caught fire, and Uncle Nick cheered him on. Pa seemed to know what was going to come of it and just stood back watching, with a half grin on his face.

It didn't take long. After only about an inch had burned off the end, Zack's face began to turn pale. All of a sudden, amid what must have been an embarrassing roar of laughter for poor Zack, he handed the cigar back to Uncle Nick and bolted for the door and outside to get fresh air. In a minute or two Pa followed with a look on his face that seemed to say that he knew what Zack was going through, while Katie and Mrs. Parrish were talking about "these ridiculous rites of passage that men insist on putting each other through," both with disgusted looks on their faces.

But even Zack's getting sick from the cigar couldn't spoil the impact of Katie's announcement about the baby coming, and the other memories of the happy Christmas Day.

Alkali Jones was right. It was a rough winter — cold, wet, with lots of snow and frost. The stream got bigger than I'd ever seen it, and the men were saying that if the rains kept up, maybe they'd wash down lots of new gold from up in the mountains. It was so wet a time or two that we stayed at the house in town for two weeks each time. The stream was so full of water rushing by that Pa and Uncle Nick had to pull all their equipment out and couldn't do much work. They worked some inside the mine, but with the cold and wet it was a miserable job. They gave that up, too, after a while, waiting for a break in the weather. But everybody was talking about the rain being good. It had been uncommonly dry, they said, for the last couple of winters, so the crops and pastures needed the rain, and the miners were glad for it, hoping it'd shake some new gold loose. Probably the only people who weren't thankful for the rain were the children, who had to stay cooped up inside the schoolhouse all day long on the worst of the wet days.

Throughout the winter, I learned a lot about the freight and mining business and took several wagon rides with either Mr. Weber or Mrs. Parrish to deliver things that people had ordered. Mrs. Parrish always introduced me real proper-like to the people we were doing business with, saying, "Mr. So-and-So, I would like you to meet my daughter Corrie, who is helping me now in the business." She had such a way of making me feel grown-up, like she respected and appreciated me! Soon I knew most of the roads for twenty or thirty miles around Miracle, and had been to nearly every little town or hamlet or gold camp around those parts. I'd never realized how many customers Mrs. Parrish had all over. Some of the places we went and people I met were pretty rough-looking. But she always marched right into wherever we had to go with her head high and without showing a bit of fear. That's probably why the men came to respect her, because she could be as tough as they were if she had to. And that was something I would have to learn, too — if I planned on making my way alone in California.

That winter some of the town leaders got together and decided Miracle Springs ought to have a mayor. The town had grown a lot in the last two years, and was still growing some, with new families coming in. There was no election, it was just announced one day that a retired banker, recently come from the East, had agreed to act as mayor. He'd had experience in that sort of thing before. So Jason Vaissade became the first mayor of Miracle Springs.

Chapter 7

Learning to Let Go and Trust God

The weather had been nice for a couple of weeks. It was warming up and folks were saying the winter had finally broken and spring was on the way. We were more than a week into March, so any other year they would probably have been right.

One morning, when we were staying at Mrs. Parrish's house in town, I woke up before dawn. I usually got up pretty early, and liked to lie in bed and read or go for walks before the rest of the family got up.

This particular morning I got up while it was still dark. I put my clothes on and sneaked out of the house as quietly as I could. The morning was beautiful. I felt as if I were the only one alive. I took in the cold morning air in long breaths. A few stars still twinkled in the sky, with just the faintest hint of the gray dawn starting to mix in with the blackness.

I walked out into the street. It was cold and I had several layers of clothes on, but I could tell the sun was going to come up and it would be a nice bright day. Everything was completely quiet. Marcus Weber wasn't out in the stable with the horses yet, and he was usually the first person to be up and at it most mornings in Miracle Springs. The roosters weren't even about their business yet either, although they likely would be before long.

I love early mornings! After I've been up a little while, my mind gets awake and active and has its best thinking times. Maybe it's the quiet, maybe being alone. As much as I like people, I never get tired of being alone either, and my brain always seems to take alone times to turn about some of its best thoughts. Morning is always the best for praying too.

I suppose the two go hand in hand — praying and thinking. When you're praying you *are* thinking, kind of thinking in God's direction, pointing your brain toward God and then letting your thoughts go *out* of you and *into* him. At least that's how I like to imagine what it's like when I'm praying. And the other side of praying, listening to God, works just the reverse — I try to pay attention to the thoughts that are coming *into* my brain. And if I've been talking to God about something, then I figure those thoughts coming toward me are the thoughts coming out of God toward *me* — his thoughts that he's sending in *my* direction.

Well, on that particular morning I was thinking and praying, and opening my thoughts toward God and trying to listen to his thoughts toward me. And I found myself remembering the talk Mrs. Parrish and I had about alternatives, and choices, things I might some day find myself doing, and how a young lady like me ought to be preparing herself for the future and thinking about what she wants to do. And pretty soon I was walking along not even paying attention to where I was going, talking back and forth with God — talking in my thoughts I mean, not out loud — and asking him what it was that *he* wanted me to do and prepare for.

My favorite passage in the Bible is in the third chapter of Proverbs, verses five and six: "Trust in the Lord with all thine heart; and lean not unto thine own understanding. In all thy ways acknowledge him, and he shall direct thy paths." That morning I felt as if God was directing my footsteps, because without even thinking where I was going, I found myself walking about the town praying and talking to God as I went.

I walked for five or ten minutes, and found myself standing in front of the Gold Nugget saloon, where we'd first met Pa and where we'd had our first church service in Miracle Springs.

Then I walked farther on down the street past Mr. Bosely's General Store. My heart was full as I recalled everything that had happened, all that God had done since those first days here.

As I passed the bank, I thought about Mr.

Royce and all the evil that had come because of him. But seeing his bank also reminded me of what Mrs. Parrish had done to save Pa's mine. Maybe that incident was the beginning of her and Pa loving each other like they did now.

God had brought me so far, would he bring me safely the rest of the way? Yet even seeing how everything had worked out in the past, it was still easy to slip into worrying about what was going to become of me.

"I'm growing up, and sometimes it's hard to know what I'm supposed to do!" I had told Mrs. Parrish in one of our talks.

"God will let you know in his time," she said. "You can trust him. If you let him, he will work in every bit of your life — you can depend on it."

Even as I was thinking these words of Mrs. Parrish's, I found myself coming back around to the Freight Company and to Mrs. Parrish's house — our house.

Oh, God, I found myself thinking, *you have been so good to me! We were so alone back then . . . and now you've given us so much! Thank you for Pa, for what a fine man he is. Thank you for Uncle Nick, for Katie, for the claim and the cabin, and for the life you've given us here, and all the new friends we have.*

I stopped and looked around me. I was standing right in front of Mrs. Parrish's office. The light was creeping up in the east, and it wasn't dark anymore, though it was still only a gray light.

Inside through the window, the office was empty and black. On the glass was painted in small gold letters: *Parrish Mine and Freight Company.*

"How can I thank you enough, Lord, for . . . for my new mother?" I whispered. There was nothing else to say — that one prayer was enough. My heart was full of gratitude for her — for all she'd been to us, for the friendship she and I had, for how she had helped me love Pa better, for all she had explained to me about living with God, for how she had helped me understand myself and my own feelings more deeply, for the talks we'd had, for our trip to San Francisco, for how I'd learned to pray and bring God into the little things of my life because of her. I wouldn't have been half the person I was if it hadn't been for Mrs. Parrish — and I sure wouldn't have been standing there praying, and thinking about verses from the Bible, if she hadn't taught me how important it was to live my life with God as part of it.

I didn't even realize it at first, but suddenly I was crying — quietly, just a few tears. And a great sadness was coming up out of my heart, although I didn't know why right at first.

I don't want to leave this place, God, I thought. *I love these people and Pa and Almeda and Zack and Tad and Becky and Emily . . . and Mr. Weber, and everybody, Lord! I don't want to leave . . . I don't want to, Lord!*

All at once I knew why I was so sad. I'd been filled with such happiness only a few moments before, in the memories of this town and people. But retracing steps along the sidewalks where I'd walked dozens of times in the last couple of years was a little like saying goodbye to Miracle Springs.

"Is that why you woke me up so early, Lord," I asked, "and drew me out of bed — to say my farewell to this place?"

My future and what was to become of me *had* been on my heart a lot — ever since the day of Pa's and Almeda's wedding. Even when my mind wasn't actively thinking about it, down deeper the question was still running around inside me. Every once in a while the doubts would surface and I'd get to thinking again about that conversation we'd had about a girl preparing herself for her future, or I'd remember what Ma had said about me needing to think about growing up. I suppose I was growing up slower than a lot of girls might — especially being a reading, thinking person always trying to figure things out in my head. But maybe now it was time that I *did* get on with the business of growing up, and I couldn't help thinking about it a lot.

The town still surrounded me, still quiet just like a moment before, but now I felt a pang of pain at the sight, as if I would not be able to hold on to it forever.

"What are you fixing to do with me, Lord?" I asked. "Where are you leading me? What do you want me to do? Where do you want me to go?"

Go! Out of my own prayer the word slammed

71

against me. "Oh, God, you're not gonna make me go away, are you? But I don't want to go! I've only had my pa back two years, and now I've only had a mother again less than a year, and I don't know if I can stand to be torn away from them! Please, God, don't make me go away! I don't want to be *Miss Hollister,* God. I want to be just who I've been all these years! I want to keep being a daughter for a while longer. I'm not ready to be a woman, a grown-up all on my own yet!"

I was crying hard now. The praying words dried up, but not the tears.

Two or three minutes later the tears began to stop. And as they did another set of words from the Bible crept into the back of my mind. I hadn't thought about them for a long time — I couldn't even remember when I'd heard or read them, but all at once there they were, as if God had sent them to quiet down my spirit and remind me of something I needed to remember right then. The words were: *Delight thyself also in the Lord; and he shall give thee the desires of thine heart.*

"Do you really mean that, God?" I asked. "Will you give me what *I* want? You won't make me leave Miracle Springs?"

I started walking again. By now the first colors of pink were showing in the sky to the east. Folks would be stirring before long. The roosters were hollering their heads off all over town.

As I walked I knew God was talking to me. I didn't hear an actual *voice* speaking out of the sky. But I had been thinking — and even crying — in God's direction. And after I'd "had *my* say," maybe it was God's turn to do the talking. Walking along I felt my mind and heart filling up with words, ideas, feelings, verses from the Bible, reminders of things Mrs. Parrish had told me or things I'd heard Rev. Rutledge say in church, about feeding on God's truth. When I look back on the experience of that morning, I think God was using everything going through my mind to speak to me. *His* thoughts were now coming in *my* direction.

I felt God speaking to me that morning. The thoughts and feelings came too fast and in such a jumble, and of course I didn't understand everything all at once. But as I wrote it down and thought about that morning after it happened, more and more of it made sense to me. It was as if God was *saying* something like this to me:

"Yes, Corrie, I *will* give you the desires of your heart. I do that with all my children who delight in me. But I cannot do it unless a man or a woman, a boy or girl . . . unless *you*, Corrie, do indeed *delight* yourself in me. That's what the psalm means. *If* you delight in me, *then* I will give you the desires of your heart."

I want to delight in you, God, I said to myself, *but I don't think I know what that means.*

Again I felt God's thoughts coming into my mind.

"Just this, Corrie — to delight in me means that you want to do what I want, not what *you*

73

want. Your desire is to do *my* will rather than your own, because you trust me to take care of you, you trust me about everything. I created you, I created all things, and I love you so much more than you can possibly realize. You can trust me to do the very *best* for you in every way imaginable — the very best!"

I don't understand. I thought that verse said you would give me the desires of MY heart?

"When you trust me completely, as your Creator and Father and friend, when you trust me so much that you know I will do the best for you, when you trust me enough to want *my* will in your life, that becomes the desire of your heart. The desire of *your* heart is to do *my* will. And when you want *my* will for your life, and you want that more than anything else, then I will give you that — I will certainly work out my will in your life. And it will be the best possible life you could ever have! You will have the desire of your heart, and everything you could possibly hope for shall be yours — because your life is in my hands, not your own. Do you remember how that whole passage from Psalm 37 goes, Corrie?"

Suddenly I *did* remember! Rev. Rutledge had preached from Psalm 37 about two months ago and I had loved the words so much I'd memorized them:

Trust in the Lord, and do good; so shalt thou dwell in the land, and verily thou shalt be fed. Delight thyself also in the Lord; and he shall give thee the desires of thine heart. Commit thy way unto the Lord; trust also in him; and he shall bring it to pass.

"I do not always fulfill the worldly desires of my children. I do not give them everything they selfishly might *want*. But for those of my sons and daughters who want *me*, who want to know me, I will fulfill that heart's desire. And everything else in life will be given in abundance along with it. I cannot give myself without giving my blessings and my love and my abundant provision."

The flow of thoughts stopped. I was outside town now, unconsciously walking in the direction of the church and school. I looked up. There was the building off in the distance. I thought of the laughing, yelling voices of the children that'd be echoing from inside it in a few hours. I thought of Miss Stansberry and wondered if I would someday be a schoolteacher too. Then I thought of the church, about that summer when it'd been built, and about Pa and Rev. Rutledge, about the dedication of the building and the picnic and seeing Mr. Grant and the soldiers. I thought about all the many church meetings and services we'd had in that building since then, and all the growing I'd done — sometimes having to do with the church services, sometimes not.

Had the Lord directed my path here, like the proverb said, so that I could say goodbye to this church and school building like the rest of the town? Something down inside was telling me a change was coming in my life, and I was afraid. I wasn't sure I liked the idea at all.

"Trust me, Corrie . . . you *can* trust me!"

This time the words came into my mind so clearly that I *knew* exactly what God was saying.

I drew in a deep sigh from the cold morning air. Even though I was all alone, I felt suddenly embarrassed, because I knew my worrying about my future was silly. Of course I could trust God to take care of me! Even if I didn't want to leave Miracle Springs, God wouldn't lead me to leave unless it was best. I *did* want my life, my future, everything I was as a person — I wanted it to be what *God* wanted, not what I wanted. I *did* want God's will. I wanted to be able to trust him, even for my future and all its unknowns.

Then I started to realize that maybe God hadn't gotten me up early like this and had me walk around town, filling me with these thoughts about my future and what I might be doing a year, two years, three years from now, because I was going to *leave* Miracle Springs. I might leave someday, or I might not, but maybe the *goodbyes* weren't to the buildings and the things I had looked at that morning, or to the people. Maybe God was trying to get me to think about my life in a new way, wanting me to say goodbye to the old way of looking at things, goodbye to worrying about what was to become of me. Maybe the future God was wanting me to move into wasn't necessarily in a new *place,* but in a new way of trusting him, of delighting in what *he* wanted for me.

Sunrise had filled the sky with brilliant reds and oranges. I could hear the sounds of the morning in the distance — dogs barking, a few wagons moving. Marcus Weber's hammer slammed down on the anvil, ringing in the distance. He was likely fixing a wheel or shoeing one of the horses.

I walked a little way off the dirt road, behind the trunk of a huge old twisted scrub-oak tree, and knelt down. I immediately felt the cold on my knees, because the grass was still wet from last week's rain and the morning dew. But I didn't mind. I bowed my head and prayed again, this time out loud, though just barely above a whisper.

"Oh, Lord, I *do* want to delight in you! I want your will for my life, whatever you want me to do. If you want me to teach children in a school, or if you want me to keep working in the Freight Company, I'll do either of those if you want me to, God. Or whatever else. I want to trust you, and so, Lord, I want to give my life to you, like Rev. Rutledge was talking about that Sunday, to make the kind of lady you have in mind for me to be. I do give you my future and whatever you want to do with it, even if it means someday having to leave Miracle Springs, though I don't want to. Please help me to trust you more completely. I'll do what you want and go where you say, 'cause I know you know what's best for me."

That was all. No more words were there. I slowly got up and began walking back toward town, breathing in deeply of the morning air.

I felt good! In church you sometimes hear people talking about "burdens being lifted" off their shoulders, and maybe that's a little what it felt like. The worry was gone. It felt as if I had given it to God, and he had taken it, just as if I'd handed him a heavy sack and now I wasn't carrying it anymore.

I'd been crying earlier, thinking about having to say goodbye to familiar sights and faces. But now I felt like smiling. The future was going to be exciting, not fearful! Because I had given all of it to God, even though I didn't know what *it* was, and he was going to make it the very best for me — because it would be what *he* wanted for me. Maybe I felt lighter and happier because for the first time I really was trusting God to make things turn out, instead of worrying about them.

As I walked into town, more thoughts from God started coming into my mind. They were different, yet still part of that psalm which said we would be fed by truth. I hadn't thought of that part of the verse before, but now I found myself considering what it might mean. Maybe I had to get to the point of saying to God "I trust you" before he could make sense out of the rest of it to me. In my mind, God seemed to say:

"Wherever you go, and whatever you do — here in Miracle Springs or far away to wherever I might send you someday — I want you to love and follow the truth, and live by it, and let it feed you. *The truth,* Corrie Belle Hollister, my daughter that I love. I am making you into a woman, and I have plans for you — whether people call you Corrie Belle or Miss Hollister. Whatever they call you, wherever you go, whatever you do — follow the truth, Corrie . . . follow *my* truth. Find out what my truth is. Then follow it, live by it, and never let it go. For in *truth* shall you be fed, and so shall you dwell in the land, and by following the truth will I be able to give you the desires of your heart."

Like so much of what happened to me and what passed through my mind that morning, I didn't fully understand those words at the time. But now, years later, I can see how the Lord was giving me those words as a way of pointing me ahead toward a certain desire that was in my heart, getting me ready for it. That morning was the beginning of where the Lord was going to take me, the beginning of the part of my life when I began learning to trust him more completely.

At the time I realized none of this. But in going down on my knees and giving myself and my future to God in a way I never had before, I see now that when I got up and walked back into town, I had left the things of my childhood behind.

Chapter 8

The Blizzard

The Lord shoved me right into something that was going to play a big part in my future almost immediately. But I didn't realize the significance in my life until I looked back on it years later.

That same day when I'd gotten up early to walk and pray and talk with God, about the middle of the afternoon huge clouds started to roll in from the North, coming toward the Sierras. By evening the cold, icy, blustery winds had begun to blow.

The next morning, just after dawn — which seemed later than usual on account of the dark clouds — it started to snow, very lightly to begin with. Even at noon there was no more than a fine layer of dust on things and it still wasn't collecting on the roads or where people walked.

But it kept falling, and by the middle of the afternoon the flakes were bigger and whiter, and an inch had collected. People were bundling up and starting to pack in extra firewood and oats and corn for their livestock.

Pa built a huge fire in the house that night, and it was warm and cozy. Every now and then he'd get up and go and peer out the window into the blackness. Sometimes he wouldn't say anything. Sometimes he'd come back into the room muttering. Once he just said, "I don't know, Almeda," and then he shook his head. "It looks like it could be a bad one!"

When I woke up the next morning, Pa was already downstairs in the parlor, standing still, staring out the same window into the morning gray. I walked to his side, he put his arm around me, and we both just looked and looked, neither of us saying a word. Everywhere was white — nothing but white. You could hardly tell there was supposed to be a town out there. It was just hills and mounds and bumps of white. It had to be over a foot deep, and still the sky was filled with the down-fluttering flakes.

"Ain't never seen it like this," Pa finally said. "Never this much so low down. Must be taller than a man's head up in the foothills! I hope Alkali got back to the cabin."

"Where is he, Pa?" I asked.

"He set out yesterday morning for Dolan's place, up to the high flat on Relief Hill above Missouri Canyon. He was aiming to get himself a mule. Dolan was in town last week and had several he wanted to get rid of. But Dolan's ranch'll be plumb snowed in for weeks now." He stopped and sighed deeply. "Alkali, Alkali

. . . I hope you made it back in time, you old buzzard!"

The day wore on slowly. School was cancelled. Most of the places in town didn't open. If they had, nobody would have come anyway. Almeda went to her office, but only for part of the day. I could tell she was worried about Pa, he was acting real fidgety. Somehow he just had a sense that things were going wrong out there in that snow. He just kept staring out the window.

It stopped snowing about noon. A few footprints and horse tracks cut through the thick white blanket, but not too many. After lunch Pa put on his heavy winter coat and started to climb into his boots.

"You're not going out?" Almeda said.

"Can't stand sitting around here any longer, Almeda. I'm going over to Rafferty's, maybe the Gold Nugget. I gotta find out if anybody's heard anything." He made for the door.

"Can I come, Pa?" asked Tad.

"I need you to stay and protect the womenfolk, son," said Pa. The gleam in his eye said he hadn't forgotten about Marcus Weber, who was pounding and working away out in the stable, but that he wasn't going to mention him.

"Zack, you come with me. Might be that I'll need you," he added.

Zack was in his boots and after him in a flash, leaving the rest of us sitting there wondering what Pa figured doing out in the middle of the blizzard.

Eventually we found out.

A couple of hours later Zack burst through the door.

"Pa said to get a couple of horses saddled up right away," he panted. "He'll be back in a minute."

"I'll get Marcus to help you," said Almeda, starting toward the back door. "What is it, Zack?"

"There's been an avalanche down on the west side of Washington Ridge. I guess the snow gathered so fast up on a ledge overlooking the little ravine that the powder couldn't hold together. Two or three cabins down in the wash was plumb buried. All the men are heading out there to try to dig the folks out."

"Who is it — any women or children?" asked Mrs. Parrish.

"No, ma'am. Just some old miners that camp out up there."

"What about Mr. Jones?" I asked. "Is *he* in danger too?"

"Don't know," said Zack. "Nobody's seen him."

"Let's go see to the horses," said Almeda.

"Come to think of it, we'll need three, cause Pa said to tell Mr. Weber to come too." The two of them closed the door behind them.

About ten or fifteen minutes later, Pa came in the front door almost exactly as Zack and Almeda returned from the stable.

"Horses ready, Zack?" he said.

"Yes, sir."

"I don't know when we'll be back, Almeda. Marcus coming?"

"He's in the stable."

"Good. Pray we'll find those fellas! There's a lot of snow up there — must be a good thousand feet higher'n we are here in Miracle. Come on, Zack."

They made for the back door where their horses waited.

"Oh, Almeda," Pa said, turning back at the door. "Hitch up a wagon — one with the highest axle to get through the snow — with two of whatever horses are left. The workhorses would be best in this weather. I ain't sure what we'll find, but if we need a wagon for hauling some gear up there, I want it ready."

"It will be," she replied. "Drum . . . be careful!" she added, gripping his hand.

Pa nodded seriously, then he and Zack were gone. Almost the minute they left it started snowing again.

Chapter 9

A Rash Decision

About an hour and a half after Pa and Zack and Mr. Weber left — the whole time it had been still as death, hardly a sound either in the house or outside — we heard the door of the livery crash open.

Mrs. Parrish jumped up and ran out back to the stable, and I followed.

"Hey!" a man's voice was calling. "Hey . . . ain't nobody in there? Marcus, where are you, man?"

Just then Mrs. Parrish opened the stable door and looked inside. "Mr. Ward!" she exclaimed. "What are you doing here?"

"No time to explain, ma'am! Where's Weber, Hollister? I can't find any of the men around. I gotta have me some help an' I ain't got time to go tryin' to track 'em down!"

"I'm afraid all the men are gone. There was an avalanche down across the Yuba on Washington Ridge."

The man swore, slapping his hand to his forehead. But I could tell it was fear he was feeling, not anger. His face turned pale and he started to collapse.

Mrs. Parrish rushed forward and caught him in her arms before he hit the floor. "What *is* it, Mr. Ward?" she said in alarm. But the moment she felt his body and saw his face close up, she knew. "The man's nearly frozen to death!" she exclaimed back in my direction. "Corrie, come help me — we have to get him into the house!"

Together we half dragged the poor man, whose legs could hardly support him another step, back into the warm parlor of Mrs. Parrish's house. By the time we got him slouched in a chair he was nearly unconscious.

"The boots, Corrie!" she said. "We've got to get his boots off!" She grabbed at one as I pulled on the other. The leather was soaking wet, and when we got his boots and his stockings off, we could feel that his feet were just like ice.

"He might already have frostbite — it's a wonder he didn't die from the exposure," she said, pulling his limp legs in the direction of the fire. "We've got to get some dry cloths around his feet."

In a few minutes Mr. Ward began to come to, and almost immediately started to ramble in a panicky, exhausted voice. "My wife and three girls," he said, ". . . trapped up on Buck Mountain . . . snow caught us last night . . . blizzard up there — had to get 'em to town . . . wind blew the storm right down on top of us . . . snowing so hard I couldn't see a thing . . . too far to turn back . . . got off the trail, and the wagon went in a ditch . . . wheel broke —"

He stopped, then looked around at the two of us. His eyes were wide, as if he suddenly had become aware he was sitting in a warm room in front of a fire. His expression showed no recognition of who we were.

He struggled to rise. "Gotta get out of here," he mumbled. "Got to get back . . . gotta find help . . ."

"Mr. Ward, you can't go anywhere," Mrs. Parrish said firmly but gently. "Your feet and hands are frozen, and all your clothes are soaked."

"I've got to get back . . . they'll die if I don't . . . got to get help!"

"Where are they?" she asked.

"Snow was everywhere . . . wagon was broke down — wheel shattered . . . couldn't get us all out on the one horse . . . sheltered them best I could under the wagon . . . unhitched the horse, took off for town. But I pushed the beast too hard in the snow . . . stumbled . . . broke a leg . . . walked rest of the way here . . . got to find some men . . . got to get back out there . . . they'll freeze to death in the blizzard!"

"Where are they — *where,* Mr. Ward?" asked Mrs. Parrish, urgency in her voice.

"Halfway down the Buck . . . off the road from our place . . . got to get back there!"

Again he struggled to rise, but fell back, unable to stand.

"There's no way this man's going out again any time soon," said Mrs. Parrish, half to me, halfway thinking aloud to herself. She paced toward the fire and back again.

Without really stopping to think, I suddenly found myself running to grab my thickest coat, putting on my gloves and hat, and then running back out to the stable and throwing the big double doors wide open. I climbed up on the seat of the wagon Marcus had hitched for Pa, and took the reins in my hands.

"Corrie, what do you think you're doing?" exclaimed Mrs. Parrish, rushing out of the house behind me.

"I gotta go after them," I said. "Mrs. Ward and the young'uns!"

"The horses can never make it! The snow's too deep, and it's still falling!"

"I can do it — I know the way."

"It'll be dark soon. Please, Corrie . . . don't. Come back inside with me." Her voice had a pleading sound in it. I could tell she was worried.

"I'm sorry, Almeda, I've *got* to. I can make it — I know I can!"

She stood there for a moment, just looking at me as if seeing me for the first time. "All right, Corrie," she said at last. "But wait a minute."

Faster than I would have thought possible, Mrs. Parrish ran into the house and came back with a package wrapped in a dish towel, with several blankets thrown over one arm.

"Some food and water," she explained. "And

blankets." She threw the blankets in at my feet and stepped back. "Be careful, Corrie," she said briefly. "And God go with you."

I flipped the reins and called out to the horses, and in a few seconds I was plowing my way through the blizzard. I didn't look back. But inside I knew Mrs. Parrish was crying, and would immediately go back into the house and get on her knees to start praying. I knew God was with me, but I was glad to have two of us praying at the same time! If Pa'd been there, I might not have done what I did, but *if* I had, he'd have probably been muttering something about "that blame fool Belle blood" as he watched me disappear up the street. He probably thought the same thing when he heard about it later.

I didn't realize it then, but that was the first time I ever called Mrs. Parrish *Almeda*. I suppose I was moving toward being a grown-up faster than I realized.

I headed out of town northward, where I could still see Mr. Ward's footsteps in the snow. But I wouldn't follow them all the way. I had made a delivery up to the Wards' place last month with Mr. Weber. He had showed me a ravine along the foot of Buck Mountain where he said the snow didn't fall. He was laughing about it then, but now it just might save those peoples' lives! I'd take the wagon to the foot of the mountain, then along the length of the ravine and up the cutoff road that joined the main ridge-road about halfway to the Wards' place. Marcus had shown me where it turned off when we'd been on our way back down the mountain.

About halfway through the canyon, I heard the bray of a donkey, a strange sound through the quiet of falling snow. I stopped, and heard it again. Then I heard a familiar voice yelling and cursing. Suddenly the sounds coming from the animal made sense!

I urged my horses toward the sounds, and as I got closer I heard the voice again, this time calling out to me. "Hey! Who's there? Hold up . . . whoever ya may be!"

I called my horses to stop. Then I heard the voice again, from part way up the hillside on the slope of Buck Mountain. But it wasn't from the trapped members of the Ward family at all. I wasn't anywhere close to them yet. Instead, the voice was coming from the mouth of a small cave.

Presently a figure appeared in the black opening, looking out into the white blizzard. It was Alkali Jones!

"Mr. Jones!" I called out in astonishment. "What are you doing here? We were all worried about you!"

"I was halfway down from Dolan's when I figured I'd better git me an' my mules hurryin' a mite faster or we'd be buried by this dang blizzard. Then one o' 'em stumbled an' went lame on me an' I figured this here cave'd be 'bout the best I could do till the blame snow quit — hee, hee, hee! But am I glad to see you!"

"But you're only six or eight miles from home.

Couldn't you have made it?"

"You ever tried t' pull a mule through a foot o' snow — an' a lame one at that? Hee, hee! I might as well o' got on my hands an' crawled home on my knees. This blasted beast won't budge! An' I jest gave Dolan six-fifty fer the blame critter, an' I weren't about to part with my investment, ya might say, hee, hee."

"Well, come on down from there and get in! We got folks trapped up the mountain!"

Alkali left the injured mule tied at the cave and tethered the healthy one behind us. The old miner jumped into the wagon with me, and we continued on to the end of the ravine, which ended abruptly about six hundred yards farther up the canyon.

"You'll never git this pile o' lumber even half-way up the hill," said Mr. Jones. "Ain't no way a wagon like this is gonna make it up that steep path. I don't know what ya was aimin' t' do fer them folks."

"I thought there was a road from the canyon up to the ridge on top. When Mr. Weber and I were up there, he pointed down this way, and it looked like a fine road leading off down toward here."

"Fine road fer maybe two hundred yards, till it's outta sight! Then it turns into a steep trail switchin' back an' forth up the side o' the mountain. Ain't hardly wide enough fer a man, much less a beast. Jest look at it! Ain't no wagon can climb up that!"

We looked up toward Buck Mountain, one side looming against the canyon on our left. Tiny flakes of snow were falling, but above us, the mountain was lost in a dense fog of thick snow.

" 'Sides that — look at it!" said Mr. Jones, still pointing upward in the direction I had been hoping to go. "Why, the snow up there's comin' down in a white blanket. There's likely a foot or two foot o' powder, maybe three, up t' the top where the other road is. That trail comin' down off the mountain t' this here ravine — why, it drops a thousand feet! Ain't no way, even if there was a road this wagon'd fit on — which there ain't! No way ya'd git it through that blizzard, not with them horses ya got."

"They're Mrs. Parrish's best," I said.

"They ain't snow animals."

"What are we going to do, Mr. Jones? Those people are trapped up there, and night's coming, and the snow's still falling!"

"That's what I was askin' you — what ya was aimin' to do."

"I thought I'd be able to get there with the wagon."

I hesitated. "What about the mule?" I exclaimed. "Could your mule make it up the steep trail?"

" 'Course he could. He could make it up a mountain with no trail."

"In the snow?"

"That critter's been with me in worse snows than this! He ain't no blame tenderfoot like that beast o' Dolan's!"

"Then we'll take the mule up to the top!" I said.

"Jest how ya figure that'll help? How many of 'em ya say there was?"

"Four — Mrs. Ward and three young'uns."

"Hmm . . . lemme see, we might oughta —"

"We could bring them out one at a time, with the mule, and get them to the wagon!"

"Take too long! I tell ya, it's a three-quarter mile o' steep, rugged trail. Time ya went back an' forth, whoever was sittin' down in the wagon waitin', why they'd be plumb froze to death! If we're gonna git 'em outta there, we gotta git 'em all at once, git back down here, an' high-tail it back to town to git them young'uns someplace warm afore nightfall brings another three foot o' snow an' they're buried till next spring!"

We were at the end of the canyon, and the trail up the mountain wound up and out of sight. I now saw the impossibility of what I had hoped to do. The wagon could go no farther. A light wet snow was falling where we were, and up higher the snow was falling in huge, thick flakes.

We stopped and I tried desperately to think.

"We'll have to try it with these horses," I said at last. "They're the best workhorses Parrish Freight has, and it's our only chance."

I jumped out of the wagon and began unhitching the straps from the two animals.

"What'n tarnation ya thinkin'?" said Mr. Jones.

"We'll both ride up there!" I answered, working my fingers as fast as I could in the biting cold. "We'll take the horses and your mule . . . leave the wagon here, then bring them all four down at once!"

"Ya got spunk, I'll say that! Let's git goin' — we still gotta find where they's broke down," said Mr. Jones, already out of the wagon and untying his mule from the back. "An' that ain't gonna be easy, neither!"

In another three or four minutes we were making our way up the narrow trail. It seemed to take forever, but we made it safely to the top. When we reached the main road that ran along the ridge, we stopped.

"Which way's the Ward place?" said Mr. Jones, half asking, half trying to remember himself.

I glanced all around. In the eerie quietness of the snowy wooded area, everything looked different.

"I . . . I'm not sure," I replied, glancing about for something I might recognize.

Suddenly Mr. Jones jumped off his mule and tromped forward in the snow several paces.

"Look . . . there's wagon tracks!" he shouted back at me as he pointed ahead. "They been along here all right!"

He glanced hurriedly to the right and left.

"The slope's climbin' this way," he said, jumping back onto his mule. "That means they was headed down."

"Let's go!" I cried, urging the horses toward the faint wheel tracks.

Alkali Jones nodded. "I jest hope we ain't too late."

Chapter 10

The Article

What happened next . . . well, I've kinda got to jump way ahead to tell you about it. You know I'd always wanted to write, and had even hoped to write newspaper articles someday — more than the one or two little things I'd done for Mr. Singleton. As it turned out, what happened to me and Mr. Jones in the blizzard was the thing that my first really big article was about. Of course, it wasn't printed in the paper till a couple months later — that's the jumping-ahead part.

But as I was writing about the blizzard, it just seemed that perhaps the best way to tell what happened would be just to let you read the article I wrote afterward. And I'm kind of proud of the article too, even after all these years, since it was the first one I got published in a big city paper. So here it is:

Sometimes danger brings with it adventures that would never have happened without it. That's how it was during the blizzard that struck the foothills northwest of Sacramento last March. Folks had already been calling the winter of '55 a bad one, and the sudden fall of snow that dropped on all the gold-mining communities of the region sure made it seem like they were right.

The blizzard brought danger, all right, because most of the citizens weren't expecting it, since it struck so suddenly and all, before anyone was prepared.

The first sign of trouble came when word got to the men gathered in Miracle Springs' Gold Nugget — one of the town's only establishments open at the time — that an avalanche had just occurred on Washington Ridge east of Nevada City, burying three cabins in the ravine below, and endangering the lives of six or eight miners trapped inside. Immediately all the town's available men set out through the snow to try to dig the men out.

No sooner had the men left Miracle Springs when another emergency came. Mr. Jeriah Ward staggered into town, nearly dead of exposure in the bitter cold and in danger of frostbite, frantically in search of help. Finding no one at the saloon or the sheriff's office, Ward made his way to the Parrish Mine and Freight Company. In a state of collapse, he desperately told Mrs. Almeda Parrish Hollister that his wife and three young girls were trapped underneath their broken-down wagon halfway up Buck Mountain.

The words had barely passed his lips when one of Parrish Freight's young employees set out through the snow with a high-axle flatbed wagon pulled by two sturdy workhorses. The Parrish Freight wagon first headed north through the snow-blanketed white countryside on the main road toward North Bloomfield and Alleghany. Following Humbug Creek, swollen full from the winter's rains, the wagon left the main road at the base of Buck Mountain, dropping down into Pan Ravine, a narrow gulch running along the south flank of the mountain. There the snow, which had been between six inches and a foot and a half deep on the main road, was only an inch or two thick. According to Mr. Marcus Weber of the Parrish Mine and Freight Company, who was interviewed afterward, this unusual phenomenon, which keeps most snowfall off the floor of Pan Ravine, is known only to the oldest natives of the region, but has been responsible for saving the lives of more than one person in winter snowstorms like this one.

Up through the ravine the young freight driver urged the two workhorses, who found the footing easier. But as the elevation steadily rose, so did the snow on the ground.

About halfway through the canyon the familiar voice of longtime Miracle Springs miner Alkali Jones was heard. Jones had left the previous day, prior to the beginning of the blizzard, for the Dolan ranch on the higher ground beyond Buck Mountain, and had been feared trapped or even lost in the snow. Like a ghost peering out from the darkness of the cave where he had been trying to wait out the worst of the storm, Jones appeared and joined the rescue effort.

The two made their way to the end of the ravine where they left their wagon. Then up the narrow trail into the blizzard they went, Jones leading on the back of his sure-footed mule, followed by his young friend on the bare back of one of the horses, pulling the other.

Steadily they climbed up the side of Buck Mountain, the snow falling heavier and heavier, but the trail under the thick foliage of the trees remaining visible. The way was slow, but all three animals proved true to their sure-footed reputations. Up the steep way they went, switching back often, always climbing, until at last they reached the main road that ran along the ridge. Snow over a foot thick covered the way.

"I hope they're still alive!" cried out the young freight driver as they began their search for the broken-down wagon.

"Ain't likely they can last long in this cold!" said Alkali Jones. "We gotta find 'em quick!"

As rapidly as they could in the thick snow, they trudged along the road, following the barely visible indentations of wagon tracks, which were growing fainter and fainter by the minute.

"I think I see it!" shouted the young driver at last. "There . . . off the road, all covered with snow!"

"Could be a wagon," replied Jones, giving his mule a hard kick in the side.

"Mrs. Ward . . . Mrs. Ward!" the two shouted as they approached, jumping down and staggering through the deep snow. "Mrs. Ward — you there?"

"Thank God!" said a faint voice from underneath the half-buried wagon. "Who is it?"

"I'm from the Parrish Mine and Freight Company. Your husband came looking for help. His horse broke a leg and he couldn't get back to you."

The two bent down. Under the wagon, protected from the snow, sat the freezing woman, the chill of death in her eyes, huddling her three children close to her under two or three blankets. The bed of the wagon, partially sloped against the wind, had kept them dry, and the blankets had preserved at least some of their body heat as the woman clutched the three children close to one another. Otherwise, all four would have been dead.

"Why, Alkali Jones!" exclaimed the woman, recognizing one of her rescuers for the first time.

"In the flesh, ma'am," replied Jones. "I haven't seen ya since last spring."

"You two can visit later! Let's wrap up the girls in these blankets. We've got to get back down to the canyon before this snow gets any deeper!"

Helping her to her feet, Jones assisted Mrs. Ward onto the back of his mule — the most sure-footed of the three animals — then handed her the smallest of the girls, tightly wrapped in a blanket. Then the other two remounted, each cradling one of the children securely.

Ten minutes later, the three animals were retracing their hoofprints toward the steep trail they had recently ascended. Downward they went this time, in tracks they had carved through the powder on the way up — still visible, though snow continued to fall. Jones, on one of the horses, with seven-year-old Julie bundled on his lap, led the way, followed by Mrs. Ward with the baby on the mule, and then the last Parrish workhorse with four-year-old Tracey in the rider's lap. In a rainstorm the footing on the steep trail would have been muddy and treacherous, but in the frozen snow the hoofs of the animals found solid footing; and though the way was slow, they made the descent into the ravine below without stumbling once.

The waiting wagon was loaded with the four Wards while the two-horse team was once again hitched to the wagon. Then the intrepid group turned for Miracle Springs.

"What about your other mule?"

"Leave it!" replied Alkali Jones, referring to the second of his two mules that he had tied back at the cave. "He couldn't make it afore ya came, an' he ain't likely t' feel none different now. I'll come back fer him when the storm breaks. You jest whip them two horses o' yers along an' git us back t' town! I'm as blamed anxious t' git outta this cold as the Missus an' her young'uns. My fingers is likely already froze clean off!"

And so the rescue of Mrs. Jeriah Ward and her three daughters off Buck Mountain took place. When her husband next saw her, Mrs. Ward was sitting trying to get warm, drinking a cup of tea, while her two older girls sipped hot milk and vanilla in front of the fireplace at Mrs. Hollister's. Waking up in a chair he could not remember being dragged to, with his family warm and safe and recovering, Ward took a cup of coffee from the hand of Alkali Jones, full of more questions than he could ask at once. Then, with many interruptions of "hee, hee, hee!" from the old miner, the relieved father and husband heard the entire story.

In conclusion, it should be mentioned that the rescue of the miners trapped on Washington Ridge was also successful, though it was after nightfall before most of the men returned to Miracle Springs.

Chapter 11

How It Got Published

Well, that's the article I wrote about what happened, though you can probably tell I had a little help with it here and there. Mrs. Parrish and the man from the newspaper office added a few words and made it sound a little better, but mostly it's mine.

The Wards all turned out to be fine, and stayed in town at Mrs. Gianini's boardinghouse for five days. It snowed on and off for another two days, then it took a while before Jeriah Ward could get a wagon back up the mountain with his wife and girls. He never let the fire go out in that cabin all winter and spring, and kept his wagon in good repair. I went up to visit them several times, and they treated me like a hero, telling me that if it hadn't been for me they might have died in the cold. I hadn't really thought about the danger, but the men around had such a respect for the mountain and for the fierceness of the weather in winter that they insisted there *was* more danger to all of our lives than I realized.

Although I never felt much like a hero, it was nice to have them appreciate what I did. And from that time on, the Ward place became kind of like a second home to me, and I got quite attached to Lynn — Mrs. Ward — and her three girls.

Alkali Jones went back to the cave off Pan Ravine the next day during a lull in the storm. I half think he was hoping the mule he'd left there would have frozen to death or run off so he'd have an excuse to go back to Mr. Dolan and try to get his $6.50 back. But no such luck. The mule was still there and still lame. Mr. Jones managed to get him back to town, and got him healthy again, although he still curses at him, calling him "the blamed orneriest dang mule I ever stuck rawhide t' the rump of!" Maybe because he figured my coming along sort of saved his and his mules' lives too — or at least saved his new mule's life by keeping him from killing it himself! — he named it *Corrie's Beast*. That's what he's been calling it ever since, though most of the time he's swearing at it so loud he never has a chance to say the critter's name at all!

I wrote in my journal all about what happened during the blizzard with the Wards — even longer than I did in the article. I wasn't in the habit of showing Mrs. Parrish everything I wrote. My journal was still a private thing I did just for myself. But she asked me what I'd said about the blizzard, and if she might see it, and I agreed.

"Corrie, this is just great!" she exclaimed after

104

she'd read only about half of it. Then she kept on reading, with a bright look in her eye. When she finally set the book down, she looked up. She was still smiling, but she tried to sound serious so I'd know she really meant what she was saying.

"Corrie," she said, "we could get this published, I'm sure of it!"

"How?" I said.

"In a newspaper. This is real news, Corrie. Papers want this kind of thing, especially personal accounts."

We talked about it some more and I asked her what I should do.

"Write it again, Corrie. Write it on separate paper, and as good as you can make it. Think of it as a newspaper story. Pretend telling folks in San Francisco or up in Oregon or back in Kansas City what it was like during that blizzard. Pretend that you're telling *real* people about what happened, and then just write it like a story."

"Should I mention my name?" I asked.

"Hmm, that is hard to know," mused Mrs. Parrish. "Why don't you see if you can write it without letting on who you are," she said after a minute. "That way it will seem more like real news reporting rather than that you're just telling something that happened to you."

Later I learned ways to do "reporting" and tell about things I was involved in without including myself. But this first time it was difficult. After I wrote everything down again as a story, Mrs. Parrish helped me make some corrections. She suggested I add a few words here and there, like *foliage* and *phenomenon.* Actually she suggested quite a few things to change, but all the time she made me think it was all my own doing.

When we were done she helped me send it to Mr. Singleton in Marysville. When he wrote back two weeks later, saying that the *California Gazette* regrettably would have to decline interest in the blizzard account, she was so upset she stormed and fumed around the house with a red face.

"That old rattlepate Singleton wouldn't know a good story if he was hit over the head with it! How he ever got into the newspaper business I can't imagine!"

All at once she had an idea. That's when she thought of her friend. "I know what we'll do, Corrie," she said. "I have a friend on the staff of the *Alta* in San Francisco. He's in advertising, but I've done quite a bit of work with him for the business. I'll send him the story, tell him it's authentic and that a friend of mine here in Miracle Springs wrote it. I'll twist his arm a bit and ask him to show it to the news editor — Kemble's his name, I believe."

"Do you really think they might print it?"

"You never know unless you try, Corrie. I've given the *Alta* a lot of my business, not just in advertising, but for various printing jobs I've needed. I think upon my recommendation, they just might consider it."

When Mrs. Parrish's friend first wrote back to us, he said, "The article's fine. Matter of fact, it's better than fine for a new reporter. But doesn't he know how important it is to identify who the hero of the story is?" He thought I was a *he* because Mrs. Parrish had suggested I send him the story as written by *C.B. Hollister,* so his editor wouldn't say no to the idea of publishing it just because I was a girl.

Mrs. Parrish answered the letter and explained why the freight driver's name shouldn't be used in the article. He responded immediately. "Kemble liked the blizzard piece. Not too well written, he said, but exciting and realistic, which is what our readers want. He complained like I did about the heroic wagon driver not being mentioned, but I told him that was a condition you'd put on publication. Anyway, he thought the piece was fine enough regardless, especially for a new reporter. Enclosed is $2.00. Whoever your friend C.B. Hollister is, Kemble says for him to get in touch. Might be that we can use something else of his in the future. Kemble likes firsthand accounts and has been looking for this kind of thing from the foothills country. We'll send you a copy of the issue when it appears."

She threw her hands in the air and let out a whoop and holler.

"Corrie, Corrie! Do you see this?" she exclaimed, shaking the check in my direction. "A check for two dollars! Corrie . . . you are going to be a published, professional newspaper writer!"

I'd been sitting beside her as we read the letter. My heart was pounding and my hands were sweating, but not because of the $2.00. In fact, I hardly even noticed that. Over and over the words from the letter spun through my brain: *Whoever C.B. Hollister is . . . get in touch . . . something else of his in the future.*

I could hardly believe it! Not just that *this* story was going to get into a newspaper — they might even want another story later, if I could write another one!

It was too good to be true!

By this time winter was over, and the story didn't appear until toward the end of April. I'll never forget what it was like sitting around the house that night after the copy of the *Alta* came, the whole family huddled near the fire, everybody looking over shoulders and around heads and through arms. Tad and Becky sat on the floor, Emily and Zack and I squatted Indian-style, Alkali Jones, Katie, Uncle Nick, Pa, and Almeda all crowded together to read the article in the *Alta* with BLIZZARD RESCUE ON BUCK MOUNTAIN in big bold black print across the top, and underneath the words: *by C.B. Hollister, Miracle Springs, California.*

Between the storm and the article, I'd turned eighteen. And there couldn't have been a better birthday present than this.

When everybody was finally done reading it, Katie congratulated me, and Uncle Nick threw his arm around my shoulder and pretended to pinch my cheek. Mrs. Parrish, bubbly and happy that it had all turned out so well, was saying things about all the articles I was going to write in the future.

But Pa was the quietest of all. He didn't say a word until the hubbub from everyone else had died down. Then he just stuck out his hand toward me. I took his hand and he gave mine a big firm shake and looked me straight in the eye.

"Corrie Belle," he said, "I reckon you're a woman now. You done this on your own, without me or your ma, though I guess you had your share of help from Almeda here. But no matter — *you* went out there after them kids. And that was a right brave thing to do — though maybe a mite foolhardy —"

Everyone laughed.

"You went after 'em. Then you thought how to write it down. You done that too. And with whatever help you had, I figure it's you that newspaper guy and them girls got to thank."

He paused, then added, "Anyhow, Corrie Belle, what I'm trying to say is that you're a mighty fine young woman — and you done your pa proud."

I held on to his hand an extra moment or two, my eyes glistening with tears as I took in the face I loved so much. God had been so good to me!

In that moment I was more full and more thankful and more proud than I had ever been in my life.

Chapter 12

Summer of '55

The snowstorm, the article, and what Pa said to me that night, all seemed to be part of the Lord pointing me toward my future. Hindsight makes it easier to see those kinds of things when your life takes new directions. And as I've looked back, I've felt that God may have brought about the events of the blizzard and then the article getting published right after the prayers I'd prayed about my future.

Even as I was still down on my knees praying in the wet grass behind that oak tree near the school, somewhere up in the clouds way up high in the sky those snowflakes were getting ready to fall. God was telling me, "You see, Corrie, even before you're through praying, I'm already sending the answers down to you. You may not realize it, but these little snowflakes are going to come down onto you, and I will use them to show you that I am answering your prayers, and will send you out into your future. I will use these snowflakes to show you that I am giving you the desire of your heart too, Corrie, which is to write."

That time of prayer and trying to give my whole self more completely to God, and then the article that came later, set me on a path I would never turn back from. I said to God, "Here is my life, my future . . . here are my worries . . . You know what I want to do . . . I am willing to do and be anything you want me to be." And then God seemed to say back to me, "I will take your life, Corrie, and I will work my will in it, and at the same time I will give you more than you could ever hope for, even more than you prayed for."

Ever since, whenever I see snowflakes falling to the ground, I think of them as beautiful tiny little remembrances of God's answers to prayer. For every prayer we pray, even before we're through praying it, God is *already* sending millions of answers down to us, answers we may not see or recognize, but they are from him nevertheless. Falling snow always helps me remember that God is so completely above us that we can never escape his quietly falling blessings and answers to prayers and his love and care.

Thus, I always look back on that time as the end of my childhood and the beginning of my being an adult. Not just because I'd turned eighteen, but because I'd let go of my worries (which kind of represented my past), and God had sent me out toward my future with a glimpse (that first newspaper article) of what it was I would be doing in the years to come. Just as Pa's and Almeda's life together was just beginning, so too was mine as a grown-up.

For the rest of that school year I kept helping Miss Stansberry at the school, and then after I was done, working at the Freight Company two or three days a week. But even before school broke off for the summer in June, I think I'd decided not to be Miss Stansberry's assistant the following fall when it started back up again. Whether it was the thinking and praying about my future, I don't know. And I still considered teaching school one of my "options" that perhaps I'd think about someday. Maybe I figured it was time to take a break from school, even though I liked being part of it. It might be that God was, like the verse said, "directing my path" by getting me to think about different things. It's hard to say. I was still too new at trying to figure out about what Almeda called "God's guidance." But I felt I ought to do something else for a spell. So my plan was to work more at the Freight Company that next year, and of course Almeda thought it was a terrific idea.

The summer of '55 was one of the happiest times I can remember. The weather was nice, and everything went perfectly. The mine didn't cave in and nobody got hurt and everybody got along real fine. We all moved permanently from the house in town out to the claim. That made Pa happy, because he'd fixed up the house so nice, and it was plenty big — big enough for all seven of us.

Tad and Becky weren't just little runts anymore, but were ten and twelve. No one worried about them getting lost as we had when we'd first come, and they were all over the place. Emily was fourteen, still quiet and beautiful. Zack was well past sixteen and was a strapping tall young man with the beginnings of a beard showing on his face and muscles gradually starting to bulge out on his arms. He helped Pa at the mine on most days, although he was over at Little Wolf's most days too, riding and breaking horses. Pa'd mutter about the two of them being "plumb loco" on account of what they did with the horses. But it was plain to see that Pa was proud of Zack's being such a tough and hardworking kid. Alkali Jones was around a lot too. His hair was gradually getting more gray in it, and he seemed to do a lot more cackling and talking and directing up at the mine than working.

Uncle Nick and Katie's son Erich, named after Katie's grandfather who immigrated from Europe, was born on the next to last day of July. Uncle Nick said he had been thinking about naming the baby after his father, Grandpa Belle, if it was a boy, or if it was a girl calling her Agatha after Ma. But in the end it was Katie's name that prevailed. So we had a new cousin in the family and were mighty pleased to have him.

As you can imagine, having Katie *and* Almeda around sure did liven up the place! When I think back to that first winter when it was just us kids and Pa and Uncle Nick in that one little cabin, all I can do is laugh. The two women sure made it different, more homey, more lively. There was more laughter in the air, more flowers on the tables, better smells coming out of the pots hanging over the fires, and everything was a lot cleaner than back then!

But I think it was a good thing there were two houses separated by six hundred yards, a stream, and some woods. Those two strong women under one roof would have been like Pa putting too much dynamite in the mine! As it was, they were able to be good friends and visit and talk and invite each other over and borrow things and help each other, while they both kept track of their own houses. Just like with the naming of Erich, Katie usually got what she wanted, and anybody who knows Katie knows she was more likely to stay Katie Morgan Belle than to become *Mrs.* Anybody! She may have been Uncle Nick's wife, but she was still "Katie" to everybody around!

I suppose you could say the same of Almeda too. She had been on her own for a long time and was used to thinking independently, unlike most women with a husband and five kids. Yet she was different than Katie in how she went about things. If Katie and Uncle Nick had a dispute about something, they'd say their mind — sometimes loudly! — and somehow or another figure out what to do. They laughed and kidded and sometimes hollered at each other — you could hear them clear down across the creek at our place! They argued, and then worked out their differences, kissed, and went on. Sometimes Uncle Nick got his way, but mostly Katie got hers.

It was different with Pa and Almeda, although they laughed and had fun together too. Maybe it was because they were older, and both had been married before. Maybe it was because there were hurts in both of their past lives. They'd each had to face the death of someone they loved very much and were now married again, but with memories still lingering from before.

Both Pa and Almeda were quieter when there'd be something to decide, more thoughtful, I guess. And if they had a difference of opinion — like earlier about the houses and where to live — it would get real quiet for a spell. In some ways yelling and arguing about things like Uncle Nick and Katie did was better for the other folks around. At least you didn't have to wonder what people were thinking! When Pa and Almeda got quiet and quit talking to each other much for a day or two, it was eerie and unpleasant in the house and all us kids would tiptoe around, not knowing what to say.

But I came to realize at such times that being quiet was their way of thinking about things. It may have been awkward for a while, but I came to see that maybe they were both quiet, not because they were angry or upset, but because they loved each other and didn't want to say something that would hurt. They needed to think and maybe pray too. And then when they did talk, you could tell they were trying hard to think of each other, not just themselves.

Both marriages were a year old that summer, and watching them develop was interesting for me. I'd never thought much about what it might be like to be married, and I wasn't thinking about it in connection with *myself.* But being older, and being Almeda's friend and getting to know Pa so much better *before* they had married made me look at them through different eyes than I could have when I was just a little kid. I did find myself wondering *if* I ever got married, way off in the future sometime, what it would be like. What kind of wife did I want to be, like Katie or like Almeda?

I didn't come to any conclusions, only that it was interesting to me, especially seeing how Almeda would try to yield to Pa as her husband. I knew that was hard for her, since she'd had to think for herself since Mr. Parrish died. And in matters like the house and how to run her business, she'd been accustomed not only to making all the decisions herself but also to thinking like a man, because she was trying to run a man's business in a man's world.

Now she was married, but she *still* had her house and business along with a husband and a family. She had to live two different lives. She'd never had children of her own before, and here she suddenly had five! Yet she still walked into her office or met with customers who looked to

116

her as the businesswoman she was.

On most days she and I would go into town together in the morning. I was learning more about how the office itself operated and would process orders that came in through the mail or write up invoices. Mr. Ashton still called me *Miss Hollister!* With me to help in the office, Almeda had more time to go out and call on miners and see potential customers, and the incoming orders picked up as a result.

"Your being here makes a big difference, Corrie," she said. "If the business keeps growing, we'll have to change the name to *Parrish & Hollister,* or *Parrish & Daughter!*"

"How about just changing it to *Hollister* Mine and Freight Company?" suggested Pa that same evening when Almeda was recounting the conversation she'd had with me earlier. "You ain't a *Parrish* no more, you know, Almeda."

I don't think Pa meant anything by it other than just a passing comment, but afterward it was quiet for a while, and I know Almeda was thinking about how all the pieces fit. I know now that she was thinking about praying about *her* future and *her* options too, just as she was helping me do in my life. Eventually she did share with me that she went through a time of real doubt and wondering about what she and Pa ought to do. She found herself wishing Pa would give up the mine and join her in the business. Then she realized maybe she wanted it because that's the decision Mr. Parrish had come to, and that it would be hard for Pa to want to be a part of *her* business if it meant sacrificing something which was *his* own, *his* dream — like the mine was. And she had to battle within herself whether she was going to be *Mrs. Drummond Hollister,* or if she was going to keep being *Almeda Parrish* with a new last name added on. Was she going to keep everything as it had been and add Pa's family, or was she going to *become* part of the family, even if it meant sacrificing some of what she had been before?

Later, when I was quite a bit older and she told me about some of these things, she said, "Every woman doesn't have to face it the same way, Corrie. Most women just get married and their husband's home and livelihood is about all they have to consider. And they're perfectly content to just be part of their husband's world. But when I married your father, it was different. And I'm so thankful that he understood. He respected me, respected that other part of my life too that had been going on before I knew him and wanted to keep going afterward as well. I think he knew I'd never want to sell the Freight Company, or would want to change the name. As proud as I was to be Mrs. Drummond Hollister, to become a 'mother' and join your family, I couldn't help wanting, I suppose, to keep a part of myself — not 'separate' exactly, but keep it as my *own,* to keep being the *me* I have always been. As much as a man and a woman become 'one' when they are married, there is still that part of you that needs to know you are your *own* person even though you are married and have given that personhood to your husband too. I don't know if other women think about it quite like that, but I have. Anyway, I *wanted* to keep the business, and to keep calling it by the *Parrish* name . . . because of something in me that didn't go away when I married your father."

And she did keep both halves of her life going just great from what I could tell — the Almeda Parrish part and the Mrs. Drummond Hollister part. I only hoped I could do as well if there ever came a time in my life when I had to.

Some days she'd go home early, in the middle of the afternoon, and get working on supper — we were a pretty big household to feed! — and I'd ride out later by myself. On other days we'd get a big pot of beans or stew prepared in the morning to sit all day on the fire, and Emily and Becky would make corn bread or biscuits to go with it. On those kinds of days we might both come home together after the office closed. It was always different. Maybe one or the other of us would be on a delivery and would be late, and the other would tend to the supper. Almeda was gracious about making me feel like I was still needed. And I suppose I *was,* even though it took some getting used to at first, not having the others depending on me for everything. Pa was a big help. He didn't mind giving the stew a stir or adding some extra water to the pot of beans or tending lunch for the rest of the kids when neither Almeda nor I was there. We were an unusual family, but Pa didn't seem to mind that.

We had Katie to think about that summer too, and most evenings one of us would go up and help her with the washing of clothes or whatever else she had to do. Emily spent half of most days helping Katie with her new little baby cousin. Becky went over there a lot too, and tried to pitch in. But Becky always thought she was a bigger help than she really was! I could tell when Emily held little Erich that she wouldn't mind being a mother herself someday!

Even with all that was going on around home, and with the work at the Freight Company to keep me busy, I kept thinking of those words in the letter to Mrs. Parrish: *Whoever your friend C.B. Hollister is, Kemble says for him to get in touch. Might be that we could use something else of his in the future. Kemble likes firsthand accounts and has been looking for this kind of thing from the foothills country.*

All summer I kept racking my brain trying to think up some other "firsthand account" I might write about to send to the *Alta*. A little dose of success was enough to make me think I was ready to be a real-live reporter!

All of a sudden, about the middle of August, the idea hit me. Of course! I had the greatest possible story right in front of my nose! If it'd been any closer it would have bit me!

The minute it came to me I was filing the

July invoices in the file drawer in the oak desk. I jumped up.

"Almeda," I said, trying to stay calm, "would it be all right if I went home early today?"

"Certainly, Corrie. Is something the matter? Don't you feel well?"

"I feel great. It's just that I think I've thought of the next story I might write and send to the *Alta*."

"Wonderful! What is it?"

"I'd rather not say till it's done, ma'am. But I'll let you read it first."

"Go, then, Corrie!" she exclaimed, breaking into a laugh. "Go and write it. Your reading public is waiting!"

I charged out the door and onto my horse and galloped all the way back to the claim. I hardly stopped at the cabin, but ran right up to the mine where, just like I'd figured, Alkali Jones was sitting on a rock and giving out advice to Pa and Uncle Nick and Zack.

"Mr. Jones . . . Mr. Jones!" I said, all out of breath as I ran up to him. "I gotta talk to you."

"Hee, hee, hee!" he laughed, looking me over from head to foot. "Can't be that one o' my mules has got me in a fix. I got one right there." He pointed to a tree where his trusty favorite was tied. "An' Corrie's Beast's tied up where she can't git loose nohow! Hee, hee, hee!"

"No, it ain't that, Mr. Jones," I said, trying to catch my breath. "Please, would you just come

121

down to the cabin with me for a few minutes?"

"Okay by me, Corrie Belle," he answered, "but I don't know if yer pa an' uncle can find any gold in that there stream without me. Hee, hee! I know this creek better'n I know that blame mule yonder. An' it ain't just nobody what gits the gold outta it. That's why I'm here, to show 'em where t' put their sluices an' pans an' where t' aim their shovels."

"We'll manage for five minutes, Alkali!" shouted Pa from where he stood knee-deep in the water. He threw me a quick wink as he spoke. "But don't you keep him long, Corrie! I don't want me and Nick and Zack wasting *too* much time when we don't know where the gold might be!"

"Okay, Pa," I answered him seriously. "I'll take care of my business with Mr. Jones as fast as I can."

The old prospector got up from his rock, grinning and cackling his high-pitched *hee, hee, hee* to himself, and followed me down to the cabin. I can't imagine what he thought it was all about, but once inside, as soon as I had grabbed a pencil and fresh sheet of paper, I started asking about his first days in California and about his discovery of gold in the creek, about how he first yelled "It's a Miracle," and how the stream was named, and then how the town started to grow. All it took was my first question and he was off retelling it all faster than I could write!

Well, that was my first "interview." And I

never had a more willing talker! I could have written a whole book just about the adventures and exploits of Alkali Jones — founder of everything in California that was of any importance, friend of everybody, who had been everywhere and seen everything and done things nobody else in the world could hope to do! I probably would have had to call the book *Alkali Jones, the Most Important Person Ever in California's History.*

As it was, I wrote a two-page story that I called "How Gold Was Discovered on Miracle Springs Creek."

I finished it four days later. That's when I showed it to Almeda.

"It sounds just like an experienced writer, Corrie!" she said. "I am excited! Do you want me to send it?"

"If you don't mind, I'd like to send it in from myself," I answered. "I've gotta try sometime."

"You're right. And they did say to have 'my friend' get in touch with them," she laughed. "Are you going to use your whole name?"

"I don't know," I answered. "Do you really think they'd mind it being from a girl?"

"If I know men, Corrie — and I do, because I do business with them all day long! — yes, I do think they'd mind. They might not say so. No man will *admit* to looking down on those of us of 'the weaker sex.' They will always talk about 'respecting' and 'admiring' us, and they'll be more than happy to be courteous and gentlemanly if it suits them. But let a woman try to *do* something on her own, especially something they think ought to be done by a man, and they don't like it. They want to keep women what they like to call 'in their place.' And they *especially* don't like a woman doing something *well* that they think is a man's thing to be doing. Don't ask me why, Corrie — but they just don't like a woman to be successful at anything except *woman* things — you know, feeding babies and sweeping floors and washing clothes and boiling water and setting dinner on the table. Not that there's anything wrong with doing those things, but a *few* of us women, like you and me, want to do some other things besides. So to answer your question again, Corrie, I would say this — I think that if you sent in your story exactly like it is, and the editor, that Mr. Kemble, figured it was from a woman — especially just an eighteen-year-old one! — I doubt he'd even read it. But if he thought it was from a man, even though the words were just the same, I think he'd read it and like it. That's just the way the world is, Corrie, if you're a woman and you want to do something that maybe is a bit out of the ordinary for a woman to do."

"Then I reckon I ought to keep being just *C.B.* Hollister for a spell longer."

She laughed. "You boil my long-winded lecture on the frustrations of being a businesswoman right down to the basics, don't you, Corrie?"

So I sent my story to the *Alta.* I addressed it to Mr. Kemble, Editor, and included a letter.

124

I introduced myself as the C.B. Hollister who had written the story about the blizzard, and thanked him very much for the two dollars. I had written another article, I said, which I hoped they might be able to use, and it was enclosed. The letter was in my best handwriting, and I tried not to make it look like it was written by a girl.

Two and a half weeks later, an envelope came to the freight office addressed to me, with a return address from the *Alta* in San Francisco.

The instant I saw it I started trembling with anticipation. I grabbed it out of Mr. Ashton's hands, and my sweaty fingers fumbled frantically to tear it open.

"Dear Mr. Hollister," the letter began — and I was so nervous that I didn't even notice the *Mr.* at first.

> We won't be able to use your article. Stories about gold being discovered in creeks around the foothills are what we call yesterday's news. Nobody cares about that anymore. We're looking for stories about people — *real* people. Your Alkali Jones sounds more like fiction than fact, and if he does exist, I don't believe a word of what he told you.
>
> I remain, Mr. Hollister,
> Sincerely yours,
> Edward Kemble
> Editor, California *Alta*.

125

I was too disappointed to think about being angry about what he'd said. As much as I wanted to be grown-up about it, I immediately felt my eyes starting to fill up with tears. I had been so sure this story about Mr. Jones was even better than the blizzard one! At that moment, I never wanted to write another word!

I dropped the letter down on the desk and quickly went out the back door before Mr. Ashton saw me start crying and blubbering right there in the office. I was glad Almeda happened to be out on the street with Marcus Weber, checking the load for an order he was taking up to French Corral.

I went out into the back of the livery, and by then I was crying. But at least I was alone, with the smells of hay and horses and leather to calm me down instead of having to face any people.

I guess I left the door open behind me, because I never heard Almeda enter. The first I knew she was there with me was when I heard her voice close behind me and felt her hand on my shoulder.

"I guess I was wrong," she said softly. "Even from a man, he didn't like the article!"

I laughed and turned around. She was holding the letter from Kemble in her hand, and a tender smile of compassion was on her face. She knew the hurt I was feeling.

But I couldn't help it — the tears kept coming!

"No matter how old a girl — or a woman

— gets, Corrie," she said, "there are times when you just have to cry. Right now, won't you just let me be — if I can say it — won't you let me be a *mother* to you?"

She opened her arms and drew me to her breast.

I laid my head against her, wrapped my arms around her waist, and melted into her tender embrace, quietly weeping. My emotions were so full, but I didn't know if it was from the letter, or from the happiness I felt at having Almeda love me as much as I knew she did in that moment. Sometimes you can't tell whether you're happy or sad, but you just keep crying anyway.

We stood there for two or three minutes, neither saying a word, holding each other tight. It was such a wonderful moment of closeness, I didn't want it to end.

Finally I felt her arms about me relax.

"You really wanted that story about Mr. Jones to be published, didn't you?" she said, looking down into my eyes, still red but at least dry now.

I nodded.

"And you thought it was . . . maybe not the best — but as good as the article you wrote about the Wards?"

Again I nodded. "I can't see that it was as much worse as Mr. Kemble said."

"But you're afraid he's right, and that you'll never amount to anything as a writer if something you liked is really as bad as he says. Is that how you feel?"

"I reckon that's about it. And he didn't say

a thing about sending them anything else. I thought he said he wanted firsthand accounts. Now I'm just back to where I was before the blizzard — which is nowhere!"

"Not quite, Corrie. There's one big thing that's changed."

"What's that?"

"You *did* write that article, and it *did* appear in the *Alta,* and you *did* get paid for it. Don't you realize what that means, Corrie — you *are* a professional writer! You have done it. Maybe only once — but that's a start!"

"But what about this?" I said, pointing to the letter from Kemble.

"It's nothing! If Singleton, and now Kemble, aren't smart enough to see a future-budding reporter right under their noses, then you can send what you write to someone else. Somebody *will* be interested!"

"In my story about Alkali Jones, do you think?"

"Perhaps. But maybe not. Kemble *may* be right about it being yesterday's news. But you can't let that stop you. You'll write another article, and then another. Some of them will be published, and some won't. But that can't stop you from writing them, not if you believe in what you want to do, and believe in yourself to do it."

She paused. "*Do* you believe in yourself, Corrie — as a writer, I mean?"

"You mean, do I think I'm a *good* writer? I wouldn't say that."

"Maybe not a 'good' writer. But do you believe

in yourself as someone who's *going to* be a decent writer someday — even if some day way in the future? Can you believe that about yourself? Can you believe that God can do that with you . . . and maybe even that he *wants* to?"

I thought a minute. "I reckon I can believe that," I replied.

"And you *want* it to happen, am I right? That is, if God opens the way for it to happen, then you want it?"

"Yes."

"Well, that's how I felt about this business, Corrie, after Mr. Parrish died. I desperately *wanted* to make the business work. I *wanted* to succeed, maybe because I figured most of the men around thought I'd pack right up and be on the next ship back to Boston. But now I *wanted* to stick it out, even during the hard times, and *make* it work. And it seems to me maybe that's what you might have to do too — stick it out, even through the hard times, and not give up, because you're *determined* to make it work . . . and to do it."

"That's what you mean by believing in yourself?"

"That's right. There are times, Corrie, when you've got to go after something you want, even when you think you're all alone and when nobody else believes in you or thinks you have a chance to do it. There are times when you've got to plow ahead with your own determination to succeed. That can be especially true for a woman trying to do something on her own. You can do it, Corrie. You *can* write . . . and you *will!* The day will come when you can march right into Mr. Kemble's office and lay your papers down on his desk and say, 'I'm *Corrie Belle* Hollister, if you please, and not *Mister* C.B. Hollister, and my story is as good as you're gonna get from any man-reporter!' "

"I could never do that!" I said, laughing.

She laughed too. "Maybe not in those words. But if that kind of determination is inside you, and you believe in yourself that much, then I can promise you, *Corrie Belle Hollister,* yours is a name people are going to see in print someday."

"So what do I do now," I asked, "if I'm going to try to keep believing in myself like that?"

"You keep looking for ideas, and you keep writing in your journal, and you keep thinking up stories and articles to write . . . and you keep writing them and sending them to Mr. Singleton and Mr. Kemble. And with everything you write you're going to learn a little something more, and one of these days those editors will start paying attention when they see your name on a story. Believe me, Corrie, Mr. Kemble has not seen the last of you!"

I laughed again. It was nice to hear her say it, though I couldn't be quite that confident myself.

The article about Alkali Jones never did get into a newspaper, though every once in a while I still think about writing a whole book about his life. Almeda's other words, however, about determination and believing in yourself — I never forgot them. Her encouragement came back to me more than once later, because that was not the last rejection I got for something I wrote. There were a lot more to come!

And her joking about what I might someday say to the editor of the *Alta* was something I remembered too. When that day came, it didn't happen just as she'd predicted, but I couldn't help thinking back on her words nevertheless.

Chapter 13

Learning to Believe in Myself . . . and Write

The following school year was very different for me. For the first time in my life I *wasn't* going to school, either as a student or a teacher's helper. It made me realize in a whole new way how much things were changing.

For everybody! Zack wasn't in school anymore either. He spent his time about equally between helping Pa and Uncle Nick at the mine and helping Little Wolf and his pa with the riding and training and selling of horses. Now that Central California had been being settled for five or six years, there were a lot more than just gold prospectors coming into the state, including farmers and ranchers. Little Wolf's pa had developed a fair business in horse selling. There seemed to be a continually increasing need for good riding and cattle horses, and they brought even more money if they were already broke and trained — which was where Zack and Little Wolf came

132

in. The two of them loved it! Anything to do with horses made them as happy as could be.

Anyhow, with Zack and Little Wolf and I gone, and Elizabeth Darien married and moved to Oregon, Miss Stansberry chose a new helper — Emily! During that year she turned fifteen, the same age as I was when we came to Miracle Springs.

Without older boys like Zack and Little Wolf and Artie Syfer in the school anymore — and there weren't any fourteen- or fifteen-year-old boys coming up in the class — Rev. Rutledge came to check up on Miss Stansberry usually once a day, to see if she needed any help moving a desk or lifting something. She was such a capable lady it was easy to forget about her being lame, but the minister didn't forget. He was always trying to find ways to make it easier for her. Sometimes when I was on my way home from town late in the afternoon just before suppertime, I'd see Rev. Rutledge's buggy out in front of the school where he was still helping Miss Stansberry. I suppose, though, with the two of them sharing the building like that, using it both as a school and as a church, they probably had plenty to keep them both occupied.

We continued living in the cabin out at the claim. Almeda and I would take a buggy into town with Emily and Becky and Tad every morning and return in the afternoon. Sometimes only one of us might go into town. Occasionally I'd want to stay home and work on something I might be writing, and other days Almeda would want to spend part of the day with Pa. By that time, whenever she did want to stay at home, I knew most of what needed to be done at the freight office. When she wasn't there, I wasn't Mr. Ashton's or Mr. Weber's boss. They knew what to do too, and we all did our jobs together and talked about any decisions to be made before Almeda got back. Yet they would ask me questions, almost as if I *were* their boss, just because of me and Almeda being in the same family now. Although it was a mite peculiar, I got used to it — but I'm glad she was there most of the time.

I didn't forget Almeda's words about having to work for something you believed in. I figured if I had the Belle blood in me, like Pa sometimes said, then I ought to put it to work for me.

So I didn't let myself get discouraged because of that letter Mr. Kemble wrote, saying he didn't believe what I wrote about Mr. Jones was true. I just said to myself: "Well, we'll see, Mr. Editor! I'll show *you* who can write around here! You're not just talking to anybody, Mister — you're talking to a Hollister, half of whose blood is *Belle blood!* Yeah, Mr. Editor, we'll see about what's true and what's not! And what's true is that I'm gonna be a reporter for your paper someday!"

That's what I said to Mr. Kemble in my thoughts. But I was nice as could be whenever I sent a story to him. And I kept signing my name *C.B. Hollister.* Almeda had talked to me about believing in myself, but I wasn't ready to believe in myself quite enough yet to start using my real name! I figured what he didn't know about who *C.B.* was wouldn't hurt him for the time being.

So I wrote stories on anything that I thought might be interesting to the folks either in San Francisco or in Sacramento. If it seemed more to do with Sacramento, I sent it to Mr. Singleton in Marysville. If it seemed more appropriate for San Francisco, I sent it to the *Alta.* Since I didn't know exactly what kinds of things a newspaper editor would be likely to publish, I tried all kinds of different approaches. Here's one I tried.

This fall the school in Miracle Springs begins its third year. Teacher Miss Harriet Stansberry reports an enrollment of twenty-four students, up eight from the previous year, though she says the average age of her children is younger than before.

When asked about the future of the school, Miss Stansberry answered: "There are still new families coming to the area, even though the rapid growth has slowed somewhat. From the age of my students, it seems as if the enrollment will probably stay about where it is for some years to come."

I then went on to tell a little about the school and what kinds of subjects the children studied, and even had a quote or two from some of the students, including one from Emily.

I sent this to Mr. Singleton, reminding him that he had printed the very first thing I had written about the opening of the school back in December of '53. I don't know whether it was that, or whether maybe he was afraid of losing the Parrish Freight advertising, but he did print this new article about the school, though he cut most of it out, including all the quotes from Emily and the others. When it appeared it was only two paragraphs long and didn't have my name anywhere on it. And Mr. Singleton never paid even fifty cents for anything I sent him. I began to wonder if that $2.00 was the last money I'd ever see for anything I wrote. But even if it was, I still wanted to write newspaper stories. I'd just have to keep doing other work besides.

I can't say that anything I wrote was any good compared to *real* authors like Thoreau or Hawthorne or Cooper or Irving or Walter Scott. But I wasn't trying to be a real author, only to write for a newspaper, and it didn't seem to me that you'd have to be as good to do that. Besides, I figured maybe writing was one of those things you had to learn how to do just by doing it a lot. So that's what I did — I wrote about a lot of different things, and practiced trying to make my writing more interesting. Like this one:

Mr. Jack Lame Pony, a full-blooded Nisenan Indian, has turned his skill in training horses into a livelihood. "When white men come to California in search of gold," says Lame Pony, "many of my people went farther north, and to mountains and hills. But I had son, cabin, land. I not want to leave."

After two or three years trying to scrape food out of the soil and sell furs trapped in the high Sierras, Lame Pony began to acquire a stock of riding horses. He was very bitter against the intrusion of gold-seekers into what he considered the land of his people. But when men began coming to him one by one in search of sturdy and dependable horses, he found that most were reasonable and not as different from himself as he imagined.

Slowly, word about his horses spread throughout the region north of Sacramento, and he had more requests than he had horses. He also found that doing business with ranchers and farmers, and even some gold miners, was not as difficult as he had thought.

"As my anger left my heart," he says, "I sold more horses. Soon had no time to trap. Had to find more horses — always more horses, then break them, train them, teach them white man's ways."

Perhaps even Lame Pony's name might have helped his reputation as the best horse trainer in the region. Wherever one goes in the foothills north and east of Sacramento, the mention of the name Lame Pony always brings a chuckle and the words, "Whatever his name says, his horses are the best." A rancher from Yuba City, who has purchased eight different horses from Lame Pony for his hands, was quoted as saying, "None of my men ever been throwed by one of his horses yet!"

Recently Lame Pony and his son Little Wolf, with the help of neighbors, enlarged their corrals and added another stable. With the continued growth of California, they foresee an even greater need for well-trained horses in the future and want to be prepared for it.

Of course I asked Little Wolf's father if I could write about him first, and Little Wolf talked him into agreeing. Mr. Singleton printed this article just as I'd written it — *after* he had signed up a small advertisement for the Lame Pony Stables to appear on the same page. The neighbors I mentioned were Pa and Uncle Nick and Zack. I didn't really talk to the man from Yuba City, but Marcus Weber knew him and heard him say those words.

I wrote a short article about Patrick Shaw, our neighbor from over the ridge, who in his spare time was getting to be a pretty well-known banjo-picker and was often invited to hoedowns from as far away as Coloma and Placerville. I drew a picture of him playing, too, to go along with the written part. But that was one of my articles that never actually made it to a paper. Mr. Shaw did ask me, though, to do a drawing of him and his banjo for him to use on a sign if he was going to be playing somewhere.

Another article I wrote was about a new church that was getting started down at Colfax. They didn't have a building yet and were meeting in a great big house. Rev. Rutledge went down there every two weeks and was more or less in charge of it, though he had people in Colfax helping a lot too, like Almeda had done when he first came to Miracle Springs.

Both the minister and Almeda were excited about the opportunity for new churches starting throughout this part of California, something I know they'd been wanting to see happen from the very first. Of course, as interested as we all were — and he would tell us what was happening in other areas on Sunday — Almeda didn't actually participate in his plans as she did at first. But at least he didn't have to make that long ride back and forth to Colfax alone every time 'cause every once in a while Miss Stansberry would go along with him to keep him company.

Religious news didn't seem to be something most folks were interested in, because that was another one of my articles that never got into a paper.

One that did, however — and I admit it surprised me, because I wrote it just for fun — was an article I called "Virginian Finds New Home After Unusual Beginning."

When Miss Kathryn Hubbard Morgan stepped off the steamer in Sacramento in May of 1854 as a mail-order bride, she could little have foretold the strange turn of events that would make her future so different from what she had planned.

Miss Morgan carried with her that day a handful of apple seeds, a seashell, a rock, a tuft of grass, some Virginia moss, and a piece of dried bark — all as remembrances of her past in Virginia and as symbols of the new life she was starting in California the moment she set foot upon the bank of the Sacramento River.

As it turned out, Miss Morgan, now Mrs. Nick Belle of Miracle Springs, did not marry the man who had paid half her passage to the West, but his brother-in-law instead.

"You cannot imagine the thoughts that were racing through my mind as I stood there in my wedding dress," Mrs. Belle said, "only to have the ceremony so suddenly interrupted and thrown upside-down."

I then went on to tell a little about the wedding and what Uncle Nick had done and the story leading up to that day, including quotes from Pa and Uncle Nick, and another one or two from Katie. When I was asking them questions, Uncle Nick got to laughing and talking and said this, which people who read the article liked best of all: "When I lit outta here on the Thursday before

140

the wedding, I figured I might never come back. I was so mad at Drum I coulda knocked his head off. But I didn't know whether to be mad at Katie and just say good riddance to the both of them, or if I oughta come back and just grab her away from him and tell her she was gonna marry me. I tell ya, I didn't know what to do. I was just all mixed up inside! And so when I rode up and saw that the wedding was going on, I don't even remember *what* I said or did!"

Then I finished the article like this:

So now Mrs. Belle, still known to all her friends simply as "Katie," has found a new life as a full-fledged Californian. Like all Californians, she came from someplace else, but now calls this her home. Her seven-month-old son will be a Californian born and bred, one of the first in a new generation of Californians who will carry the hardy breed of pioneers — from Virginia and every other state of the union — into the future of this western region of these United States.

When Katie looks out her window, if she lets her eyes go to the edge of the pine wood, she will see a thin apple tree, still too young to bear fruit, but a growing reminder of where she has come from. At its base, a different variety of grass and moss than can be seen anywhere in the surrounding woods is growing — also a reminder that this is a big land, and that its people have roots that stretch far away.

One day Katie's young son will eat apples from that very tree, Virginia apples, and Katie will be able to tell him the story of how its seeds ventured to a new and strange place called California, and put down roots and began to grow, in the same way that his own mother did.

The "hardy breed of pioneers" and the "venturing to a new and strange place called California" and "roots that stretch far away" were all Mr. Kemble's words. But the ideas, even at the end were my ideas, and he just helped me to say it better.

Having this article published surprised me, especially since most of the things I'd written had been sent right back to me. But Mr. Kemble was real interested in this one. He sent me $3.00 for it — the first time since the blizzard article that I'd gotten any money. And afterward, about a week after the story had come out in the paper (we sent for ten copies! Katie had lots of folks back east she wanted to send them to), a letter came to me from the *Alta.* I hadn't sent anything else to them and couldn't imagine what it was. But when I read the letter, the tears that came to my eyes were not tears of disappointment like the last time the editor had written to me.

Mr. C.B. Hollister
Miracle Springs, California
Dear Mr. Hollister,

Your recent article "Virginian Finds New Home," etc., has been very well received, both by the staff and the readership of the *Alta*. I must say, your writing has improved very much since your first story with us, "Blizzard Rescue on Buck Mountain."

As I read those words I couldn't help thinking of what he'd said when he sent back the Alkali Jones story about finding gold in the creek. I wondered if he remembered. I read on —

I would be interested in seeing other such pieces in the future. There have already been two inquiries as to when the next piece by C.B. Hollister is going to appear. I hope to hear from you soon.

Sincerely,
Edward Kemble,
Editor, California *Alta*

I sat down and handed the letter to Almeda. She read it.

"There, you see," she said. "You never know what can happen if you believe in yourself and just keep moving in the direction you think God wants you to go."

And if you practice your writing a lot, I thought, *and don't mind getting most of your things sent back to you!*

But in an instant this one brief letter seemed to make the earlier disappointments all forgotten.

Chapter 14

I Write to Mr. Kemble

I took the letter from Mr. Kemble not just as an encouragement but also as an opportunity.

There was that determination in my Belle blood coming out again! But I figured I ought to make the most of the fact that he'd written and seemed interested.

So I decided to write back and ask him some questions so I'd be able to know what to do differently in the future. I had thought the story about Alkali Jones was good, and hadn't expected anybody to pay much attention to what I'd written about Katie. As it turned out, my figuring was exactly opposite from Mr. Kemble's. Not only that, two months after his letter, *another* letter came, telling me that a paper from Raleigh, Virginia, had written to ask permission from the *Alta* to reprint the Katie story! The name C.B. Hollister was going to be read clear back on the East Coast!

I wrote to Mr. Kemble and asked him just what it was about the "Virginian" article that his paper liked and wanted more of.

About three weeks later I got a reply.

"There're two kinds of stories," he told me. "First, there's straight news reporting. That's when you've got to tell your *who, what, where, when, and why.* Those are your *w's,* and no reporter better forget them for a second.

"But then you've got your human interest kind of stories. They're more personal. The *who* and the *why* are still important, but you're telling about people instead of just facts, so the other things aren't quite so important.

"Now, you take your 'Virginian' story. That was human interest if ever I saw such a thing. Once you got folks interested in your Katie Morgan, they kept reading. They weren't trying to find out news or facts; they were reading because you were telling a story about a *person.*

"I've got lots of reporters who can give me the five *w's.* One rambunctious kid on my staff chases around this city night and day and is the first person on the scene of anything that happens. Now *he's* a newshound!

"I'm not saying that if you brought me some noteworthy news like that I wouldn't print it. Maybe I would. But from the two stories of yours we've run so far, something tells me your talent tends more toward the human interest side. You seem to see interesting things in people. And if you can keep doing that, keep finding interesting people and keep finding interesting ways to tell folks about them, then I don't doubt you might just have a future in this business. Leave the five *w's* to the newshounds like that Irish kid on my staff I was telling you about. Stick to the personal angles, Hollister, and let me see anything you come up with."

He didn't say it in that same letter, but much later when he and I were talking about similar things, he said some other things along this line.

"Women and men are different in how they read a paper," he told me. "Now we've got more men than women in California, but we still have thousands of women readers, and we've got to please them, too.

"Men want to know news and not much else. They're your five *w's* readers. Give them what happened, where, when, and why and they'll put the paper down and get on with what they got to do. Men want to know whether it's likely to rain, what kind of damage the flood caused, what price gold is fetching, whether there've been any new strikes, and how much a new pick or a fifty-pound sack of beans is going to cost.

"But a woman'll look through the paper while she's drinking her tea, and she'll want to read about Polly Pinswiggle's garden that the rain washed out. That woman reading about Polly doesn't care a hoot about how many inches it rained or about what the seed is going to cost to plant a new garden. All she's thinking about is poor Polly!

"The women are your people readers. And that's why we've got people like you writing

147

human interest stuff. You've got to go out and find interesting people who are involved in interesting things and then write about them, mixing in a little news too, and getting three or four of the *w's* in there to please your traditional men-editors like me.

"In other words, you've got to sort of *pretend* to be a reporter, a newsperson. But really you're not. What you are is a journalist, a writer about people, not facts. And as long as you keep writing about people, you can count on having readers, whether you ever dig up any hard news or not."

All this he didn't tell me, as I said, until later. But even now, without realizing it, I think this was the way my interest in writing was heading. I'd been keeping a journal all this time, not just to record the facts of my life, like where I went and what I did and what the weather was like — what Mr. Kemble would have called the five *w's*. I kept a journal to write about a person — a person who happened to be *me* — and what she was thinking and feeling inside.

In a way, the other writing that I was starting to do now — about Mr. Jones and Katie and the Wards and Jack Lame Pony — was kind of like the writing I did in my journal, but about other people instead of me.

Having Mr. Kemble tell me about the two different kinds of writing helped me understand it a lot better. But besides the five *w's* and the human interest kind of story, there was one other ingredient that I came to see was an important part of *any* writing that anybody did. Maybe it was the most important ingredient of all.

And I have Rev. Rutledge to thank for putting this other factor in focus for me.

Chapter 15

A Sermon About Truth

One Sunday morning Rev. Rutledge preached about *truth*. Nothing he said had that much to do with writing, I suppose, but I found myself listening carefully, trying to understand everything and applying it to my own life.

"Truth means different things to different people," he was saying. "To some people truth means a set of *ideas*. Therefore, if we were talking about five statements, we might ask which of them were true:

"The sky is blue and the sun is shining today.

"California is smaller in size than New York.

"It is raining outside.

"There is no gold in Miracle Springs Creek.

"This building is used for a church and a school."

He paused a minute and let the words sink in, and then repeated the five statements.

"Now then," he went on, "which of those are *true* and which are false? We can look outside and see the sunshine and the blue above, so we know that it is *not* raining. How about New York and California — which is larger? Any of you youngsters of Miss Stansberry's school know the answer?"

Someone piped up that California was the second biggest state behind Texas.

"Right," said the minister. "So saying California is smaller than New York is a *false* statement. How about the gold? *Is* there gold in the creek?"

Some laughter spread through the room.

"Depends on who you ask, Reverend!" called out one of the miners whose claim was known not to be doing so well.

More laughter followed.

Rev. Rutledge joined in the laughter. "However, I think we would all agree that there is *some* gold still around," he said, then added, "even though it might be unevenly distributed!"

He let the chuckling gradually die away before he went on. "Then, finally, is this building used for both a church and a school?"

"Yes!" went up a chorus of young voices, enjoying being able to participate during the sermon time for a change.

"Right you are again!" said Rev. Rutledge. "Now, think back to the five statements. How many were true, and how many were false? Let me repeat them for you."

He did so. Then he waited a minute.

"All right, now — how many statements were true?"

"Two," answered someone.

"Are you all agreed? Two true, three false?" said Rev. Rutledge.

A nodding of heads and general murmur went around.

Again he waited until everyone had quieted down. When he finally started speaking again his tone was different and he was more serious.

"I must confess that I tried to trick you," he said finally. "I hope you will forgive me, but I wanted to get across a point that many people misunderstand. Now — let me answer my own question. How many *true* statements were there? My answer is . . . *none*."

He waited to let the word sink in. I don't think anyone in the whole church understood what he meant, but we were all listening for what would come next.

"Two statements were *correct* — two statements of fact; three statements were *incorrect* — three statements of *error*. But my point this morning is that *truth* is a very different thing from correct 'facts.' That's why I said in the beginning that to most people truth has to do with the factual correctness of a set of ideas. But in reality, as the word *truth* is used in the Bible, it means something very different."

He stopped, opened up his Bible, then went on. "Let me read to you what the Bible calls truth. In John, Jesus says, 'I am the truth.' He doesn't say that such-and-such an idea, or a certain set of statements or facts are the truth, he says that *he* is the truth.

"Do you remember when I said that truth means different things to different people? Let me show you two people in the Bible to whom truth meant completely different things. In the eighteenth chapter of John, after Jesus had told his disciples that *he* was the truth, Jesus stands trial before Pilate, and he again brings up the subject of truth. Jesus says to him, 'Every one that is of the truth hears my voice.' And then Pilate asks one of the most profound questions in all of the Bible. He says to Jesus, 'What is truth?' — the very question we're examining this morning.

"Can you get a picture of these two people in your minds — Pilate and Jesus — both talking about truth?

"But they mean very different things by the word. When Pilate asks 'What is truth?' he is asking for a set of ideas, facts, opinions — just like the list of statements we talked about. Pilate wants Jesus to tell him what facts and ideas comprise what he calls 'truth.' But Jesus gives him no answer. Jesus says nothing. Why doesn't Jesus answer him?"

Rev. Rutledge paused a moment.

"Jesus doesn't answer him because truth is not at all what Pilate thinks it is. There are no *ideas* that would make up what Pilate calls truth. Not even any religious ones.

"What is the truth, Pilate wants to know. Jesus *himself* is the truth, and he is standing right in

153

front of Pilate. Pilate *has* the truth but doesn't know it!

"In other words, the truth is a *person,* but Pilate wants mere *ideas.* And even true ideas, even correct facts, are not the truth. 'The sky is blue today' is a correct statement of fact. But it is not a truth. Only a *person* can be true."

Rev. Rutledge stopped again, and took in a deep breath. I was concentrating hard to understand what he was saying.

"I hope I've made myself clear," he said, "about the difference between truths and facts, and about the contrast between Jesus and Pilate. I know I've gone on a long time, but there's one more very important point I must make. If I don't say this one last thing, then my whole sermon may mean nothing to you. My whole sermon could amount to nothing more than just a nice set of 'ideas' that I have given you, without there being any *truth* in it.

"So, here is my final point: Jesus is not the only person who can be of the truth. So can you and I!"

Again he stopped to let his words sink in.

"Jesus said that everyone who is *of* the truth hears his voice. In other words, Jesus is *the* truth, but others — people like you and me, people who hear his voice and obey him — we can be *of* the truth. Jesus is the first truth, but we can be *of* the truth if we follow him and do as he did."

As I pondered Rev. Rutledge's words afterward, what he said next was the thing that stood out most in my mind. "Truth is people and how they live. If we want to *be* of the truth, like Jesus said, it's in how we live and what we do, not in what we think about ideas and facts. Someone sitting right here this morning — one of you in this church building — may have been mistaken in all five of those statements I gave. You might have missed every one. Yet you might be more an of-the-truth person than another one sitting here who got every answer correct — if that person with all the wrong answers went out and *lived* the truth by what kind of person he was — lived following Jesus' example.

"Was Pilate a true man?

"After asking 'What is truth?' what did he do? Knowing Jesus was innocent, knowing the charges against him were lies, and even admitting that he could find nothing wrong in him — knowing all this, Pilate still gave Jesus over to the Jews to be crucified. Pilate may have wondered what truth was, but he was not a 'true' man. He did not stand up for what he knew to be right. He was weak. He was not *of* the truth."

The minister paused again, took a breath as he closed his Bible, and went on.

"Truth is not ideas, not even religious ideas, not even Christian ideas, not even correct ideas. Truth is *life*, not thoughts. Truth is a person. That person is Jesus. And he wants us to be *of* the same truth as he is — by how we live.

"As Christians we are to be *true people*. Jesus

was of the truth. Pilate was not. Jesus *is* the truth. Pilate wanted ideas, but was not a strong enough person to *live* truthfully.

"Each of us has to make the choice which of these two men we are going to be like. How are we going to live? By the truth or not? Who is going to be our example? Are we going to *live* truth, or only think and talk about it?"

Chapter 16

A Talk About Growth

It probably seems like I was forever taking walks and thinking and writing in my journal about what was going on in my mind.

But I did also try to write down things I was doing — however, the most important thing about life to me was what was going on inside me. Maybe it isn't this way for everyone, but I liked to try to figure out the meanings behind things. When I read a book, I think about what the author said, and I like to read for the ideas as much as the story. I reckon that's why I liked Mr. Thoreau so much. There was hardly *any* story in *Walden* but it was full of ideas that made me think.

Maybe that's why I wanted to be a writer, so I could think on paper, and so I could get to know other people and find out what they were thinking and write down their ideas for others to get to know too.

Ever since I began keeping my journal and started learning more about what it really meant to live as a Christian, something inside me wanted to grow, to learn, to stretch and think and explore and be more than I was. I wanted the inside part of me to get bigger so it could hold more. Thinking and talking to God and reading and writing down my thoughts and feelings in my journal were all ways to stretch and enlarge that deep-down part of me and make it grow.

Almeda and I talked once about growth. I told her this feeling I had inside about wanting to stretch that inside part of me, and to be more than I was.

She thought for a long time, and then said that she felt the process of growth inside each person's heart and mind was one of the greatest gifts God has given to us.

"There is nothing in all the world," she said, "quite so wonderful as an individual soul expanding, reaching out, coming awake to itself, to its Maker, to other souls around it. The awakening of the soul, then its growth and development, then its reaching out to touch other souls that are similarly growing along the same journey — there is hardly anything in all of life so wonderful."

Her voice became quiet and her eyes misted over.

"Like you and me?" I suggested.

"I think so, Corrie," she replied in a soft tone. "I truly think so."

"What makes some people want to grow like

that, and others content just to stay where they are?" I asked.

"That's a huge question, Corrie! Who could possibly know the answer to that?" she laughed.

"Is it because some people are made to be thinkers?"

"People like you, I take it you mean?"

Now it was my turn to laugh. "You know what I mean," I said. "Not everybody keeps journals and thinks about everything like I do."

"Maybe people should think more."

"But I figured God made some folks to be thinkers and others not to be. Isn't everyone different?"

"That's true. But I have the feeling God wants *everybody* to think, though maybe in different ways and to different degrees. It has nothing to do with being smart, but with using the brain you do have. The book of Proverbs, the whole of Scripture really, is full of urgings and promptings to learn and understand. One of my favorites is 'Apply your heart to understand, incline your ear to wisdom.' That sounds to me as if God meant for every person in the world to try diligently to understand things, and to get wisdom. It also says to *seek* for wisdom like silver, and to *search* for it like hidden treasures. That sounds to me like we're supposed to think!"

"It sure doesn't seem as if everybody thinks like that. Or at least they don't talk about it so you'd know."

"Most people don't think, Corrie, not like God wants them to. They aren't searching for wisdom and applying themselves to understand, and that's why not even very many people who call themselves Christians are growing as they could be."

"You mean you can't grow if you're not thinking about everything?"

"No, that's not it exactly." She paused and thought for a little bit. "Let me try to explain it another way," she said finally. "To grow, I would say — yes, you *do* have to apply yourself to understand, and you have to search and pray for wisdom, just like the Bible says. Both those things imply not only prayer but also a lot of thought. And if you're *not* doing those things, your thinking and growth and wisdom muscles, so to speak, are going to lose their power to think and grow. If you don't use a muscle, it gets weak. In the same way, if you don't think and make an effort to grow and, as Proverbs says, *apply* yourself to understand, then pretty soon you won't be able to, and you will stop growing. You become capable of thinking by thinking. You become capable of growing by growing. And thus you grow as a Christian . . . by growing. And certainly thinking and praying and searching for wisdom are all part of that process.

"But growth isn't *only* a matter of thinking — most important of all is the *doing* that goes along with the thinking. Thinking all by itself won't stretch that inside part of you. It won't make you bigger inside, won't draw you closer to God, won't make you *more* than you are now, as you said. The real growth comes *after* the thinking, when you *live* what you've been thinking about. The growth comes when we *do* what God wants us to.

"In other words, Corrie, it's a process that has two parts. First we have to try to understand, we have to search and pray for wisdom. But then after that, as the second part, we have to *live* out what our understanding has shown us. We have to *do* what Jesus says. We have to put others first, we have to be kind and do good, speak pleasantly and behave with courtesy and trust God and pray, and do all those things Jesus told us to do. That's the active part of getting understanding and wisdom.

"There's the thinking part and the doing part. And growth only happens when *both* are at work in your life together. That's how the inside part of you, the *real* you down in your heart, will stretch and grow, and will always be becoming more than it was the day before."

Chapter 17

A Walk in the Woods

After the church service, I needed time alone to try to understand Rev. Rutledge's sermon more clearly. I had a feeling God might have more meaning for me in his words than I could know just from sitting in the church. I had to think about it some more.

So I told Pa and the others to go on ahead home without me. I'd walk back in a while. Then I went out into the woods behind the church, the same woods where Becky'd gotten lost. On the way as I walked, the conversation I'd had with Almeda about growth came back to me, and I found both her words and those of the minister mingling in my mind, trying to sort themselves out.

As all of it was tumbling through my mind — living truth instead of just thinking about it, growth, understanding, wisdom, the thinking kind of person I was, everything Almeda had said about growth and doing and Proverbs — it came to me how important all of it was if I was going to be a writer.

You couldn't even write the five *w's* without being able to think and understand things, I thought to myself, because one of them was *why*. So if you were going to write, you'd *have* to think and understand!

Then I found myself thinking, not just about the kinds of writing that Mr. Kemble had talked about, but about *why* I wanted to write in the first place. At first it had just started with journal writing. I had only needed to express myself, to think out loud.

But now I realized there was more to it. I still liked to think on paper — whether in my journal or in something I was trying to write. But now that I thought about it in light of Rev. Rutledge's and Almeda's words, I found myself realizing that I wanted my writing to amount to something more than *just* writing. I wanted it to *mean* something, even though I'd never really stopped to think about it before.

Then I found myself reflecting back on that early morning walk I had taken just before the blizzard began, when God had shown me so many things and when I had prayed about my future. I recalled how on that day I had thought about the *truth* too, and had felt God telling me to find the truth and to follow it and live by it and be fed by it. The scripture I had thought about that morning came vividly back to me: *In truth shall you be fed, and so shall you dwell in the land.*

Suddenly it all made so much more sense!

The truth was so much bigger than just giving a factual account of the five *w's*. Anybody could do that. That was the Pontius Pilate side, the facts, the statements, the lists of ideas that might be half correct and half wrong. That might be "reporting," but that wasn't what I wanted to spend *my* life doing.

I wanted to *grow* — in understanding, in wisdom . . . in truth.

And I wanted my writing to be true. Not just with correct facts, with the five *w's* — though that might be part of it too. But true like Rev. Rutledge talked about truth — true to the kind of person I was, true to the Bible, true to the man who *was* truth — Jesus, God's Son. I wanted my writing to point to the truth, to be *of* the truth. I wanted it to make people think and help them to grow. Even if I was writing a story about something other than Jesus, who was the truth, I wanted how I said it to make people think in a true way, not a Pontius Pilate sort of way. I wanted people like Katie, who didn't believe in spiritual things, to read my writing and think in a little more of a true way. Katie herself had said, after my article about her, that she could never think about the apple tree in quite the same way after reading what I wrote. Well, maybe if I could get her thinking about apple trees and people and roots in a true way, someday that might lead her to think about God in a more true way too.

That's what I wanted my writing to be able to do, even when I was writing about something that didn't have anything to do with God on the surface.

I remembered the verse Rev. Rutledge had quoted in church just a little while ago, the words Jesus had said: "Everyone that is of the truth hears my voice."

"Help me, God, to hear your voice," I prayed. "I want to hear your voice so that I can grow and understand. I want to hear your voice so I will know your wisdom, and so that what I write will be true."

I was deep in the woods now, the church and all the buildings of the town long out of sight.

I stopped and dropped to my knees among the decaying leaves and dead pine needles of the forest floor. I clasped my hands and closed my eyes.

"Oh, Lord," I prayed aloud, "make *me* a true person! When I hear your voice, give me strength to do what you say. Give me your wisdom and your understanding. Be the guide to my thoughts, God, and then help me to *do* what you want me to. Make my life be a true life, so that my writing will be *of* the truth."

I drew in a deep sigh, and my nostrils filled with the fragrance of the forest. It was such a lovely smell, and I couldn't help thinking right in that moment that God had made it only for me. It reminded me all over again how much he loved me.

Me — just me! The God of the universe loved

little me, Corrie Belle Hollister!

Almeda had been telling me that simple truth for three years, and now I really grasped it on my own. Now maybe it was my turn to find ways to begin telling *other* people the same thing, as she had told me.

I stood and turned around and began retracing my steps out of the woods. Everywhere I looked were the signs of growth, from the fresh buds on the tips of the pine branches to the shrubs and undergrowth of the forest. Overhead the early afternoon sun poured through in tiny rays split into millions of arrows by the infinite, green needles on the trees.

I had always loved the woods, the mountains, the streams, the sky, the clouds. Yet the older I grew the more alive it all became to me. Every time I went out alone something new revealed itself to my consciousness. This was not the first time I had walked in this pine wood. But I think it was dearer to me on this day than it had ever been before. The mystery of its loveliness was somehow almost sacred. From the church building that the men of Miracle Springs had built, I had stepped into God's presence itself — into his greater, living church. All about me were signs and reflections of God himself, things he had made.

And as I left the wood that afternoon I found myself wondering about the *truth* contained in the trees and the bushes and the grass, even the truth of the blue sky and the sunshine and the smells I so enjoyed. Were all these things "true," as a man or woman might also be "true," because they came out of God, and reflected part of his nature?

That was far too big a question for my mind! I thought about it all the way home, and was no nearer to figuring it out than when I left town.

Chapter 18

New Times Come to Miracle Springs

By the time I got back to the claim, the afternoon was half gone and it was snowing again. Not real snow — it was toward the end of May, and though snow that late wouldn't have been out of the question higher up in the mountains, down in the foothills where we lived it would have been close to impossible.

A storyteller might call it snowing "figuratively." Sometimes a writer says something that has more than one meaning, like the apple tree when I was telling about Katie. So when I say it was snowing, I mean that God had already begun to answer my prayers again, my prayers about wanting to be true and to write in a true way. Like the last time, when it was *really* snowing, I didn't recognize the things that happened as God's little answering snowflakes coming down into my life.

The invisible snowflakes of answered prayer are

falling down all around, millions of them. But it takes a special kind of sight to see them, and most folks never know that kind of snow's falling. You have to learn to hunt for them, learn to see them, train your eyes — your *inner* eyes, the eyes that look out of your heart and your mind. Just about everything having to do with God and the spiritual side of life is like that — they're things you have to train yourself to see.

And so I've been trying to train myself to look for buried, hidden, *invisible* things the more I grow as a Christian — the hidden meanings that are all around us, the invisible little glimpses of God that most folks don't notice.

When I got back to the house, there sat Rev. Rutledge's buggy out in front. I didn't think anything much about it until I went inside. Everyone was sitting there all quiet and talking in low tones. The reason the minister'd come was to tell us that our mayor, Mr. Vaissade, had just died, and the pastor was making the rounds to tell as many people as he knew would be interested.

Mr. Vaissade was an older man, and I don't suppose his death was all that much of a shock. But he had been in church with us just three or four hours earlier, and now suddenly was dead. He'd collapsed right on his own front porch after walking back to town from church, and was found lying there by a neighbor an hour later.

Although we all liked Mr. Vaissade, we weren't close friends, so his passing away like he did wasn't in itself an event that changed everything for me or for our family. But it turned out to have a huge effect on the future of the town, and an even bigger effect on our family.

Mr. Vaissade had been mayor of Miracle Springs for a year and a half. I don't think during all that time I heard of one thing in particular that his mayoring had done or changed. He just *was* the mayor, and everybody went on about their business as usual. Maybe he had to sign papers or something, but I never heard anything about it, and didn't really see what difference having a mayor made to Miracle Springs.

But folks had gotten kind of used to the idea of having a mayor, and almost immediately talk began to stir up about who was going to replace him. Miracle was a respectable town now. Including all the folks round about in the foothills and farms and ranches for several miles around town, there were fifteen hundred or two thousand people, and the area was growing back into the kind of size it'd boasted right after the first gold strikes. No town of the importance of Miracle Springs, they said, could be without a mayor. And in addition, political fever was in the air that summer of 1856 after Mr. Vaissade's death.

California had changed so much, even in the four years we had been there. *We* were by now among the old-timers, the early settlers in the West. For the first several years, just about everybody coming to California from out East was coming because of the gold. Right at first it was the gold miners themselves, then later the people like the Parrishes and others — businessmen and suppliers and merchants and others who hoped to make a living *because of* the gold rush, though they may not have been directly involved themselves.

But by now, people were pouring into the West to settle it and live here, just because there was space and freedom and adventure, and because they heard the land was good. Schools and churches were being built all over the state, and thousands of families were putting down roots. Farmers were turning the valleys into land that produced food. Cities and towns were growing. Railroads joined the different parts of California, and there was even talk of a railroad someday to hook up California with the rest of the states back East.

California wasn't the only place that was growing. People were coming west — the *whole* west. California'd been made a state in 1850, and by this time there was lots of talk that Oregon would be the next new state. Settlers were coming across the Oregon Trail by the thousands.

It wasn't only because of all the new people coming west that folks were more interested in politics that year. In the only other election since California'd been in the union, statehood had been so fresh and the gold rush so much on people's minds that folks just didn't pay that much attention. After all, Washington, D.C. was thousands of miles away, and Californians didn't figure it made much difference whether they voted for

Franklin Pierce from New Hampshire or General Winfield Scott.

But now in 1856, everything was different!

A new political party, the Republicans, had been formed only a couple of years earlier. The issue of slavery, though not really involving California too much, was still talked about, because the new party was more or less based on anti-slavery. I suppose Californians were interested in the Republican party too because one of the state's most well-known men, John Charles Fremont, was one of the leaders in getting it established. Fremont was rich from the gold that had been discovered on his huge estate. He had been one of the first explorers to California, had fought the Mexicans, and was one of the first new senators in 1850 right after California became a state. All in all, John Fremont was the most famous Californian there was.

And now, for the presidential election of 1856, the new Republican party had chosen John Fremont as their nominee.

That made all of California stand up and take notice of national politics. Now it made a big difference who people voted for — James Buchanan from far-away Pennsylvania, or John Fremont *from California!* We may have been the newest of the Union's thirty-one states, but all of a sudden we were one of the most important.

"Why, just think of it," everyone was saying, "a Californian in the White House!" That election of 1856 was just about the biggest thing to hit

California since the discovery of gold!

John Fremont was one of those kinds of men that not everyone liked. When people talked about the election, lots of folks like Alkali Jones didn't have that much nice to say about him. But one thing was for sure — he was *our* John Fremont . . . from *our* own state! And folks figured that made him worth voting for no matter what else they thought.

So politics and John Fremont and Washington, D.C., and slavery and Republicans and Democrats were all topics in the air and on people's minds and lips that summer.

And as part of all that, and maybe because of it, almost immediately after Mr. Vaissade's death, folks started saying Miracle Springs needed to have an election for mayor.

Chapter 19

The Candidate

An election for mayor in a little town like Miracle Springs may not sound like a big event, especially with an important presidential election going on at the same time. But around the Hollister-Belle claims, the minute Franklin Royce announced that he intended to run for mayor, all discussion about Buchanan and Fremont faded completely into the background. The Miracle Springs mayor's election was all at once the only election anyone cared about!

"I told ya afore, an' I ain't changed my mind none since," said Alkali Jones. "The man's a pole-cat!"

"A snake!" put in Uncle Nick.

They were sitting around the table in our house talking about Royce and the election. Alkali Jones' high laughter had ceased. The men didn't seem to know whether to be angry or miserable over the turn of events. So they wound up being a little of both.

"You talked t' Rafferty again, Drum?" asked Mr. Jones.

"I've talked to him half a dozen times," Pa answered, "and so has every other man in town. But he says he's got all he can do as sheriff, and he don't want to be mayor too. None of us can convince him."

"Ol' Vaissade didn't do nuthin'. What makes Rafferty think he can't jest combine the mayorin' an' the sheriffin'?"

"He says the town's growing, and needs both a mayor and a sheriff."

"Well, one thing's for sure," added Uncle Nick. "The mayor's job won't be a do-nothing job no more with Royce in it."

"Simon says he can keep him from doing any mischief," said Pa. "That's another reason he doesn't seem too worried."

"What harm *could* he do?" asked Katie, who had been listening from the other side of the room, where she and Almeda were sitting. "After all, he's still got his bank to manage."

Pa turned his head, then gave a shrug in answer. "Who knows? But if you give a man like Royce a chance, he'll find *some* way to turn it to his advantage, and I reckon that's what has the rest of us worried. Especially if we just let him have the job for the taking."

"I'll tell you what he could do," said Almeda. "Once a man like that's in power, he can do all kinds of things. I've seen it happen in other towns. There's been corruption in the governments of Sacramento and San Francisco, and any time you have money involved in political de-

175

cisions it can be dangerous. As mayor *and* the town's only banker, Franklin Royce could control this town. He could bring in his own people and set up a town council. He could control decisions that were made. He could levy taxes, commission building projects, change laws. He already dictates how the money in this community flows. He could put Parrish Mine and Freight Company out of business if he wanted to. What if, as mayor, he wanted to get rid of Simon Rafferty as sheriff and appoint one of his own men? I'm sure he could find a way to manage it. Before we knew it, warrants on Drum and Nick would start to appear from the East. I tell you, the possibilities are frightening. I don't trust Royce, even though I'm forced to do business with him."

"But the mayor's never had that kind of power. Vaissade couldn't have gotten rid of Simon if he'd wanted to."

"Power has a way of sneaking up on you if you put it into the wrong hands. Once you start something, it's sometimes impossible to undo it. I for one would feel a lot more comfortable if the door were not opened in the first place."

Uncle Nick now spoke up again. "He's always wanted this land of ours," he said.

"An' every other piece he could git his slimy white hands on," Jones added.

"Then, why doesn't one of the other men in town run against him?" asked Katie.

"No one wants to," replied Pa. "Bosely, Simon, Lewis, Miller, Griffin — me and Nick and Rutledge, we talked to all of them. I even tried to get Avery to consider it, but he keeps saying religion and politics don't mix."

"Wouldn't do no good anyway," said Uncle Nick. "Royce would win, whatever anybody else tried to do. He holds mortgages and notes on eighty percent of the property in the whole area. Nobody's gonna cross him up when it could mean he'd call due what they owe him."

"But they could still vote against him," I suggested. "I can't see why everyone can't simply choose not to vote for him, or vote for nobody. He'd never know."

"Economics, Corrie," said Almeda, looking over toward me. "Sad to say, money dictates power. If Royce doesn't win, he could call *everyone's* mortgages due. When they can't pay, he forecloses on whatever properties he wants, and winds up owning all the land for miles. Such a prospect might even be worse than calling him our mayor. Nobody *knows* whether he'd do that, but just the threat can be enough to frighten people into doing what a man like that wants. He wouldn't even have to say anything — a mere rumor circulating that foreclosures would result if he wasn't elected would probably be enough to insure his victory. That is *if* someone was running against him. As it is, he probably won't even have to go that far."

Chapter 20

The Two Campaigns

Mr. Royce continued to be unopposed in the election for Miracle Springs mayor, which was scheduled for November 4, the same day as the presidential voting between Fremont and Buchanan. He gave a couple of speeches in town in June, but nobody paid much attention since he was the only one running. And after that, he didn't do much else. About the only sign that would let a stranger know there was even an election going on was a banner in the window of the bank that said, "Royce for Mayor."

Nobody liked the idea of Franklin Royce being mayor of Miracle Springs, but gradually they got used to it and the hubbub and complaining slowly died out. Out in the open, no one really said much. I guess what Almeda said was true — they didn't want to get on Royce's bad side for fear of what would happen. Royce didn't have any "paper" against our claim (that's what Pa called it), but Parrish Mine and Freight still had business dealings with the bank, so we had to be careful like everyone else.

One other thing quieted down all the initial worries, something that was a surprise to everybody. Mr. Royce started making himself agreeable. He didn't give any more speeches, but he walked around town, smiling, shaking people's hands, visiting in the stores. He even came into the freight office a time or two for a minute, saying he was checking up on his customers, seeing how they were doing, wondering if there was any way the bank could be of service to them. He was so polite and friendly you almost couldn't help liking him!

The words "election" or "mayor" were never mentioned once. He never said a thing about asking people to vote for him. Of course, he didn't need to — there was no one else they *could* vote for!

Mr. Royce knew, I suppose, that folks were suspicious, not only of him but of bankers in general. And he probably knew that he wasn't the best liked man in Miracle Springs, and that people were nice to him only because they had to be since he was the banker.

That could hardly make a man feel too good about himself, knowing people had more fear than liking for him. I can't imagine anyone finding it pleasant inside to know that people were afraid of him. But I figured that Mr. Royce decided he'd rather have people liking him as mayor than being afraid of him, so he had vowed to himself to change his ways and be nice from now on.

Rev. Rutledge talked sometimes about giving people what he called "the benefit of the doubt" — thinking the best of them. Maybe that's what I was trying to do with Mr. Royce.

When he'd come around, I'd watch his face real careful and look into his eyes to see if I could see the change. I like to watch people and try to imagine what they're thinking. But I couldn't see anything in Mr. Royce's face. His mouth had a nice smile on it when he talked, but there was just no way to tell what he was thinking. His eyes didn't seem to look exactly at you when he spoke. It was like he was looking just a little bit off to one side, and so the conversation back and forth was just a tiny bit crooked, though such a little bit that I doubt anyone else even noticed. I didn't talk to him much myself, only to answer when he'd come into the office and say "How are you today, Corrie?" before going on to talk a minute with Almeda or Mr. Ashton. So maybe that crookedness was just something I noticed that he didn't do with everyone else. But his eyes didn't sparkle, they just kind of looked past me.

I watched other people, too, as they talked to him. I was real curious about this changed friendly Mr. Royce. Mr. Ashton seemed to be drawn into the banker's friendly smile, and their words back and forth were jovial and lighthearted. Almeda, however, always seemed to be looking into those dark gray eyes of Mr. Royce's as if she was trying to figure out the thoughts behind them too. She smiled and was very gracious, and their talk was polite. Her eyes didn't sparkle at such times either. Despite the smile on her lips, her eyes remained serious and seemed to be turning over more thoughts inside than her words let on.

Even Pa and Uncle Nick gradually started speaking more kindly about their future mayor.

"We may as well get used to him," said Pa one evening. "I never liked the man, an' I'd rather see someone else run. But we're stuck with him. He's gonna be the mayor and he's gonna be the banker, and it's for sure we don't want to be on the wrong side of *his* fence once he's *that* important."

"I reckon you're right," said Uncle Nick, "though I'll still feel a sight better once I get the $450 I owe him for lumber paid back. I don't like to be indebted to no man, least of all him. Politicians *and* bankers are both a mite too full of smiles to suit me!"

"I don't trust the varmint nohow!" put in Alkali Jones. "Jest like I don't trust ol' Fremont neither. Anyone what's been in California as long as me knows too much 'bout what Cap'n John's *really* like! I ain't gonna vote fer neither o' the skunks!"

"And a big difference *that's* gonna make, Alkali!" said Pa, laughing. "Fremont's gonna carry California so big they might as well take Buchanan off the ballot, and Royce don't need nobody's but his own vote to win."

"It's the preenciple o' the thing, I tell ya, an' I ain't gonna vote fer neither o' 'em!"

181

Pa chuckled to himself, but said nothing more.

"Well if *I* could vote," said Katie, who had been following the conversation with interest, "I would vote for anybody, just to have my say in what happens. You men are lucky, Alkali, to be able to vote. You shouldn't throw the chance away just because you don't like the candidates."

"Aw, but Drum's right. What blame difference is it gonna make anyhow who we votes fer, or even iffen we votes at all?"

"It's the American way, Alkali," said Pa, smiling, and giving his friend a poke in the ribs. "When you came out West it was just a wilderness. Now we're a state and our man's running for the White House, and we got our duty as citizens to do. Come on, Alkali, you got to get into the right spirit for this election!"

I couldn't tell at first how serious Pa was, but when I saw him throw Uncle Nick a quick wink, I knew. I think he meant the words but was using them to make Mr. Jones squirm a little.

When they'd get to talking about Mr. Royce, Pa was pretty kindly disposed toward him and seemed willing to forget about the past. Uncle Nick was more cautious, but not as critical as they had both once been, though he did say one time, "It's easy for you to forgive him, Drum. You don't owe him a dime. Why, you got four thousand dollars *in* his bank! But me, I gotta still worry some, till I get that house all paid for."

Pa only laughed. He'd worked hard in the mine

these last two years, getting enough to add on to the house, and save money besides. Since they'd both got married, Pa and Uncle Nick had kept their earnings separate, and as much as Uncle Nick had settled down, he still wasn't half the worker Pa was. And Zack had by now begun to make a pretty big difference in the Hollister share of the output of the mine. I didn't know how Pa's and Almeda's money was being handled now that they were married — the Mine and Freight Company, that is. That's something they never talked about to me.

All through the conversation about Royce and Fremont and the elections, Almeda remained silent, although I don't think it had anything to do with the money. I could tell she was listening to every word and was *very* interested in what was being said — that much was plain from one look at her face. Just as clear was that she was thinking real hard. But what she was thinking about, she didn't let on so much as one little peep.

The weeks of summer went by. Royce kept up his pleasantness campaign. The leaves on a few of the birch trees started thinking about turning yellow. Both Mr. Singleton's *Gazette* and Mr. Kemble's *Alta* were full of the Fremont-Buchanan election, and there wasn't much room left for an aspiring girl-writer from a little foothills gold town. I hadn't seen anything of mine in either paper since May, though I kept writing. Mr. Kemble was still looking at two more articles I'd sent him — one called "Summer in the Foothills of Gold Country," and the other one of what he called his "human interest" stories about Miss Stansberry and the school, and especially about how she had learned to use her lameness as a strength instead of a weakness.

The Summer-in-the-Foothills one was mostly about the beauty of the countryside and how summer was such a special season. I had the idea out walking one day, watching Pa and Uncle Nick and Zack and Mr. Jones all working away in the stream and mine from where I was standing up on a hill behind the house. I had been thinking how much I loved the countryside God had made, and when I saw them laboring away after little pieces of gold, the realization came to me that the land itself was really the treasure, not the gold. The "real gold" — that's what I called it in the article — was the land and its people, not just the nuggets that they were digging out of the streams and rivers. Someday, I said, there might not be any gold left, but there would still be this wonderful land, and there would still be people to love and cherish the land, and that was more lasting than any riches any miner could ever dig out of even the wealthiest mine. So the article had one of those "double meanings," because I meant the word "gold" in the title to stand for the wealth of the land itself.

Anyway, I figured Mr. Kemble would be sending it back to me some time real soon. But I hoped the article on Miss Stansberry might get published. And in the meantime, the papers were full of editorials about the election and reprints from papers out East and articles about the slavery question and where the two presidential candidates stood on that and all kinds of issues. There were also other elections going on for California's senators and representatives in Washington. So much was happening so fast. Everything was growing. Sacramento had just been made the capital of all of California two years before in 1854. Now that we were so close to the center of politics, the elections for state offices had gotten everybody's attention too, and even a time or two men came through making speeches and telling everybody to vote for them, though half the time no one had ever heard of them.

Chapter 21

Almeda Surprises Everybody!

One evening toward the latter part of July, Almeda was late coming home from town. I'd been home for some time. Supper was all ready, Pa had quit working and was cleaned up, but still she didn't come. Finally Pa said we should just go ahead and eat, though it wasn't like her to be so late. At first I think he might have been a trifle annoyed, but by eight o'clock, when she still wasn't home, he started to worry.

Finally Pa got to his feet. "I'm going into town," he said, "to find out where she is and if she's okay."

He walked out the door and toward the barn to saddle his horse. But not two or three minutes later, Almeda's little buggy came around the bend and up the road toward the house.

A moment or two passed before she and Pa came through the door together. From the look on Pa's face, she still hadn't told him what had caused her delay.

Without sitting down, she waited until everyone was quiet. We all had our eyes fixed on her, wondering what she was going to say. Her face was serious but bright, and it was obvious something was brewing inside her head that she was dying to tell us all about.

"I'm sorry to be so late," she said. "I didn't expect this, but as I got ready to come home, suddenly a great . . . a great sense . . . of God speaking to me began to come over me and I knew I had to be alone for a while. As it turns out, I've been thinking, praying, and crying for over two hours! But now . . . I believe I know at last what he's been trying to tell me."

She stopped and took a deep breath. Then she got a big smile on her face, and was clearly excited about what she had to say.

"I've reached a decision," she said. "Hopefully with God's help —"

She paused again, then announced:

"I've decided to run against Royce . . . for mayor!"

Silence fell like a heavy cloud throughout the house. No one said anything. Everyone was too shocked.

Becky was the first to break the silence by bolting past Almeda and through the door.

"Where ya going?" called Pa after her.

"To tell Uncle Nick and Aunt Katie!" shouted Becky back at him, already halfway to the bridge over the stream.

That was all Pa said for a while. He was real quiet, and from the look of expectation on Almeda's face I could tell she was waiting for him to say something.

"Well, if that don't beat all," he finally said. "You are a lady full of surprises, I'll say that for you."

Almeda laughed, and finally sat down, showing some relief. I brought a plate and set it down in front of her at the table.

Pa didn't say anything more, just sat there thinking about this turn of events. From looking at him, I couldn't tell whether he approved or not. I guess it was quite a thing for a man to get used to, his wife saying she was going to run for politics. It wasn't the kind of thing women did, or that men usually approved of!

I decided to break the silence myself. "What makes you think you can do it?" I asked. "If a woman can't vote, I wouldn't think they'd let you *run* for an office."

"Well, women *ought* to be able to vote," she replied, "and I intend to run whatever anyone thinks."

"Anyone . . . including me?" said Pa finally, looking over at her.

"Well, I . . ." Almeda hesitated. "I just thought, Drummond, that you'd be all for it. I've heard you say yourself you didn't like the thought of Royce as mayor."

"You're right, I don't. I reckon I just wish you'd said somethin' to me first, that's all."

"I'm sorry, Drummond," she said, genuinely surprised, as if she'd never thought about talking to Pa ahead of time. "If you'd rather —"

"No, no," interrupted Pa. "I ain't gonna stand in your way."

Then he tried to lighten the tension some by letting out a laugh. "Who knows, maybe I'll like the notion of bein' known as the mayor's husband! But what about Royce?" he asked, serious again. "He ain't gonna like this one bit!"

"Franklin Royce can think what he will. If he calls my notes due, I'll borrow the money from *you!* I don't owe him more than a couple thousand dollars."

Pa laughed again. "Well, you're determined enough," he said, sounding as if he was getting gradually used to the idea. "I reckon I'll give you my vote. But since women can't vote, and men being what they are, I can't see how you'll get many more."

"What about everything you and Nick have been saying about none of the men around caring for Royce?"

"That was before. Now that he's changed, I ain't so sure most of the men wouldn't still prefer him to voting for a woman."

"Are *you* prejudiced against the idea?" asked Almeda, still wondering what Pa thought.

"I'm just tellin' you how folks'll see it, and you know as well as I do how men are about women doing 'men's work.' "

Almeda sent a glance in my direction, as if

189

to remind me of the conversations we had about that very same thing.

"We'll see," she said. "I'm not so sure Royce has changed as much as everyone thinks. I have a feeling he's just as conniving as ever, and if folks have a choice in the election . . . well, we'll have to wait and see. I just think they ought to have a choice."

In a few minutes Katie and Uncle Nick, led by Becky, came in. Uncle Nick was carrying fourteen-month-old Erich, but set him down as soon as they were inside. He'd been walking about three or four weeks, and now he went toddling about while Becky and Tad tried to keep up with him. Still sitting at the table, Almeda did her best to eat some supper and answer everyone's questions. Her surprise announcement caused an uproar in the house. No one knew what to think, but everybody had plenty to say in response!

"I think it's exciting!" said Katie over and over. "If I'd thought of it myself, why *I'd* have run!"

"Being the wife of this character," said Pa, tossing his head sideways toward Uncle Nick, "I wouldn't exactly have recommended you as qualified for the position."

"Why, Drummond, how dare you!" she said.

"I'm only saying," laughed Pa, "that Almeda here's got a reputation as a businesswoman that goes further back in Miracle Springs even than Royce's — when *did* he come to town, Almeda?"

"I think it was late '51 . . . maybe early '52."

"There, you see," continued Pa. "Parrish Mine

and Freight has been doing business in town since '50." He stopped. "Hmm, now that I think about it, maybe you *can* put up a campaign against Royce."

"Sounds like a campaign slogan to me," said Katie. " 'Hollister for Mayor — Part of Miracle Springs from the Beginning!' "

"How about being my assistant, Katie?" said Almeda.

"No, no, no!" interjected Uncle Nick. "If a woman's gonna try to go up against a man, at least you gotta have a man runnin' it for ya."

"Are you suggesting, *Mister* Belle," said Katie, "that two women would not be able to do it?"

"*Three* women!" I added.

Katie and Almeda cheered and clapped to have me joining their debate. "Now we three outnumber you two!" said Katie. "Perhaps we should *vote* on who should be the campaign manager, right here and now!"

"Make it three against three!" chimed in Zack. "I'm sixteen. My say oughta count as much as Corrie's!"

"Now you're talking, son!" said Pa. "You just stand aside, Katie, and let us men figure out the best way to go about this thing!"

By now we were all laughing, including the kids, who had never seen a family squabble line up quite so definitely with the women against the men. It was sure good to see Pa entering into the spirit of it now, after his initial hesitation.

A lot more lively discussion followed throughout the evening. Despite all the suggestions the rest of us were free to give, the wisdom of the candidate prevailed when she said, "Perhaps the best idea is that we let this whole *committee* manage my campaign. What do you say — we six, three men, three women? That way we'll be able to give even voice to the concerns of the men *and* the women, the young *and* the old, the married *and* the unmarried, the business persons *and* the miners. We'll have our whole Miracle Springs constituency represented right on our 'Hollister for Mayor' committee — do you all agree?"

Everyone looked around at each other. What she said made sense.

"Maybe you *are* cut out to be a politician, Almeda," said Pa. "That sounds just like the kind of solution a mayor oughta be able to figure out — with a little speechmaking thrown in!"

We laughed.

"And the first thing for the committee to get busy on," she said, "is publicity. That, I think, would be your department, Corrie," she added, turning toward me.

The result could be seen the next afternoon in the window of the Parrish Mine and Freight Company, with a hand-lettered poster where the words *Vote Almeda Hollister for Mayor of Miracle Springs* suddenly declared to the whole town that the poster in the bank's window wasn't the only political message to be heard anymore.

This election had now become a two man — that is, a two-*person* — race!

It took only the rest of that day and half of the next morning for the poster to be seen and for word to begin to get around. But when it did, the news spread like a brushfire in a hot wind. Before the week was out there wasn't *anything* in the mouths of people for miles around other than what they thought of Almeda going up against Franklin Royce. Some folks thought it was ridiculous. Others said privately they would vote for her if they could, but they just couldn't afford to rile Royce. A lot of the men said women ought to stay where they belonged and keep out of politics. Of course, all the women admired Almeda and loved the idea, but none of them could vote. And most of the men, whether they liked the idea or not, said she had guts to try it, although some added it would probably ruin her business in the end. Royce wasn't the kind of man you got on the wrong side of, they said.

All of a sudden, the Fremont-Buchanan election seemed far away and uninteresting!

Chapter 22

The Campaign
Gets Started

With the town all a buzz, there was still not much active support for Almeda against banker Franklin Royce.

People were talking *about* the election, but nobody was coming out and saying they actually supported Almeda. If anything, business around the office was quieter than usual. Almeda was right in the middle of a hurricane of talk and interest and discussion, but the Parrish Mine and Freight office was quieter than a tomb. And even the people who did come in seemed reluctant to mention the election. They just took care of their business and left without more words than were necessary.

"You know what it is," said Almeda one day in frustration to me and Mr. Ashton. "They're all afraid Franklin is standing behind his window over there watching!"

The bank and freight office, two of Miracle's

busiest places and biggest buildings, sat looking right at each other across the intersection of the two main streets. There they sat, with the General Store and the sheriff's office and jail on opposite corners and lots of other little stores and buildings in between, making up the central square block of Miracle Springs.

And there stood the posters in the windows of each, saying nothing out loud, but silently saying so much about what really made Miracle Springs work and operate and "function" every day as a town. *Royce for Mayor,* said the one, promoting the man who owned the bank and who as a result co-owned or part-owned three-quarters of all the farms and ranches and businesses and homes for miles around. And in the other window folks read the sign I had made that said *Vote Almeda Hollister for Mayor of Miracle Springs.* Everyone knew that it was Almeda who had gotten them their gold pans and sluice boxes and their bags, shovels, wagons, spare parts, picks, saddles, ropes, and nails. At her livery half their horses and mules were tended, and at her blacksmith's forge Marcus Weber repaired their tools, re-shod their horses, and fixed their broken wagon wheels.

I don't suppose any two people had done more to make Miracle Springs what it was in 1856 than Franklin Royce and Almeda Parrish Hollister. Yet it seemed more than likely that most folks would end up on Royce's side. Even though through the years Almeda had given credit to most of the men of Miracle Springs one time or another, she didn't hold mortgages on their property. And if she went out of business, as sorry as they might be, they could always get what they needed someplace else. If she was gone, probably Royce himself would set up a new business to replace hers!

"What we need is a flyer, a pamphlet!" Almeda exclaimed, after a few moments pause, still staring out the window, looking toward the bank. "Folks are just too nervous to be seen talking to me. But if we distributed something they could take home and read when they're alone, then they wouldn't have to worry about being seen by you know who."

She spun around and faced me. "What do you say, Corrie? A flyer — you can help me write it, and I'll take it down to Sacramento to have it printed up. We'll get five hundred, even a thousand printed up. We'll scatter so many of them around that everybody will see it eventually!"

We got started on it that very afternoon.

Almeda told me what she wanted to say. I wrote it down in the best way I could, she made some changes, and then I wrote it over again. I started to work on a couple of pictures for it, too, so that it would look interesting — a sketch of Almeda's face, and another one of the front of the Freight Company office, as a reminder of what Parrish Mine and Freight had meant to the community.

During the evening we all sat around and talked — what Almeda still called her campaign "committee" — trying to figure out what we ought to say. Katie kept talking about needing a campaign slogan, and Almeda finally settled on: Almeda Hollister — A Hard-Working Part of Miracle Springs' Past Who Will Be Faithful to Its Future. She Will Put *Your* Interests First."

That slogan would go on top of the handbill. Under it would be my sketch of Almeda. At the bottom would be words like: Integrity, Experience in Business, Familiar with Needs of Miners, Dependable, Friend of Miner and Rancher and Farmer, Working Hard for Your Prosperity.

All that would comprise the front page. Inside the fold, people would open it up and read the written part about how Almeda had come to Miracle Springs, how the business had been started, and how much she had done for the miners through the years — helping get what they needed, giving them extra time to pay if needed, delivering things at odd hours or even in rain or snow if something was needed right away, opening up her livery or blacksmith's shop in an emergency even if it meant getting Marcus up in the middle of the night — and finally saying that as mayor she would continue to do all those things for the community, always looking out for the interests and well-being of the people she represented.

During those first couple of weeks, Mr. Royce continued to be his same smiling, friendly self.

In fact, three days after the poster went up in our window, we were astonished by another personal visit by the opposing candidate himself. Mr. Ashton had spotted him out the window walking in our direction from the bank.

"Here comes Royce!" he said, and he hurried back to his chair and tried to busy himself with the papers in front of him. Almeda and I braced ourselves for — well, we didn't know what, but I don't think either of us expected it to be pleasant.

But Mr. Royce walked in the door, a big smile on his face, and went straight up to Almeda.

"Well, Almeda, I must say this is a surprise! Welcome to the race!" he said.

"Thank you, Franklin," she replied, shaking his hand. "You are being most gracious about it."

"Whatever our differences in the past may have been, I congratulate your intrepid decision. California needs more women like you!"

Almeda smiled, the two wished each other well, and then the banker departed, leaving Almeda with a question on her face. "Have I completely misjudged that man?" she said after a moment, speaking more to herself than to either of us. Her eyes remained fixed on the door Mr. Royce had just left for another few seconds. Then she shook her head and went on with her work. Was she doubting whether she had done the right thing?

Thereafter, Mr. Royce kept being nice about

the whole thing. Whenever anyone asked him about the election, or mentioned Almeda's running against him, his response was something nice and friendly.

"It's a free country," he might say. "Anyone is able to do as his conscience leads him, and I salute Mrs. Hollister's courage to stand up for what she believes in."

Or: "She is a strong woman, and Miracle Springs should be proud to have her as one of its leading citizens."

Or: "It is remarkable, is it not, what women are able to achieve when they persevere? She has done a great deal for this town, and I for one have the greatest respect for her as a businesswoman in what is predominantly a man's occupation."

Whether he was truly being nice, or just didn't think he had to worry about Almeda's hurting his election, I didn't know. One thing was for sure, folks were starting to change their opinion of him, and his nice comments about Almeda only made them like him all the more.

But some people didn't believe a word of it. Like Katie. When she heard that last remark he'd made to Patrick Shaw — which his wife had told Katie — she got downright riled.

"I tell you, Almeda, he's talking out of both sides of his mouth!" she said. "All those nice words don't fool me a bit."

Almeda laughed. "Why do you say that?" she asked.

"He may be saying nice things about you, but he makes sure he always mentions that you are a woman, and that this is a man's world. He doesn't *have* to say anything — it's obvious he wants people to think for themselves that being a mayor's no job for a woman."

"He's never said a word to that effect, Katie."

"He doesn't need to. He's relying on the men around here to draw that conclusion for themselves. Patronizing, that's what it is. He's being nice to you so that folks won't take you seriously. It's almost as if he treats your running against him as a joke that doesn't *really* mean anything as far as the election's concerned."

"I don't know, Katie," Almeda replied with a thoughtful look on her face. "It just may be that Franklin Royce has changed his ways after all."

Chapter 23

I Surprise Myself!

Right in the middle of all the excitement of getting the handbill ready and everything else to do with the election, a letter came from San Francisco that caught me by surprise.

"Dear Mr. Hollister," it read. "I would like to run your article about Summer in the Gold Country in the *Alta* next week. Enclosed is $4 for it. I have to admit your pieces continue to surprise me. Some of the people on our staff tell me your writing is among the most favorably received of anything we print among our women readers. I don't know how you do it, but you seem to have a good feel for the kinds of things that women enjoy reading about. Keep it up! I am confident we will be able to sell this article to several eastern papers as well." It was signed, "Edward Kemble." Then underneath had been added: "It may be that we will also run your story about the lame schoolteacher. It will depend on whether we have space to spare. You're getting the picture about 'human interest.' But of course, right now we're swamped with election news."

I was elated. This was the most positive thing he'd ever written me! He actually said there were people who *liked* reading what I wrote!

Over the next two or three days, I read his letter several times. My conscious mind couldn't help feeling good at the words "favorably received," "good feel for what women enjoy reading," "keep it up" and "you're getting the picture." But down deep something was bothering me.

At first I didn't know what it was.

Then gradually thoughts began coming back to me about that Sunday when Rev. Rutledge had preached on truth. He had talked about *people* being true rather than *ideas*. I found myself wondering about it further, questioning how to make my writing "true." It seemed like I was getting to do what I had always wanted to do. Writing for a newspaper had been my dream, and now here I was actually doing it! And if I was going to keep on doing it, I wanted to write truthfully.

I thought about the two articles and about what I had written, and about what Mr. Kemble had said about them. The more I thought about them, the more I did feel like I could be proud of those articles as truthful. I honestly *did* feel there was something more special about the gold country than just the gold itself — and that was the land. And I hoped what I'd written about Miss Stansberry overcoming her lame leg would show folks something about her down inside that was a good thing for them to see, a part of her true character.

Yet something kept eating at me inside. I'd written about ideas and thoughts and feelings and people in a good and honest way, even in a way that people might like reading about. But something was still wrong.

I remembered Rev. Rutledge's words: *Truth is not ideas . . . only a person can be true.*

All at once I knew what was wrong with the two articles. It wasn't anything I said about Miss Stansberry or the gold country. It was in Mr. Kemble's letter. All the nice things he'd said were pleasant to hear. But the words that now suddenly jumped off the paper as I looked at his letter again were the very first ones: "Dear Mr. Hollister . . ."

Mister Hollister . . . Dear *Mister* Hollister . . . *Mister . . . Mister . . .* !

That's what was wrong! Truth wasn't the ideas, it was the person, and I was the wrong person! Mr. Kemble didn't even know who I was! He thought I was a man. How could I possibly be a writer who was trying to write about true things when I *myself* wasn't being true?

Then the words that had come out of my own mouth that same day came back to me, the words I had prayed to God in the woods after the church service: *Lord, make me a true person!*

If my writing was going to mean anything, no matter what it was I happened to be talking about, then I had to be true *myself!* And maybe this letter from Mr. Kemble was my opportunity to start. After all, being a true person isn't something you put off and figure you'll get around to some other time. You either are or you aren't. And if I had let this little lie slip in about who I really was — even though neither Almeda nor I had a thought of deceiving Mr. Kemble at first — I couldn't wait for some other time to set it right.

Setting something right is a thing you have to do now, not later. So I figured I'd better do something about this situation . . . and soon.

I'd gotten the letter at the office in the morning. All day long I thought about it. And by the middle of the afternoon I'd made a decision that surprised even me.

So that night, in as calm but determined a voice as I could, I said to Pa and Almeda:

"I'm going to San Francisco."

Almeda's eyes opened up wide as Pa exclaimed, "What in tarnation for, girl?"

"If I'm gonna keep writing for his paper," I said, "there are a few things I need to talk to Mr. Kemble about. And I just don't figure there's any way to do it but in person."

I reckon they both sensed from the resolution of my tone that there was no way I was going to let them talk me out of it.

But that didn't stop them from trying. In fact, at first Pa said if I was determined, one of them would have to go with me. But in the end, after endless instructions and warnings, they sent me off with the boys keeping me company for at least half the way.

Chapter 24

Face to Face
with Mr. Kemble

Zack and Little Wolf went with me on horseback as far as Sacramento. We camped out for one night somewhere between Auburn and Folsom. We lay around the fire and talked until after midnight before I finally drifted off to sleep.

I left my horse at a livery in Sacramento and went on to San Francisco alone. Zack and Little Wolf said they'd keep busy and see the city and would meet me back at Miss Baxter's Boarding House in three days. Miss Baxter could hardly believe it was us, and said she'd never have known Zack if he bumped into her on the sidewalk. What a feeling it was, the three of us — still kids inside, I reckon, but alone in the city and knowing we could handle ourselves. Well, Zack and Little Wolf could handle *them*selves, and I felt safe enough as long as I was with them!

Not until I was alone on the steamer floating down the Sacramento River did it begin to dawn on me what I was doing. I was on my way to the biggest city in the West — alone!

I'd climbed tall trees when I was little — terrified that I was going to fall, too frightened to look down, yet tingling with excitement as I kept climbing higher and higher . . . afraid, but glad to be afraid! And not so afraid that I didn't want to get as high up as I could.

That's how it felt as I looked out over the river and watched the shore glide past and felt the warm breeze on my face and in my hair. I was nervous, and thought that anyone who saw me would have noticed my knees shaking under my calico skirt. But I wouldn't have wanted to be anyplace else.

I thought of traveling to San Francisco with Almeda exactly three years earlier. I was so dependent on her back then. It had been *her* trip about *her* business. *She'd* made the arrangements. *She* knew what to do and where to go. I had been just a little girl.

And now here I was, not only going to San Francisco alone, but going there on my *own* business, about something that concerned *my* life. It had been *my* decision to come, and I was on my own to figure out what to do. I had the name and address of a boardinghouse run by a friend of Mrs. Gianini's, but that was all.

I still felt young, but I knew I was starting to grow up. I was going to San Francisco by myself and, as fearsome as it might be, I knew I could figure out what I should do. And if I couldn't, then maybe it was time I learned. I had to grow up sometime. And maybe the best way to learn how to stand on your own two feet without your pa or ma helping you is to just go out and start walking on them without anyone's help.

I thought too about how dependent I had been on Almeda spiritually. She had been the one who had first told me how God felt about us, and about how he wanted us to think and live and behave. I hadn't known anything about God and his ways back then. When I think back to some of the questions I used to ask her, I can't help but be embarrassed at how naive I was. But on the other hand, that's how you grow and learn — by wondering, by asking, and by having someone you can look up to who can help you as you're trying to figure things out. So I'm glad I wrote in my journal about some of those lengthy conversations Almeda and I had. I still go back and reread them now and then — the talk we'd had about what sin meant when Mrs. Gianini was working on the dresses, the talk we'd had right on that same Sacramento River steamer about faith, the Easter Sunday afternoon just after I turned seventeen when I'd prayed that God would make me into the person he wanted me to be, and the long talk on the way home about obeying. Every one of those talks remains so special in my memory, and makes me love Almeda all the more as a mother.

Now those truths she had given me were part

of *me*. She had taught me, helped me, encouraged me, and loved me. But the most important thing she had done for me was to help me stand on my *own* spiritual feet. She had helped me to think for myself, helped me as I learned how to pray, and encouraged me gently as I grew.

I had been grappling with the whole prospect of what growing up meant, and about my future. But the fact that I was thinking about options, about writing, about what truth was, and about growing to be a woman, the fact that I was asking God about them, showed that maybe I *was* growing up after all — or at least starting to.

And now here I was on my way to San Francisco! I would never have imagined it just a few months ago. But now . . . who could tell what the future might hold.

If being so far away from home wasn't enough to make my knees quake, the thought of facing the editor of one of California's biggest newspapers sure was! The more I thought about it, the more foolish this whole thing seemed. Yet I still knew I had to go through with it, even if it meant I never saw another word of mine in Mr. Kemble's newspaper . . . or any other newspaper! If growing as a Christian and being a "true" person had anything to do with becoming an adult, then I had to do this thing I had come to do, no matter how hard it might be. I'd never *keep* growing if I didn't do the thing that was set before me.

Another idea had been running around in my

mind since just before we got to Sacramento. The closer we got to the big city, the more I found myself thinking about it — and it had to do with the election back home between Almeda and Mr. Royce. By the time I walked into Mr. Kemble's office the next day, I had figured out exactly what I wanted to say to him.

Of course, the conversation didn't quite go the way I had planned it!

The lady in the *Alta* office seemed a little surprised when I asked to see Mr. Kemble. I don't know why. I tried to look as professional as I knew how, and I had brought along my best clothes to wear. But I couldn't hide my age.

She asked if he was expecting me. I said no. Then she asked my name, and I said he didn't know me and that I wanted to wait to tell him my name in person.

That kind of annoyed her, and she told me to sit down and wait, which I did. It was a *long* wait, and I think maybe she hoped I'd get tired and go away. But I kept sitting there, and finally she got up and went somewhere out of my sight. When she came back a minute or two later, she said, "Mr. Kemble will see you now, young lady," and she led me down a hall to the editor's office.

The instant I walked in the door, a panic seized me, and I forgot everything I'd intended to say!

There sat the man I took to be Mr. Kemble behind a big desk, looking up at me with a half gruff expression that said, *I don't know who you are or why you're here, but I'm busy. So get on with your business and say what you have to say before I throw you out!* Before he had a chance to say anything, all of a sudden I was talking, hardly knowing what was coming out of my mouth.

"Mr. Kemble," I said.

"That's right," answered the man.

I walked forward and stood in front of his desk.

"My name is —"

My throat went dry suddenly and I couldn't get out the words.

"I'm not going to hurt you, Miss . . . Miss whoever-you-are. You don't need to be afraid to tell me your name."

"That's just it, sir. When I tell you my name, you may say you never want to see me again."

"I doubt that. But come on — out with it. I haven't got all day."

I tried again. "My name is — *C.B. Hollister.* Corrie Belle Hollister."

"What? You're C.B. Hollister? I don't believe it!"

"I'm sorry, Mr. Kemble. I never meant to not be truthful . . . it was just something that happened at first, and then I never had the courage to say anything once you started calling me *mister* in your letters."

I was shaking from nervousness and fear and from wondering what he would do. But at least I had said it.

"You're just a kid," he said at length. "And a girl, besides!"

"But I want to be a newspaper writer," I said, though my voice was trembling. "I *am* sorry," I apologized again, "and that's why I came here to see you, to tell you the truth about who I was, and so that the rest of any articles I write can have my full name on them, so that everybody else will know too."

Mr. Kemble leaned back in his chair, thinking for a moment.

"You came all the way to San Francisco for that?" he asked. "Just to see me and set the record straight on this *C.B.* business?"

"Yes, sir."

"Hmm," he mumbled. "That shows some spunk — I like that." He paused again. "But as to your doing any more writing for the *Alta* . . . most of my reporters are older, and —"

"I'm nineteen," I said. "Halfway to being twenty."

He chuckled. "That's hardly old in this business!"

"You said folks liked reading what I wrote," I ventured cautiously. "They didn't care how old I was . . . or that I was a young lady instead of an old man."

He leaned forward and eyed me hard for a minute. Now I *was* afraid I'd said too much!

All of a sudden he threw his head back and laughed. "You *do* have spunk, young Miss Hollister! And you're not afraid to say what's on your mind," he added more seriously, "or to come a hundred and fifty miles to make something right, even if it's for something you shouldn't have done in the first place. I like that. Those are good qualities for a writer — spunk and courage. So tell me, what's on your mind to write about now — same kind of human interest stuff our former friend C.B. Hollister's been sending me?"

He smiled at his own humor, but I had my answer ready. I'd been thinking about it all the way from Sacramento.

"I want to write about the election in Miracle Springs," I said. "I'd like to write three articles on it."

He laughed again. "The election's being covered by more experienced reporters than there are gold miners in the Mother Lode. If Fremont ever so much as sets foot in the state, there will be a hundred writers waiting. You'd never get near him!"

"I don't mean that election," I said. "I mean the Miracle Springs election — for mayor."

"What could my readers possibly care about that?"

"They'd be interested because a woman is running against the town's banker. You've heard of Parrish Mine and Freight Company."

"That's right," he said. "Run by Almeda Parrish — fine woman, from what I hear. And you say *she's* running against the town banker?"

I nodded.

"What's his name?"

"Franklin Royce."

He let out a low whistle. "I've heard of him too. A slick operator, and with plenty of dough. And you think you can write something my readers will be interested in?"

"You mentioned your women readers liking my articles — don't you think they'll want to read about a businesswoman in politics?"

"Yeah, you're probably right," he said thoughtfully, nodding his head slowly. "The thing is unheard of — though everything's new in California these days."

After a minute of silence he went on. "Now you understand, Miss Hollister, that if I agree to print something of yours about this election — well, for that matter, anything of yours in the future —"

"Three stories on the election," I reminded him.

"Whatever — whether it's the Royce-Parrish story or something else — you understand that I can't pay you near what I did before. Women only fetch a third or a half a man's wages, and a girl who isn't even twenty yet . . . let me see — I doubt I'll be able to give you over a dollar an article."

A *dollar!* I shouted inside. Whether it was my mother Agatha Belle Hollister or my stepmother Almeda Parrish Hollister rising up inside me — or some of both of them! — what Pa called my Belle blood started to get riled. Why should the exact words that might have been worth three or four dollars a week ago be worth only *one*

dollar now? Because he had found out that I was
a lady instead of a man, and a young lady besides?
It didn't seem at all fair!

But before either of us said another word, the
door of Mr. Kemble's office opened behind me.

Chapter 25

A Familiar Face

Into the editor's office walked a tall young man, carrying a stack of papers. He wore a cap tilted to the right down over his forehead, which kept me from being able to see his eyes at first, though there was immediately something familiar about the way he walked and the few blond curls coming out from beneath his cap.

The instant he spoke I remembered the voice as if I had just heard it yesterday!

"Mr. Kemble," he said, "I've got those files you asked me to dig up on —"

He stopped, apparently just as surprised to see me as I was him.

"If I didn't know better . . ." he said, pausing to look me over from head to foot. I couldn't think of a single word to utter as I stood there, probably with my mouth hanging open.

"It *is* the girl from off in the backwoods gold country!" he finally exclaimed. "Are you still trying to get into the reporting game?"

"You two know each other, O'Flaridy?" asked

a bewildered Mr. Kemble.

"We ran into each other a couple years back, though I can't remember your name," he added, looking again at me.

"Robin O'Flaridy, meet Corrie Belle Hollister," said Mr. Kemble.

"Hollister, that's it!" he said. "Miracle Springs, right?"

I smiled and nodded. "It looks as though you've moved up a few notches from delivering papers yourself," I said. "Are you really a reporter now?"

He shifted his weight onto his other foot, as if he was embarrassed for the editor to hear me ask the question, and the pause gave me a quick chance to assess the changes that had come over the first acquaintance I had ever made in San Francisco.

In the last three years, Robin O'Flaridy had shot up, and stood a good head taller than me. But he was still lean, with a smooth face and blond hair, though a bit darker than before. And his voice, though not boyish, was still high-pitched for a man. All that made it just as hard to tell his age as the first time I had seen him as a scrappy kid delivering papers and hanging around hotels. I figured him for twenty or twenty-one, and he certainly looked as at home and comfortable in the offices of the *Alta* as he had in the lobby of the Oriental Hotel. Maybe he hadn't been exaggerating as much as I thought back then about his association with the paper. He seemed every bit the newsman now.

"Of course I'm a reporter," he answered, a little defensively I thought. "I told you that back then."

"Don't listen to a word he tells you, Miss Hollister," laughed Mr. Kemble. "To hear him talk, you'd think the *Alta* couldn't possibly put out a single edition without him. But he does occasionally bring me something I can use."

Robin's neck reddened slightly. He tried to get the conversation off himself. "So I take it you're here because you still hope to write for a newspaper someday, eh? But I can tell you from experience, just being a pretty face won't get you anywhere with this editor!" He grinned and threw Mr. Kemble a wink.

"Now don't get too cocky, O'Flaridy!" said the editor. "Miss Hollister has already written several articles for us — a couple of them have appeared back East. You may have seen the name *C.B. Hollister*."

If Robin was surprised, even halfway impressed, he wasn't about to let it show.

"What do you know about that!" he said. "So you've moved up from that other rag from the sticks! Good going, Hollister!" He gave me a slap on the back.

Now I remembered what had so irritated me about Robin O'Flaridy before. I smiled, but my heart wasn't in it. My Belle blood was flowing again!

"Careful, O'Flaridy, she may be taking your job someday! I was just about to offer her three articles on an election they're having up her way," said Mr. Kemble. "That's besides the two I've already got in the files. Can't recall *you* ever bringing me good writing quite so fast as that." He was kidding Robin O'Flaridy, that much I could tell from his tone, but whether he was being serious about my writing or making fun of me — that I *couldn't* tell.

"Three articles, huh!" he said. "That *is* something! I guess I better get my pencil busy. I can't let some girl cub reporter from out in the hills of the Mother Lode show me up!"

He set the files on Mr. Kemble's desk and then turned to leave. "See you around, Hollister!"

"Well, I think that about concludes our business too," the editor said to me before O'Flaridy was even out the door. "A dollar an article, as agreed. When will I see the first piece?"

"Uh . . . in a week or two," I said, trying to get my mind back on what I had come for and off the surprise interruption by Robin O'Flaridy.

"That sounds fine."

Mr. Kemble stood up behind his desk and offered his hand. I shook it.

"Good day, Miss Hollister," he said.

I turned and left his office, my mind half numb from all that had gone on inside, part of me thinking of the things I had intended to say to Mr. Kemble but hadn't. The whole interview now seemed awkward, even though I had accomplished what I'd wanted — he now knew who I really was, and he had agreed to let me write about the election. But somehow I still felt unsettled inside.

"Hey, Hollister, where you staying?" said the familiar voice of Robin O'Flaridy from where he was leaning against the wall of the hallway, apparently waiting for me.

I told him, then began walking toward the door where I had entered the building. He pushed himself off the wall, skipped a couple of steps to catch up with me, then continued to walk alongside me.

"That older lady with you again?" he asked.

"No."

"You came to the big city alone, eh?"

"That's right."

"And how long you planning to be around?"

I said I didn't know. To be honest, I had thought about remaining for another day or two. It was such an adventure being there on my own, I wanted to see a little of the city. However, I wasn't so sure I wanted Robin O'Flaridy escorting me around — even with his blue eyes, blond curls, and air of confidence, as if he considered the whole city and everything in it his own personal domain. I suppose most nineteen-year-old girls would have been dazzled and flattered. But something about his attentions caused me to squirm.

He started in telling me all about his latest escapades as he moved closer to my side. I felt his hand slip through my arm. Immediately I knew my cheeks were turning red.

"Say, how about I come over to Miss Sandy Loyd Bean's Boarding House tonight," he said, "and you and me, we'll go out to dinner someplace, and then I'll show you San Francisco by night?"

We were just about to the door. He opened it for me with his free hand, then continued on outside with me.

"What do you say, Corrie?"

"I . . . I don't know — I'd made plans to eat with Miss Bean. I told her I'd be back for dinner. Besides, I couldn't possibly go out with you — alone!"

"Aw, forget Miss Bean. You can eat a home-cooked meal anytime! And who needs a chaperon? Who'd ever know about it, anyway?" He laughed. "When else are you going to have an invitation to go out to a San Francisco restaurant with one of the city's well-known journalists? You're a good-looking girl and I'm not too bad-looking a fella, and it just seems right that we ought to spend some time together, you being here alone like you are. Especially with us both in the same profession now. What harm could there be in one evening of fun?"

"I really don't think I ought —"

"Listen," he said, cutting me off as I hailed a horse-drawn cab for myself from the corner of the block, "you talk to your Sandy Bean and put your mind at ease. I know she won't mind your not being there once you explain that you ran into an old friend who invited you out for the evening. I'll be by at seven o'clock."

Without giving me an opportunity to say anything further, he took my hand, helped me up onto the cab seat, gave the cab driver fifty cents and told him where to take me, then turned back toward me, smiled, tipped his cap, and as the horse's hoofs clopped off, said, "See you tonight!" He turned and pranced off down the street, obviously pleased with himself.

Chapter 26

What to Do?

I tried to see some of the city during the afternoon, and even took a cab out to Point Lobos where Miss Bean told me the Pacific Mail steamship was due to reach the Bay with letters and newspapers from the East. But all day I was distracted by thoughts of Robin T. O'Flaridy! There was such a battle going on inside my head that I could hardly enjoy myself.

One side of me kept thinking that I ought to throw caution to the wind and go with him. I imagined putting on my nice cream dress with the pink lace around it. He was a decent-looking young man — he'd been right about that. And we were both interested in newspapers and writing. And how many opportunities was I going to have like this? He had talked about showing me the town and it was bound to be fun.

I could hardly believe that the thought of marriage would cross my mind at a time like this! I'd never in my life thought *seriously* of getting married! But now all at once I couldn't keep the idea from entering my brain. I always figured Ma was right about me not being the kind of girl that fellas would stand in line to marry. Maybe I ought to take the few opportunities that come along and not let them pass by.

Why shouldn't I go with Robin? I might have a good time, and he probably wasn't such a bad fellow. It might be years before another young man took an interest in me. And even if he wasn't a Christian, maybe I could do him some good, or even talk to him about some of the things Mrs. Parrish and I talked about.

But the other side of me said something entirely different. I couldn't help thinking of the people who mattered to me, and what they might think. What if I did go out to dinner with him? Would I be proud to tell Almeda or would I be embarrassed? I couldn't help wondering if Robin T. O'Flaridy was the kind of person I *wanted* her to know I had been with. Was he a good person, the kind of young man she would respect and admire? And what would Jesus think to see me alone with someone I hardly knew?

The more I thought on it, the more doubts I had about what they might think. If Mrs. Parrish walked in on us together at some fancy restaurant, I *would* be embarrassed. He wasn't her kind of person — unselfish, kind, and thoughtful of others. In fact, he'd always struck me as a little egotistical and conniving. That certainly wasn't the sort of person I wanted to marry, if I ever *did* get married. If I didn't think enough of him to figure he was worth marrying, and if I would have been embarrassed to have Almeda see me with him, then what possible reason could I have for accepting his invitation? To accept would not be true to what I was thinking and feeling inside. Something about him made me very uneasy.

When Mrs. Parrish and I had first come to San Francisco, the desk clerk had said, "Nobody even knows where the boy lives. He's always on the street looking for some likely target to fleece." Robin just delivered papers, but he had told me he was a reporter. He wasn't a very honest person.

Robin T. O'Flaridy and I were different sorts of people. I couldn't believe he was a very godly young man. What would he say if I told him about how I prayed every day to obey God more and to be true?

He'd probably laugh. Or if he didn't laugh, at least he'd probably make some comment like, "Well, all that religious stuff is okay for girls and women. But I'm a man and I can make it just fine on my own without all that stuff about God."

Was that someone I wanted to spend time with, see San Francisco with? We'd be talking together and smiling and trying to have a good time, but our *real* selves would be miles apart. That didn't seem right, didn't seem honest or truthful, didn't seem any way to have a friendship between a young man and a young woman — pretending on the surface to be people we really weren't. There was really no decision to make. I couldn't even say I actually wanted to be with him. To go with him would be compromising my convictions.

By the time evening came, I had made up my mind.

He came to the door promptly at seven. I heard the knock, and my stomach lurched with a queasy feeling. I said a quick prayer as I went to answer it.

"You ready?" he asked. He stood there dressed up in a coat and tie, flowers in his hand. "These are for you," he said, holding them out toward me.

A giant knot suddenly tightened in my stomach. This was awful! A hundred doubts shot through my mind about the decision I had come to earlier. Maybe I had completely misjudged him. He probably wasn't such a bad young man after all! Yet in spite of my last-minute misgivings, I found coming out of my mouth the words I had been practicing to myself for the last hour:

"I . . . I've decided . . ." I stammered.

"Decided? Decided what?"

"I've decided that I really shouldn't go," I finally blurted out. "I'm . . . I'm very sorry."

He stood staring at me blankly, as if he hadn't heard.

"I don't believe it," he said at last. "You can't be serious?" I could see him getting angry.

"I'm really sorry. I — I — just feel I shouldn't . . . And I never really said I would go with you."

"But I had so much planned for us. I've dressed up and brought you flowers," he said, glancing at the bouquet still in his hand. "I just can't believe you'd do this to me!"

I didn't know what to say. I felt dreadful.

He just stood there staring at me, his face gradually filling with color — not the red of embarrassment, but of anger.

"Well then, enjoy your ridiculous meal in this dull boardinghouse, and your evening alone! You'll probably sit in your room reading some boring book when you could have been having the time of your life out in the city!"

With a last spiteful, glaring look, he spun around and started to leave. Then he noticed the flowers in his hand. With an angry motion, he threw them into the dirt in the street. Then he looked back at the door.

"But just don't you come crawling to me when you're a lonely old spinster!" he said vengefully. "Or when you realize you can't make it as a reporter without the help of people like me. Robin T. O'Flaridy doesn't get made a fool of twice!"

He strode off down the street with long steps, and never looked back.

I shut the door slowly and turned back into the boardinghouse. Then I ran back up to my room and lay down on the bed and started to cry. All I could think was how hard it had been to refuse him when I saw his face so alive with expectation. I had almost given in and walked out the door with him. Yet even as I lay there crying, I knew that something inside me had been strengthened, and that I would look back on this moment as one more marker on the road of my spiritual life.

Robin was right. I did spend the rest of the evening alone in my room, mostly reading. I'd brought along a book of Mr. Fremont's about his exploration of Oregon and Northern California in 1843–44. Since he was running for President, I was interested in his early years in the West.

My adventure in San Francisco had lost its excitement. I had never in my life felt so lonely and far away from everybody I loved. But still I knew I'd done the right thing.

Chapter 27

The Campaign Heats Up

I tried hard to enjoy the city the next day. Miss Bean told me some things I ought to see, and I walked around a little, and took one cab. But I was afraid I'd run into Robin O'Flaridy around every corner. So it was with a great sigh of relief that I boarded the steamer the next morning back to Sacramento. And I was so glad to see Zack and Little Wolf later that afternoon that I gave them bigger hugs than I ever had before.

"What's that for?" asked an embarrassed Zack as he half returned my embrace.

"Just to remind me how much I love you," I answered. He was satisfied, in the boyish sort of way that avoids talking about such things, and I wasn't inclined to explain any further.

Little Wolf hugged me back, smiled, and pretended to give my face a little slap. Even though we were two days from Miracle Springs, I already felt like I was home! Without people to love, you can get awfully lonely in a big hurry!

Back in Miracle, the mayor's campaign had

started to heat up. While I had been gone, Almeda had gotten the box of completed handbills back from the printer in Sacramento — one thousand copies printed on bright colored paper. Already Tad and Becky and Emily had been putting them around town, and Almeda had begun to call on some of the leading townsfolk, both to take them a handbill and to explain what she was doing and why. With the excitement over seeing the handbill, and then telling Pa and Almeda about my trip and the incident with Robin O'Flaridy, it was late in the evening before I remembered my most important news of all.

"But guess what?" I said. "Mr. Kemble said he'd print three articles on the election if I'd write them!"

"The state election?"

"No — Miracle Springs . . . you and Mr. Royce."

"That is something — and *three!* My goodness, you *are* turning into a genuine newswoman, Corrie!"

"For pay?" asked Pa.

"More or less," I answered. "A dollar each."

"Three dollars!" exclaimed Almeda. "They paid you four times that just two weeks ago for that countryside article."

"That was before he found out I was a girl."

"Why — why, that is the most despicable, low —"

"Now hold on to your breeches, Almeda," said Pa. "Don't get all riled. You know how the world

229

is. If Corrie's gonna try to do a man's job, she's gonna have to expect this kind —"

"A man's job! Drummond Hollister, not you too! Corrie can write just as well as any man her age, and better than some a lot older, and there's no reason she shouldn't be paid according to her ability."

"Maybe you're right, but then I figure that's Corrie's decision, not yours or mine. And if she doesn't want to write an article for a measly eight bits, she don't have to. And if she does, then it ain't nothing for you or I to stick our noses into."

Pa's practicality silenced Almeda for a minute, then she smiled broadly. "Well it's a start, Corrie." She paused. "I'm really proud of you. Proud of your courage in standing up to a powerful man like Mr. Kemble, but even more proud of your honesty, your integrity." She reached over and squeezed my hand. "Proud to have a young woman like you as my daughter."

I thanked her, inside thinking how much I would like to have known what Robin O'Flaridy made for each of *his* articles.

With the handbill circulating and Almeda making visits to people, the whole feeling of the mayor's campaign changed. People had been talking earlier, but I think it was mostly from interest's sake, almost curiosity. Just the fact that Miracle Springs was going to have an election was an event in itself. Having two of the town's most well-known people in it against each other made it all the more a topic of interest and conversation.

But now the initial novelty had worn off, and people were starting to ask more serious questions about the election. Which one of the two, Royce or Hollister, would actually make the best mayor? Who would do the most for Miracle Springs?

Almeda's visits and the handbill got people to thinking about more than they had at first, and wondering if maybe she just *might* be a better person to vote for than the banker. But she *was* a woman, and having a woman for mayor just wasn't done. And Royce was not only a man — he was the banker, and he still had financial power in one way or another over just about everybody around Miracle.

After several days Mr. Royce made another call at the freight office. This time none of us had seen him coming down the street, so when he walked in it took us by surprise.

"Almeda," he said, "I'd like to talk with you for a minute."

His voice was more serious than the last time he'd come into the office. He was trying to smile as he said the words, but you could tell he had more than just lighthearted conversation in his thoughts.

"Certainly. What is on your mind, Franklin?"

"In private?" he suggested.

Almeda nodded, then led him around the counter and into her small office. But when they went inside she made no attempt to close the door, and he did not particularly keep his voice down.

There was a pause while they both sat down. Mr. Ashton and I looked at each other sort of apprehensively and kept about our work as quietly as we could.

"Are you really sure you want to do this, Almeda?" asked Royce.

"Do what — you mean the election?"

"Yes, of course that's what I mean. What's the purpose? You're doing nothing but getting people stirred up and confused. And what good can it possibly do in the end?"

"The last time you were in, Franklin, you welcomed me to the race and said you congratulated my intrepid decision, as I believe you so eloquently phrased it." I could almost see Almeda smiling faintly as she said the words.

"That was then," he replied, a little quickly. "I had no idea you were going to take the thing so seriously. I thought perhaps it was a ploy to help your sagging business."

"My business is not sagging. We are managing just fine."

"Nevertheless, you have taken it beyond the casual point, Almeda, and I simply suggest that it is time you paused to consider the implications. People are talking and, quite frankly, some of the talk has negative features to it that are not going to help *my* reputation and business if they persist."

"And therefore you want me to withdraw?"

232

asked Almeda. She wasn't smiling now, that much I knew.

"Be reasonable, Almeda," Mr. Royce said. "You've had the excitement of the campaign. You've thrust yourself into the center of attention. People respect you. It cannot help but heighten your image as a businesswoman. But now it's time for you to face the realistic facts. No town is going to elect a woman mayor, and the longer you continue, the more the potential damage to *my* reputation and *my* business. And if I'm going to be the next mayor of Miracle Springs, both the bank and my image in the people's thoughts need to be solid. And all this is not to mention the lasting impression your loss will leave. Right now you are riding high in the public mind. But after the election, your image, and perhaps even the reputation of your business itself, will be tarnished and you will be seen as a loser. All I'm attempting to convey to you in the most reasonable manner I can — from one business person to another, from one *friend* to another — is that it is time you stand aside and let Miracle Springs move forward without all this dissention and strife your being part of the election is causing — for your own good, Almeda."

A long silence followed.

"So then, Franklin, you consider the outcome of the election a foregone conclusion?" said Almeda at length.

"I didn't think there was ever any doubt about that," said Mr. Royce, with the hint of a laugh.

"Maybe not as far as you're concerned," replied Almeda. "But I didn't join this race to help my business or my reputation, as you call it, or anything else. I joined it to make every effort to win."

"Surely you can't be serious?" Royce sounded genuinely surprised.

"Of course I'm serious. I wouldn't do something of this magnitude for frivolous or self-seeking motives. If you think I care about what people think of me, Franklin, then you do not know me very well."

There was another pause.

"Well, if you're determined to see it out to the bitter end," Mr. Royce finally said, "I wish you'd at least discontinue the distribution of this brochure of yours, and visiting people — a good many of them my friends, Almeda — and stirring everybody up and spreading talk about me that isn't true."

"Franklin, I have not said a single word about you to a soul! I'm surprised you would think I would stoop to such measures."

"People *are* talking, Almeda. How can it be from anything other than your stirring them up against me?"

"I tell you, I am doing no such thing. I have never even hinted anything about you. I have only been talking to people about what I feel I would be able to offer Miracle Springs as its mayor."

After the pause which followed, Mr. Royce's

tone cooled. He apparently realized he was not going to dissuade Almeda from anything she had her mind made up on.

"You can't win, Almeda," he said. "The thing's simply impossible."

"We'll see," she replied.

"You're wasting time and money."

"You may be right."

"You're determined to go ahead with it?"

"I am."

"Will you stop making calls on my friends and customers?"

"They are my friends, too, Franklin. You are free to call on them yourself."

"In other words, you will not stop?"

"No."

"Will you withdraw the brochure?"

"I will not. Again, Franklin, you are free to circulate one of your own."

The next sound was that of Mr. Royce's chair scooting back on the wood floor as he rose to his feet. "At least it appears we understand each other," he said.

"So it would appear," repeated Almeda.

"Good day, Mrs. Hollister," said the banker, and the next moment he reappeared from the office and walked briskly to the street door and out, not acknowledging me or Mr. Ashton in any way as he passed. We both pretended to be busy with the papers and files in front of us.

Two or three minutes later Almeda came out of the office. Her face was red with anger.

"That pompous, egotistical man!" was all she could say before she started sputtering and pacing around the office like a caged animal. "The nerve . . . to say that I stood no chance whatsoever! To ask me to withdraw from the race, because — because of his reputation! *His* reputation — ha! Calls on his *friends!* I doubt he even has that many friends around town — everyone is too afraid of him! What harm could *I* do *his* reputation!"

She walked around the office another time or two, then burst out again:

"I've got to get out of here!" She looked at the two of us. "I'm going for a ride. I'll be back in about an hour."

With that she left the room with as much grace as she could manage. When Mr. Ashton and I heard a yell and hoofbeats galloping away down the street a couple minutes later, we looked at each other and laughed. It was plain her horse was in for a time of it!

Almeda didn't pull out of the mayor's race, which continued to get livelier and livelier as we got into the month of August.

Mr. Royce paid no more visits to the Parrish Mine and Freight Company office.

Chapter 28

I Try My Hand at Something New

I wanted to get right to work on my first article about the election. It was early August, and there were only about thirteen weeks to go.

I began by just trying to tell the five *w*'s of the situation. I figured the first article needed to be a straight "news" kind of story that told folks about the election and what was unusual about it. Then for the next two I'd maybe try to write what Mr. Kemble called "human interest" things about the election and the two candidates, and maybe even about Miracle Springs itself.

I started off writing down the facts like I had for the poster about Ulysses S. Grant that Almeda had put up.

The mining town of Miracle Springs, sixty-five miles northeast of Sacramento, will hold its first mayor's election in November of this year. The local election will be held at the

237

same time as the general election for President and other offices. But what has the people of Miracle Springs all roused up isn't just that they're having their first election, but *who's* running in it!

Then I talked about Mr. Royce and Almeda being two of the town's leading citizens, about the bank and the Freight Company and how everyone for miles around depended on both of them for different parts of their livelihoods. But of course the fact of Almeda being a woman couldn't help but be the main thing that would make folks interested in the election — and in my articles.

The Miracle Springs mayor's election is one of the most unusual elections in all of California this year because a woman, who herself cannot even vote, is running against one of the wealthiest and most powerful men in the community. It is not known whether a woman has ever before run for such a high position as mayor in the United States, but Mrs. Hollister must certainly be considered one of the first. One might say she is a pioneer in a state full of pioneers. And if she wins, the rest of the state — if not the entire country — will be watching her, just as it is now watching the most famous Californian of all, John Charles Fremont.

I was planning to write a little bit about both of their businesses and how they both came to Miracle Springs, and then finish off the article with the last of the *w's* — a quote from both Mr. Royce and Almeda about "why" each had decided to run for mayor.

But before I got quite finished with the first article, an idea came to me that I just couldn't wait to get started on. I started putting together what I'd need for the second article, and so I got delayed a while getting the first one finished and in the mail to Mr. Kemble.

My idea was this: I'd go around to people around Miracle Springs, in private without either Mr. Royce or Almeda knowing what I was doing, and I'd ask them questions about what they thought of the election. I'd ask them their reaction to the two candidates, about what things would probably decide who they voted for, about whether they had business dealings with either candidate, and what difference that made. I would ask what they thought a mayor of Miracle Springs ought to do, what they thought was going to be the future of the community, what they themselves were most concerned about. I might even ask them who they planned to vote for.

It was such an exciting idea, I could hardly wait to get started!

If I could, I would get quotes, but if people wanted me not to use their names, I would promise not to. I'd just tell everyone I wanted to get an idea how the whole town and its people were feeling about the election but without giving away any secrets or making it awkward for anyone.

Mostly, since they were the ones who could vote, I figured I'd talk to all the men I knew, and then to those I didn't know. And then another idea came to me! I could interview women too. Even though they couldn't vote, it would be interesting to get their opinions — especially since, according to Mr. Kemble's letter, it was the women readers of the paper who liked the kinds of things I had been writing. And I could ask the men (the married ones, at least!) if they might vote any different on account of what their wives thought.

What a great "human interest" article I could write if the women all put enough pressure on their husbands that they actually voted for Almeda! Even though the women couldn't vote, might it be possible that they could still influence the outcome? Or were there even enough women around Miracle Springs to make a difference? If the women started putting that kind of pressure on their husbands, what might the unmarried men do? There were still more unmarried men around than families. And what might Mr. Royce do?

I didn't know the answers to all my own questions. In fact, I kept thinking up new questions. And I figured the only way to find out some of these things was to get out and start talking to people and getting their ideas.

This would make a great article! It'd show Mr. Kemble I could write an article of news *and* human interest. And one worth more than $1!

The first people I talked to weren't the kind you could get a fair opinion from — they were all people who were friends of Almeda's — Pa, Uncle Nick, Katie, Mr. Ashton, Marcus Weber. But I had to begin someplace, so those were the folks I started with. I hadn't ever done anything quite like this before, so I had to learn how to ask questions and write down what people told me.

Gradually I started to talk to other people — the Shaws and Hermon Stansberry gave me some interesting ideas, so did Mrs. DeWater, though her husband didn't say much. Rev. Rutledge was visiting Mr. and Miss Stansberry when I called on them, and so I got to talk to all three of them at once. The minister tried to be gracious toward both sides. Though obviously he had always felt fondly toward Almeda, he said some nice things about Mr. Royce too. Miss Stansberry took the woman's point of view completely, just like Katie had.

So far most of the people I'd talked to favored Almeda. But I knew to be fair I had to get the opinions of Mr. Royce's friends too. It would probably be harder than I thought to write an article that fairly represented both sides and all the people in the town!

But even as I interviewed people, I knew I had to get my first article finished up and in the mail. I went back to it, added the few parts that had been missing, rewrote it all, and then

241

put it in the mail to Mr. Kemble. Then I got right back to visiting people, asking them questions, and writing down as much as I could about what they thought.

Chapter 29

I Get Angry

By this time there were daily stage runs from Sacramento up the valley and into the foothills. Mail usually took two or three days from Miracle Springs to San Francisco. And we'd get San Francisco newspapers most of the time just two days late. They'd get the issue right off to Sacramento on the morning steamer up the river, or across the Bay and onto the train line that was now running between the two cities. Then the next day the papers would be taken by stage up the main routes to the north, which usually took a day and a half by the time it reached Miracle.

Almeda had always gotten the newspapers from Sacramento and San Francisco, besides Mr. Singleton's *Gazette*. But now that I was writing for them, I was more interested than I used to be, and the minute the stagecoach arrived in town at between two and four every afternoon, I'd be out of the office and on my way over to the depot to get whatever mail there was for Parrish Freight *and* our newspapers. On most days I spent the next ten or fifteen minutes looking over the paper, seeing what other reporters were writing about, getting ideas, reading some of the news. Then usually at night Pa and Almeda and I would pass the paper around until we all three had read every word.

The day of August 8 is a day I will always remember. At about four-thirty in the afternoon, I was sitting down in the freight office, scanning through the copy of the *Alta* that had arrived about an hour before on the stage. Mostly it was full of election news. There were quotes from a speech Mr. Buchanan had made in Philadelphia, and a lot about Mr. Fremont, including two long editorials. He had been campaigning all through the East, but news of his travels and the issues surrounding the election continued to make daily news in California. The slavery situation, events in Kansas, the question of Fremont's religion had all contributed to heated debate and discussion, as well as legal battles involving title to Fremont's Mariposa estate down in the foothills east of Merced. There was a short article entitled "Fremont Estate Embroiled in Campaign Controversy," though I didn't stop to take time to read it.

A few moments later my eyes fell on a small article on the bottom of page four. When I read the caption, my pulse quickened. There was no way they could have gotten my article into print this soon, yet there were the words in bold black type: "Woman Pioneer Seeks Office in State of Pioneers."

Hastily my eyes found the small print of the article and began to read:

The place is Miracle Springs, foothills mining town some seventy miles north of Sacramento on a tributary of the Yuba River. The occasion: an election for mayor between two of the area's most prominent citizens and members of the business community — one, the town's only banker; the other, the owner of one of the largest mining supply and freight companies in the northern foothills.

What makes this an election that many observers will be watching with interest, however, is that it pits a woman — who cannot even vote in the election — against a man of great influence in the community.

I couldn't believe it! This wasn't my article, but it might as well have been — all the information was the same!

With my heart pounding, I read on:

According to research done by this reporter, the Miracle Springs mayor's race marks one of the very few times a woman has sought higher public office in these United States, and never has a woman held office west of the plains. It should prove a groundbreaking election insofar as the future of this great state of California is concerned.

Almeda Parrish Hollister, owner of Parrish Mine and Freight Company and recently married to one of the town's miners, has thrown her hat into the ring against Franklin Royce, Miracle Springs' only banker and financier.

There were three more paragraphs telling a little about Miracle Springs itself, and then a brief background of Mr. Royce and Almeda and their businesses and how they had come to California, with the final sentences: "Experts interviewed for the purpose of this article give Mrs. Hollister no chance to win the election. They say that besides the disadvantage of being a woman, she has taken on a man owed too many favors by too many people. But just the fact that she is in the race is of interest in its own right."

If those words weren't enough to make me downright furious, those immediately below them were:

Reported by Robin T. O'Flaridy, staff reporter for the California Alta.

I threw the paper down and jumped to my feet. How could he do this to me? The rat!

And what about Mr. Kemble? He had no right! Why, they'd stolen my ideas, my words! And if Mr. Kemble wasn't in on it, how did Robin ever get his hands on my article in the first place? They must have done it together! It wasn't so much losing the dollar. They'd taken *my* idea — and even used some of my exact words. And then, most of all, they put Robin's name under them!

I was so angry I would have clobbered Robin if he had been there! I knew why he'd done it. He wanted to get even with me for the incident over the dinner and the flowers. He was paying me back for making him feel foolish.

Well, Mr. O'Flaridy, I thought to myself, thinking up all kinds of things I could do to *him* in return to get revenge, *we'll just see who gets the last laugh!*

I fumed around the streets of town, my brain reeling back and forth, not even stopping to think about whether my anger was right or wrong, not once thinking about God or what he might think. All I could think about was Robin O'Flaridy and how I could fix him!

And what made it even worse was that his article was *better* than mine. I couldn't stand to admit it, but he was a better writer!

I don't know how I spent the rest of the day. I think I walked around town a while longer — but for sure *this* walk wasn't one I spent in prayer! I must have gone back to the office, but whether I did any more work, I can't remember. I was just so mad!

By evening I had cooled down. In fact, I was embarrassed at myself and had to go outside for a while alone to talk to God a little about it. I told him I was sorry for getting so angry, because I knew it wasn't right. I'd been thinking so much recently on being true and everything that *truth* involved. I suppose that's what vexed me so much about what they had done — that they weren't being truthful at all, not to the people reading their paper or to me. But after a while I realized I had no business thinking about whether *other* people were truthful or not. There was only one person I had the right to criticize for not being truthful, and that was me. It was none of my affair what Robin O'Flaridy did about living honestly and doing things right. But what I did — that *was* my affair!

I walked around a while and thought and prayed. But when I went back inside I still didn't have everything figured out.

We talked about it, and Pa said something that helped me see a little more inside the situation. I had just told him and Almeda about realizing that I had to take care of myself and whether I did the right thing, rather than criticizing others for what they did.

"That's right, Corrie," Pa said. "One of the biggest things about growing up is to take responsibility for yourself without forever blaming other folks for everything that you don't like. That's something me and your Uncle Nick's had to learn — and sometimes the hard way. It still ain't easy for Nick, who gets to blaming your grandpa for things he done. And I used to blame Nick for things that I later had to face up to myself. Blame's a terrible thing, Corrie. A mind that's set to blame other folks all the time is eventually gonna destroy any chance of setting things right, 'cause all it's doing is looking at everything that's wrong."

He stopped for a minute and gave the log in the fireplace a poke with a stick.

"But on the other hand, Corrie, if you're gonna write for this man Kemble, and you're gonna work for his newspaper, then you gotta be able to trust him, and you gotta know where you stand. It's a sight different than blaming a fella when you try to get your business dealings straight so you know what's up and what's down. If I'm gonna have some kind of a deal going with your uncle or Alkali or if I walk into Royce's bank and say I want to borrow some money, then there ain't nothing wrong with saying, 'Now, Nick, here's what you gotta do, and here's what I gotta do,' and since we're both men of our word, then we'll do what we say. Then we shake hands and agree on it, and that's that. Or I might say, 'Now, Mr. Royce, I don't exactly like you, but I want to borrow some money. How much'll it cost?' And then he might say, 'I don't like you either, Hollister, and I don't like your wife running for mayor against me, but if you want to borrow money, it'll cost you 6 percent.' Then if it's agreeable, we shake hands and that's the deal. We don't have to like each other, but everybody's got to know where everybody else stands, otherwise you can't do business together."

He stopped, and I waited for more. But he was finished.

"Is that all, Pa?" I asked. "What is it you think

I ought to do now?"

Almeda, who had been listening to everything, laughed.

"In his wonderful roundabout way," she said, "I think your father's been trying to tell you that even though you may have to get over your anger and blaming, you still have to find out where you stand and why they did what they did. Otherwise, how can you go on writing for the *Alta*?"

"Maybe it ain't as bad as it looks, Corrie," added Pa. "Are you sure it's your article?"

"Some of the exact words, Pa. I told you about the pioneer in a state full of pioneers."

"And you and Kemble had a deal for the article."

"Well, we didn't shake hands that I can remember," I said, "but he told me he'd pay me a dollar each for three articles on the election."

Pa shrugged, and nodded his head thoughtfully.

"It sounds to me, Corrie Belle, reporter of the Mother Lode, that you need to get some things straight with your editor," said Almeda.

I gazed into her earnest face, and realized she was right. I let out a deep sigh, then got up and went into my room, where I sat down and immediately began a letter to San Francisco.

"Dear Mr. Kemble," I began. "I have to admit I was given a considerable surprise when I opened the copy of the *Alta* that arrived in Miracle Springs this afternoon. . . ."

I then went on to ask all the questions that

were on my mind, as nicely as I could, though I did ask him right out if he'd let Robin put his name on my article — and if not, then how was it that I found some of my very words appearing in the paper?

It was a long letter, but I finally got everything said I wanted to say. Once I'd done it I felt a lot better. For a writer, getting your thoughts said to *somebody* — even if it's just on paper — is always a great feeling of relief. I wondered if I ought to send it at all — this might be the last I'd ever hear from Mr. Kemble. But like Pa said, I had to know how things stood if I wanted to keep having dealings with him.

The letter went south on the next morning's stage.

Chapter 30

Mr. Kemble's Reply

The next five days were torture!

I knew I couldn't possibly hear anything back from Mr. Kemble for at least six days, yet even on the fifth day I couldn't help being there to meet the stage and frantically looking through the mail.

During that time I must have wished I had the letter back a thousand times. *What an idiot I was!* I kept saying to myself. *He's never going to print another thing I write! He's never going to even answer my letter!*

But that didn't keep me from meeting the stage every day.

I tried to do my work and to keep up with my interviews about the election just in case I got another chance with the series. But I was so distracted I finally just gave up.

On the eighth day, the seventeenth of August, there among the rest of the mail was an envelope with the return address: The California *Alta*, Montgomery Street, San Francisco, California.

I grabbed it and ran off down the street. I had to be alone. I was so afraid of what might be inside that envelope!

Finally I wound up inside the livery of the Freight Company, up in the loft. No one was around, and the silence and smells calmed me down like they always did. At home the barn was still one of my favorite places.

I took several deep breaths, then looked down at the envelope in my hands. My fingers were shaking. My whole future as a writer might be at stake. It might even be over already.

Finally I scratched off an edge of the stuck-down part, then jammed a finger through and tore the top off the envelope. Then I reached inside with two fingers and pulled out the letter, unfolded it, and began to read:

Dear Miss Hollister,

Your letter raises some interesting questions.

First, you said you thought we had a deal about you writing on the Miracle Springs election. But we had no such "deal." I said I'd pay you a buck a piece *if* you sent me something acceptable. But at the time in question I hadn't seen a word from you yet. And time was wasting! We are a *news*paper. People buy the *Alta* to read news.

In the meantime, O'Flaridy came to me with a legitimate news article. He'd researched it in our files and the limited library we have here at the *Alta* and it was a decently done bit of writing. What am I to do, turn it down? I'm an editor, he's a reporter; he brought me news, I printed the story. It's as simple as that.

Face it, Miss Hollister, he scooped you on this one. You may not like it. Maybe it doesn't seem fair. But then nobody ever accused the newspaper business of being fair in the first place. And maybe that's why you don't see too many female reporters. It's a tough business, and the reporter who gets the goods gets published. There's no place in this business for feminine emotions and for getting your feelings hurt. Talk is cheap. If you don't deliver, you get left holding the paper and reading it, while somebody else does the writing and reporting.

Now as to your chief complaint, the O'Flaridy article was set to go before I received yours in the mail. He did not take a word of yours. You can trust me on that. I would never condone such a thing. If I'm tough, you'll also find me a fair man. The title for his piece was taken from your words. That was my doing. It was a clever phrase that caught my eye and I would have written you acknowledging the fact except that your letter beat me to it. I apologize if I overstepped my bounds. I will make it up to you in the future.

As to your question about pay, I gave O'Flaridy $4 for the article. It was solid news, and before you think of complaining, remember that he's a young man with plenty of experience that you don't have. That's why he's on our staff and why I offer him a bonus incentive like this one for bringing me something in addition to his regular assignments. If you think it's unfair, remember, this is a man's business. If you don't like the offers I make to you, then take your writing elsewhere.

Now to something more serious on my side. Given the false impression you gave initially over the whole business about the *C.B.* name, I do not feel that the payment I offered you is unfair, since you are a woman. But it does not seem you have learned your lesson about false impressions! Robin tells me this woman running for mayor is no longer Mrs. *Parrish* as you told me, but rather Mrs. *Hollister,* and none other than your own stepmother. I must tell you, Miss Hollister, I was highly annoyed when I learned that fact. You should have been clear on that point up front. It could look like you were attempting to further the campaign of your stepmother rather than to carry out objective news writing. That fact did, I must confess, contribute to my decision to run Robin's story.

We have a term in this business called "conflict of interest," and it looks to me as if you have landed yourself squarely in the middle of it. How do you possibly expect to remain objective and unbiased in writing about an election of which you are such an intrinsic part?

My first inclination was to withdraw any and all commitments and cancel all plans to publish anything else of yours, including the two prior ones I am still holding. But upon further thought I realized you may not have intentionally tried to deceive me. Thus, I have decided to keep an open mind, and if you present me with anything publishable on the election, I will run it as per our one dollar per article arrangement. Given the circumstances, I do not feel obliged to hold to our two-dollar "deal." I originally offered you one dollar, and one dollar it will be. But it will have to be well-done and objective, or I will have no choice but to send it back to you.

The two previous articles will also be run at payment of $1 each rather than the $4 stated originally. Under the circumstances, I think that is more than generous. The article received last week concerning the Royce-Hollister election, I will obviously not be able to use.

I remain, Miss Hollister, sincerely yours,
Edward Kemble

By the time I was finished reading, I was crying. Part of me couldn't help but be outraged at Robin for "scooping" me, as Mr. Kemble had called it. He'd done it on purpose, just to spite me — I knew that. And I was angry at Mr. Kemble for talking down at me about my "feminine emotions" and my "hurt feelings." No, it didn't seem fair that Robin would get $4 and I only $1! The whole thing wasn't fair!

But then my logical mind reminded me that Robin's article *was* better than mine had been. That made me mad all over again — but mad at myself, mad for being so stupid as to think I could be a writer.

I was no writer! My writing was nothing compared to everything else in the *Alta*! A dollar was too much to pay for my writing.

I thought about all the rest Mr. Kemble had said. I hadn't meant to hold back the truth about Almeda. It just never came up about our being related. I'd never even thought about what he called a "conflict of interest." That made me mad all over again. Mad at myself.

I *had* made a mistake! I hadn't told him the complete truth. Maybe it hadn't been on purpose, but what difference did that make? Why should he trust me after twice giving him the wrong impression?

I sat and cried for a long time — sad, angry, disappointed, hurt, and irritated at myself. I couldn't help but feel like a complete fool. I had wanted to be a writer, and now I realized I wasn't fooling anyone.

For years I have kept Mr. Kemble's letter. Every once in a while I get it out and read it again, because in a lot of ways — though I don't think he intended it necessarily — Mr. Kemble's words helped me in the growing-up process. Writing the letter to him had forced me to face a situation squarely. And his reply helped me to see for the first time what was involved in being part of the newspaper business. Although I didn't want to admit it, Mr. Kemble was right — it *was* a tough business.

It was time I gave it up and tried to get on to doing something else with the rest of my life.

Chapter 31

"How Bad Do You Want It?"

I moped around for a few days, keeping mostly to myself. I didn't even talk to Almeda or Pa. I was too dejected and defeated to want to talk about it.

They gave me room to wallow around in my self-pity for a while. But then eventually they both began to try to encourage me out of my despondency. When you're in one of those holes where you feel everything in your life has failed, part of you doesn't even want to get out of the hole you've dug for yourself. Strange as it seems, you almost enjoy feeling sorry for yourself.

But Pa and Almeda wouldn't let me do that.

"Ain't it about time you got back to your article writing?" Pa asked me the second evening after I'd got the letter.

I shrugged and said I didn't know if I'd do any more articles.

"What?" he exclaimed. "This from my daughter who wants to be a newspaper reporter more than anything? What're you talking about, girl?"

Finally I showed them the letter.

They both read it quietly and seriously, and neither of them said much else that night. But over the next couple of days both Pa and Almeda found a time to be alone with me.

"There's times when a body's just gotta force himself to keep going," Pa told me, "even though maybe inside everything's screaming at him to do something else. If something's the right thing to do, then you just gotta do it."

He looked at me carefully. "You want to keep writing, don't you?" he said.

"Of course I do, Pa. But everything Mr. Kemble said is true. And besides, my writing is terrible, and he doesn't think I was honest with him."

"But it's something you still want to do?"

"Yes."

"Then how else you figure on gettin' any better at it if you don't do it? And how you figure on gettin' Kemble to trust you if you don't keep going to him and writing for him and showing him he *can* trust you? Ain't no other way but to keep at it."

"I just don't know how I can, Pa, after that letter of his."

"I reckon it's a setback for you, all right. And I can understand how it'd hurt a mite, those things he said. But don't you want to prove him wrong, prove to him that you *can* do it, prove that a woman *can* write as well as that O'Flaridy kid?"

"Yeah."

"Then you gotta toughen up, Corrie! Get that Belle blood working for you. Toughen up, fight back, keep writing and don't let either Kemble or O'Flaridy take your dream away. Maybe they stole your idea, and even your words. But don't let them steal your dream. Fight for it, Corrie. And if Kemble doesn't like what you write, then do like he said and take it someplace else. But don't let him rob you of what God gave you just 'cause he don't have the good sense to see what a fine writer you're gonna be someday."

He gave me a hug and a kiss, and I cried a little again. It made me feel better just knowing that *he* still believed in me.

Almeda told me what it was like for her after Mr. Parrish died.

"After my husband died, Corrie, I was absolutely despondent. I felt so alone and out of place in this world. We hadn't been in California much longer than a year and our business was just getting going. I was the only woman in Miracle Springs besides the saloon girls. Mr. Parrish and I had dreamed of the life we would build in the new west, and all of a sudden it was shattered."

"But you probably didn't fall apart like me," I said.

"Oh, I did," she answered.

"I cried thousands of tears, so I think I know a little of what you are feeling right now. I wanted to just sit down and die at times. Then at other

261

times I would decide to pack everything up and go back East. I had my reasons for not wanting to go back to Boston. Someday, when the time is right, perhaps I'll tell you about that period of my life. In light of what I've seen and been through, Corrie, God has been so wonderfully good to me. But it wasn't because of being afraid of my past that I decided not to go back. No, Corrie, it was because I finally realized I couldn't give up. That wouldn't have been fair to my husband and to the dream we'd had of a new and happy life in California. And it wouldn't have been fair to me!"

She stopped, and it was real quiet. I hadn't seen that distant look in her eyes since she and Pa had been married, but there it was again. I knew she was thinking about another time and another place, and I didn't want to disturb her.

But as usual, the silence only lasted a few moments. Then her face suddenly brightened and she spoke again.

"In every person's life, Corrie, there come times like you're going through right now. Usually everyone has several such moments, when everything you think you wanted seems suddenly gone, destroyed, unattainable. At those times a woman's got to stop and take stock of herself. Just like in business. We have to do periodic stock-checks, inventories of supplies — just like you and Marcus did out in the supply room last week. We had to know what we had on hand so we'd know what to do in the future.

"A person has to do that too — take inventory, check the supply room. Especially when you come to what you might call 'crisis' times, or times of evaluation and question, when you have to ask yourself where you're going as a person, where your life is headed. You have to take stock. You have to find out if where you've been going is still where you *want* to go, or if you need to *change* directions."

"And you think maybe that's where I'm at now?"

"Quite possibly.

"Sometimes God allows difficulties and hardships and questions and heartbreaks to come our way because he wants us to change directions. And so whenever they come we have to stop and try to listen to his voice and ask him what he's trying to get through to us. But there are other times when the disappointments come not to get us to change directions at all, but to strengthen and toughen us, so that we will be all the more dedicated to accomplishing what we felt God was leading us toward in the first place. Do you see the difference, Corrie?" she asked.

I nodded. "Like how hard it was when us kids and Pa got together," I said. "I think we all wanted to find some way out of that situation — especially Pa!"

Almeda laughed.

"But we knew we had to stick it out because it was the right thing."

"Exactly! And that's why I decided to stay here

263

rather than go back East. After taking stock of myself, I realized that I *wanted* to make it work. I had to ask myself how willing I was to fight for what I wanted to do. And I decided I was willing to fight for it, even though I knew it would be hard and that men would probably be against me at first. But I was determined to fight for what I believed in, to fight for my dream.

"Now you're facing almost exactly the same thing. You've had a bad letdown. You're a woman up against stiff odds. The man you're up against — in my case it was the men of the community whose support and business I had to have to survive. In your case it is an editor you have to prove yourself to — such men don't necessarily make it easy for us. Now you have to take inventory of the direction you've been going and ask yourself if it's *still* the direction you want to *keep* going.

"What it boils down to, Corrie, is this — how bad do you want it?"

"I *do* want to be able to write," I said.

"I had to ask myself the same question. How bad did I want to see my business succeed? What sacrifices was I willing to make? Was I willing to fight for what I believed in? In the same way — how bad do *you* still want to be a writer? Are you willing to fight for it? What sacrifices are you willing to make? If you don't think you're a good writer now, how hard are you willing to work to improve? Are you willing to work twice as hard as a man would have to, and get only half the pay?"

She paused and looked into my eyes. "How much do you want it, Corrie?"

"I think I want it," I answered lamely.

"Well, if after taking stock of yourself, you decide you *do* still want to be a writer, then don't let Kemble or O'Flaridy or anyone else stop you. Go after it! It's your dream — so fight for it, and don't let go of it."

Chapter 32

My Decision and What Came of It

Even before Almeda was through talking, I knew what my decision was!

This was one time when I didn't need to go out in the woods for a long time to think and try to figure things out. I knew what I wanted — and that was to keep writing! And if it meant working even harder than before and trying to make my writing better than it had been, I'd do it! If it meant getting only $1 an article, maybe I'd do that too. But then maybe I'd tell Mr. Kemble I wanted more. And if he said my articles weren't good enough to pay more, then I'd *make* them good enough! I'd improve my writing. I'd practice. I'd learn.

How bad did I want to do what I'd dreamed of doing? I figured I wanted it bad enough to fight for it, just like Almeda had.

Within ten or fifteen minutes I was in the saddle and on my way back toward town. It was Saturday afternoon, a good time to interview some more people about the election. If my first article wasn't good enough for Mr. Kemble, then I'd make my second one all the better — with facts and the five *w's* and human interest all put together! I'd make it so interesting even *he* would enjoy reading it! And since I'd gotten behind during this last week, I couldn't afford to waste another minute. Most of the people in town had seen Almeda's flyer. Mr. Royce had put up a great big new banner on the side of his bank building just three days ago, which said in big letters and bright paint: ROYCE FOR MAYOR. MIRACLE SPRINGS' FUTURE PROSPERITY DEPENDS ON YOUR VOTE. Folks were really interested and were talking a lot about everything. Now was the time to see everybody to get their thoughts and reactions while interest was high and they were willing to talk.

But about halfway into town a huge new idea suddenly hit me! It was such a great idea I completely forgot about Mr. Royce and Almeda and Miracle Springs in an instant. If I could write an article about someone *really* important, about news that was significant to the whole country, not just a little town like Miracle Springs, then Mr. Kemble would *have* to print it! And he'd see that I could be a reporter who could write about more than just pretty leaves and sunsets and interesting people nobody'd ever heard of.

I yanked back on the reins, swung my horse around on the trail, dug in my heels to her flanks, and galloped back to the house.

I ran straight inside and began searching through the pile of old newspapers Pa kept by the fireplace to start fires with. I hoped it was still there!

Then I remembered. I'd saved the August 8 issue with my own articles. I ran into my room. There it was, right with the others! Hurriedly I scanned through the paper until I found it. I read the brief article again, then went back into the big room where Pa and Almeda were sitting with puzzled expressions watching me scurry around.

"Look!" I exclaimed, pointing to the paper still in my hand. "It says right here that there is a controversy about Mr. Fremont's estate, but it doesn't say what it is. What if I could find out? That would sure be a story Mr. Kemble couldn't refuse!"

"There ain't no mystery there," laughed Pa. "Everyone knows they been trying to claim jump and get his gold mines away from him ever since he found gold on his land."

"Who, Pa? Who's *they?*"

"His enemies, people who want his gold — neighbors, claim jumpers, drifters, Mexicans. Anybody who's rich and powerful always has a pack of people trying to do him in, and John Fremont's both. All this time he's been back in Washington senatoring and now running for President, folks back here's trying to get their hands on his gold."

"But *who,* Pa?"

"I don't know. I suppose there's lots of 'em."

"Well, I'm gonna go find out," I said determinedly.

Pa laughed again. "What you figure on doin', girl?" he said. "The man's running for President of the United States! And *you* figure on uncovering some mystery about him that no one else knows?"

"I don't know, Pa. It's probably downright foolish — but I *know* there's a story there. I can *feel* it! A story for me . . . if I can just find it!"

"And how you figure to find this story that's waitin' just for you?" I know the smile on Pa's face wasn't meant to be making fun of me, but at the same time he just couldn't keep from chuckling. I was serious.

"I don't know. Maybe I'll just go out there and start looking around. I guess maybe that's what a reporter's got to do sometimes, and maybe it's time I learned how."

"Go where — Mariposa? That's a hundred and twenty, maybe a hundred and thirty miles."

"Through the mountains," added Almeda. "Through Sacramento and the valley roads, more like a hundred seventy-five."

"If that's what I gotta do for a story, then maybe that's just what I gotta do."

I reckon I'd been swept along in this conversation by the emotion of the moment. But the minute those words were out of my mouth, suddenly the reality of what I'd said seemed to strike us all. There was silence for a moment, and I guess somehow in the very saying of the words a determination rose up within me to *do* what I'd said, even if the words had been spoken lightly. I think Pa and Almeda realized, too, that a change had come in that instant. And maybe inside, both of them had to face how they were going to react to my growing up.

Almeda's next words were not what you'd expect from a mother who was worried about what her son or daughter was about to do, and who wanted to talk them out of it.

"I think it's a sensational idea, Corrie!" said Almeda. "If you are going to go after something and follow a dream you have, you might as well go straight to the top."

Pa had been serious for a minute, but now he chuckled again. "You're a determined one," he said. "Once you make your mind up about something, I wouldn't want to be the one standin' in your way. But how do you figure on going all that way . . . how do you figure on findin' something out that other folks don't know?"

"I don't know," I answered again with all my innocent youthful enthusiasm. "I'll find a way."

"You want me to take you down there, maybe go with you?" he asked.

I hesitated a minute before answering. "I don't know, Pa," I said finally. "Something inside me wants to do this alone, though I'm afraid at the same time. Maybe one of you should go with me . . . if you could." I was already starting to get cold feet about my idea.

A little frown passed over Almeda's forehead and I could tell she was thinking. But the reply she gave startled me.

"I don't think we ought to, Corrie," she said after a minute. "This is your idea, and you're the one who wants to go down there and uncover a story you think is waiting for you. I think it's time you figured out the best way to go about it yourself. I can give you the names of good boardinghouses all the way, people I know and that we can trust. But I think perhaps it's time you saw what you were capable of. You can do it — I know you can."

"It is a fearsome thing, to go so far alone, not even knowing what I am looking for, not even knowing who to talk to, not knowing if anybody will listen to me." My earlier resolve was fading fast.

"They will listen to you, young lady. You can be very determined . . . and very persuasive! Besides, part of the process I was telling you about of fighting for your dream — part of it is learning to stand alone if you have to, facing the dangers and uncertainties, and learning to go where maybe no one else has gone in just the same way, or asking questions no one has voiced before. That's part of growing up — finding your own inner strength with God. Something inside tells me this might be one of those times. If there's a story there meant for you, then you have to be the one to find it."

"I don't know, Almeda," said Pa. "I ain't so

sure I agree with you. There's bears and varmints and who knows what kind of hoodlums all the way up an' down that way. I don't like it. I'll go with her, just to keep an eye on things."

Neither of us said anything more. From the sound of it, Pa had made up his mind, and I knew what he said was the logical way to look at it. So I was surprised the next morning when he announced that he'd changed his mind, and that if I wanted to make the trip alone, he wouldn't forbid me. He'd still rather he or Zack went with me, but he'd trust me to make the decision.

Naturally I was fearful at first as I anticipated such a trip, such a quest for the unknown. Later I looked back at this as another one of those growing experiences. And I came to thank Pa and Almeda afterward for not doing it for me, for giving me encouragement but not actually helping me, and for forcing me not just to believe in what I wanted to do — but for forcing me to believe in myself too. Whatever I felt at the time, Pa and Almeda didn't try to make it easy for me. They pushed me out from under their wings to go after this story — whatever it was! — by myself, showed me that they really did believe in me, and were ready to treat me like an adult. There's just no other way to get your legs strong unless you stand on them without holding on to someone else. And that's what I was about to do.

I would have to finish my interviews and articles

about the Miracle Springs election for mayor later. Whatever was waiting for me at the Fremont estate, I figured it had more potential for being something that Mr. Kemble would take notice of.

Two days later, my decision had been made!

With saddlebags full of a week's supply of food, and with blankets in case I couldn't put up at a boardinghouse for any reason, I set off on my faithful horse Raspberry alone, headed for Sacramento.

Chapter 33

To Mariposa

The two-day ride to Sacramento was by now a familiar one. I had traveled the road three or four times in each direction. It was almost like coming to another one of my "homes" to stay at Miss Baxter's boardinghouse again. When I told her where I was going, she gave me several names of people she knew along the way where I could lodge.

"If you go down the valley," she said, "there are nice women who will put you up in Lodi, Modesto, Turlock, Merced. I'll write their names down for you, dearie."

I thanked her.

"But if you take the short route through the foothills, it's rougher, and mostly men. I don't know of a single reputable place from Angels Camp down through Chinese Camp and Moccasin Flat. No, you'd best stick to the valley and then cut east from Merced."

She wrote the names down for me, and having them in my pocket gave me a feeling of security.

Then we talked a little about our old trail boss, Captain Dixon. She said he was just about due, and I told her to give him a hug for me.

"He'll be so proud when I tell him how you've grown and how you're a real reporter for a San Francisco newspaper!" she said.

"Not a reporter," I corrected her. "Just barely a writer, and only sometimes at that!" I laughed.

"Perhaps that will change when you find what you are seeking in Mariposa," she said.

I hoped so, too, although inside I was getting more and more fearful that I was on what Pa would call a fool's errand. But I wasn't about to turn back now, even if I did come back empty-handed.

I left the comfort and security of Miss Baxter's and Sacramento early the next morning, and went straight south on the road leading through Lodi, Stockton, and Modesto. It was hot and dry and dusty, and I was glad I had plenty of water with me. There weren't too many people on the road — now and then a rider on horseback, and two stagecoaches headed to Sacramento.

At first I rode pretty hard, but before the morning was half gone, I knew I had to slow down or poor Raspberry would drop from exhaustion in the heat. Stockton was fifty miles, and I'd thought of spending my first night south of Sacramento there. But I passed through Lodi well before noon, so I decided I'd try to make it all the way to Modesto, where I had the name of a boardinghouse. That extra thirty miles in the afternoon sun nearly wore me out, and when I got to Modesto that night I didn't think I could ever get in a saddle again in my life!

I didn't start nearly so early the next morning. I only had to go thirty miles that day, though on my sore rump it was far enough! I got to Merced in the middle of the afternoon, found Harcourt's Boarding House, took a bath, and then fell fast asleep until dinnertime.

The next morning I prepared to go to the Fremont estate, only fifteen miles from Merced. I told Mrs. Harcourt that I might be back that night, but that I couldn't be sure.

When I set off east from Merced toward the foothills, the rising sun was in my eyes. As it rose in the sky, the hills came closer and closer, with the mountains in the distance behind them. It was probably ten-thirty or eleven in the morning when I approached the Rancho de las Mariposas, estate of presidential candidate John Charles Fremont. In my heart, I must confess, I felt about as uncertain, scared, and intimidated as I had ever felt in my life. If this was "following my dream," as Almeda had put it, I began to wonder if it wasn't time to just give the whole thing up and turn around! I had no idea who I'd run into or what they'd say to me . . . or what I'd say to them!

Lord, I prayed silently, remembering my prayers before the blizzard and the article I'd written about the Wards, *I don't know what I'm supposed*

276

to do next, but please guide my steps . . . and show me what you want me to do.

And then, taking in a deep breath of the warm dry air, I rode forward toward the gate of the estate, about half a mile outside the little village of Mariposa.

I learned later some things about the estate I didn't know at the time. In 1847, the explorer John Fremont gave a friend $3,000 to buy some land for him near San Jose, just south of San Francisco where he hoped to settle with his family. By mistake, however, the man bought a huge estate eighty miles too far inland, across the flat, dry San Joaquin Valley. At first they were disappointed, but as soon as the Fremonts saw their new land, they realized perhaps the mistake had been a blessing in disguise.

And as I entered the estate, I understood why! The Fremont ranch covered over 44,000 acres, with mountains and streams, waterfalls, trees, forest, pools, meadows, areas of rich soil, and even two small towns. I had already been through the first, for which the ranch was named, and I would later get to know the town of Bear Valley, and spend several nights in Oso House, the small hotel owned by Fremont himself. Fremont named his estate *Mariposa* after the millions of beautiful, tiny winged creatures that flew and fluttered all about it — Ranch of the Butterflies.

Even before Fremont had set foot on the land himself, farther to the north James Marshall and John Sutter discovered gold at Sutter's Mill along the American River, and the California gold rush was on. Only a year later, in 1849, huge amounts of gold were also discovered at Mariposa. Overnight John Fremont was a rich man. He had been well known already because of all the exploring he had done throughout the West for years; he became even more famous for the stories of the gold found on his land. When California became a state in 1850, John Fremont was immediately elected one of its first senators. Fremont's wife Jessie was the daughter of the well-known United States senator from Virginia, Thomas Hart Benton. Fremont was therefore a nationally known politician throughout the whole country. So when the new Republican party was formed in 1854, they nominated John Fremont to run as their candidate for President.

Fremont had not even been back to California during the whole campaign, so I didn't know what kind of story I figured to get by coming here. And as I rode up to the gate I desperately wanted to turn around and go home. But I was here, and it was too late to turn back, so I might as well see what happened.

A man was sitting in a little shed by the gate, which stood open. A painted sign on the fence read *Rancho de las Mariposas*. The man looked like a Mexican, and he stood up as I approached and glanced over me and my horse. He wasn't carrying a rifle, though he had a pistol in his holster at his waist, and he didn't seem too friendly. I suppose he was standing guard on account of the trouble Pa talked about with the Fremont mines.

"I . . . I'm a newspaper writer," I said hesitantly. "I've come to —"

But he didn't wait for me to finish and didn't seem to care what I was doing there. With a wave of his head, he motioned me to come through the gate, then pointed along the road toward some buildings in the distance, which I assumed was the ranch itself. I urged my horse along slowly, and the man sauntered back to his shed and sat down, never speaking a word.

Well, I thought to myself with relief, *at least I made it past the outside gate!*

As I approached the house, which wasn't big and fancy at all like I had expected, I could hear the sound of machinery and voices and wagons and workers in the distance. I knew that must be the gold mining going on. And as I got closer I saw more and more people about — all men, lots of Mexicans — but none of them paid any attention to me. There were several buildings, mostly adobe, a barn with corrals and stables attached with both horses and cattle in the enclosed areas. Several log buildings were scattered about, with a few men going in and out of them, and I figured maybe that's where the mine and ranch workers lived. The main house was made of wood planks, but it didn't look impressive like the house of a U.S. President. The Fremonts had never actually lived here, however. They spent most of their time back in Washington, D.C.

I stopped, got off my horse, tied her to the hitching rail in front of the house, and took in a deep breath. I looked around again. Still no one had taken any notice of me. I walked up onto the porch, then knocked on the door, my knees shaking.

The door opened and another Mexican appeared. He could not have been much older than I was.

"Hello," I said, trying to sound confident, "I am a newspaper writer and I have come to write an article —"

I paused just for a second, wondering from the fellow's blank stare whether he understood English. But even before I opened my mouth to continue, he spoke quickly.

"Sí, you come see Mrs. Carter!" He motioned me inside. "Venga aquí, you seet down . . . you seet here," he said, pointing to a chair. "I get Mrs. Carter — she veesit you!" And before I realized it, the young man had left the room and I was alone again.

A minute or two passed. Then I heard footsteps coming down the hall in my direction. A woman appeared and came toward me.

"I am Ankelita Carter," she said. "Felipe says you want to see me about something for a newspaper."

I liked Mrs. Carter immediately. From her dark brown skin it was plain at once that she was Mexican, and her broad smile of white teeth put me instantly at ease. Despite the color of her skin and her overall appearance that seemed to me at first glance that of a servant or maid, she spoke flawless English without even the hint of an accent. There was even a cultured sound to her tone, which made me immediately curious.

She was a stocky woman, not fat, but strongly built, and looked well accustomed to work. She might have reminded me of Katie, though she was taller and her broad shoulders had almost a manly quality. She was not "pretty," although her brown complexion was clear, her eyes bright, and her smile so infectious that you couldn't help but consider her attractive to gaze at and converse with. Her hair was pure black without a trace of gray, but from the rest of her appearance I would have guessed her to be somewhere in her mid-forties.

"I write sometimes for the *Alta*," I said, "and I was hoping to be able to write something about the estate or the Fremonts. My name is Corrie Belle Hollister."

"Well, Miss Hollister," replied Mrs. Carter, "I am very pleased to make your acquaintance." She held out her hand, and as I shook it I was further reassured by this woman with the friendly smile. "You must have come a long distance." She sat down in a chair opposite me.

"I have ridden four and a half days," I said.

"My, you *are* dedicated! But I must admit to some surprise. You are a woman, and a very young one at that. How do you come to be a reporter? I've never heard of such a thing."

"I don't suppose I'm *really* what you'd call an official reporter," I replied. "I try to write things I'm interested in, and then I hope the editor will want to print them."

"And he is willing to print something written by a woman?"

"Actually, the first few things he's printed appeared under the name C.B. Hollister. To tell you the truth, he hasn't printed anything of mine since he found out I was a girl not even twenty years old yet."

"How old are you, Corrie?" Mrs. Carter asked.

"Nineteen."

"Well, you are brave to try what you're doing." She paused. "Hmm . . . C.B. Hollister, you say?" She seemed to be thinking. "Did you write something about, let's see . . . it's coming to me — something about a lady from Virginia who went out to California as a mail-order bride and planted an apple tree?"

"Yes, yes!" I answered excitedly. "Did you actually read it?"

"I did indeed," she said. "It was very well done."

She smiled at me again, and gave a little nod, as if she was looking me over again for the first time.

"My, but isn't this something! For us to meet like this — a year later and all the way across the continent."

"What do you mean?" I asked. "I've only just come from north of Sacramento."

She laughed broadly. "That's not what I meant," she said. "I read your article in Virginia, when I was there with Mrs. Fremont."

"It really did get printed back there?" I said. "Mr. Kemble said it was going to be, but I never knew if it really did."

"Oh, yes, we all read it. Mrs. Fremont, the Senator."

"You were there with the Fremonts?" I asked, my surprise showing through.

"I've been with Mrs. Fremont since they were in Monterey in 1850. Her father, you know, is Senator Benton, and we were at their Virginia estate of Cherry Grove often, until the house burned down two years ago. After that and the death of Mrs. Fremont's mother, we went south less frequently. Though that is still where we encountered your article. Jessie herself is a writer, or at least she helped her husband a great deal with the memoirs of his travels. She hopes to write again one day. Just wait until I tell her I've met you! She will be thrilled. I know she will recall the article and your name because it made an impression on her at the time."

"I can hardly believe it," I said, in wonder. "To think that someone that far away actually read something I wrote out here!"

We continued to visit, and Mrs. Carter turned out to be as interesting herself as the Fremonts or the election or the estate. From a wealthy Mexican family, she had been well-educated in eastern United States, had returned to Mexico

283

where she had married a California businessman. Her husband had been killed and most of her family's wealth lost during the Mexican war, and in Monterey, Jessie Fremont had taken her into her household, at first as a domestic. But soon realizing Ankelita's training and education, Mrs. Fremont put her in charge of most of the household, including the Fremont children. The two women fast became friends, and Ankelita had been part of the Fremont home ever since — in Washington, D.C., during Mr. Fremont's term as senator, back in California, accompanying them to Europe. Only two months earlier had she left the Fremonts to return to California.

"But this recent trip," she concluded, "was *so* much more pleasant, now that there is a railroad across the Isthmus instead of having to walk or ride a donkey or be carried and pulled in carts by Indians." She laughed at the memory.

"Why did you return to California?" I asked.

"I felt it would be best for the campaign," Ankelita replied. She stopped as a look of sadness crossed her eyes. "I love Mr. Fremont," she went on, "and Jessie is like a sister to me. But politics is a field that attracts many enemies, where cruel things are said and done in order that men might gain their selfish ends. And many things have been said about Mr. and Mrs. Fremont that are untrue, things that others would use to defeat Mr. Fremont in the election. Some newspapers began to report that he was a Catholic. Though it is not true, the mere report has damaged him greatly. His own father-in-law, Jessie's father Mr. Benton, has spoken out harshly against Mr. Fremont, even against his own daughter."

"But why?" I asked.

"Because Senator Benton is a Democrat and his son-in-law is a Republican. The Republicans are against slavery, and most of the Democrats are in favor of slavery. And though Senator Benton himself is from the slave state of Virginia, he is personally against slavery. Yet he cannot make himself cross the party line to support his own son-in-law, though he shares his views. I find it appalling that his party has more influence than his own conscience."

"Is that why you left?" I asked.

Mrs. Carter drew in a deep sigh, and I saw a look of something like sadness on her face, even pain.

"I came to feel that my presence would ultimately do him more harm than good in the election," she said at length. "Being raised as a Mexican, I am Catholic. It was only a matter of time before Buchanan's press writers would have discovered about my religion, and they would have used it against the Colonel. And there were those who were beginning to talk against Jessie because of me, implying that I was Mrs. Fremont's 'Mexican slave,' as they called it. Not a word of it was true. But just the darkness of my skin was enough to feed prejudices, and the hint of such a thing would have been enough to hurt the Colonel because of his strong anti-slavery position. All through the campaign people have been trying to link Mr. and Mrs. Fremont to slavery, digging up Jessie's Virginian upbringing, and asking pointed questions about their black servants, all of whom were perfectly free just like me."

"It doesn't seem fair," I said.

"Politics is never fair, Corrie. Politics is politics, and it's a matter of winning however you can and by whatever you have to say about your opponent. But *fair* — no, politics is rarely fair."

"It just doesn't seem right!"

"No, I don't suppose it's right any more than it is fair. But if you're going to be in politics, that's just the way it is."

"Did the Fremonts ask you to leave?"

"No, Jessie would never have done that. But when I told her of my decision, she knew it was best. She gave me money for passage and asked me to come back here to watch over their household affairs. Not that I could really be of much help with the business of the mine, but they want to know there is someone here they can trust completely who can tell them what is happening. So I returned, and I have been here a little over a month. After her husband is elected President, Jessie wants me to come back and live with them in the White House."

"Oh, wouldn't that be wonderful!"

"And then *you* could come visit us, Corrie, and write a story about President and Mrs. Fremont. *That* would surely make that editor of yours stand up and take notice of you — even if you are a young woman!"

I laughed. But just the thought of me ever visiting the White House was too unbelievable to fathom.

"But you cannot have come all this way just to listen to me," Ankelita said. "You must have known the Fremonts have not been in California for five years. What did you want to write an article about, Corrie?"

I shrugged sheepishly. We'd been talking for almost an hour and the subject of my writing had hardly yet come up. If Mr. Kemble wanted "human interest," Ankelita Carter was the perfect subject. She was as "interesting" a person as I'd ever met! I could write several stories about her, without having to worry about the Fremonts or the election or the mine or anything!

"Actually, I didn't have anything to write about," I admitted. "I saw the article a few days ago in the *Alta* about the mine here having some controversy, and I just decided to come here and hope that I might find out about it. The editor of the paper has been pretty hard on me after the C.B. Hollister business, and I just have to find something to write about that'll make him see that I can be a reporter even if he doesn't like the fact that I'm a young woman."

"So you didn't knock on the door asking to see me as Felipe said?"

"No, ma'am," I said. "I just knocked on the door and was praying that somebody would be here who would take the time to talk to me and wouldn't mind that I had come."

"Well, I don't mind a bit!" she said. "And I have enjoyed talking to you."

"What is the controversy about the estate?" I asked.

"Oh, nothing new. The Colonel's mine has been in legal battles from the very beginning. Most of the miners in California believe in 'free mines' — whoever first stakes out a claim has right to the area. Colonel Fremont bought all this land before anyone knew there was an ounce of gold anywhere around here. But after 1849, miners invaded his property, and he has been having to fight them off ever since. The miners feel entitled to stake claims even though the land belongs to Mr. Fremont. And just a few months ago the Supreme Court back in Washington confirmed his title to the whole estate and Mr. Fremont had all the independent miners driven out by force. That all happened earlier this year. But it hasn't been the end of the trouble. That's why you saw Hector out at the gate wearing a gun, and there are guards posted all around the main mining areas. Some of the anti-Fremont newspapers are stirring up the Mariposa title issue again, trying to make sure the miners of the state stay mad at Fremont until the election."

"Won't Mr. Fremont win easily here in California?" I asked. "That's what my pa says."

"I don't know, Corrie. Money and greed and power do strange things to men. Many powerful

Californians are jealous of Mr. Fremont because of his fame and good fortune. They want him to fail. And they will stop at nothing. There are bad men involved, ruthless men. I have even heard Mr. Fremont say there are politicians willing to have people killed to further their own causes. It is hard to believe such people run our government. And such men are fanning the fires of contention about the title to the estate, and spreading many other false rumors about the Fremonts."

"That's terrible!" I exclaimed.

"I agree. But gold is not the only issue involved. Here in California the issue over mine ownership is big in the minds of the miners. But on a national scale, slavery is the overriding issue. And there are millions of dollars at stake over the future of slavery in the South, just as there are millions of dollars at stake over where a man is entitled to mine here in California. The pro-slavery forces of Buchanan are equally ruthless at times. They are determined to keep John Fremont out of the White House. If Fremont is elected, he will probably abolish slavery, and then their whole southern way of life will be ruined. They feel they *have* to stop him."

"Are *all* politicians like that?" I asked. "Greedy and mean?"

"No, there are many good men. Yet when otherwise seemingly good men support something intrinsically evil like slavery, it does something to them. They become different, and in a bad

289

way. But during my years with the Fremonts, I have met many good men too. I've never forgotten the time I met a young Illinois lawyer by the name of Lincoln. The look in his eye told me that *he* was a different breed than these kinds of men I've spoken of. In fact, this Lincoln was almost Mr. Fremont's running mate for Vice-President this year, but lost out to Mr. Dayton. Lincoln is staunchly anti-slavery, just as is Mr. Fremont, and I overheard the Colonel say to his wife shortly after the nominating convention in Philadelphia last June, 'That fellow Lincoln is one to watch. I doubt the country's heard the last of him.' "

She stopped and the room grew quiet for a minute or two.

"But all this can't be that interesting," Mrs. Carter said finally.

"It's interesting to me," I replied.

"But nothing so interesting you could make an article out of. The papers have been full of this kind of thing for a year."

"But not from a woman's perspective," I said with a smile. "Maybe I could write something about Mr. Fremont in a different way that women readers would enjoy more."

"You want something women would like to read?"

"Mr. Kemble says that's one of the reasons he printed some of my articles, because women enjoyed them."

"Well, if you want a woman's story, I'll give

one to you!" said Ankelita excitedly.

"What is it?" I asked eagerly.

"The best story of all in this election isn't the candidate or the election at all. It's the candidate's wife. If Mr. Fremont wins and gets to the White House, he's going to have Mrs. Jessie Benton Fremont to thank for it. *She's* the real story!"

"Should I get out my paper and pen?" I asked.

"You get them! And then you sit right here and I'll tell you all about Jessie. And when we're through, Corrie Belle Hollister, young woman reporter, we're going to have an article that editor of yours won't be able to refuse, an article that will make your name read in newspapers all over the country! Jessie's story is one that only another woman could write, and you're the first woman writer I've ever met. Oh, how I wish Jessie herself were here! She would so love to talk with you!"

I started to get my things out of my satchel, but before I got seated again, Ankelita was out of her chair.

"Let's eat some lunch together first, Corrie," she said. "Felipe!" she called down the hallway, then turned to me again. "Then afterward we'll sit down and I'll tell you everything."

Felipe appeared and she spoke a couple of hasty sentences to him that I didn't understand, then indicated for me to follow her.

Chapter 34

Hearing About Jessie

An hour later we were seated in the same chairs again, each with a cup of tea in our hands.

Lunchtime had been an interesting assortment of people coming and going as we sat around a wooden table eating beans and tortillas. There were several children, an older woman, Felipe and two or three other young men about his age, and Ankelita and I. Most of the conversation among the others had been in Spanish. The ranch and mine workers must have had their midday meal someplace else, and I never did quite figure out how Ankelita was involved with everything that was going on. She could not have been in charge of the whole household, because she had only recently arrived, yet I saw no one else who seemed to be higher in authority. At least she spoke to those in this particular house in a confident manner. Maybe this wasn't the main house, even though it had been the first I had come to. There were a few other buildings about with people coming and going from them.

Once we were alone again and had seated ourselves, Ankelita began telling me about Jessie Benton Fremont, from their first days together in Monterey, right up to the present.

"It was just before I had become part of their home,⁎ she said, "that gold was found here. I've heard Jessie tell the story so many times I feel as if I'd been there: how Colonel Fremont rode up on his horse and ran into the room they were renting in Monterey and plopped down two big heavy sacks in front of her. 'Gold, Jessie!' was all he said. 'Gold! The Mariposa is full of it in every stream!' "

She told me about the Fremonts' life in Monterey before that.

"Monterey was then the capital of California, but it was a hard life for Jessie. They had no money, and Jessie had little fresh food. They had no milk, no fresh eggs. Jessie talks about eating rice and sardines and crackers during those days."

She paused and chuckled.

"A couple of months ago during the campaign, a woman started criticizing Jessie for being rich and pampered, for having tea and cake between meals.

" 'I find it a comforting break in my often wearying day,' Jessie answered her.

" 'But you allow yourself to be served by a maid?' the lady asked, thinking to make Jessie look foolish. But Jessie turned the tables on her.

" 'Yes, I confess it,' she whispered. 'But just between us, I think I make better tea myself. I had no maid in Monterey. I heated the water in a long-handled iron saucepan over a smoky fire. And instead of French cakes to eat, I lifted a sardine from his crowded can and gave him a decent burial between two soda crackers.'

"The lady and all the people around laughed, and in the next day's paper it was reported that Jessie Fremont was a good down-to-earth woman who could cook over a campfire."

We both laughed at that, and I found myself wondering if the story had made its way to the California newspapers. If not, it would be the perfect thing for me to use!

Then we talked about the Fremonts' trip to San Francisco following the discovery of gold on their estate. At San Jose, which later replaced Monterey as the capital of California, they hired some Indian women to wash their clothes by pounding them with stones in a brook. They were met there by a workman from the Mariposa, bringing buckskin bags filled with gold dust and nuggets — wealth from their foot-hills mines.

After Colonel Fremont's election to the Senate to represent the newest state in the Union, the Fremonts set sail for New York. For the next year, Jessie, who had long been a senator's daughter, now found herself a senator's *wife*.

"The years came so rapidly and were so full," Ankelita said. "Colonel Fremont was in the Senate only a year, and then we returned to San Francisco in 1851 to a beautiful big home. But within months there were two terrible fires and the house was gone. Then we spent a year in Europe before returning to the East. Jessie's mother died, her father lost his Senate seat, and the house at Cherry Grove also burned, all within a few months. And now they are running for the White House! The Fremonts' lives, especially with three young children, have been so busy and eventful."

We talked most of the afternoon. I must have asked a hundred questions. It was all so fascinating! Ankelita told me what Jessie looked like and what she felt about some of Mr. Fremont's political decisions, about the heartbreak of their decision to become Republicans, knowing that it meant driving a wedge between them and Jessie's southern relatives. She told me about the children, about what it was like for Jessie to try to be a good mother in the midst of Washington politics. She told me how Fremont would consult Jessie about political decisions, not something very many politicians did. That, too, would be perfect for an article women would really enjoy. Even though they couldn't vote, women were more interested in current events than men sometimes thought. And Jessie Fremont was the shining example of what impact a woman could have standing beside her husband in American politics.

"During the early part of the campaign, Corrie," Ankelita said, "Jessie was sometimes as popular as her husband. Crowds would call out her name after the Colonel's speeches, wanting to see her too. One campaign song went like this:

And whom shall we toast for the Queen of the
  White House?
We'll give them "Our Jessie" again and again.

"I only wish I could be there to see the election through, although I know it's best that I am here."

By the end of the day, I truly felt as if I knew Jessie Benton Fremont myself. If I could just figure out how to best put it down on paper, Mr. Kemble was sure to print it! And if he didn't, I would take it to another newspaper. The Fremonts hadn't been in California since 1851 and things had been much different back then. Now Jessie Benton Fremont was only a month or two away from being the most important woman in the whole nation, and I had personal stories about her that Mr. Kemble could not possibly have heard before.

I was so excited, and hoped I'd be able to somehow write about Jessie Fremont in as interesting a way as Ankelita Carter told about her!

By the time our conversation was over, the shadows were starting to lengthen outside. The day had gone by so quickly, and had been better than my wildest dreams.

"Well, young lady," said Ankelita, "we'd best get Felipe to see about getting your horse put up for the night, and then getting you settled in your room."

From my puzzled expression she could tell I didn't understand.

"You weren't thinking of riding back down the

296

mountain to Merced, were you?" she asked in a voice of astonishment.

"I figured I would," I answered. "To tell you the truth, I hadn't really thought about it since this morning."

"Well, you're not going anywhere, Corrie. You're staying here with us tonight. I have an extra bed in my room. Besides, you have to get started on that article of yours. And what better place than right here?"

I had supper with them around the same table, with most of the same people. Then later, at a little table with a candle, I pulled out several sheets of blank paper, got out my pen and ink, spread out my notes, and began to write the article I had come to Mariposa to find.

At the top of the page I wrote for a title: "The *Real* Jessie Benton Fremont: The Woman Behind the Candidate."

Chapter 35

Mr. Kemble Once More

Five days after I'd first set foot on the Mariposa estate, I once again walked through the doors of the offices of the California *Alta* on Montgomery Street in San Francisco.

I'd arrived in the city late the evening before. I spent the night at Miss Bean's Boarding House. After a bath and a change into fresh clothes, I felt much more confident than the first time I had been there. In my hand I held eight sheets of writing, an article I was genuinely proud of as being different and publishable, and something that no other reporter could have, especially no San Francisco reporter. If Robin O'Flaridy had scooped me last time, now it was my turn!

I didn't feel like a little girl begging a powerful editor to publish my little article. For the first time I guess I felt like a real "reporter" who had uncovered a story. As I walked down the hallway — and was I ever glad there was no O'Flaridy in sight! — I felt tall and good inside.

I went straight to Mr. Kemble's office, without

even asking anybody if he was in or if I could see him, and knocked on the door.

I heard a muffled sound from inside, so I opened the door and walked right up to his desk, where the editor sat just like last time. His head was down and he didn't even look up right at first.

"Mr. Kemble," I said, trying not to let my voice quiver, "I have a story for you."

At the sound of my voice he glanced up.

His eyes surveyed me up and down for a second, then it seemed to gradually come to him who was standing there in front of him in his office.

"Ah, Miss Hollister," he said, leaning back in his chair. "Come to deliver your next article in person, eh? So you can be sure no one steals any of your precious words? Long ways to come, isn't it, just to deliver a short piece?"

I think he was trying to be humorous, but I didn't smile.

"This isn't on the Miracle Springs mayor's election," I said. "It's got to do with the national election."

"Oh, national news! My, oh my!" he said, still with a little grin on his lips. "You've broken some major new story that all the other hundred newsmen in this city have never heard?"

"No, it's not a major new story," I said. It's 'human interest,' I believe you call it. However, I think you will find it of interest to your readers. And to answer your question, no, I don't think any of your other newsmen do have access to this information."

I stood straight and confident before his desk, the papers still in my hand. Gradually the smile disappeared from his face, and he eyed me carefully. I think he was starting to realize I was serious.

"All right, Hollister," he said at last. "Let me see it."

He held out his right hand. I handed him the top page.

He took the sheet, glanced over it quickly. His eyes darted up to mine again, as if looking for some clue. Then he looked down at the sheet again and read it start to finish. As he completed the last line he again held up his hand.

"I'll give you more when you agree to publish it," I said.

"Don't toy with me, Hollister!" he snapped, dropping the page. "I don't play games with my reporters, especially nineteen-year-old women!"

I reached forward and took the page from his desk, then turned around and made a step toward the door.

"Okay, okay," he said, still brusquely but apologetically. "I'm sorry. That was rude of me."

I turned back and faced him again.

"It looks good, Hollister," he went on. "I'm sure I can use it. May I please see more?"

I shuffled through the sheets and handed him page five.

He took it, and the moment he saw what I had done, he glanced up at me again, bordering on another outburst, I think. But he controlled himself, and read the page through. He set it down on his desk, leaned back in his chair, put his hands behind his head, and looked at me for a long moment.

"What is this little game you're playing with me?" he finally said.

"I just want to protect my article," I said. "What happened before was very upsetting to me. I felt we had an agreement, even if we didn't shake hands on it, and I don't think what you did was right. Now, I'm very sorry I didn't get the chance to tell you all about Mrs. Parrish being my stepmother. That was wrong of me. But it was an honest oversight. When Robin O'Flaridy walked in, I forgot a lot of what I had intended to say. But all that's past, Mr. Kemble. You explained yourself very clearly in your letter, and you were very plain about how things are if I intend to write for your paper. Therefore, it seems best to me that I make sure we come to an agreement beforehand. And after we've reached an agreement, then you can see the entire article."

While I spoke his face changed first to red then to white. I don't know if he'd ever been spoken to by any of his reporters that way, but he certainly wasn't used to it from a nineteen-year-old woman!

When I finished, I stopped and stood still. I half expected him to yell at me, or throw me out of his office and say he never wanted to see me again.

There was a long silence. I don't think he knew

what to do with me either. He probably *wanted* to throw me out! But then again, I knew he wanted the article on Jessie Fremont!

Finally he spoke again.

"Where did you get this stuff?" he asked.

"My sources are confidential," I answered. I'd been practicing that line all the way from Mariposa! Ankelita told me that's what I ought to say if asked where I'd got my information.

"Nobody could know some of the things you say unless they knew the lady personally. *You* don't know Jessie Fremont . . . do you, Hollister?" His voice was incredulous at the very thought, even though he *knew* I couldn't possibly know her.

"Confidential," I repeated. "I can tell you nothing about where any of this came from."

He squirmed in his chair. I could tell he hated not being in control.

There was another long silence.

"All right . . . all right, Hollister, you win! I'll print it. I don't know how you got it, but it's good, it's original, and I want it."

"And the matter of pay?" I said, still holding the rest of the pages.

"I told you before I would pay you a dollar an article . . . until you've proven yourself."

"I think this is worth more than what I've sent you before."

"So now it's you who's welching on a deal, eh, Hollister?" He chuckled.

"I never agreed to a dollar," I said.

"Okay, you're right, this is worth more. You've done some good work here. I'll pay you two dollars for it."

"I want eight dollars."

"Eight dollars!"

I didn't say anything.

"That's highway robbery! I can't pay that kind of money for a single article. If word got out that I'd paid a woman eight dollars, the men would be wanting sixteen for every little thing they brought me."

"This has nothing to do with whether a man or woman wrote it. Somebody had to do the work to uncover this story, and whether it was a man or a woman, it seems to me the words would be worth the same. And I figure the words of *this* story are worth eight dollars. She might be our next first lady, and nobody else has some of this stuff I've written here."

"You are a huckster, Hollister, a downright rogue! All right, I'll give you four. I can't pay a penny more!"

"I'm sure the Sacramento *Union* or maybe the *Courier* would like to take a look at it."

"You can't do that. You're under contract to me — don't forget, we have a three-article deal on the other election."

"A deal you did not feel you needed to honor a couple weeks ago," I said. "I'm under no obligation to the *Alta*; I simply wanted to offer the story to you first."

I reached for the page five still lying on his desk.

"Good day, Mr. Kemble," I said, and again turned to go. This time I made it almost to the door before I again heard his voice. Even as he said it I could tell from the grating tone that it killed him to give in to the demands of a woman.

"Six" came his voice behind me.

I stopped, and slowly turned around. He was standing behind his desk, both hands resting upon it, sort of leaning toward me, his face glaring.

I stood where I was and returned his stare. Two seconds went by, then five. It seemed like an eternity that we stood there, looking deeply into each other's eyes. Whether it was a struggle of wills, or a contest of stubbornness, I don't know. But in that moment, I was thankful for Ma and her Belle blood!

Finally I spoke. My voice was very soft, but very determined. I had made up my mind even before I'd entered his office, and I wasn't about to back down now.

"Mr. Kemble, I said I wanted eight dollars. I believe the article is worth eight dollars. And if you want it for the *Alta*, you are going to have to pay eight dollars. Otherwise I am going to walk out this door and take what I have to one of your competitors."

Several more seconds went by.

Finally Mr. Kemble sat down and exhaled a long sigh.

"All right, you win. Eight dollars." His voice

sounded tired. I could hardly believe it — I had beaten him.

"I'd like the money today," I said.

"Do you never stop, Hollister?" he asked in disbelief. "Don't you trust me for payment?"

"You told me yourself, Mr. Kemble, that the newspaper business was a tough business. I'm just following your advice. You also told me that if I thought it was unfair I could take my articles elsewhere. It seems that your own advice would apply to you too. If you do not like my terms, you do not have to accept them. I'm simply saying, my terms for this article are eight dollars in advance, and then you may have my article on Jessie Benton Fremont."

He sighed again.

"Go see the cashier," he said. "Tell him I'm authorizing payment for an article. He'll check with me, and then you'll have your payment."

I turned and left his office and did as he said. An hour later I was walking back up the street to Miss Bean's. I felt like shouting at the top of my lungs.

I had done it!

Chapter 36

Last Night Alone
on the Trail

Two nights later I was camping between Auburn and Colfax beside a blazing fire. I'd be home the next day.

I'd spent the previous night with Miss Baxter in Sacramento, and I could have slept this night in Auburn. But somehow I felt that I wanted to finish off this adventure alone, by myself, beside a campfire I had built, sleeping under the stars. I suppose it was a dangerous thing for a young woman to do. After all, even if Buck Krebbs was gone, there were a thousand more just like him, and California was still no tame land.

But I wanted to do it. By the time I rode back into Miracle Springs tomorrow, I would have spent eleven days alone. It was like nothing I'd ever done before. I'd gone off chasing a dream — in search of a story I didn't even know existed. I had found it, written it, and sold it for eight dollars! I'd met some interesting people. I'd taken care of myself. I'd faced some scary situations and come through them. I was eleven days older, but I felt about eleven years older! Something inside me had changed. I had learned some things about myself, about what I was capable of. And this seemed the fitting way for me to spend my last night.

I had also learned to pray in some new ways, and to depend on God more than I'd ever had to before. And now I knew a little more about what that verse in the Bible really meant about God guiding our steps. He had really guided mine!

I guess I felt I had grown up a little bit. Well . . . grown up a lot. Especially standing there staring back at Mr. Kemble and saying if he didn't pay me the eight dollars, I was leaving. I had met a lady who knew the man who might be the country's next President. The next first lady had read one of my articles, and now I'd written an article about her. Why, I practically had an invitation to the White House! I felt like I'd gone halfway around the world in those eleven days. I'd talked about and thought about some big and important things. And now here I was going back to little Miracle Springs in the foothills of the California gold country. Yet another part of me had been opened to a bigger and wider world, and I knew I'd never be the same again.

I *could* be a writer now; I already was a writer. Maybe I'd do other things. Maybe I would teach or keep working for the Freight Company. But at least I knew I *could* do it. I could go into the office of an editor of a California newspaper and put my pages down on the desk and say, "There's a story that Corrie Belle Hollister wrote, Mister. I wrote it, and folks are going to want to read it!"

So I sat there staring into my little fire, eating dried venison and hardtack and some apples Miss Baxter gave me. I felt peaceful inside. Peaceful and thoughtful and even a little melancholy. This had been an adventure, but now it was over. I knew I'd face disappointments in the future, and probably write a lot more articles that wouldn't get printed. And there would probably be times Mr. Kemble would win and would stare *me* back into a corner and make *me* give in and do it his way.

But I would always have the memory of this journey, of feeling a story calling out to me though I didn't even know what it was, of going out and uncovering it. Next time I'd have more courage to ask questions and to knock on doors and to search and try to uncover something. I was lucky this time, meeting Ankelita Carter. But I had met her because I struck out and tried something scary. Maybe next time, though it would be different, God would lead me to someone else, to a different set of circumstances that would take me in the direction of the story I was after.

There were no sounds around me but the crackling of the fire and the crickets in the woods. I hoped no wild animals came. I was especially afraid of bears and snakes, and I didn't even have a gun — only a small knife.

But God would protect me and take care of me. He had so far. Why would this night be any different?

Maybe that's one reason I wanted to spend the last night alone like this on the trail. I had been nervous and anxious plenty of times in the last ten days. Yet I hadn't been in any situation that was downright "dangerous." I wasn't really in any danger now. But I wanted to prove to myself that if I had to, if I was out tracking a story again sometime, and I did have to fend for myself — up in the mountains, or down in the valley where there was no town — I could do it. Maybe someday I'd even travel farther from home, or back East — or maybe I *would* go to the White House someday. Wherever I went, I wanted to know that even if I was all alone, I could stand on my own two feet and say to God, "Well, it's just the two of us, Lord. And that's plenty to handle just about anything that comes along!"

My eyes were fixed on the bright orange coals of the fire, and I found myself praying quietly as I sat there.

"Lord, I am grateful to you for doing like you promised, and for guiding my footsteps on this trip. I don't know whether I trusted you very well or not. I tried to, but then sometimes it's hard to remember. Yet you just kept taking care of me, anyway. And, Lord, I thank you, too, for the article, and for all the ways you have been helping my writing this last year. You showed me a while back that trusting you is the way you give us the desires of our hearts. But you've let me be a writer too! You've given me that dream, Lord, and I am so thankful to you! Help me to write just like you want me to. And teach me to trust you more! I really do want to, God. I want to do just what you want me to do, and I want to be just exactly the person you want Corrie Hollister to be."

I drew in a deep breath. I felt so peaceful. God had been good to me!

The night air was getting chilly. I lay down and pulled my blankets tight around me. And still staring into the fire, the sounds of the crickets in my ears, I gradually fell asleep.

Chapter 37

Home Again

I'd left Miracle on a Monday. It was now Friday afternoon, a week and a half later, the 29th of August. I wondered if Almeda would be at the office, but I was actually relieved when she wasn't. I wanted to see everyone at once.

I can hardly describe the feelings I had inside as I went around the last turn in the road and the house came into view. I felt as if I'd gone to a foreign country and was now returning after many years. Yet it had only been eleven days!

Almost immediately Becky saw me. But instead of coming to meet me, she turned around and ran inside, then out again, then up the creek, screaming at the top of her twelve-year-old lungs, "Corrie's here! Corrie's home . . . it's Corrie . . . Corrie's back!"

Within seconds people were pouring through the door of the house, and out of the corner of my eye I saw Pa and Uncle Nick and Mr. Jones running down from the mine. By then my eyes were full of tears; everybody was hugging and laughing and shouting and asking questions, and I could hardly tell who was who. I was so happy, yet I couldn't stop crying even at the same time as I was laughing and smiling and trying to talk. And I don't even remember getting off my horse, but there I was surrounded by the people I loved so much, arms and hands and voices all coming at me at once. Every once in a while I'd hear a voice I knew — Katie's one minute, then Alkali Jones's high *hee, hee, hee,* and of course all my sisters and brothers shouting at once. The only two voices I don't remember hearing were the two whose sound I loved more than all the others. But Pa and Almeda and I got a chance to visit quietly alone later. The three of us stayed up and talked around the fire way past midnight, and I told them everything.

"I've got to tell you, Corrie," said Almeda when I was through, "we were mighty concerned about you."

"I know," I said. "I'm sorry."

"You're starting to remind me of myself, girl!" said Pa with a smile. "Maybe it ain't just the Belle blood, but some of the Hollister too. Tarnation, but I'd like to see you in ten years! You're gonna be some woman, that's all I got to say."

I could tell that in spite of Almeda's concern, Pa was proud of me. I suppose he'd figured I was a mite timid — which I was! — for a daughter of his. So I think he liked what I'd done. He'd been acting a little different toward me all evening — not just treating me like I was older and wasn't a little girl anymore, but also more like a son who had done something brave. Being gone a few days wasn't all *that* courageous a thing. But because it was *me,* timid little Corrie Belle, I think it gave Pa kind of a special feeling to see his daughter do it. Zack acted different, too, as if I'd proved my right to be the oldest Hollister.

Once the article on Jessie Fremont appeared in the August 30 issue of the *Daily Alta* — on the *second* page with a big bold caption over three columns, with my name right under the title! — my life would never be the same again. Whether I liked it or not, ever after that I *was* a reporter, a writer, and much would change as a result. How many times I must have read those words over: "The Real Jessie Benton Fremont . . . *by Corrie Belle Hollister.*" I was so thankful inside, so thankful to God. More and more, as I reflected back on those eleven days, I realized that none of it would have happened had he not been guiding my steps just as he promised. Even though I wasn't aware of it at the time, and even though I hadn't even been thinking of him through some of it, he had been there all the time, going along the path just in front of me.

As I read over the article and the caption and my name underneath, I couldn't help wondering if I shouldn't have used my full given name, *Cornelia.* But when I later suggested it to Mr. Kemble, he said, "Too late, Corrie. Folks know you now. And once you're writing with one name, you can't change it any more than you can change horses in mid-river, as the saying goes. No, you stick with Corrie. It's a good name, and folks are starting to recognize it."

The excitement of my trip and the article died down, especially after church on Sunday when everybody asked me all about it, and then the following Monday I went into the office with Almeda and spent a regular day working in town.

I'd almost forgotten about the Miracle Springs election. Almeda hadn't said much about it since my return, but all of a sudden the church service on Sunday seemed to stir it up again, even more than before. People came up to me afterward, welcoming me home, asking me about the trip and what I'd done, and most everybody said something about my interviewing them earlier about the mayor's election. Sometimes it was just a little comment, like, "I been thinking about that conversation we had," or they might say, "I might like t' talk t' you again, Corrie, if yer still gonna do interviewin' about it."

Most of the folks were quiet about it, as if they didn't want anyone to hear them talking to me. And Mr. Royce acted pretty friendly at the service too, like I reckon a fellow ought to be if he's trying to make people vote for him. He was greeting the men and their wives and shaking hands. And he even came up to me and gave me a light slap on the shoulder and said "Good to have you back, Corrie!" before he went on to visit someone else.

But in the background amid all the hubbub of the after-church visiting, lots of people seemed as if they wanted to talk to me again about the election. My getting back to town seemed to stir up people's thinking in a new way.

All day Monday my mind was on the interview article, going over what I'd done and things people had told me and thinking of how to go about starting to write the article. There were only two months left before the election, so I couldn't delay too long. On Tuesday, the *Alta* came with my article in it, which set my mind running in a hundred directions at once! So it wasn't until Wednesday that I really settled myself down enough to think about the interviews and article again. That morning I gathered my papers together and put them in my satchel to take with me into town to work. I hoped to see some of the people who'd talked to me at church. There were still a few people in town I hadn't interviewed yet. As I went through my notes and quotes from what people had told me before and started to consider actually beginning to write the article in a way that Mr. Kemble'd like, I found myself getting enthusiastic about it again.

But that very evening something happened that suddenly changed my thoughts not only about the article I wanted to write but about the whole mayor's election.

Chapter 38

Threats

Not long after Almeda and I got back home from town, we heard a single-horse carriage approach outside and then slow to a stop. Pa went to the window, and when he turned back inside, his face wore a look of question and significance.

"Franklin Royce" was all he said, half in statement, half in question.

We all looked at one another, but the knock on the door came before we had the chance to wonder fully what the visit could possibly be about.

Pa opened the door.

"Good evening, Mr. Hollister," I heard the familiar voice say, "might I have a word with your wife?"

Pa nodded, stepped aside, and gestured Royce into the room. Almeda stood and offered her hand. Royce shook it, though without conviction.

"Mrs. Hollister," he said rather stiffly, "I would appreciate a few moments of your time."

"Of course, Franklin," she said deliberately.

It was clear from his tone this was no social call. "Please . . . sit down." She pointed to an empty chair.

"In private, if you don't mind," he added.

"Anything you have to say to me can just as well be said in front of my husband," she replied, her voice betraying a slight edge to it. I think she was perturbed by his unsmiling seriousness. She continued to look right at him, but neither said another word.

Pa had a hesitant look on his face, not seeming to know what he ought to do. But finally he spoke up.

"It's no never-mind to me, Almeda," he said. "Come on, kids, let's go outside. But I'm warning you, Royce," he added to the banker. "I'm going to be right outside this door, and if you say something my wife don't like, I'll be right back in here and throw you out on your ear!"

Every one of us was curious what Mr. Royce's visit was about, but we all got up and started trooping silently toward the door that Pa held open for us. I was the next to last one, but before I reached the door, I heard Royce's voice again.

"Perhaps *Miss* Hollister could join us," he said, speaking to Almeda but gesturing his head in my direction. "What I have to say concerns her as well as you."

I glanced up at Pa. He shrugged. "If he wants to talk to you, it's okay by me." But as he said it he was staring daggers at Mr. Royce.

I turned around and went back to where I was

317

sitting, while Pa and Zack filed outside with the others and closed the door. Once we were alone, Mr. Royce still did not take the seat Almeda offered him, but began speaking immediately.

"Almeda, when you first announced that you were going to run against me for mayor, like everyone else I was surprised, interested, even curious. And for a while I was willing to play along with your little charade of pretending to be a politician. But when matters grew more serious and when people began to talk and I began to fear for the business of my bank, then I grew concerned. You were visiting people and rousing them up against me. I came to you in your office, and I tried to be reasonable. I asked you as cooperatively as I was able to cease and desist, and to withdraw before more harm was done. But you refused. You have persisted in your efforts to undermine my reputation. Your flyers continue to circulate. And now you have set your stepdaughter to do your dirty work, talking with everyone in town, asking their opinions."

He stopped, but just long enough to take a breath of air.

"Now," he continued, "I'm here to tell you — both of you — that I want this to stop. It's futile, it's useless. You cannot win the election, Almeda, and I will not have you stirring up the community against me any longer. I've been patient for as long as I can, but it's time I put my foot down. I want it to stop. And as for you, young lady," he said, turning and looking me straight in the face, "I do not want you talking to anyone else about the election."

"You leave Corrie out of this, Franklin," said Almeda heatedly. "This election campaign is between you and me."

"Then *you* tell her to stop with these ridiculous interviews."

"I will do no such thing. She is a newspaper reporter in her own right and I will not tell her what she can or cannot pursue."

"Newspaper reporter! That's a good one," he laughed. "That's almost as humorous as a woman mayor!"

By now we were *both* more than a little annoyed!

"My editor in San Francisco is paying me for two stories about the Miracle Springs election," I said. "I have done nothing to hurt you in any way."

"Except get people talking."

"It's hardly *our* fault if people talk," I said. "And you can't blame *us* for what they think of you."

I shouldn't have said it, but the words were out of my mouth before I realized it. Now Royce was angry too, and he made no more attempt to mask his true intentions.

"Look," he said, "Hollister may pamper the two of you in your little schemes! But he never did have much backbone. It's a rough world out there, and no two interfering women are going to spoil my plans, no matter what their fool of a husband and a father lets them get away with.

Two can play this little game of yours, and you don't want to play it against me. Stop now, or I'll make life miserable for all of you!"

"How dare you talk that way of the finest man in Miracle Springs!" cried Almeda, rising from her chair.

I expected to see Pa burst through the door any minute and slam his fist into Royce's face.

"You are meddling in what is not your business, and he is a weakling if he cannot prevent you."

"You are the fool, Franklin Royce, for not knowing a real man when you see him! And as for the election, my campaign is *not* a charade. I have not roused a soul against you, and have never once even mentioned your name in a single discussion with anyone. Corrie is absolutely right — you can hardly hold *us* responsible for what people may think of you! I have done *nothing* to undermine your reputation. And I would never think of resorting to dirty work, as you call it, still less of asking Corrie or anyone else to do it for me. I resent your charges against me, Franklin, and I will *not* withdraw from this election!"

"It will not go well with you, Almeda, if you do not reconsider."

"What's more," she added, "not only will I see it through to November, after today, Franklin, you have shown me more clearly than ever that for Miracle Springs to elect you its mayor would be a grievous mistake. You have made me more determined than ever to *win* that election!"

"If you do win, Almeda," and his voice was

deadly serious, "you will live to regret it! I will make life so miserable for you and your family that you will have no choice but to resign, and I will be made mayor eventually anyway."

"What can you possibly do to us?" she shot back. "You hold no mortgages on either my property or Drummond's. The little my business owes you is unsecured."

"The people of this community who *are* indebted to me will find themselves compelled to reconsider where they purchase their supplies. In fact, I have been thinking of opening a supplies outlet and freight service myself, as an adjunct to the bank."

"Dare to go into business against me, Franklin, and you will find I am a strong businesswoman, with more contacts and experience than your money alone will buy you."

I had never seen Almeda like this. She was seething.

"Perhaps that is true," replied Royce, with a sly smile. "But you will not be able to survive long without customers. And the men of this community will know they had better deal with me or else find themselves foreclosed upon. Most of the mortgages I hold have a thirty-day call."

"You are an unscrupulous man, Franklin!"

"It's called 'the fine print,' Almeda. Every standard banking contract has its share, and I simply use it to my own advantage, as does any wise businessman when it comes to matters of finances."

"When the people find out you are trying to blackmail this town into electing you its mayor, they will never stand for it!"

"They will have little choice. If they do not vote for me, I will simply call their loans due. Within a year I'll own the whole town. In the meantime, you'll be out of business for lack of customers."

"Well, you don't own *us*, Franklin! You may blackmail the rest of this town, and you may put Parrish Mine and Freight out of business. But you will never control me, or my husband, or our family! If it comes to that, I will leave the business and move out to the claim. We will manage with or without the Parrish Freight."

"Ah yes . . . the *claim*," said Royce, drawing out the words with a significant expression. "That brings up an interesting point which I have been looking into. You are correct, Almeda, in that I hold no mortgage on the property your husband and his brother-in-law claim as their own. However, according to my investigations there may be some question as to the validity of their ownership of the land."

"That is preposterous, Franklin!" Almeda nearly exploded. "You know the doctrine of *free mines* as well as anyone else in California. Whoever first stakes out a claim has exclusive right to the land. Drummond and Nick have been on that property since 1849, long before you ever got to California!"

"Granted, they have right to *use* the land, but

322

that does not make the land itself theirs. I have been looking into the deeds to actual land ownership in and around Miracle Springs, and let us simply say the results may surprise many people."

"You wouldn't dare try to run the miners around here off their land! You wouldn't survive a month as mayor!"

"There are laws, Almeda," Royce said, trying to sound calm. "California is a state now. There are legalities to be observed. Surely you know of the recent Supreme Court decision in the Fremont case *against* free mines. I tell you, Almeda, your husband's position may be very tenuous indeed, and he may find it more pleasant to have me as his friend rather than his enemy. Especially when the authorities who might be compelled to look into the matter discover his criminal record, and learn that he is still wanted by the law in the East. I very seriously doubt that they'll uphold his claim to the property, especially given the Mariposa ruling."

"You are full of threats, Franklin," replied Almeda, and she had now grown calm as well — calm and cold. "But Sheriff Rafferty put the matter of my husband's past to rest long ago."

"Rafferty is a weakling, too!" Royce spat back. "There are others who might find his failure to uphold his duty cause for his removal as well. As mayor of Miracle Springs, I may well find that I must —"

"You will never be mayor, Franklin! Not if

I can help it. You will not get away with all this!"

Suddenly the room grew silent. Royce stared back at Almeda with piercing eyes. When he next spoke, all anger, all passion, all intensity from his voice was gone. His words were icy, measured, and the look in his eyes hateful.

"I have tried to be as reasonable as a man can be, Almeda. But you have left me no choice. As a gentleman I am loathe to stoop to such measures, but you force my hand."

He paused, and his eyes squinted in a glare of evil determination.

"If the hurt to come to the rest of the town, if the loss of your business, if danger to your husband, and if the loss of all this property here on your so-called claim — if all these things do not convince you that it is in everyone's best interest for you to withdraw from the race, then perhaps what I have to tell you now *will* convince you.

"There are men in this state, even now, who will stop at nothing to see Fremont defeated in the general election, men whose interests will be more preserved under a Buchanan presidency than one led by an anti-slavery westerner."

He looked over in my direction.

"Our budding reporter here is taking a decidedly pro-Fremont stand in the *Alta*. Should these men I speak of learn that she is perhaps, as the daughter of a miner herself, planning to come out with an appeal for the miners of California to vote for Fremont, they would take such news very badly, and I would hate to see anything happen to Corrie as a result."

"I am planning no such pro-Fremont story," I said quickly. "I only wrote a story about his wife."

"Ah, but don't you see, Corrie," replied Royce, "these men do not take kindly to *any* such favorable articles. And word could begin to spread that you intended to take a more affirmative stand, and — well, you can see how a man in my position would . . . be powerless to stop such a rumor."

"Franklin, you are despicable!" said Almeda, practically shouting. "Are you now threatening Corrie with what is purely a false and —"

"Enough, Almeda!" Royce interrupted angrily. "I will do whatever I have to do! I have had people investigating you too, Almeda, as well as your husband and his daughter. If danger to your stepdaughter from the slavery people does not pound some sense into that stubborn brain of yours, then perhaps the people of Miracle Springs would like to read a little flyer that I might circulate just prior to the election concerning what I have recently discovered from my contact in Boston. You have an interesting past, Almeda!"

At the word *Boston*, Almeda's face grew white. She spoke not another word, and sank into a chair as if she had been suddenly struck a devastating blow.

"Forgive me, Almeda," said Royce. "I do not want to use the information I possess, either

325

against you or your stepdaughter. I admit it is not the gentleman's way. But you are a stubborn woman, and I will do what I have to!"

He spun around and quickly left the house.

Chapter 39

Meeting of the Committee

The rest of that night and all the next two days Almeda was practically silent. Not a word was said about Royce's visit. Pa asked no questions. I guess he knew Almeda would tell him about it when the time was right. I didn't say anything either. I figured it was her business to share, not mine.

On the evening of the second day, Almeda got the six of us together — Zack and I, Katie and Uncle Nick, and she and Pa — for what she called a campaign committee meeting. Then she told everyone else about Mr. Royce's visit and that he'd promised to do some pretty bad things to a lot of people if she kept on with the election.

"I believe you men have an expression," she said, trying to force a smile, "when you are playing poker and realize you can't possibly win the pot. Well, I finally realize there is no way I am holding a winning hand, and it's simply time for me to throw in my cards, as you say. So I've decided to pull out of the mayor's race."

A few groans went around, but then it got quiet again.

"I am very disappointed too," she went on. "And I am convinced that Franklin Royce is more of a louse than when I began. But it just is not fair for me to continue. Too many people could be hurt. And it isn't worth it just for my pride to try to defeat him."

"But you *can* defeat him, Almeda," insisted Katie.

"The price would be too high. Many of the miners and families around Miracle Springs could be hurt."

"How?" asked Uncle Nick. "What can he do if you win?"

"He's a banker, Nick," she replied with a thin smile. "He can do whatever he wants. Specifically, he can make it very hard for folks whose mortgages he's holding. He as much as threatened to begin foreclosures if I didn't withdraw." She told them what Royce had said.

"The man is a ruthless skunk!" muttered Pa.

"But it isn't only the townspeople I'm concerned about," Almeda went on. "He threatened all of you too." She told about the questions he'd raised about ownership of the land, and about his threats to reopen Pa and Uncle Nick's problems with the law.

By now Uncle Nick was pacing about the floor angrily.

"We can fight him!" he said, waving his hands in the air. "Me and Drum ain't afraid of him.

We been up against worse odds dozens of times!"

"He's a powerful man, Nick," said Almeda. "I'm not willing to run the risk of us losing our land here, or the mine. We've got a good life and I just can't take that chance. And besides all that, he threatened Corrie as well."

"He what?" Pa roared, his eyes flashing. "If he dares lay a hand on any of my —"

"Only on account of my writing, Pa," I said quickly. "He's not about to hurt me himself."

"What can your writing have to do with it? What did he say?"

"I didn't really understand it all myself, Pa," I answered, "but he said there were rich and powerful slave-state men who were determined to see Mr. Fremont lose in California, and who would do anything they could to stop him."

"His implication was that something could happen to Corrie if she got in their way," said Almeda seriously.

"What could Corrie possibly have to do with the outcome of the election?" asked Pa.

"After her article in the *Alta* about Mrs. Fremont, she could be seen as a Fremont supporter, especially if she wrote more such articles."

"Then she doesn't need to write any more."

"That's what I told him too, Pa," I said.

"Franklin implied that he knew some of these men, and that if I didn't do as he said, he would start a rumor to the effect that Corrie Hollister, a miner's daughter, was planning a major story to try to persuade California's miners to vote for

Fremont. Even if it wasn't true, if he did what he said, it could endanger Corrie . . . and every one of us. The man has no scruples, and I have no doubt that he would do it just to spite me."

The room was quiet. I think any of us would have been willing to go up against Mr. Royce if the only danger was to himself. But when harm could come to so many others, no one was quite willing to take that chance.

"So you see," Almeda said at last with a sigh, "why I just cannot continue on with the election. The risk to all of you whom I love, and to others in the community, is simply too great. I'm afraid I'm just going to have to go into town and face Franklin again. And as much as it galls me to have to give in, I'm going to have to tell him he's won."

She took a deep breath, looked around at the rest of us, then got up out of her chair and slowly walked outside and away from the house. No one followed. We all understood that she needed some time alone.

During the whole discussion she had not once mentioned Royce's threats to her business, or what he said he had discovered about Boston. And after seeing the look on Almeda's face just before Royce had left, I certainly wasn't going to bring up the subject. Whatever it meant, it was clear there was a great deal of pain involved for her. Still, I couldn't help wondering how much these words of Royce's influenced her decision.

After about five or ten minutes Pa followed

Almeda outside. It was an hour before the two of them came back inside. Almeda's face was red, and I knew she'd been crying. Pa was serious, but the rest of that evening whenever he'd look at her, his face was more full of love than I'd ever seen it.

Both of them were quiet, and neither said a word about their time alone together outside.

Chapter 40

A Surprise Letter

The rest of that week things were pretty sullen and quiet around the office and at home. We were all disappointed and angry, yet there was nothing we could do. Mr. Royce had us over a barrel.

I didn't write a word or interview anyone. As much as I hated to quit on something I'd started, a dollar or two wasn't worth getting Almeda or Pa in trouble with a man like the banker of Miracle Springs. As for what he'd said about me, I have to say I didn't think of it that much. I didn't see how anything I wrote could possibly put *me* in any danger. Almeda didn't say anything to Mr. Royce, though she took the banner down from our office window.

The thought did occur to me that perhaps I could still write an article or two about the election, even maybe with some of the quotes from talking to people, if I showed it to Mr. Royce first and he didn't see anything wrong with what I'd said. I would hate to do that! But it did seem like a possible way to be able to do the article. Maybe this was the other side of the question Almeda had put to me before I went to Mariposa: How bad did I want to write? Did I want it bad enough to crawl to Mr. Royce for approval? I didn't know if I wanted it *that* bad.

Fortunately I didn't have to decide. All of a sudden I was thrown into the middle of a new story, one that made the Miracle Springs election — or what was left of it, anyway — seem small and far away.

The following Monday a letter arrived for me in the mail. I immediately recognized the *Alta* envelope. I opened it and read:

Miss Hollister,

A major story is about to break which will doom Colonel Fremont's chance for election. We can still stop it, but time is short and I need your help. After your article on Mrs. Fremont — which I must confess turned out to be worth the $8 from all the favorable response it has received — it could well be that you have the necessary contacts to get to the bottom of this scheme to ruin the Colonel's reputation.

I must warn you, however, there could be danger. Powerful men with great resources behind them are involved. If you want to help, the *Alta* version of the story will be yours to write. I hope this reaches you in time. If interested, I will be at the offices of the *Daily* and *Weekly Sacramento Times* at two o'clock on the afternoon of Wednesday the 12th. Meet me there.

Edward Kemble
September 8, 1856

I could hardly believe my eyes! Mr. Kemble was asking *me* for help!

I ran across the street and burst through the door of the office. "Look at this!" I cried, waving the letter in my hand.

Almeda took it and scanned it quickly. Then she just looked up at me with raised inquiring eyebrows.

"I've got to ride home and pack my things," I said. "I've only got forty-eight hours to get there!" I reached for the letter and was ready to head back out the door.

"Are you sure you know what you're doing, Corrie?" asked Almeda.

"This could be my big chance!" I answered.

"And the danger?"

"How bad could it be? No one would try to hurt me."

"People do awful things sometimes when you try to thwart their plans. You remember what Royce said."

"This doesn't have anything to do with that."

"Just be sure, Corrie, that's all."

I paused, my hand on the knob of the half-opened door, and looked back at Almeda. Her eyes were filled with concern.

"I'm not sure," I said. "But maybe the only way I'm going to be sure is to go ahead, and see what God does. But I'll talk to Pa . . . and I'll pray. I'll try hard not to do anything foolish."

"Then God go with you, my daughter. I love you . . . and I too will pray!"

For one moment our eyes met, and in that moment worlds were spoken between us. The next instant I was out the door, onto my horse, and dashing toward home as fast as Raspberry could gallop, my hair streaming out behind me, the early autumn wind chilling my nose and ears.

I was at home in less than an hour. I threw together what food I could find, rolled up three blankets, and repacked my little tin fire box. It wasn't cold yet, but the nights would be chilly so I dressed up as warm as I could, and put extra clothes, a warm coat, an extra pair of boots, a rain slicker, and several old newspapers in a bag. Then I got together my writing satchel.

Once Pa read the letter, he figured it was too late to try to stop me. He probably wouldn't have tried, anyway. The look in his eyes said to me that he thought I was ready to face whatever the world might throw at me. And if I wasn't, then maybe it was high time I learned to be.

"You go and do your name proud, Corrie Hollister," he said. "You're a Belle *and* a Hollister. And when anyone tries to give you a hard time, you just remember that, and remember you're tougher'n any of 'em. And you're God's daughter and Drummond Hollister's little girl too — and

I figure that gives you a winning hand against just about anybody. Now you go and show that fella Kemble what kind of stuff you're made of!"

"Thanks, Pa," I said.

"I love you, Corrie Belle," he added. His voice was soft and shaky.

I wheeled Raspberry around. I couldn't say anything back because of the big lump in my throat and the tears in my eyes. I dug my heels into my mare's sides and took off down the road. Before I was out of sight, I glanced back and waved. There was Pa still standing in the same place, his hand in the air.

Chapter 41

Sacramento

I walked into the office of the Sacramento *Times* at ten minutes after two on Wednesday.

I had ridden my mare as hard as I dared, spent both nights on the trail, and arrived in Sacramento just in time to go to Miss Baxter's to take a bath, change into presentable clothes for seeing an editor, and get directions where to go. I didn't know Sacramento very well, and it was growing so fast that it seemed to have changed every time I came.

A man sat at a desk inside an open office just inside the main door. He walked out and looked me over.

"I'm here to see Mr. Edward Kemble of the *Alta*," I said.

"Yes, I was told to expect you," he replied. "Right this way, Miss Hollister."

He led me down a hall and opened a door for me. I walked inside. He stayed outside, closing the door behind me.

Mr. Kemble sat at a table in the center of the

small office. There was no one else in the room.

"I'm sorry I'm late," I said. "I came as quick as I could. I left the minute I got your letter."

"Good . . . good, Hollister," he said. "Sit down." He pointed toward the chair opposite him.

I sat down and took off my coat. He started right in.

"I don't know how much you know about California politics," he said, "but it's a real mess this year. You would think that with Fremont's ties to the state, he'd be a shoo-in to win California."

"That's what my pa says," I added. From the look on Mr. Kemble's face, I gathered this was a time he wanted to listen to himself talk, and wasn't particularly interested in my responses. I settled back in my chair and listened.

"Well, it isn't necessarily so. Fremont's in a bunch of trouble here, and California's one of the critical states that's going to decide this election. It's all split right down the middle of the Mason-Dixon line — Fremont and the Republicans above it, Buchanan and the Democrats below it. But even with all Fremont's exploring and connections to the West, and the anti-slavery sentiment of the North, his chances are still shaky in some places — like California and Pennsylvania. The Republican party is too new. The Democrats are just plain a stronger party. They've got the South all sewed up, while at the same time there are bad fractures in the Northeast and West.

"The trouble is, there's a lot of folks who don't

like the idea of slavery, but they have always been Democrats. And there's some of us who are afraid that in this election we're going to find out they're more *for* being Democrats than they are *against* slavery.

"Now, you take the Germans. There's likely a hundred, maybe a hundred and fifty thousand Germans who are going to vote next month; most of them are Democrats and always have been. They don't like slavery, but they're Democrats and nobody knows how they're going to go. And so both parties are trying to win them over and are giving them money, and there are editorials aimed at the immigrant vote in the New York *Tribune* and the Cleveland *Herald* and the *Ohio State Journal* and the Detroit *Free Press* and the Cincinnati *Enquirer* and every other paper in the country. And the Democrats are stirring up fear of a Southern secession from the Union if Fremont wins. The Philadelphia *Daily News* and the *Pittsburgh Post* and the Washington *Daily Globe* are full of that stuff. The fear is worst in Pennsylvania. Listen to this."

He stopped a minute and rifled through several papers on the table in front of him. I didn't understand everything he was saying, but it was interesting, and I didn't want to interrupt again. He found the paper he was looking for.

"Listen — this is from the *Daily Pennsylvania* just a couple months ago: 'There is no disguising the fact that the great question of union or disunion has been precipitated upon us by the mad fanatics of the North, and that it is a direct and inevitable issue in the presidential contest.' "

He put the paper down and glanced across the desk at me. I think he was almost surprised to see that he'd been delivering his political speech to no one but me, who barely understood half of it.

"Do you get what I'm driving at, Hollister?" he asked.

"Some of it," I answered.

"I'm talking about this country splitting apart — that's the kind of fear the southern Democrats are putting into the people of the North. They're blackmailing the voters, threatening to pull the South out of the Union if Fremont is elected. But if Buchanan is elected, then the South wins . . . and slavery wins. The Democrats are saying, 'Give us the victory, put our man in the White House, let slavery remain, and we won't destroy this nation.' Now I ask you, can we allow this country to submit to that kind of blackmail? Of course we can't. Slavery is wrong, Hollister, and that's what John Fremont stands for, and that's why he must be elected in November. The southern states will never secede from the Union, even over slavery. The secession issue is a bluff."

He stopped, took a breath, but then went right on.

"It's the Southerners, the Democrats, these blackmailers holding the threat of secession over the rest of the country, who are trying to ruin Fremont. They're spreading all kinds of lies and rumors about him — saying that his parents weren't married until after he was born, ridiculing him for his beard, claiming that he had once been a French actor, saying that he is secretly a Catholic, that he hates Germans because of his French blood, and hinting at improprieties, even illegalities, in how he came by his wealth. And the rumors involve his wife too — that's where you come in, Hollister. There are reports circulating that Jessie Fremont has never forsaken her Virginia upbringing, that she still keeps slaves and even watches while they are beaten at her orders, and that she herself was suckled by a slave mammy on her father's plantation.

"They're all lies. Vicious lies. But they are damaging Fremont's chances. And I don't have to tell you what that means to California. Buchanan stands for the interests of the South. His election will mean that the West will be forgotten.

"Many people feel that the future of California depends on a rail line between Chicago and Kansas City and the Pacific. Mark Hopkins, Charles Crocker, Leland Stanford, C.P. Huntington, and others like them are backing Fremont for that reason. They know that the only hope for a transcontinental railroad lies with the Republican party. And that's why our paper, the *Alta*, and the *Daily* and *Weekly Times* here in Sacramento are doing our best for him. But our competitors are working just as hard to discredit him. The Sacramento *Union*, the *Courier*, the *Democratic State Journal* are all backing Buchanan. And the worst is the *Morning Globe* in my own city, where some of my own former colleagues have defected.

"Fortunately, I have a spy at the *Globe* who keeps me informed, and only last week I learned that they are planning a major story to run just a week before the election, a story they hope will utterly ruin Fremont and insure his defeat. Their timing is intended to sway last-minute voters, and I fear they may have similar stories they will break in some of the eastern papers as well."

He paused and gave me a long, serious look.

"You understand what it's all about, don't you, Hollister?" he said after a minute. "It's slavery . . . and power . . . and greed. You've got to understand all this so you'll know the kind of men we're up against. We may be fifteen hundred miles from the nearest slave plantation, and California may be a free state. But there are men here who work for some of the most powerful and wealthy men in the South. And they're doing whatever it takes to put Buchanan in the White House and keep their power from eroding. The South controls the country right now, and they don't want to lose their hold on Washington. Men like Fremont, and that young lawyer from Illinois, Lincoln, who aren't afraid to speak up, are in danger. And *we* may be in danger too. But we've got to do what we can, and we've got to try to scoop them on their story before they print it. We've got to discredit everything they say before they say it, and print our own major new pro-Fremont piece. We may not be able to change what they do in Pennsylvania. It's too late for that. But if we can swing the vote in California, it may be enough to put your friend Jessie Fremont in the White House."

"I didn't say she was actually my friend," I corrected him.

He looked at me crooked for a second. "I thought you did," he said finally. "Well, that makes no difference. You obviously have *some* connection."

"What do you want me to do?" I asked. "I don't know anything about politics. I don't see how I can be of much help."

"One of Senator Goldwin's men is supposed to be up in the Mother Lode somewhere, digging up the last of the dirt they're planning to use against Fremont."

"Who's Senator Goldwin?"

"Herbert Goldwin — just about the most powerful man in the U.S. Senate, an entrenched slave owner, and filthy rich from his huge cotton plantations in South Carolina. Also one of the most unscrupulous men in Washington. He'd lie or cheat, steal, maybe even kill to keep his little empire secure. Fremont's spoken out against him, and Goldwin hates the Colonel. Of course he'd never soil his lily-white hands with his own dirty work. But he has plenty of people to do it for him. And one of them's up Sonora way rousing up all kinds of mischief — getting falsified documents against Fremont, getting interviews from miners Fremont supposedly ran off the Mariposa at gunpoint. Then there's the Catholic angle, and the rumors against Mrs. Fremont. My contact at the *Globe* says this guy's due back in San Francisco in a week and a half with the last pieces of the article which will, his editor claims, 'nail down the coffin on the presidential bid of John Charles Fremont.' We've got to locate that guy and find out what he's got so we can see if there's any substance to it. If they're making claims, we need to find out whether they're true or false."

"What's the man's name?" I asked. This was getting mighty interesting!

"We think Gregory, or something like that. Only heard the name once, so we can't be sure."

"And you don't know exactly where he is?"

"I had someone else on it, but they lost his trail. Sonora's the last scent we had, which makes sense — there's a lot of anti-Fremont talk among the miners that close to Mariposa. Lot of 'em think they ought to be entitled to the gold on Fremont's estate, and they don't like him getting rich while they're scratching away for tiny little nuggets. And just between you and me, I wouldn't doubt if what Goldwin *really* wants is the Mariposa for himself! Rich guys like him can't stand when a man like John Fremont comes into a lot of dough overnight. They want all the wealth and power for themselves, and it makes them crawl to have to share it."

"What do you want *me* to do?" I asked. "Why do you think *I* can help?"

"Maybe you can't, but it's worth a try. So here's

what I want you to do. Find this Gregory, or whoever he is, and find out what he's got. If he has something on Fremont or his wife that's not true, then use your contact to write an article discrediting Goldwin's charges."

"How could I possibly find him? I'm just . . . a girl!"

Mr. Kemble laughed. "Here all this time you've been wanting me to overlook that fact. And now when I drop something really important in your lap, you tell me you're not old enough to do it!"

"I didn't say I wasn't old enough. I just don't know what you expect me to do when your other man couldn't do it. I don't have experience tracking someone like that."

"Don't you see — you're the perfect one, Corrie. No one will suspect you of a thing. I doubt if anyone who's involved with Goldwin will even recognize your name. I could send one of my experienced men. But they'd spot him right off. No, I think you might be able to find out things someone else couldn't. You shouldn't even have to lie."

"I couldn't do that."

"I don't think you'll have to. But you won't be able to tell them what you're after."

"I still don't see why you want *me* to follow somebody."

"I'm not just sending you to track this fellow. I'm sending you after a story. You've got to get on the trail of this thing, find out what's at the

345

bottom of it, and then write a story that tells the truth and shows up their lies for what they are. Once their story runs, it's too late. You've got to find the guy and uncover what he's trying to do. I don't know how, but that's what you've got to try to do. I can't do it, and none of my regular guys can do it because they know them all. But you can, Corrie — at least I hope you can, 'cause the outcome of the election in California may depend on it. You get to the bottom of it, find out the truth behind the things they're planning to say, and I'll make you a reporter, Corrie Hollister. You find this guy and uncover what Goldwin's up to, and get me the story I want *before* their charges can appear in the *Globe*, and I'll give you a monthly article of your very own, as an *Alta* regular."

I was stunned. It was the very thing I'd dreamed of. Yet how could I *possibly* do all he asked? I must have said something, or asked what I should do first, though I don't remember. But I do remember his answer.

Mr. Kemble's expression changed from concern to relief. "The first thing you do is get yourself out to Sonora and start asking questions and nosing around. Real quick you'll start to find out if you're *really* a reporter, or just a kid who wants to be one. And whatever you find out, it's got to be on my desk by noon on the 22nd or else we're done for. That's ten days, Hollister. By then we'll know what kind of stuff you're made of."

Chapter 42

Sonora

Everyone in California had heard about Sonora. Except for the area around Sutter's Mill farther north, it was one of the heaviest populated, roughest, and richest regions of the Mother Lode. There were stories told — and we'd heard them all the way up in Miracle Springs, thanks to Alkali Jones — of single nuggets worth thousands of dollars. One was found that was supposed to have weighed twenty-eight pounds!

The whole place had been fabulously rich in the few years after the rush. There were twenty or thirty separate little towns all within ten miles of Sonora. Every one had seen thousands of hopeful miners pass through, all with a hundred stories to tell. In Shaw's Flat, only a mile away, eighty-seven million dollars had been taken from its streams. Columbia, four miles away, supposedly had a population of 30,000 with over a hundred gambling houses, thirty saloons, twenty-seven food stores, a stadium, and a theater. Farther north, Mexican Flat and Roaring

Camp and Columbia and Angels Camp and Saw-mill Flat — they all could have laid claim to equal riches and equal notoriety. I'd heard stories of fights and jumped claims and even murder. Most of what I'd heard, coming from the mouth of Alkali Jones, was probably considerably bigger in the tale than in the reality, but that only made it all the more fearful for me as I rode into the heart of the Mother Lode — alone, and not even knowing what exactly I was looking for. I had been praying harder than ever before in my life since leaving Sacramento! And I hadn't been about to spend the night alone in this country — at least not my first night. I'd stayed at the National Hotel in Jackson, although it wasn't much better than sleeping outside. I'd heard yelling and singing and piano playing all night, and a couple of gun-shots. But at least I'd been able to lock the door to my room!

Late the next morning I rode into Sonora, still praying, still thinking every other minute of just forgetting the whole thing and galloping back to Miracle Springs as fast as I could! But I knew I couldn't. Even though Pa didn't really approve of me riding down here alone, Mr. Kemble was counting on me. And maybe Mr. Fremont too, and Jessie Fremont, and even Ankelita Carter. So I had to do what I could. Even if I failed, I had to try.

I walked my mare slowly through the main street. I hoped I could find a boardinghouse in town instead of a hotel, because most of the hotels were connected with saloons, and stayed pretty loud and raucous all night long. But I didn't see anything that looked even halfway civilized. Every other building seemed to be a saloon, and from the sounds coming from them they all seemed full of men drinking and yelling. The people on the streets were all men, and I didn't see a friendly face anywhere. The ones who noticed me looked me over as I passed, and a few yelled and whistled at me. But I just kept going and tried to keep my face from turning red. I was beginning to think I was the only female in the whole place when two or three saloon girls came out of a place called the Lucky Sluice. They started calling out worse things than the men. I didn't like their looks at all!

Finally a little ways farther on, I spotted a building with just the word "Hotel" printed across the door. I rode toward it, stopped, got down and tied my horse to the hitching rail, and walked inside.

I was glad there was hardly anyone inside, though a few tables in the lobby indicated that probably card playing went on at night. A man stood behind a counter, and I walked toward him. But before I even got across the floor, a whistle behind me let me know that the man at the counter wasn't alone after all. "If it ain't a real live female woman!" someone said.

"Hey, Fence," a voice called out, "check her into my room!"

I ignored the noises behind me and went up

to the counter. Before I'd said a word the man they called Fence pushed the register in my direction.

"Excuse me," I said, putting on my bravest-sounding voice, although I probably didn't convince anyone, "do you know if there's a boardinghouse in town?"

"I got a boardinghouse, Missy!" called out a voice, followed by footsteps slowly coming across the floor.

"Shut up, Jack!" said the hotel man. "Can't you see she's just a kid?"

"So much the better!"

"Get outta here, Jack. I don't want no trouble." Then looking down at me, the man said, "There's Miz Nason's place, little lady. Down the next street to the right, 'bout a quarter mile down."

Just as I was about to turn to leave, a thought occurred to me.

"You don't have a man by the name of Gregory registered here, do you?" I asked. I glanced down at the register and tried to scan the names on the page without being too conspicuous.

"Nope. But half the fellas what come to the diggin's ain't usin' their real names anyway."

"Thank you very much," I said, turning around to go. As I did I almost bumped into the man the hotel manager had called Jack. He had been standing right behind me. I didn't know how I couldn't have known it, because he smelled terrible. He must have been working for a month without a bath! He looked even worse, and I walked on past him toward the door without even looking into his face, though he muttered a few words as I went by. Just as I was going through the door, the hotel man's voice called out after me, "If you don't find no room, Missy," he said, "I got one you can have fer four dollar a day. The lock works, an' I personally keep Jack an' his kind off the second floor."

Four dollars! When Almeda and I went to San Francisco, she'd only paid six dollars a night at the fancy Oriental, and that was for *two* of us! And he wanted four, just for me, in this ramshackle place that looked like it hadn't been cleaned since the day it was built! I kept walking back out to the street, ignoring the voices and laughter coming from behind me.

I mounted my horse again and set off again in the direction that I hoped would lead me to Nason's boardinghouse. In five minutes I found myself approaching a decent-looking two-story wood house. At least the paint wasn't peeling and some grass was growing in front. A small hand-painted sign on the fence simply said "Nason."

I stopped, got off my horse, and walked up and knocked on the door. In a minute or two a stout, broad-shouldered black-haired woman opened it. She looked me over up and down, without the slightest change in her expression, then just stared at me, waiting.

"I'm interested in a room," I said, "if you

have any available."

"Rooms? 'Course I got rooms!" she said back, a little too gruffly to make me feel altogether comfortable. "How many you got with ya?"

"It's just me, ma'am."

"Just you!" she exclaimed. "You expect me to believe a young thing like you's travelin' in *this* country alone?"

"I'm sorry, ma'am, but I really am by myself."

"Well, then, guess I can't hardly send you away. Yeah, I got a room, if you got two-fifty a night."

"Two-fifty!" I said in astonishment before I could keep it from slipping out.

"Two-fifty, and a bargain at that! Only two other houses in town — one of 'em's full of dance-hall girls, and the other's full of drunken miners. An' both charge the same. If you want to stay in one of the hotels, you'll take your life in your hands — someone's gettin' shot over some gold fracas every week. An' you'll pay more besides. So it's two-fifty a day — in advance! Breakfast's included, but if you want supper, it's another two bits."

Every other boardinghouse I'd stayed at was a dollar a night, including supper — except for Miss Bean's in San Francisco, which was a dollar-fifty. It was a good thing I'd brought money along!

Finally I nodded my head and said that would be fine. Mrs. Nason opened the door and led me inside.

I followed her through a large parlor and toward a flight of stairs. "Might you have a man by the name of Gregory lodging with you?" I asked.

"Never heard of him," she answered without turning around.

We continued up the stairs in silence, and she opened the third door we came to. "This here's the room," she said. "How many nights?"

"I — I'm not altogether sure just yet, ma'am. I guess I'll pay you for two to begin with."

"With supper?"

"Yes . . . thank you."

"That will be five dollars, four bits. And I believe I did say in advance?"

"Yes, ma'am. I'll go down and fetch my things from my horse."

"Ain't a good idea to keep nothing of value unattended in this town. They'll steal you blind. You better go down and make sure your horse is still there."

"Yes, ma'am," I said, turning back the way we'd come.

"If you want to put your horse up, there's a barn out back, with stalls an' fresh oats."

"Thank you, that will be fine."

"It's another two bits for the horse," added Mrs. Nason. I sighed, and walked back outside to where my mare was waiting patiently.

An hour later I sat down on the edge of the bed in the bare little room. I'd fed and groomed Raspberry and put her up in the barn for a well-deserved rest. Now I had to think about what I was doing here.

I supposed if I was being a newspaper reporter investigating something, then about the only place to begin was by asking questions. No doubt Mr. Kemble might have other ideas. He'd probably have all kinds of sneaking-about-kind-of notions how to find this fellow who was working for the *Globe* and for that Senator Goldwin. But I didn't know anything but just ask around and try to find him. And if I did, then try to find out what he was up to, even if it meant just going up to him and asking him. I didn't have to blab right out that I was working for the *Alta* and that my editor told me to sabotage him.

I wasn't sure how to do what Mr. Kemble sent me to do and still be honest at the same time. This was a part of being a reporter I'd never thought about. I had always wanted to write just to express myself and tell interesting stories to people. Now all of a sudden here I was in the middle of trying to investigate a situation where wrong was being done. But even if wrong *was* being done, I couldn't do wrong myself to try to uncover it. I just hoped I'd be able to keep straight what was right myself, no matter what anyone else was doing!

I got down on my knees beside the bed.

"God," I prayed, "I'm not sure what's going to happen here. But I ask that you'd show me what to do and where to go, and guide my thoughts as well as my steps. Help me to be true, like I prayed before, and help me to find out the truth behind this article they're trying to hurt Mr. Fremont with. Help me to be a good reporter, and to be a good daughter of yours."

Chapter 43

The Lucky Sluice

All that afternoon I walked around the town of Sonora.

After a while I got used to the rowdiness and the yelling and the horses running through the streets, and even the men talking to me and calling after me. I saw a few other women about who didn't look like they belonged in a saloon, and that helped. And luckily there hadn't been rain for a while, so the streets were dry instead of muddy.

I went into several stores, peeked over the swinging doors into a saloon or two, and got up my courage to go into two or three more of the town's hotels to ask about the fellow named Gregory. I felt rather foolish just wandering about, and it didn't seem like I was having much luck. Later on I saddled my horse and rode out of town.

I took a ride clear around through Jamestown, Rawhide, Shaw's Flat, Springfield, and Columbia. I saw signs pointing off to Brown's Flat, Squabble-

356

town, Sawmill Flat, and Yankee Hill. I had no idea there were so many little towns and mining camps — though most of them were just a few buildings surrounded by claims up and down the streams. Once I got out of Sonora no one bothered me much. The men I passed would stare or watch to see where I was headed, but most of them were too intent on their work to mind me. All around were the sights and sounds of gold mining — men panning in the streams, mules laden down with equipment heading off the roads up toward the high country, the sounds of heavy equipment and dynamite and quartz machinery. It seemed that every square inch of this country was being dug up or mined by somebody!

Riding back to town, I decided that the only way to go about this search was to start at the beginning of Sonora and go to every hotel and boardinghouse and ask about Mr. Gregory. Then I'd go ask the sheriff. After that, I'd have to do the same things in whatever places there were in the little surrounding towns where he might be staying. I'd never find him just wandering about. There were thousands of people around here! I'd have to go to every lodging place one by one until I found where he was staying. At least by then I'd know for sure if he was in Sonora or not. If he wasn't, then I'd be able to tell Mr. Kemble I'd done everything I knew to do.

I arrived back at Mrs. Nason's just in time to unsaddle and put up my mare before supper. When I went in, Mrs. Nason introduced me to the others around the table, including her own husband who'd been out working their claim all day. Besides Mrs. Nason I was the only woman, but the men were all nice enough, although they spent most of their energy gulping down the biscuits, potatoes, roast beef, and cooked cabbage.

"She's lookin' fer a feller named Gregory," said the landlady to her husband. "You ever heard o' him, Jed?"

"Can't say as I have," the man answered. "What you want him for, Miss?"

It was the first time I'd been asked that, but I'd already planned out the answer to give.

"We're in the same line of work," I said. "And I need to ask him a few questions."

" 'Bout what? You look kinda young to be in *any* line o' work in these parts. What do you do?"

"We're in the newspaper business."

This seemed to satisfy Mr. Nason. His wife's expression didn't look like she approved, but she hadn't smiled once since I'd arrived, anyway.

Just then one of the other men at the table spoke up.

"There's a Gregory over at the saloon, least he was a couple nights back. But he weren't no newspaper man, I can tell ya. A shyster's more like it! The guy took me for my whole two days' worth of dust in an hour of five-card stud."

"Where was that?" asked one of the other men.

"The Lucky Sluice."

"The Lucky Deuce, you mean!" said the other.

"They play a game of faro there with deuces countin' triple and always goin' to the player, *if* you lay down a double bet ahead of time. So if you hit it wrong, the house gets rich and you lose everything in a hurry. But they keep bringin' the suckers in! I gave it up after losin' my whole wad to 'em twice."

"When was the last time you saw this man?" I asked.

"Couple nights ago, don't remember exactly. I ain't been back since."

"Maybe I'll go over there and see if he's back," I said.

"It gets mighty wild there, Miss," said Mr. Nason. "You don't want to be mixing with drinkin' men, especially if they happen to be losin' their gold at the same time."

"Well, if it's the man I'm looking for, he's not a miner, so I won't have to worry about that. And as for the drinking, I reckon I'll just get my business done and get out before anything rough gets started."

Nobody said anything else. None of them seemed to think I was too smart to think of walking into a saloon alone. But on the other hand, they didn't seem to care that much either way. Sonora was the kind of place, I guess, where folks were in the habit of doing whatever they pleased, and where everyone else minded their own business.

After supper I went out to the barn. I was about to saddle up my horse when I remembered

Mrs. Nason's words about the stealing that went on around here. Maybe it wasn't such a good idea to tie the horse on the main street of Sonora at night. I decided to walk up to the middle of town instead.

Even while I was still a block away, I heard the laughing and yelling and music coming out of the Lucky Sluice. There weren't many people out. I'm sure all the respectable people were in their homes — if there were very many of those in this town! — and the rest were already inside the brightly lit saloons.

When I got to the double swinging doors of the Lucky Sluice, I took in a deep breath, breathed a silent prayer, and, trying to hide my shaking knees, pushed through the doors and walked inside.

I was dressed in denim breeches and a man's flannel shirt, and most of the men were absorbed at the dozen or so card tables, so I didn't attract too much attention at first. If I had, I probably would have turned back around and run right out! Against the right wall a man was playing lively music on a piano, and a few women in short, bright-colored dresses were lounging about and talking with some of the men.

I walked straight to the bar, ignoring the few heads that turned and watched me. The big burly man behind it walked toward me, still finishing something he was saying to somebody else. When he looked down at me, surprise showed on his face, and I think he might have been about ready to throw me out because of how young I looked. But I didn't give him the chance.

"I'm looking for a man named Gregory," I said quickly. "I was told he might be here."

The bartender stared at me like he might *still* be thinking of throwing me out. Nobody in this town did much smiling, but they sure stared a lot! Maybe I was funnier looking or more out-of-place looking than I realized.

But finally he turned his head and shouted off toward a table near the piano, "Hey, Hap, that friend o' yers from Frisco here tonight?"

"Naw . . . who wants t' know?"

"Little lady here's askin' fer him."

The man named Hap sat up in his chair and looked in our direction. If I'd hoped to be inconspicuous, there was no chance of that now! The rest of the men he was playing cards with glanced up too, and a round of whistles and catcalls followed. But I tried not to pay any attention to them.

"I'm afraid yer luck's done run out, Miss," said Hap. "Derrick lit off fer Chinese Camp yesterday. But maybe I can help ya out, Miss," he added with a smile, and a wink at his friends. "I'm better lookin' than him by a dang sight!"

"Can you tell me where I might find him?" I asked.

"Try Shanghai Slim's at Chinese Camp, or else he might be stayin' at old lady Buford's place in Jacksonville."

"Is that a boardinghouse?"

"You can call it what ya want, Miss. Derrick's called it worse things than that! But if ya mean a place where a body can get a bed an' a meal, then that's what it is."

"Thank you kindly," I said, nodding toward him and the bartender. Then I turned and walked out as fast as I could!

I went back to Mrs. Nason's. I'd paid for the night, and it was nearly dark and much too late to think of doing anything else. I'd head south to Jacksonville in the morning. I had no way of knowing if Hap was talking about the same man as I was trying to track down. But the bartender did say Gregory was from San Francisco, and that's where the *Globe* was. So I figured I ought to follow the lead and see what came of it.

Chapter 44

Derrick Gregory

Chinese Camp was about ten or twelve miles south of Sonora. I figured I'd ride there first.

There probably wasn't much chance of finding anybody in the morning, but I could look around, ask, and then I could go on to Jacksonville three or four miles farther on and see about getting a room for the night at that boardinghouse. I didn't much relish walking into strange hotels and saloons and asking about a man I didn't know. I still couldn't figure out why Mr. Kemble had sent *me* after this Gregory when, like he said, he had other more experienced men. I couldn't believe it was only that he wouldn't recognize me. Especially when I didn't have any idea what I was supposed to be doing, or how I'd find out the information Mr. Kemble needed. But I noticed that every time I walked into a strange or uncomfortable situation, it got easier the next time.

So when I saw the sign above the door advertising "Shanghai Slim's" as I rode into Chinese

Camp, I didn't feel nearly so queasy in the stomach at the thought of walking inside. I wasn't looking forward to it, but at least I knew I could do it.

I got off my horse, tied her to the rail outside, and went in.

It was obvious in a minute where the place got its name — both the town and the saloon. Inside, the decorations looked more Chinese than anything I'd seen before in California. And although there weren't very many people there, more than half of them were Chinese. A man wearing a green apron was sweeping the floor in front of the bar. From his appearance I thought he must be the owner.

"Pardon me," I said, "are you Mr. Slim?"

He stopped his broom, glanced up at me, and answered in a thick Chinese accent, "You bet. I Shanghai Slim." The look he gave me seemed about the friendliest I'd seen in a long time, and he almost hinted at a smile. But I couldn't be sure.

"I'm looking for a man by the name of Gregory," I said.

The short little man pointed behind me, then without another word returned to his sweeping.

I turned around and saw, among the half dozen empty tables in the room, a group of men involved in a poker game at one of the tables. From the looks on their faces, I wondered if it had gone on all night, or if it was just getting started on a bad note. The only one apparently having a good time was one jovial Chinese man with a pile of money and some little bags of gold sitting in front of him. Several others who had apparently dropped out of the game stood by watching.

Slowly I approached them. No one even saw me. A pile of coins, some paper, and a couple of small nuggets of gold lay in the middle of the table, and all six of the men had their fingers curled tightly around their cards. Most of them had creases on their foreheads and were examining their hands intently. Finally a Chinese man broke the silence.

"Not me. I fold," he said throwing his cards face down in front if him. "I out this hand."

"I'll stay," said the man next to him. "That is, if you'll all take this nugget as good for the fifteen-dollar call." He held up a piece of gold between his thumb and first finger that looked to be about a half an inch thick all the way around.

"Okay by me," said a player across the table, and his words were followed by various nods and mutterings of approval.

The first man tossed the nugget into the middle of the table, where it sounded against the other coins there and rolled to a stop.

"I'm in," said a third man, laying two paper bills into the pot.

The next man eyed his cards carefully, then sent his thin Oriental eyes squinting one at a time around the table of his companions as if trying to penetrate either their thoughts or see through the backs of their cards. Finally he spoke.

"I only once see man draw two cards to inside straight, and his face not look like yours. So I think you bruffing."

The look of satisfaction I had noticed on this man's face at first from his obvious winnings had now disappeared.

"I call your fifteen," he said. "And another fifty."

He reached into the pile in front of him and first tossed in two coins for the fifteen. Then with great deliberation he dropped five more ten-dollar gold pieces one at a time into the pot.

Sighs and exclamations went around the table. A couple of the men threw their cards down immediately.

To the left of the rich Chinese, a grubby looking miner laid his cards down and leaned back in his chair. "Well at least I'm glad you did that before I called with the fifteen. It's all yours, Ling. I'm out."

To his left, however, a well-dressed man, who looked somewhat out of place among both Chinese and dirty unkempt miners, cracked a tiny smile as he glanced again at his cards, then looked over into the eyes of the Chinese man who had just raised the bet to fifty. When he spoke, in spite of a deep serious look in his eyes, there was humor in his tone.

"Now, Ling," he said, "you asked for two, I took one. You figure me to be going for the inside straight. And I figure since you're so confident, then you must have three of a kind. My gut tells me you didn't pick up either the four or the full house, and that you're still standing with the same three you were dealt."

He paused, and now smiled broadly at the man called Ling.

"So if you want to see if I *did* hit on my inside straight, I'm going to make you pay for the privilege."

Still with his eyes on the other man, his hand went down in front of him and found five coins, which he tossed into the pot. It left him with only five dollars in his own pile.

One by one, all those who had previously called threw in their cards until it came again to Mr. Ling.

He laid his cards down in front of him, face up. "Three kings," he said.

"Well, Ling," said the man who had raised, "it appears at last your string of luck has come to an end. For you see, I picked up the straight . . . jack high!"

He laid down the five cards with a triumphant look of satisfaction and let out a great laugh, while various reactions and exclamations went round the table on the part of the others.

While he was scooping up the pot he had just won, I walked timidly the rest of the way to the table. He didn't see me until I was almost beside him.

"Uh . . . excuse me," I said shyly, "would you by any chance be Mr. Gregory?"

"That's me," he answered, still raking in his

money. "Who wants to know?"

At last he glanced up to where I stood, and before giving me a chance to say anything more, let out an exclamation.

"Well, well! It looks like you came just in time to change my luck, honey! Derrick Gregory, at your service!" he said, flashing a grin.

He stood, took off his hat, and gave an exaggerated bow. As he rose from the table I saw that he was taller than I had realized, with curly black hair and eyes of the same color. He appeared to be in his early thirties. The smile revealed his teeth, though his voice and look didn't appear altogether genuine.

"I would like to talk with you," I said.

"Oh, I'd be right pleasured t' speak with ya, Miss," interrupted one of the other card players, a dirty man with a leering face I didn't like at all. "Now you jest come right over here t' me, an' —"

"Snap your big trap shut, Frank, or I'll stuff my fist into it!" said Mr. Gregory in my defense.

"Tarnation, Greg, I didn't mean nothin' by it."

"Well, just stay out of it!"

And though Frank didn't say another word, I still wasn't sure what to think of Derrick Gregory either.

"Now, girl," he said, towering in front of me, "who are you, and what are you hankering to tell me?"

"I'm Cornelia Hollister," I said, "and I understand you're a newspaper writer."

The smile faded from his face. He started to lead me toward the other side of the room, saying as he did, "You fellas go on without me. I figure I owe this little lady a few minutes, the way she won that pot for me!"

As we moved away, a few whistles and jeers followed us.

"Don't pay any attention to them," he said to me. "And don't one of you think of touching my pot!" he called out over his shoulder. "I'll count every penny when I get back!"

He led me out the door and into the bright sunlight.

"You see, none of those men in there — they don't know *exactly* that I'm a reporter. They know I've been around a while asking some questions, but as long as they can keep winning some of my money at poker, they don't care too much about what I'm up to. And that's the way I'd like to keep it. So what is it *you* heard about me — what'd you say your name was?"

"Cornelia."

"So what makes you think I'm a writer?"

"I just heard about you, that's all."

"And what did you hear?"

"That you're writing about the election," I answered.

He sat down on the edge of the wood sidewalk, his long legs stretching out into the dirt street. Then he looked up and scanned me up and down as if taking stock of me for the first time.

"So you're interested in the election, eh, Cornelia?"

I nodded.

"That all?"

"I've always wanted to be a newspaper writer too," I said.

He smiled again. "A girl wanting to be a writer!" he exclaimed. "And so you figured I could give you a few pointers, eh, is that it?"

I didn't answer right off, but he didn't seem to mind.

"Cornelia what?" he asked.

"Hollister."

"Hmm . . . Hollister . . ." He rubbed his chin thoughtfully, then after a few seconds went on. "Well, Miss Hollister," he said, "I'm not saying anything one way or another about what I may or may not be. But I figure I owe you one. Ol' Ling in there'd been beating me all day and all night and had just about cleaned me dry till you walked up. So just maybe this is your lucky day as well as mine."

He didn't seem to take me seriously. But on the other hand, he didn't mind talking to me either, which was all I could have hoped for.

"Where do you come from, Cornelia?"

"I rode down from Sonora."

"Well, I'll tell you what," he said, getting back to his feet. "I've been staying at a place down in Jacksonville, and I got some folks I gotta see down at Big Oak Flat. If you want to ride along with me, I'll tell you a thing or two about this

370

election, and maybe let you watch me conduct a real live interview in person. You game?"

"Oh yes, thank you very much!" I said enthusiastically. "I would like that."

After just a few minutes with him, I wasn't worried about riding off alone with Derrick Gregory. There was nothing about him that frightened me, although I couldn't help being on my guard. He talked to me as if he were sharing his great experience and wisdom with a little kid, which in this case I didn't mind.

"Let me go back in there and get my loot and tell those old coots that we're leaving. And then we'll hit the trail, *Miss* Hollister."

Chapter 45

I Find Out More
Than I Ought To

For the rest of the morning we rode south and chatted easily. Mr. Gregory seemed perfectly willing to talk to me about his work, and didn't appear to mind my questions. Gradually I learned a lot about him and what he was doing. Apparently he thought of me as nothing but a raw novice who knew absolutely nothing.

In a way I guess I *was* just a raw novice. But I knew more than he thought I knew, and I wasn't so innocent of motive as he thought. I wondered if I was doing wrong to deceive him. But I hadn't actually said anything that was untrue, he had drawn his own conclusions. I wasn't trying to hurt anyone but was just trying to get at the truth, and I thought that what I was doing was justified. If it wasn't, and if I was doing wrong, I'd have to deal with my conscience when it started to nag at me. It was a hard question, and wouldn't be the first time as a reporter when

I'd wonder about the line between honesty and not saying enough. Maybe it's a problem a reporter never completely gets a handle on.

One thing was for sure, Derrick Gregory wasn't in the least concerned about truthfulness in what *he* wrote. He treated me nice enough. But he didn't care if he was fair to Mr. Fremont. Before we'd gone very far at all, he'd confided in me that his job was to get whatever he could in order to destroy John Fremont's reputation.

"But what if you write something that's not true?" I asked.

"Nobody pays you for truth, Cornelia. They pay you to watch out for their interests."

I reached into my saddlebag and pulled out a notepad and a pencil. "A *real* reporter's supposed to take notes, isn't she?" I asked innocently. "Do you mind if I write down some of what you say? I want to learn as much as possible."

Derrick looked flattered. "Atta girl, Cornelia! You wanta be a writer, you gotta *act* like a writer!" He paused, and an expression of importance crept over his face. "Now, Miss Hollister, listen close, and you might learn something about being a real newsman."

Writing notes on horseback is not an easy thing to do. My pencil went all over the page, but at least I got down the important parts. Mr. Kemble wouldn't print anything unless I was sure I had the facts straight, so I wanted to make sure I could back up what I wrote.

"If you're writing about election news," I asked

Mr. Gregory, "don't you have to report the facts?"

"Facts are slippery things. One fella might look at a fact one way, and somebody else in another way. The people who hired me pay me to dig up facts that they can use against Fremont. They don't care how I get them, or even whether they're true. If they can make people *believe* they're true, then they'll have what they want, and I'll get paid handsomely for my efforts. You see how nice it works out!"

"But that's not being honest to the people who read what you write, Mr. Gregory," I said.

"What is honesty? Like I said, I don't get paid to be honest, but to do a job. And the senator who sent me out here always gets what he wants. So why shouldn't I profit from his greed?" He patted his saddlebag. "So I've got a whole lot of things here that are just what the senator wants, sworn statements, quotes from guys who saw Fremont do such and so. Why, by the time I get through writing it up, the election's as good as decided in this state. And by the way, Cornelia, no more of this Mister Gregory stuff. If you and I are going to ride together and I'm going to teach you the business of being a reporter, then you at least ought to call me by my name. Fair enough?"

I nodded. "But then why — uh, Derrick — why did you come clear out here, all the way from the South, to write stuff about Mr. Fremont?"

"That's the beauty of the senator's scheme! Right here's where Fremont kicked around before he got famous. Why, his estate runs clear up to just a few miles from here. Anything we can uncover here, people'll believe it just like it's gospel, because it's from the man's *real* past, what he was like before he got into politics."

He stopped, with a serious expression on his face, and looked around behind us.

"You hear a horse back there?" he asked, pulling his own mount to a stop. I reined in alongside him and listened. I didn't hear anything.

"Maybe I'm just too jumpy," he said, urging his horse along again. "But I've had a feeling like I'm being followed for more than a week now. Maybe I'm just nervous till I get this article written and these papers back to Frisco. But I still don't like not knowing who's watching me."

"Who would be watching you?" I asked.

"Fremont's people — maybe even Senator Goldwin's people, for all I know. Politics is a dirty business. Those guys play for keeps. To tell you the truth, it wouldn't surprise me if the senator had eyes on me, to make sure Fremont's people don't buy me off. If I will do *his* dirty work for a price, then he's got to figure I'd pull turncoat for a higher offer. You always gotta be figuring how these powerful guys think. Those slavery people are the worst. Right and wrong means nothing to them — it's strictly dollars and power."

"*Would* you turn your information over to

Fremont's side — for a higher price?" I asked.

"Nah, they couldn't pay me enough to make me cross Goldwin. He'd have me killed inside a month."

"What do you have that's so valuable to him?" I asked.

"I've got the election in my saddlebag — the end of Fremont's political career forever, that's what. Once this stuff hits the press, Buchanan's election is secure. Goldwin's happy; he and his slavery boys stay in power in Washington. The anti-slavery forces go down in defeat with their champion, John Charles Fremont, caught with mud on his face and skeletons in his closet. Just think, the Union may owe its preservation to none other than an investigative reporter and man of the hour, Derrick Gregory! And you, Cornelia Hollister, had the good fortune to take it into your head to ask his advice about becoming a reporter right when he was about to finish the story that would sway the election of 1856! You are witnessing history in the making, Miss Hollister!"

"But I still don't see what you could have discovered way out here in the middle of nowhere that could be so damaging to Colonel Fremont," I said.

"All right, just for an example, take that little place where you found me, Chinese Camp," he replied. "My time there was spent doing more than playing cards. You might have seen it on your way in — little Catholic church, St. Xavier's.

I've got a quote from a Chinese man back there as an eyewitness that he saw John Fremont going into the church with a priest last time he was out here, for a private Mass."

"That can't be true," I said in disbelief. "John Fremont isn't a Catholic . . . is he?" I added, suddenly unsure of myself.

"Who knows? But haven't you been listening to anything I been telling you about this game of political reporting? Doesn't matter if it's true. Doesn't matter that I had to slip the guy ten bucks to encourage his memory along after I hinted at what I was looking for. If folks think it's true, it's good enough and you've done your job. No one's gonna come checking up on it. They couldn't check it anyway. The source's name will never be mentioned. My name won't appear on the story, won't have anything to do with it as far as the public's concerned. The story's untraceable. But the charge will persist, and even if it is only a rumor, it will do its job."

"It hardly seems right."

"Right, wrong — who cares? A reporter has a job to do, and he gets paid by people in power with money to pay him. A writer doesn't decide right and wrong, he has to do his job. Facts are just what you make of them, no more, no less. There was another reason I was at Chinese Camp. You know about the Tong war a few months back at Crimea Flat? Well, I've got it on good authority that Fremont's men rode up from Mariposa and instigated the whole thing because

Fremont hates the Chinese and doesn't like so many of them so near his estate."

"What kind of authority — same as about the church?"

Derrick laughed. "Now you're catching on, Cornelia! No, it's a little more reliable than that. Miners in these parts hate Fremont. They're jealous of his gold, they think some of it's theirs. A few of them who got run off the Mariposa at gunpoint for poaching are willing to say just about anything to bring down Fremont. I've got sworn statements that Fremont used Chinese slave labor along with the Mexicans when he first started mining the Mariposa, that he falsified surveying reports to change his boundaries to include the richest claims. I got quotes saying they saw Negroes in chains on the Mariposa, and even that Fremont used to get away at night with barmaids, leaving his wife alone at home. I got all kinds of stuff from interviewing people around here. Fremont's dead when it all gets out."

"What are you after today? Some other quote from someone who doesn't like Mr. Fremont?"

He laughed again. "In a manner of speaking. We're almost to Big Oak Flat. I'm gonna see Jack Savage, Jim Savage's brother — they founded the place and got rich from it. The Savage brothers and Fremont go back a ways. Savage and his brother led the Mariposa Battalion. Jim got himself killed by the Indians. They were the first white men into the Yosemite valley, and he has a thing or two to say about how Fremont got his clutches on all that land when he wasn't even here in person. From what I've gathered, the senator's promised Savage a big chunk of the Mariposa if he can give him enough information to contest Fremont's title. If I can get what I need, it not only makes Fremont out a crook, it might put the Mariposa right in Senator Goldwin's lap. Half of the old fat judges on the Supreme Court owe their appointments to him, and they would back him up if it came down to a law suit between Fremont and Goldwin."

"Do you think this man Savage will go against Fremont?"

"Sure. Disputes over money make men more unforgiving than anything. Gold men and slavery men — there aren't any two groups in this country to hold a grudge longer. It would gall Savage to the core to see his old arch-rival over these gold fields be made President of the United States. I have no doubt he'll say anything and everything I want him to. And to make matters even better, Savage was involved with the Palmer & Cook Company back then at the same time Fremont was. He'll be able to confirm Fremont's role in that as well — and that one *does* happen to be in the area of true facts."

"What's that all about?"

"Just a couple months back, Palmer & Cook got into trouble for an illegal breach of faith in handling some securities belonging to the state of California. Fremont was closely involved with them when he was last here. It's the perfect smear."

We'd been talking a long time, and within another ten minutes we rode into the little village of Big Oak Flat. Derrick seemed to know where he was going. We rode straight through town, made two or three turns, and eventually arrived at the ranch called the Savage Diggings, the original name of the town in 1848. Mr. Savage must have been expecting him, because we went right in and sat down and the two men started talking. I just watched and listened, and they paid me no heed. But as I glanced around the room I noticed some old copies of the *Alta* lying around, and a momentary panic seized me.

As I sat there listening, I was astonished at what I heard. Mr. Gregory didn't just ask questions and write down Mr. Savage's answers. The two of them talked back and forth and discussed what would make it look the worst for Mr. Fremont — sometimes laughing, even making up situations and other people. By the time Mr. Gregory got to writing down some of the things they'd talked about, it might as well have been fiction. He wasn't trying to find out what *really* happened at all, but to make up what he called "facts" and quotations that he and Mr. Savage could agree on that would put Mr. Fremont in a bad light. They said things about Jessie, too, that I was sure were untrue, and I got angrier and angrier. Everything Derrick had told me on the way there was bad enough, but now I saw the deception and lies going on right in front of me, and it made me mad. How could he call himself a reporter, a newsman? He was telling lies to the whole country for that rich Senator Goldwin.

"But you say Fremont got out of the Palmer & Cook Company several years back?" asked Derrick.

"Oh yeah," answered Savage. "He's got nothing to do with this current mess of theirs. But it doesn't matter. His financial involvement in the company can be documented, and by the time he has a chance to refute it, the election will be over. Use it, Gregory. It'll bring him down in the business circles in Frisco."

Derrick was busy with his pen. He had written several pages since we'd got here, full of accusations, quotes, names, dates, places, illegalities, rumors — all slanderous against Colonel Fremont.

"But don't forget what I told you about the purchase of the Mariposa," Savage went on after Derrick's pen stopped. "It all hinges on Thomas Larkin, the guy Fremont used to buy the estate. Larkin was U.S. Consul at the time, but he had dealings back to the mid-forties with Alvarado and Michelorena, who owned the property first. I've never been able to get to the bottom of it, but if the senator could get to Larkin and, shall we say, win him over with a few hundred dollars on the side, I have the feeling Larkin might be able to provide all the ammunition the senator needs to mount a challenge to Fremont's title and get the Supreme Court to overturn their ruling."

Derrick was writing as fast as his fingers could move. Finally he glanced up.

"You are a devious one, Savage," he said. "I'm sure the senator will be deeply indebted for all your help in putting the final pieces of this article together."

"I am counting on it," smiled Savage.

"I will pass along your sentiments when I next see the senator after the election."

A pause followed. Derrick looked over his several pages of notes, then put them in a leather case along with his pen and ink. He snapped the buckle shut, patted the case with his hand, and let out a long sigh.

"Well, it's all here," he said. "I'll be writing up the article in the next few days, and within a week you should be reading the political obituary of one John Charles Fremont in the San Francisco *Morning Globe*. I'm sure future President Buchanan will be grateful for your part in effecting the demise of his opponent."

Derrick rose and extended his hand. Mr. Savage shook it, then offered me his hand also as I got up.

"Nice to see you too, Miss —"

"Hollister," I reminded him.

"Ah, yes — hmm . . . Hollister . . . seems as if I know that name. You from these parts?"

"My father's a miner," I said, evading the question. I hoped his mind didn't wander to the *Alta* right then!

"Hmm . . . well, I don't know . . . your name just seems familiar, that's all."

Derrick and I left the house, got on our horses, and started back north the way we had come.

"Looks like I've got everything I need, Cornelia!" Derrick said with a smile. "All I have to do now is write it up and take it to the city and my job's done!"

"Why do you bother with interviews," I asked, "if you're just making everything up, anyway?"

"You've got to at least give the appearance of credibility, you know! Besides, if anyone does question my sources, I want to have a credible list to give them."

We rode on a while in silence.

"Why so glum?" Derrick asked. "You've just seen political reporting at its best, firsthand. Why, you're watching how Presidents get elected!"

"It just doesn't seem right, somehow," I said.

"Still worried about honesty, Cornelia?"

"I reckon."

"Forget it. If you want to be a news reporter, this is how it works — who you know, and what kind of deal you can make with them. And watch out for your own best interests! It's the only way to get ahead in this game — just like in politics."

We were quiet again for a while.

"Are you going to Jacksonville now?" I asked.

"Nah, we still got plenty of daylight left. I think I'll get on back to Sonora and bunk there for another day or two while I'm writing this all up. I got a nice room above the Lucky Sluice where I can work."

"Maybe I could come and see what a finished article looks like," I suggested.

"Sure. Come on around, that is if your folks'll let you into a place like that." He hesitated. "But I guess if you're old enough to be tracking me down to learn how to be a reporter, you're old enough to go where you like without your pa's permission." He laughed, then sobered and asked, "Your pa's a miner, huh?"

I nodded, and immediately felt a pang of guilt for not telling him that I didn't actually live in Sonora.

All the rest of the way back that afternoon, Derrick seemed to be watching and listening, as if he still thought someone was following him. But we never saw anybody and nothing ever came of it.

Chapter 46

An Unexpected Reunion

We didn't get back to Sonora till pretty late in the evening.

We parted at the edge of town. "See you around, Cornelia," Derrick Gregory said, then took off toward the middle of town and the Lucky Sluice. I rode back to Nason's boardinghouse, hoping I wasn't too late to get my room back — payment in advance! — for the night.

Mrs. Nason almost seemed glad to see me, in her grumpy sort of way. She even heated up some of the supper things for me to eat and said that because they had already gotten cold she wouldn't charge me for the meal.

As I lay in my room that night, I couldn't get to sleep. All I could think of was the day I'd spent and Mr. Kemble, and the election, and what I ought to do with everything I'd learned. Finally I got up, lit a lamp, and for the next couple of hours went over my notes and tried to remember everything I'd seen and heard that day. I wrote it down in as much detail as I could.

Whatever came of it all, at least I had to be sure of the truth of *my* facts. I had to be accurate about Derrick's falsehoods if I was going to tell them to Mr. Kemble in a way that would help Mr. Fremont. My notes weren't very neat, but I managed to get down most of the names of people Derrick said he'd talked to and quoted from, as well as what he'd told me about making things up and bribing people to say things. And I tried to reconstruct as much of his conversation with Jack Savage as I could so that I'd be positively accurate in my *own* quotes when it came to disproving the lies that were being told against Mr. Fremont.

When I finally got to sleep, it was after midnight and I slept late the next morning. But when I woke up my thoughts were less confused and my head was gradually coming clear about what I ought to do. I didn't really stop to consider that the plan was probably foolhardy and dangerous.

First, I'd have to find out what room Derrick was in. After that I'd have to watch him and try to figure out his writing habits. If they were anything like mine, every once in a while his hand would cramp up and his brain would get dizzy and he'd have to take a break and go for a walk or something. And after that . . . well, then I'd just have to hope for the best!

A little after noon I decided to walk up to the saloon just to see if I could run into Mr. Gregory. I didn't really know what I'd do or say, but whatever happened I had to keep him in my sights. If he left town without my knowing it and got back to San Francisco ahead of me, everything was lost.

There weren't many men in the Lucky Sluice at that hour, but a couple of tables were occupied. Almost before I was fully inside I heard Derrick Gregory's voice raised in laughter and talk. He had just won a hand and was celebrating at the expense of his companions. As I walked toward him, I noticed something awfully familiar about the tall thin form sitting beside him with his back to me. Across the table facing me as I approached sat two mean-looking men — one with a beard who looked like a miner, the other clean and well dressed in an expensive suit. If they were together, they sure made an odd-looking pair!

Derrick half turned and spotted me out of the corner of his eye.

"I should have known you were somewhere close by, Cornelia!" he exclaimed. "Gentlemen," he said to the rest of the men sitting at the table, "this is my good luck companion, Cornelia Hollister. Whenever she's around, I win!" Then glancing back at me, he added, "Cornelia, these two fellas are the men I was telling you about that work for the senator and are supposed to keep me in line." He threw me a quick wink, as much as to say that in spite of their rough appearance, *he* wasn't worried about them. "And this young buck just got in from the big city," he said, indicating the young man sitting next to him.

"Meet Rob Flaridy."

It was all I could manage to keep from stumbling over my feet and gasping in amazement! I'm sure the shock must have shown on my face. I must say, if he was as surprised to see me as I was him, Robin hid his reaction better than I did mine.

"Charmed," he said, half rising from his chair and tipping his familiar cap with a smile. I knew he enjoyed my discomfort.

"Sit down . . . sit down, Cornelia!" said Derrick. "Bring me some more good luck!"

"I . . . I really can't stay," I fumbled. "I was just . . . I thought I'd find out how your article was going. I didn't mean to interrupt."

"No interruption at all!" he said boisterously. Now that I was close to him I could tell he'd been drinking, although he wasn't really drunk. "I'm half done, Hollister . . . the election's practically in the bag! I'm just having a little break with my friends here! By tomorrow at this time I'll be on my way to San Francisco, and the boys here will be on their way overland with a copy of everything I've found for the senator's use in the East."

"You have a loose tongue," growled the man with the beard.

"Relax. Miss Hollister's on our side!"

In spite of his expensive suit, the expression on the other man's face was anything but friendly.

"You just keep your mouth shut and your hand busy, and get those papers copied out for us! We're a day behind schedule as it is."

I couldn't help but notice that both the strangers had rifles leaning against their chairs. The man with the beard also wore a gun belt. The other eyed me with a questioning look.

I turned to leave.

"You come back around tonight, Cornelia," said Derrick. "I'll be right here at this table, and I'll be ready for another dose of your good luck."

I nodded sort of noncommittally.

"And maybe by then I'll be rid of these two brutes," he added, gesturing across the table, "and we can have some fun!"

I left the saloon without looking at Robin again.

I walked straight across the street into the dry goods store and pretended to look around. I kept close to the window with one eye on the swinging doors of the Lucky Sluice. In about twenty minutes the two men came out and walked up the sidewalk toward the north end of town. Five minutes later Robin emerged. He stopped, looked up and down, then started in the opposite direction, crossed the dirt street to the side I was on, and continued on toward the first hotel I had gone into when I'd got into Sonora.

I watched for another minute or two to make sure Derrick wasn't coming out. I didn't want him to see me chasing down the street after Robin. But finally I figured he'd gone back upstairs to his room. I left the store and walked southward as quickly as I could without attracting attention. I saw Robin up ahead of me, sauntering along slowly. I went out into the street so my boots wouldn't make a pounding noise on the wood walkway, and started running after him. I caught up with him just as he was passing a narrow alleyway that ran along the near side of the hotel.

Before he saw me coming, I ran alongside him and gave him a hard shove sideways into the alley and behind the building. He lost his balance and let out an exclamation, while he struggled to get back his footing. I jumped behind the edge of the wall after him, and grabbed him before he could yell.

"What are you doing here?" I exclaimed as loudly as I dared without attracting attention.

"I could ask you the same thing," he retorted. "And get your hands off me!" I hardly realized that I had hold of his coat and had pushed him up against the building.

I relaxed and took a step back.

"I am here because Mr. Kemble sent me," I said.

"As am I."

"He sent *you?*"

"How can I put this delicately, Corrie?" he said, finally cracking a meaningful grin. "He wasn't sure a girl of your tender years could — shall we say — *handle* such an important assignment. So he sent me along to make sure you didn't foul it up."

"Foul it up?" I cried, getting angry. "*You're*

the one who's going to foul it up. I've practically got Gregory's whole story!"

"Ah, but I know that he's in room fourteen, and I know where those other two men are staying, and I know their whole scheme."

"How long have you been tracking him?" I asked.

"Couple weeks."

"Kemble told me he had someone on this but that it dried up and they lost Gregory's trail."

"Well, that was unfortunate. He eluded me for a while, but then Kemble told me to follow you up here and see what you turned up, and to move back in if I could. Experience, you know," he said with a superior smile. "He felt even if you did track down Gregory, I'd be better able to get what we need in the end."

"Why, that conniving rascal!" I said. "He gave me all that runaround about me being the perfect one for the story and about the election and truth all hanging in the balance, and all the time he was just using me! And you're trying to tell me that I was just a decoy so that *you* could get the story in the end?"

"The truth is sometimes painful, Corrie," said Robin, still smiling with that look of superiority.

I turned away and strode off a few steps deeper into the alley. I felt like crying and screaming all at once!

But if I was going to prove that I could compete with men like Mr. Kemble and *Mister* Robin T. O'Flaridy, I couldn't do either. I couldn't give in to all the female emotionalism flooding through me right then. I couldn't cry. I couldn't scream. I couldn't go over and punch Robin in the nose. Somehow I had to see this thing through, and prove that I was made of stronger stuff than either of them might think.

I took a deep breath, then turned back around.

"So it *has* been you following Derrick recently," I said calmly. "And you were on our trail down to Big Oak Flat yesterday."

"And you've got to admit I did a pretty good job too," said Robin. "Neither of you saw me, did you?"

I shook my head. "But Derrick knew somebody was back there."

"Nah, he knew nothing. He was guessing."

"Don't be too cocky, Robin," I said. "If you're not careful you could put your foot right in the middle of it and get us both killed."

"What could go wrong?"

"Plenty. You just watch your step. We're too close. I don't even want to think what those two men might do if they catch us or if they find out we know each other."

"They'll never find out a thing!"

"Just watch your step. Both of our names have been in print recently. It wouldn't take much and we'd be in way over our heads."

"I tell you, you worry too much, Hollister."

"And maybe it'll be my worrying that'll get you through this," I replied. "Where you staying?"

"Right here," he said, indicating the hotel.

"Well, I'm in the boardinghouse down the street. Which is where I'm going now — I've got to do some thinking. You stay out of trouble!"

In reply, he only flashed another smile of unconcerned indifference.

As I left the alley and walked off alone down the street, it hardly occurred to me how much everything had changed. I wasn't afraid of Robin anymore, as I had been in San Francisco. In fact, I'd acted as if *I* were the older and more experienced one of the team.

And for better or worse, I suppose that's what we were now, at least for a couple more days — a team. Something inside me told me it was up to me if we were going to get out of this in one piece. Robin was too cocky for his own good.

Chapter 47

Discovery and Betrayal

I didn't see either Robin O'Flaridy or Derrick Gregory for the rest of the afternoon. I spent three hours finishing writing down what I'd learned.

I didn't really know what to do next. But I had to get my hands on Derrick's batch of papers before those other two men headed east with them. If I waited too long to figure out some plan, Robin might louse it up and get us both into a heap of trouble.

Finally, late in the afternoon, I went outside. I had to do *something*. I'd been praying and thinking all afternoon, but without any ideas coming to me.

I wandered up the street toward Robin's hotel. I went inside and walked up to the counter.

"Do you know if Rob Flaridy's in?" I asked the man called Fence.

"Left an hour or two back, Miss."

"Alone?"

"Couple of men with him. They'd been lookin' fer him earlier."

"Friends of his?" I said.

"Didn't look too friendly to me," said Fence. "Looked to me they was takin' Flaridy against his will. But I don't ask no questions. You get too curious in this town, Miss, an' it's a good way t' git yerself a plot o' ground out in the cemetery."

I went back out into the street and walked back in the direction of the Lucky Sluice.

I approached the saloon on the wood walkway, but the instant I reached it and started to push one of the swinging doors open, I froze. Over the top of it I saw Robin seated at a table, his hands tied behind his back, with the three other men standing facing him, asking questions and talking among themselves. It was obvious in a second they'd discovered he was trying to foil their scheme. But how much they knew, I couldn't tell.

I backed up quickly so they wouldn't see me in the doorway, leaned against the wall, and strained my ears to hear through the door just to my right.

They were speaking softly to avoid attracting attention, but because they were so close to the door I could hear them clearly. It was still early. The saloon was nearly empty, and the piano player hadn't started.

"I say we take him out and put a slug through his head right now," said the man with the beard.

"No, no, Jake — too messy," said the other friend of Derrick's. "There are certain rules to be observed, even in our business. No, we'll wait till we're set to leave town, then there'll be no tracing us."

"I don't like it," I heard Derrick mutter. "I knew there was somebody trailing me!" He swore a couple of times, giving Robin a cuff on the side of the head. "But I never thought they'd send someone the likes of you after me!"

"Who's in it with ya, kid?" asked the bearded man, grabbing Robin's shirt around his neck and giving it a yank. "Tell us, an' maybe we'll go easy on ya!"

"Please . . . please! I don't know anything about what you're doing. They just told me to follow you, that's all, but I didn't find out anything. Please . . . let me go . . . I'll never say a word to anybody."

While he was whining, the nicely dressed man was apparently rummaging through his clothes.

"Well, look at this!" he said. "We shoulda searched him when we first found him snooping around your room, Gregory. It would have saved us the trouble of trying to beat the information out of him. His name's not Flaridy at all, but *O'*Flaridy — Robin O'Flaridy . . . and he works for the *Alta.*"

"I should have known!" said Derrick. "Kemble's rag. They sent him here to kibosh the story! They've been backing Fremont from the beginning!"

"Look," pleaded Robin in a forlorn tone, "you caught me red-handed, and you know I've got nothing that can hurt you. Let me go, and you go your way and do whatever you want about the election, and I'll never say a word. You can trust me to —"

"Shut up, ya whimpering brat!" shouted the bearded man. I heard the back of his hand slap across Robin's face, and he cried out in pain.

"Wait a minute!" said the man in the suit, snapping his fingers as if he was thinking. "Wait . . . it's coming to me . . . Derrick, that girl you were so friendly with — the one you said brought you good luck."

"Yeah, what about her?"

"What'd you say her name was?"

"Hollister."

"Her first name, you idiot!"

"Cornelia . . . Cornelia Hollister. But what has she —"

"You are a bigger fool than I thought!" the man said spitefully. "I knew there was something familiar about her name the minute you said it! Blast, why didn't I think harder — don't you know who she is?"

"Yeah, she's just some miner's kid from around here who wants to be a writer."

"And you thought you'd give her a few pointers, eh?"

"I didn't see any harm in —"

"You lunkhead, she *is* a writer. And she doesn't need any pointers from you! She writes for the

Alta, too! The name Corrie Hollister mean anything to you?"

Derrick shrugged.

"You dolt! She wrote a big pro-Fremont piece just a couple of weeks back. She's a friend of Fremont's wife! She's in it with this snivelling little creature here!"

"That's impossible — she's just a kid!" cried Derrick in disbelief.

"Impossible, huh? I saw that look in her eyes. She was watching and listening to a lot more than you thought."

"I can't believe it."

"The senator will love to hear this. What did you tell her, Gregory?"

I could hear Derrick sitting down and letting out a bitter sigh. "She was with me all day yesterday. I told her everything. She was there for the Savage interview."

"Well, you know what you got to do, Gregory," said the bearded man viciously. "The senator don't like mistakes like this. You make a mess, then you clean it up — that's what he always says."

"Yeah . . . yeah, I know," sighed Derrick. "I kinda liked the kid too, and she did seem to bring me luck at cards."

"Yeah, she brought you luck all right. *Bad* luck! She's got to be eliminated, along with this trash here!" snarled the man in the suit. "Jake'll do the boy, but *you've* got to pull the trigger on the Hollister girl, Gregory! Otherwise the senator won't know if he can trust you in the future."

"I know," sighed Derrick. "You don't have to tell me. I know the senator as well as you do. If we let these two survive, he'd be after me next."

"Where's the girl?" the suited man asked Robin.

I'll have to say this much for him, he didn't give me away immediately.

The next sound I heard was a blow to the side of the head. I was terrified! My first thought was to flee. But something held me back. I *had* to find out all I could. I looked around the corner, just in time to see Robin crashing to the floor. The terrible-looking man grabbed roughly at him and raised his fist to smack him again. "The man asked you a question!" he yelled. "Where is she?"

"You'll . . . you'll let me go if I tell you?" whimpered Robin. His mouth and forehead were bleeding. "I don't know anything . . . it's her you want, not me."

"Yeah, okay — you win, kid," said the suit-man. "Take it easy, Jake — let him loose." They set him back down in the chair.

"Okay, you got a deal, O'Flaridy. You tell us where she is, and we'll let you go."

"She's . . . she's staying at a boardinghouse — down the side street from my hotel."

I leaned back against the wall in disbelief. He had *betrayed* me!

But I didn't have time to stop to consider the implications. Immediately I heard the sounds of chairs being pushed aside and boots on the wood floor walking my way.

I turned and ran, darting into the alleyway, running alongside the edge of the saloon. I hurried into the darkened passage, and ducked quickly down behind some big oak beer kegs sitting by the back door. A few seconds later I heard the three men pass by along the sidewalk, dragging Robin along with them.

"We'll take O'Flaridy out back of the livery and tie and gag him," the suited man was saying. "You finish what you got to do, Gregory, and later you go down to that boardinghouse and sweet-talk that Hollister kid into coming out for a walk with you. We'll grab her and stash her with the kid."

"Hey, you promised to let me go!" cried Robin. "I told you what you wanted to know."

I couldn't hear what they said back to him, because by now they were too far down the street. But the man with the beard let out a huge laugh that sounded full of glee and evil intent at the same time.

I waited a few minutes after they had passed, inched out to the edge of the alley, looked both ways to be sure it was clear, then I darted across the street and made my way back to Mrs. Nason's through the back streets and alleys and over a few fences. I knew it was dangerous to go back there after what had been said. But I had to risk it.

Chapter 48

A Risky Plan

I gathered my things quickly and stuffed them into my bag.

I'd already paid for the night's lodging, but I thought it best to slip out and not tell anyone at the house. The less they knew, the less chance Derrick would have of finding me.

Dusk was just settling as I sneaked out my window and down the back stairs outside the house. I could still hear workmen's voices inside the Nasons' barn, so I crept out behind it, sat down in the grass and waited. It gave me time to collect myself, catch my breath, and rest. I was hungry, but food would have to wait! I had to spend my time thinking of a plan, not my stomach.

When time came for supper, I heard the men in the barn leave for the house. A few minutes later I heard Mrs. Nason call my name a couple of times. But eventually she gave up, and I knew everyone was at the table eating. I crept into the barn, saddled my horse as quickly as I could in the dark, then led her out and around back.

I didn't know Sonora very well, but I thought I could make a big circle around to the other side without going through any of the main streets where I might be seen. It took me twenty or so minutes to get where I was headed. I rode out past the edge of town, but stopped where most of the buildings were still visible. I got off my horse, tied her securely to a tree. I had my bag tied down behind the saddle too so I would be able to make a quick getaway when the time came.

The only thing I took back toward town with me was a handful of blank writing pages from my satchel.

Now I retraced my steps back to Nason's boardinghouse. I found a place across the street, behind some bushes, where I could see both the front door and up the street toward the hotel and the main street of town. I was sure Derrick would come that way when he came looking for me. I just hoped I wasn't too late!

I waited for a long time. I started to shiver from the cold, and I could tell the dew was beginning to creep up out of the ground. But eventually my patience was rewarded. Sure enough, in the distance down the street from the main part of town came Derrick Gregory walking toward Nason's boardinghouse.

The thought that he was coming to lure me away was incomprehensible! But I didn't have time to reflect on that now. I had to get to the

Lucky Sluice and safely away before he found out I wasn't there and had time to get back to his room.

I jumped up and ran in the direction I had planned, through a couple of gardens, over a fence or two, through an alley, across a back street, into somebody's yard, through another alley, until I arrived at the main street just next to the dry goods store across from the saloon. Looking right and left I darted across, behind the saloon, and had arrived at the back stairway just about the same time, I hoped, as Derrick was knocking on the door and asking Mrs. Nason to see me.

Now came the risky part! If he got suspicious from my not being there and ran back, or if I had trouble getting in, he could catch me right in the act of breaking into his room — then I'd be a goner for sure! I only had five minutes at the most to get in, grab what I wanted, and get out!

I took the saloon's back steps two at a time as quietly as I could on the toes of my boots. I tried the door. It was open! I crept inside. The hallway had a narrow strip of carpet down the middle, which kept my footsteps quiet. I walked slowly forward.

There it was! Room 14, the second room on the right.

I tried the latch. It was locked!

The next minute I heard voices coming up the stairway from the saloon below at the other end of the hall.

I turned and bolted back for the back door, and had just closed it behind me when I saw a man and a woman come into view. I watched through the window from the landing where I stood. Luckily they didn't come much farther, but stopped and went into a room at the far end of the hall.

Now what should I do? The door to Derrick's room was locked, and he was probably already on his way back here from the boarding-house!

I glanced around where I stood on the landing of the back stairs.

A thin ledge ran around the building at the height of the second floor, a board about six inches wide. I stuffed my batch of papers inside my pocket, then I climbed over the railing and began slowly easing myself away from the landing. If I could just keep my balance and find enough for my fingers to grasp on to!

Slipping along sideways across the ledge, my fingers barely keeping me upright by holding on to window moldings, gutters, and other projections from the building, I came even with the window of the first room. Luckily it was empty!

I continued on, my heart pounding so hard that I was afraid its beating would knock me off backward. I didn't know which would be worse — to die from a gunshot through the head, or to die of a broken neck from falling twenty feet onto hard-packed dirt!

I came to the second window. This should be Derrick's room!

As I had hoped, the window was open a crack. I got my fingers under it and jerked upward. With a great scraping sound, it gave way and opened about nine inches. I got both my hands underneath and yanked again, but only managed to open it another two or three inches.

It would have to be enough.

I leaned down, stretched one leg through, then my left arm, then squeezed the rest of my body through.

In a few seconds I was standing alongside Derrick's bed, with visions of him already walking into the Lucky Sluice below and hurrying up the stairs three at a time to catch me red-handed!

There was enough light from the moon showing through the window for me to see his writing table. I walked toward it. There was his satchel, full of papers, as well as a stack of the papers he had just been working on. A half completed sheet lay on top of them, his dried-out pen lying across it.

Quickly I opened his satchel and grabbed out all his papers. There must have been twenty or thirty pages — interviews, quotes, names, dates, lots of notes of his own. I picked up the fresh pages off the table, apparently his completed article about Fremont and the copy he was making for Senator Goldwin. I put them all in a stack together, folded them once, and stuffed them into my coat pocket.

Then I took the blank pages I had brought with me and replaced about the same number into his satchel, and on the tabletop. I hoped that at a quick glance, seeing papers still there and still in his case, he wouldn't stop immediately to think they weren't his papers.

I hurried back to the window and started to squeeze my way back through to the outside.

Suddenly a thought struck me. One look at the table and he would instantly know his writing had been tampered with!

I reached into my pocket and grabbed the papers. I removed the half-completed top sheet. Quickly I read it over in the light of the moon. Still I heard no voices. I read it again so that it would stick in my memory.

Then I went back to the table, replaced the half-written sheet of Derrick's on the stack of blank pages I had put there, and smoothed out the fold. I laid the pen down exactly as it was before, then stuffed the rest of the pages back in my pocket, and left through the window.

It closed easier than it had opened. I crept back across the ledge, over onto the landing, and back down the stairs onto the street.

Just as I started down I heard the heated voices of Derrick and the other two men entering the hallway from the saloon. They sounded like they were in a hurry. "We'll ride out of here early tomorrow and dump the kid and the girl in a ravine up in the mountains someplace," one of the men was saying. "Then you can put a bullet into both of them. You got it, Gregory?"

I didn't want to stick around to hear any more. I leaped down the stairs three at a time, and dashed off into the night.

Chapter 49

Escape

Taking back streets and finding my way as best I could by the light from the night sky, I hurried toward where I thought the livery stable was.

The smells and the sounds of the horses and mules inside told me I had reached the right place. I approached from out in the back of the livery. There wasn't a door into it from where I was, but I could hear two men talking on the other side of the wall. They weren't voices I recognized, probably only stable hands cleaning up and tending to the animals.

I glanced around. Where could they have stashed Robin? Inside one of the stalls? Not likely, or those two workers might have spotted him.

What had they said? I tried to remember their words. *Out back of the livery* — that's what they'd said.

He must be here someplace. There were several shacks nearby. I ran to the first and opened the door.

It was pitch black and cold inside — must have

been the ice house. "Robin . . . Robin, you in here?" I said just a little above a whisper. There was no reply.

I shut the door and ran to the next little out-building. From the smells of leather and dirt and the shovel and pitchfork I nearly stumbled over, I figured this to be where they kept tools for repairing harnesses and wagons. "Robin . . . Robin!" I whispered. Again, I heard nothing.

I looked around yet once more. The last possible spot was a shed for storing bales of hay and straw, made of three walls and a roof, with the one open end facing southwest, probably to protect it from the wind and rain.

I ran to the shed and inside. All I could make out in the dim light were piles of baled hay.

"Robin . . . Robin?" I called out, a little too loud, I'm afraid. But I was getting desperate. I knew those men were going to be after me any minute!

"Robin O'Flaridy, you low-down rat . . . where are you?"

I stopped and looked all around, wondering where else I could search.

Then I heard a muffled groan!

"Robin, is that you?" I cried.

The sound came again, from the back of the shed. I ran toward it, struggling to throw aside bales, and climbing over them to get to the back of the shed.

There he was, tied up in the corner — wrists and ankles bound tight, a rag stuffed in his mouth, lying on his stomach, his face buried in loose straw, and a couple of heavy bales leaning sideways on top of him. He'd probably been trying to free himself, and they'd toppled over on him, knocking him into the ridiculous position where I found him. Luckily there was no one guarding him.

As fast as I could I went to work at the ropes around his legs. But they were too tight!

I fumbled in the darkness for the knife I'd tucked at my waist, found it, and quickly slit the cords.

"Get on your feet!" I said. "Let's get out of here!"

I pulled at him to get him up. He moaned and motioned at his hands and mouth.

"After what you did to me," I said, "you want me to set your mouth free to start yapping again? You betrayed me once tonight already, Robin O'Flaridy, and I'm not likely to forget it anytime soon. And if I'm going to save your life, I don't want to have to listen to your explanations or excuses! I'll just leave your hands tied behind you and your mouth gagged until we're safe. Now come on, before those ruffians get here!"

I yanked at his arm and half-dragged him back over the bales the way I'd come. If I had seen the dried blood on his face and the welts above his eye and the bruises on his shoulders, I probably would have been a little kinder. As it was, I was both angry at him and terrified that we'd be caught any second. And by the time we got out of the shed and back out into the moonlight and I did see his condition, we were in too big a hurry. My compassion for loose-tongued and cowardly Robin O'Flaridy would just have to wait until later!

"This way!" I said, still holding on to his arm, pulling him to follow.

I ran toward the woods behind the livery, toward where I'd tied my mare earlier.

Robin was stiff and sore from being tied up, and he could barely keep to his feet. I knew I'd have to untie his hands or he'd keep stumbling along and falling every other step. I stopped and got out my knife again. But just as I was slitting through the last of the cords, I saw a figure come running out from the front of the livery to the back. He made straight for the hay shed, then stopped the instant he saw us standing about thirty yards from it toward the woods. There was no chance to hide. We were exposed in the pale glow of the moonlight.

It was Derrick Gregory!

Robin and I froze. Derrick walked slowly toward us. I hadn't noticed him wearing a gun before, but he had one now, and he pulled it from his holster.

I could feel Robin trembling and he began pulling away. I went with him and we inched backward.

"You're a clever one, Cornelia Hollister," he said, still advancing. "You had me completely fooled."

"I'm sorry, Derrick," I said, "but I had to know if you were going to write the truth about Mr. Fremont."

He gave a laugh, though this time it rang with bitterness. "I told you before, a reporter can't worry about that. You've got to do your job, that's all. And right now *my* job's to get those papers back from you."

"What papers?" I stammered nervously.

"Come on, Cornelia," he said with a sneer. "You know as well as I do you took them from my room. Now, hand them over!" He waved his pistol at us, but still we kept inching back.

"How did you know?" I asked.

He chuckled again. This time there was a little of the old humor in his tone.

"Every writer has his own little secrets, his own way of doing things. You must know what I mean, Cornelia. One of mine is that I never fold my pages. I can't stand papers with folds in them! You tried to smooth it out, but it didn't work. Very clever of you to leave the top sheet. If you hadn't folded it first, I'd never have noticed it till hours later. But then I saw all those blank papers substituted for my own, and I knew it had to be you. You're a smart girl, but I've got to have those papers back!"

"Where are the other two men?" I said.

"I sent them on a wild goose chase to the boardinghouse to look for you. I figured you'd be here, trying to save that coward who turned you in to save his own skin."

"And if I don't give you the papers?"

"Look, I don't want to hurt you, Cornelia. But I've got to have those papers! The other men'll be here any second. Now just give me the papers and get going. I'll tell them you got away. But if they get here first, they'll kill you both! Now come on, Cornelia, don't make me do something I don't want to have to do!"

He quickened his pace toward us. Robin and I began moving backward toward the woods. Derrick was still twenty or twenty-five yards from us.

"Robin," I whispered. "Make for the woods. My horse is straight up that little rise about fifty yards away. Untie her. I'll be right behind you! And you wait for me, you scoundrel!"

He hesitated.

"Get going!" I yelled, shoving him up the hill. He needed no more encouragement. He'd broken the last strand of rope on his wrists and took off for the woods as fast his spindly legs would carry him.

"Stop, Flaridy!" cried Derrick. "Stop, or I'll shoot!"

Robin kept going and in a couple of seconds was out of sight.

"Derrick," I implored, still walking backward after Robin, "you don't want to shoot anybody. I don't think you're willing to kill either of us for the sake of your rich senator."

"You'll never get away from them," he said.

"I'll just have to get back to San Francisco

413

before you or your friends."

Behind him I heard the sounds of running footsteps and shouts.

I turned and sprinted into the woods!

My heart nearly stopped when I heard the explosive fire of Derrick's gun behind me. But he couldn't have missed! I was sure he intentionally shot wide and over my head! I heard shouts again and I knew whose voices they were. Derrick's pistol echoed in the blackness with two more deafening shots.

"They got away!" I heard Derrick yell. "After them . . . this way!"

More shots sounded, but they were not close. I reached the horse only seconds after Robin. He was fumbling with the rope.

"I'll get it!" I cried.

I loosened the rope from the tree, then jumped into the saddle and helped him up behind me. "Hang on!" I called. "If you fall off, I'm not stopping for you!"

I dug in my heels and off we galloped.

Hearing us, more gunfire rang out. It was the sound of rifles this time! Bullets smashed into trees and clipped off branches around us. But we kept on. Finally the gunshots stopped.

"Get to the horses!" I heard the man with the beard cry out. "We'll chase 'em down . . . they can't get far!"

I lashed poor Raspberry on as fast as she could go, circling the town and working our way down onto the main road west toward Chinese Camp and Modesto. Reaching the road, we pushed on as fast as we could go. But I knew the other three riders were only a minute or two behind us.

We rode hard for a couple of miles. When we came to the junction of the southern road, I eased up on the reins, then found a place to pull off the road and hide behind several boulders and large pine trees.

A couple of minutes later, the thundering hoofs of our pursuers' three horses approached and passed us, continuing on the westward route. Once the sound had died away, I led my horse back out into the clearing, and onto the road leading south.

The stop had given Robin his first opportunity to pull the rag from his mouth.

"Hey, this isn't the road to San Francisco," he said as I urged the mare to a gallop again.

"Is that all you have to say after I just saved your skin?" I shot back at him over my shoulder.

"Of course, I'm grateful, but I only wondered where we're going."

"Well, for the moment at least, we're *not* going toward San Francisco. That is the direction they think we're going, and I don't want to make it too easy for them to find us. I happen to value my life, Robin, even if *you* don't!"

"They would never have hurt you, Corrie. I knew that. I would never have said a word if there'd been any *real* danger to you!"

"Ha!" I said. "I don't believe that for a second!"

"Where are we going?"

"Don't worry, I'll get you back to San Francisco. But first I've got a little unfinished business with regard to Mr. Gregory's article."

"Where?"

"At the Fremont estate."

The moon was practically full and I could see well enough to ride with tolerable speed. I couldn't see my map too well, but I had studied it back at Sonora. There were enough markers along the way so that I knew we were on the right road to Mariposa.

We rode pretty hard for half an hour, then eased back. The horse wouldn't be able to keep it up all night at this pace, and all I wanted to do was get far enough from Sonora so that I'd know we were safe.

We stopped about midnight. We hadn't gone very fast, but we had ridden for several hours and had covered a good distance. By my reckoning we were only eight or ten miles from Mariposa and could make it there easily in the morning. I pulled off the main road, and found a clearing two or three hundred yards away where we could spend the night.

We got down off the horse. I built a small fire, making sure to use dry wood so as not to give off any visible smoke, then got out some dried food and my canteen. I tried to wash Robin's wounds as best I could, then gave him something to eat and tried to make him comfortable with two of my blankets.

"You get to sleep, Robin," I said. "You're going to need it. I'll keep watch for a couple of hours, just till I'm sure no one's tracking us."

He was real quiet, not like his usual self. When I'd look over at him, he was just staring into the fire like he was thinking.

"How'd you learn to do all this stuff, Corrie?" he said finally.

"All what?"

"Ride a horse, escape from guys with guns, build a fire, take care of yourself out in the wilderness."

"I don't know," I said. "I never thought about it. I just did it. I guess I've been taking care of myself for a lot of years."

"Yeah," he said after another minute of staring into the fire. "I suppose it's the same for me in the city. I can take care of myself there, just like you do out here."

"The city scares me," I said, laughing. "But out here, I don't know, for me it's more like home."

"Give me buildings and lights and people and city-sounds any time!" said Robin, and for a minute I thought he might be going to laugh too.

"Not me," I said. "I love the crickets and the far-off howl of some animal and the wind in the trees and the sound of a stream."

It got quiet again.

"How's your face?" I asked. "They roughed you up pretty bad, didn't they?"

"It hurts some, but I'll be okay." He paused,

417

but then added, and I could tell from his voice that the words were hard for him to say, "Thanks, Corrie, for what you did back there. I didn't deserve it."

"Aw, think nothing of it."

"Why did you do it? Why'd you risk everything to save me?"

"Anybody'd have done the same," I said.

"I doubt that. I'm not sure I'd have had the guts to do what you did, especially after what I did."

"Well, look at it this way," I said. "I couldn't very well go back to Kemble with the lowdown on Gregory's article and with all the papers of his, and then at the same time tell him I left his star reporter for dead. How could I tell him *that?* Don't you see, Robin, I had no choice. I *had* to save you to keep on Kemble's good side!"

Now he did let out a little chuckle, but quickly put his hand to his mouth from the pain.

"Well, whatever your reasons, thanks anyway."

"Any time," I said. "And I'm sorry I was so hard on you back there, Robin," I added. "I didn't mean to yell and call you names. I was just upset, that's all."

He nodded, then turned over and pulled the blankets around his shoulders. In two or three minutes I could tell from his breathing that he was sound asleep.

I took off my coat, wrapped my blanket around me and lay down, staring into the fire, thinking of the terrifying, unbelievable day I'd just had.

At least it felt good that Robin O'Flaridy was no longer my adversary. That was one positive thing to emerge from the dangerous escapade of this night.

Still I stared into the fire, growing sleepier and sleepier, until at last I knew no more.

Chapter 50

Mariposa Again

When I awoke, the gray light of dawn was just giving way to the reds and oranges of the coming sunrise.

The fire was out cold.

I glanced around. Robin wasn't where I'd left him. He must have gone down to find a stream to wash and get water.

I got up, stretched, and wandered in the direction where I figured he had probably gone. But before I had gone far, I stopped and turned back.

It was too quiet. Something wasn't right!

I ran back to the clearing where we had slept. There was no sign of Robin anywhere. And my horse was gone!

Frantically I looked around. There was the blanket I'd slept in and my coat — that was all. He'd taken both my two other blankets, my canteen of water, and all the food. I checked my coat. My notes! Every single sheet of Derrick's notes and the article he had written

420

for the *Globe* were gone!

"Why, you underhanded rascal!" I cried.

At least he'd left me my carpetbag! There it lay on the ground right where he'd thrown it off the horse. I walked toward the bag, and then spotted a scrap of paper on the ground alongside it, torn from the bottom of one of Derrick's pages. I picked it up.

I'm sorry, Corrie. It's an awful thing to do to a colleague. But I just couldn't afford to miss a shot at a really big story. I always wanted to write politics, and this is my chance! I'll make it up to you someday.

Fond regards,
R.T. O'Flaridy

Fond regards!

I crumpled up the paper and threw it to the ground. "And *I'll* make it up to *you* someday too, Mister O'Flaridy — just you wait and see!"

I grabbed my blanket, stuffed it inside my carpetbag, put on my coat, and headed back to the road, so angry I could have walked for a week! The only trouble was, time was short and I was stuck out in the middle of nowhere!

I soon found out that even anger in the absence of food won't keep your energy up forever. After two hours, I was beat. My feet hurt, my legs ached, and I was hungry!

But still I trudged on, my carpetbag getting

heavier and heavier. I don't know how far I walked. It had to be at least ten miles, although it felt like thirty! Somewhere in the middle of the morning, when the sun was getting high in the sky and the day was beginning to get uncomfortably warm, I finally reached the little village of Mariposa.

Half an hour later I was sitting with Ankelita Carter, telling her my story. Watching the various expressions on her face change from shock to grief to anger to sympathy to outrage was nearly enough to take my mind off my own trouble. As irritated as I was at Robin, Ankelita's chief concern was for her mistress and her husband.

"You must stop them, Corrie!" she exclaimed when I was through telling her everything that had happened. "You must not let them print such lies! The Colonel and Jessie are good people — these are nothing but lies!"

"I'm will do my best," I said. "But I will need your help."

"Anything!" she replied.

"First, I need to borrow a horse," I said. "A fast horse. Robin will have at least a twelve-hour lead on me. Though I doubt he will be able to ride straight through to San Francisco," I said with a smile. "He does not exactly have the adventurous pioneering spirit! Still, I have to catch up with him before he does any mischief with Gregory's parcel of papers. For all I know, he might try to sell the pack of lies back to the *Globe* rather than take it to Kemble."

"We have horses. I will have Felipe saddle for you the fastest in the stable."

"Then I need to ask you some questions, Ankelita," I said. "I need whatever proof I can get that will disprove the claims Gregory was going to make in his article. You probably know the Fremonts better than anyone in California."

"You get out your paper and pen and ask, Corrie!" she said enthusiastically. "You've got to get back to San Francisco and write the truth about Colonel Fremont! He's *got* to win that election, for the sake of the Union. We just can't let a slave man into the White House!"

"Before we start," I said with a sheepish expression, "would you mind if I had something to eat?"

She laughed, jumped out of her chair, and was on her way to the kitchen before all the words were out of my mouth.

A couple hours later, we had gone through just about everything I could remember of Derrick Gregory's charges against Colonel Fremont. I don't suppose the words of a Fremont friend and maid would constitute proof in a court of law. But perhaps they would shed sufficient doubt on the credibility of the *Globe* story to keep them from running it. I hoped so, at least.

"You can't trust anything Jim Savage might say," Ankelita said. "Why, he's been mad at the Colonel for years because he didn't get his hands on this land! And as for all that foolishness about Negroes in chains and Chinese slave labor and false surveys — why, they're just lying to make Mr. Fremont look bad. Felipe!" she called out into the other end of the house.

The young Mexican appeared after a minute. She spoke to him in Spanish, and he ran outside.

"I told him to get Bernardo. You couldn't ask for a more honest and upright man than Bernardo Garcia. He has been the Colonel's foreman here since the Colonel purchased the property. He will tell you himself that these things are not true."

"Thank you," I said. I was writing down everything as rapidly as I was able, though my fingers were already getting cramped. I would have to rely on the old newspaper gimmick of quoting "reliable sources at the Mariposa estate," and my words could be persuasive enough to convince people that what I was writing was the truth.

"As for the Colonel and barmaids in the village," Ankelita went on, incensed at the very thought. "I can tell you that Jessie never believed such things. She once told me that neither of them had ever been unfaithful to the other. She said —"

"Wait," I said, "just let me get that written down."

She paused until I caught up, then finished her sentence as I kept writing.

"What about his stirring up the Chinese in that Tong war?" I asked.

"I don't know what to say about that, except that the Colonel had nothing against the Chinese any more than he did the Negroes. But you should ask Bernardo about that. If anything like that did go on among the men here, Bernardo will know of it."

"And the rumor that Mr. Fremont is secretly a Catholic?" I asked.

"Ridiculous!" exclaimed Ankelita. "The Colonel and I had more than one discussion about matters of faith, and I know he always took the Protestant view and I the Catholic one."

"How did the rumor get started?"

"Mr. Fremont's father came from France, you know, and so I presume he was a Catholic. When he was young Mr. Fremont was educated for a time at a Catholic school, and he and Jessie were married by a priest. From all this, people merely assumed he was personally a Catholic, and his enemies stuck the label on him. He is such a private man in religious matters that he never went out of his way to refute it. His enemies knew that if it could be proven, he could never be elected President. That is undoubtedly why they are trying to dig up this old story about St. Xavier's. But don't you believe a word of it, Corrie! John Fremont may have attended some services when he was at school as a youth, but the grown man John Fremont never attended a Catholic Mass in his life!"

"How can you be so sure?"

"Because when we were in Charleston two years ago, he showed us the church where he was baptized at the age of eight — a Protestant church!"

425

"Then why doesn't he make a public statement?"

"I don't know, Corrie. But just before I left the East he and Jessie had given all three of the children's baptismal records to the *Daily News* to be made public, with their admission into Protestant churches."

"Then that refutes Derrick's story completely," I said.

Just then Felipe returned, followed by a man Ankelita introduced me to as Bernardo Garcia. His English was not as flawless as hers, but I was able to understand him well enough to get along. I questioned him on all the points that were still fuzzy, especially the charges about the boundary surveys, the Chinese and Negro labor, and the treatment of local miners over squabbles about the ownership of the land. He confirmed what Ankelita had told me about Jim Savage, and was definite about everything else as well. We spoke for an hour, and when we were through I knew I had all I needed.

Bernardo went back out to the mines. Ankelita and I stood. It was already midafternoon.

"Now I must get your bed ready for you again, Corrie," she said.

"Oh no, Ankelita, I mustn't stay!"

"The article cannot get into print in less than a day," she replied. "You should stay with me again, get some rest, eat well, and sleep. Then leave early in the morning."

I stopped to think. If I took the rest of today

and this evening to write my article, then I would be prepared the moment I saw Mr. Kemble. Whatever Robin might tell him, I had to have my own facts straight. And if I could have an article completed, so much the better.

I nodded. "You're right, of course. I'll stay tonight and leave with the first light of the morning."

She led me into the room where I had slept before. I immediately began spreading my notes and previous papers over the table. I had to make sense of everything I had learned, and try to put it together into an article that was factual and true.

I worked long into the night. And when at last I laid my head down to sleep, it was with a satisfied feeling. Despite the fact that I had a journey of a hundred and fifty miles awaiting me, and even then I didn't know what might be the outcome of my efforts, at least I knew in my heart that I had uncovered the truth of what I'd been sent here to find, and I had done what I'd set out five days earlier to do.

Tomorrow was the 18th. If I gave it everything I had, just maybe I could make it to San Francisco before the offices closed on the 19th.

I might even make up the ground I'd lost and beat Robin O'Flaridy at his own game!

Chapter 51

Showdown

Ankelita awoke me the next morning before dawn.

She had packed food, a canteen, and an extra blanket, and Felipe already had the horse saddled and waiting for me.

"Her name Rayo Rojo," he said. "She . . . este caballo corre como el viento!"

"She's the filly of Jessie's favorite mare," added Ankelita. "She's of good stock, and Felipe's been training her to race one day."

"She run like no horse miles 'round," said Felipe excitedly. "Rapido . . . like tornado!"

"If any horse in California will get you to San Francisco ahead of that O'Flaridy scamp, Rayo Rojo will!" said Ankelita.

"What does her name mean?" I asked.

"Do you see the reddish star on her white forehead?"

I looked and did indeed see the reddish-brown star. The rest of the top of her head was white, though her predominant color was a tan or light brown.

"That red star was there from the moment of her birth. Jessie had always called the horse's mother Big Lady Red because of her color. So when the foal was born, they called her *Little Red* — until they saw how fast she could run! Then she became Rayo Rojo, or *Fast Red*. I had never seen her until I arrived back here at Mariposa recently, and Jessie has still not seen her. But we both have felt we knew her from the reports Bernardo sent. She is a favorite with all the men on the ranch."

Felipe handed me the reins, then offered his hand to help me up into the saddle.

The moment I was on her back I felt a surge of the animal's life and energy. The look in her eyes did not fully reveal the power contained within her frame and her thoroughbred legs and muscles.

"Now go!" said Ankelita, giving Rayo's rump a little swat. "Go . . . and may God be with you, our friend Corrie."

"I will get Rayo Rojo back to you as soon as I can," I shouted over my shoulder. But already I was halfway to the gate. At my slightest urging, the young filly accelerated with an ease that was astonishing. The breeze flew through my hair and I leaned forward to be sure of my seat. With my right hand I grasped the saddle horn and reins, while my left sought to make sure my hat was tied securely around my chin.

This was going to be like no ride I had ever experienced. Truly this was a faster animal than

I had been on top of in all my life. I had never known such speed. Perhaps I would overtake Robin after all!

We flew through the village and eastward along the Carson Creek road, past the quarry at Negro Hill and around Cathey's Mountain, and were already in Cathey's Valley before the sun had risen over the last of the mountains in the east. I was to the central valley and Bear Creek by midmorning, and Merced by noon. I stopped and looked up Mrs. Harcourt and asked her if I could feed and water and rest my horse in her stable and refill my water canteens. The hottest and driest part of the journey still lay ahead.

It was midafternoon the following day before I reached San Jose. Poor Rayo Rojo! She was indeed fast, but I had pushed her hard, and her stamina was not equal to such a sustained effort. Now we had to walk and take many rests between gallops. She was a brave one, though, and whenever I would urge her forward, she would obey faithfully.

I rode up to the office of the San Francisco *Alta* at about half past five that afternoon. I tied Rayo outside and ran to the door. I turned the handle and it yielded. I raced down the hallway to Mr. Kemble's office.

The door was closed. I tried the handle. It was locked. I rapped on the marbled glass. There was no reply.

I turned and walked slowly back. I stuck my head in at one of the other offices where I heard someone busily at work.

"Is Mr. Kemble here?" I said.

"Gone home for the night, Miss," was the answer.

Dejectedly I left the building. Well, at least it would give me time to clean up and take a bath, I thought — and to put the finishing touches on the article I planned to present to the editor in the morning. I just hoped Miss Sandy Loyd Bean had a room left! Rayo Rojo would no doubt welcome the rest much more than I did!

Miss Bean did have a room, and I slept very soundly that night after two days of bouncing along on Rayo Rojo's back.

At seven-thirty the following morning I was standing on the walk outside the lobby of the *Alta* building, my writing satchel in my hand, awaiting the arrival of head editor, Mr. Edward Kemble.

A little while later Mr. Kemble approached along the sidewalk, with none other at his side than Robin T. O'Flaridy, walking along laughing and talking amiably together. No lady would say the things that came into my mind at that moment. Fortunately, I swallowed them and managed to keep my mouth closed. Robin wore a bandage over one corner of his mouth and chin, and one eye was pretty badly swollen and discolored, but otherwise he didn't look too much the worse for wear.

"Ah, Miss Hollister!" exclaimed Mr. Kemble the moment he saw me. "Robin told me to expect you sometime soon."

Robin gave me a nod and a smile, and I gave *him* back a look that shot daggers. I wasn't feeling much like a loving and forgiving Christian at the time!

Mr. Kemble led the way inside and down the hall to his office, and I followed in silence.

"Quite a business you and Robin got into up there, eh, Hollister?" Mr Kemble said the moment the three of us were alone. "And it looks like he scooped you again! Tough break too. I thought this was the one where you might really prove yourself."

"Scooped *me!*" I exclaimed, at last finding my tongue. "What are you talking about?"

"Right here," he replied, slapping his hand a couple times on a stack of papers that sat on his desk. "When Robin arrived yesterday afternoon — looking a mess, I have to tell you! — and put this in my hands, I knew everything had paid off in the end. Not only had he unearthed the whole of that bum Gregory's story, he had actually made off with the thing — notes, interviews, quotes and all! Can you believe it, Hollister? He scooped the whole *Globe* story — stole it out from under their noses! With this in our hands, they can't run it against Fremont!"

"What?" I stammered.

"How was I to know that he'd go back out there on his own after I pulled him off the story and sent you? Mighty determined reporter he's turning out to be! It really is too bad, Hollister, for O'Flaridy to scoop you twice in a row. Lucky for you he was there, though — to save you from those ruffians!"

The whole time Robin was standing by with a smug smile on his face, not saying a word.

"He — he told you all that, did he?" I said. I'm afraid my voice did not sound too calm.

Mr. Kemble chuckled. "He *also* told me you'd be furious and would try to tell me *you* had done it all. Look, Hollister, you're young . . . you're a bright kid. But another thing you've got to learn in this business is not to be a sore loser. When you're up against someone more experienced than yourself, like Robin, you've got to expect to be beat out for a story now and then. But you're learning."

I sat down finally, took some deep breaths, and tried to calm down. It would do no good to argue or yell or complain or call Robin a liar. That would only confirm what Mr. Kemble already thought, that I was a young and emotional female not able to think rationally. And I suppose the first two *were* true, but this was one time I had to *force* myself to think rationally!

Finally I looked up at the editor and spoke again, softly and without anger.

"And just what sort of article did Mr. O'Flaridy provide you to run in opposition to this information of Gregory's that *he* brought you?" I asked.

"We hadn't exactly settled on our response. Perhaps Robin will write a pro-Fremont piece.

Perhaps you could even join that effort. Perhaps nothing need be done with regard to this aborted *Globe* information." He patted the stack of Derrick's papers again.

"I see," I said, then paused thoughtfully. "And has it occurred to you that Derrick Gregory is also an experienced writer with perhaps more at stake than either of you, and that he would be well able to reconstruct from memory much of what he was planning to divulge? Do you think that just because you have his notes and perhaps a rough draft of his article, you have stopped him entirely? I wouldn't doubt that he is already back in Sacramento or right here in San Francisco, in a hotel someplace, writing furiously to redo the very article that you think you have stopped." I pointed to Mr. Kemble's desk and the papers that I had taken from Derrick's room.

Mr. Kemble and Robin were both silent, thinking over what I had said.

"If that is true, your possessing his notes and original material will do you no good whatsoever. He'll still run his story in the *Globe*, and Colonel Fremont will suffer just as much damage as ever."

I paused and looked straight at Mr. Kemble. "What you need," I said, "is a story that refutes Gregory's charges and strengthens Mr. Fremont's position."

"And where can I get such a story?"

"I happen to have one — right here!" I patted

434

the writing satchel on my lap. "Completed, ready to print, and refuting nearly all of Gregory's charges."

"May I see it?" asked Mr. Kemble. I think he was beginning to wonder if he'd misread the whole situation.

"Not until we have worked a few things out," I replied. "For now, I will just hold on to it myself."

"If it's what you say, Corrie, I'll pay you well. I'll give you your eight dollars without an argument this time."

"You can't buy my submission quite so easily now, Mr. Kemble. You sent me up to Sonora, as you said, to find the truth. Well, I found it. I found Mr. Gregory when Robin couldn't. I found what he was going to print. I found what I am satisfied is proof against his charges. I risked my life to steal that for you —" I pointed to the papers on his desk.

Suddenly I stopped, and the impact of what I had done hit me square in the face. I had determined not to lie to get my story, and yet I had done something just as wrong — I had broken into Derrick Gregory's room and stolen his papers, and at the same time I hadn't given it a second thought.

"Mr. Kemble," I said at last. "When I took Mr. Gregory's article, I didn't even stop to consider if it was right or wrong — I just knew I had to get my hands on that information. I had to stop his article from being published, to save

435

the Fremonts from his deception." I paused, then went on.

"Maybe that makes me just like Derrick — willing to do anything for a story. But maybe it's different because my reasons for doing it were better. I don't really know, and I haven't had time to sort it all out yet. Maybe it doesn't matter at all to you, but it matters to *me,* and it may take me a while to get over what I've done. But your willingness to believe falsehoods about *me* is just as bad as the *Globe* being willing to print lies about John Fremont!"

I stopped, trembling with both anger and apprehension as I thought about my actions.

"I am deeply sorry, Corrie, if there has been some misunderstanding," Mr. Kemble said.

"There has been no misunderstanding. It seems simple enough to me. What Robin brought you is nothing." I turned to Robin. "That was your one mistake, Robin, leaving me my carpetbag," I said. "That's where *my* notes were. I had been with Derrick the whole previous day, and had written down everything he'd told me. He even admitted to bribing half the people he quoted! He as good as told me himself which of the charges against Mr. Fremont were false. And all *that* was in my carpetbag, which I still have. And at the Mariposa I got the rest of what I needed to destroy the credibility of Derrick's story. But you had none of that, which is why stealing Derrick's papers from me didn't do you a bit of good!"

I was angry again, and even the pale look on

Robin's bruised face wasn't enough to renew the kinship I'd briefly felt with him four nights ago around the campfire.

"And you know what else you don't have?" I continued. "You don't have the last page that Derrick was in the middle of writing when everything exploded back there in Sonora. I left it behind. But I know what that page contained, and it would be dynamite if used against the Colonel. I know what that page said, and I am able to refute it. But neither of you have any idea as to either."

I looked around again at Mr. Kemble as I said these last words. I stopped and the room was silent. I had the best of the argument, and both men knew it.

"Now, Mr. Kemble," I said. "When I left, you told me to get to the bottom of the story and to find out the truth, and to have it on your desk by the 22nd. Today's the 20th. I've done everything you said with two days to spare. I reckon it's time for you to decide what you want to do about this matter, and it's time for me to decide what I want to do with what I've found and with the article I've written. I'll be staying at Miss Sandy Bean's Boarding House if you want to contact me. Otherwise, I'll be back to see you, perhaps tomorrow. That is, *if* I don't decide to take what I have to another paper!"

I got up from the chair and approached his desk, where I reached over and took hold of the stack of papers. "And if you don't mind, I think

I will take these with *me*. I'm sure Robin will be glad to tell you how things *really* happened in Sonora."

I took Derrick's papers, put them under my arm with the satchel full of my own, and walked out of the office.

Chapter 52

Countdown to November

The trip back to Miracle Springs from San Francisco was peaceful and thoughtful for me. I'd gotten my Raspberry back from Robin, and would return Rayo Rojo to Mariposa later. With both horses it was a much slower ride, and it gave me a chance to reflect on all that had happened.

After my conversation with Mr. Kemble, I went through all sorts of doubts about what I had done. Even though I was trying to stop others from doing wrong, the thought kept coming back to me that I had taken what didn't belong to me. And as I sat at Miss Bean's wondering what to do, I couldn't help finding myself confused. Finally I just had to say to myself, "Well, right or wrong, I *do* have Gregory's papers, so now I have to decide what to do with them." Maybe I'd never find any hard and fast rules that would help me know the answer to every situation I was in. I had to trust somehow that God would lead me through the dilemmas I might face as a writer.

In the end I left my entire Fremont article — explaining the charges that were being brought against him, and then showing how many of them were fabricated just so that he would not be elected — with Mr. Kemble. He said that its appearance would be a major boost to the Fremont campaign and should insure that the Colonel carried California in the election.

I took Derrick Gregory's papers to the *Globe* for them to return to him. He couldn't do much damage with them any longer, and I didn't feel right about keeping them. Without my even having to dicker for it, Mr. Kemble said he'd pay me $10 for the work I had done. He called it a "major effort" in the Fremont cause. He also said the *Alta* would pay the expenses of my trip to Sonora. He would have a check sent to me for $29. We didn't get around to discussing the pledge he'd made earlier to give me a regular article in the *Alta*. But I hadn't forgotten, and I planned to remind him of it before long!

On the afternoon of September 26 I finally rode into Miracle Springs. I was so glad to be home — I'd had enough adventures for one month!

I rode up to Parrish Mine and Freight Company, stopped, dismounted, and walked inside. Almeda wasn't there, but Mr. Ashton and Marcus gave me greetings and hugs enough for all three of them.

"Miz Hollister, she left for the claim," said Mr. Weber. "She got big news for ya all, Miss Corrie! You best git on yer horse an' follow her as quick as you can."

"Can you take care of Raspberry for me, Marcus?" I asked. "As you can see, I came back with an extra horse."

"No trouble, Miss Corrie."

"Then I'll see you both again tomorrow," I said, and hurried back outside. Now I was ready to give Rayo Rojo a run, and she was ready! We flew out of Miracle Springs so fast I'm sure a few heads turned as we passed the Gold Nugget. We clattered across the first bridge over the creek and headed up the incline in less than two minutes. Never had I covered the distance so fast. *Just wait until Zack and Little Wolf see this magnificent animal!* I thought.

I galloped all the way home. As I was dismounting, all the family poured out of the house, and just like after my other trip, there were hugs and tears and shouting in plentiful measure.

I was anxious to find out the "big news" Marcus Weber was talking about. A flood of questions came out. I had all but forgotten that nobody else knew a thing of what *I'd* been through for this last two weeks. The only responses I heard were the clamoring questions of six other people shouting out and wondering what had happened to me!

Finally Pa managed to make his voice heard above all the rest. "*Everybody* inside!" he shouted. "The only way we're gonna get to the bottom of all this is to take it one question at a time!"

We trooped inside, still loud and laughing and

talking. It was a happy moment. Every one of the others had big smiles on their faces and I knew they had something to tell me.

Pa got us all sat down and got my brothers and sisters to quiet down. Then he said, "Now, Corrie, tell us all about your trip."

"Oh, Pa," I groaned, "there's too much! It'll take *days* to tell you everything that happened! I want to hear *your* news! Something's up — it's written all over every one of your faces!"

The laughter erupted all over again. I had never seen Almeda so gleeful. She was laughing like a little girl.

"Come on . . . out with it!" I exclaimed, looking around at everybody. "What is going on here?"

"Well, Almeda," said Pa, looking down on her with a smile, "I reckon it's more your news than anyone else's. Go on . . . tell her!"

Almeda, who was sitting beside me on the couch, took one of my hands in hers and looked me tenderly in the eye.

"You'll never believe it, Corrie, but your father and I are going to have a baby!"

"That's . . . that's wonderful!" I exclaimed.

Without even realizing it, I discovered that I was crying. All the emotions and fears I'd had to keep to myself for the past two weeks broke loose into a well of tears that spilled over to everyone in the room. Even Pa was half laughing and crying at the same time!

When I finally dried my tears, I found that I still could not find any words to express all that was in my heart. Every word I tried to speak only started up the tears all over again.

Almeda finally came to my rescue with a long, tight hug that only a mother can give and only a daughter can receive.

At length we did manage to take some deep breaths and get back to some normal conversation. I had so many questions, especially with the election now getting so close, and wondering what had been going on in Miracle Springs. But they were nothing compared to all *I* had to tell about my adventures!

So much had happened in two weeks, and so many stories remained to be told! In the *next* few weeks the Hollister-Parrish-Belle clan would witness a whole new series of events that would turn our lives topsy-turvy again — permanently.

All of our lives were changing. In a period of two weeks, I had found myself facing more adventure and danger, struggle and doubt, than I would have ever thought possible. I had grown so much! I'd gone out on the trail of the truth, and in finding it, I had found a little more about myself as well.

And yet in some ways the adventures were still only beginning!

The employees of G.K. HALL hope you have enjoyed this Large Print book. All our Large Print titles are designed for easy reading, and all our books are made to last. Other G.K. Hall Large Print books are available at your library, through selected bookstores, or directly from us. For more information about current and up-coming titles, please call or mail your name and address to:

G.K. HALL
PO Box 159
Thorndike, Maine 04986
800/223-6121
207/948-2962